I'd known for a long time that
I wasn't sure it had a face and
one that would show itself to
a subway platform, fidgeting nervously, with
luminescent eyes, dark, limp hair, and a cocky-bastard
smile that could boil water.
But I knew.
I could tell.
And I would've done anything for him.

HOW TO KILL A ROCK STAR

Funny and irreverent, and at the same time it
has a depth of emotion that should resonate
with readers of all ages. A cool love story with
unexpected twists and turns.

—Eileen Goudge, bestselling author of
Otherwise Engaged.

HOW TO KILL A ROCK STAR

a novel

HOW TO KILL A ROCK STAR

tiffanie debartolo

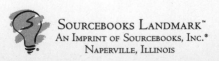
SOURCEBOOKS LANDMARK™
AN IMPRINT OF SOURCEBOOKS, INC.®
NAPERVILLE, ILLINOIS

Grateful acknowledgment is made for permission to reprint the following material:
"The Day I Became a Ghost" by Douglas J. Blackman
© 1977 Soul in the Wall Music
All rights reserved. Used by permission.

"Eliza" by Paul Hudson
© 2001 ScrawnyWhiteGuy Music
All rights reserved. Used by permission.

"Rusted" by Loring Blackman
© 2000 Two Fathoms Music
All rights reserved. Used by permission.

"A Thousand Ways" by Loring Blackman
© 2002 Two Fathoms Music
All rights reserved. Used by permission.

"Save the Savior" by Paul Hudson
© 2002 ScrawnyWhiteGuy Music
All rights reserved. Used by permission.

Excerpt from the novel *Hallelujah* by Jacob Grace.
All rights reserved. Used by permission.

The characters and events portrayed in this book are fictitious or are used fictitiously. Any similarity to real persons, living or dead, is purely coincidental and not intended by the author.

Published by Sourcebooks, Inc.
P.O. Box 4410, Naperville, Illinois 60567-4410
(630) 961-3900
FAX: (630) 961-2168
www.sourcebooks.com

Library of Congress Cataloging-in-Publication Data
DeBartolo, Tiffanie.
  How to kill a rock star / Tiffanie DeBartolo.
    p. cm.
  ISBN 1-4022-0521-X (alk. paper)
  1. Women journalists--Fiction. 2. Aircraft accident victims' families--Fiction. 3. New York (N.Y.)--Fiction. 4. Fear of flying--Fiction. 5. Rock musicians--Fiction. 6. Roommates--Fiction. I. Title.

PS3604.E233H69 2005
813'.6--dc22

                                                    2005012501

Printed and bound in the United States of America
LB 10 9 8 7 6 5 4 3 2 1

We are the music-makers,
And we are the dreamers of dreams,
Wandering by lone sea-breakers,
And sitting by desolate streams;
World-losers and world-forsakers,
On whom the pale moon gleams:
Yet we are the movers and shakers
Of the world for ever, it seems.

—Arthur O'Shaughnessy

This one is for the music makers
and the dreamers of dreams.

I was only a child
when I learned how to fly
I wanted to touch the colors of the bleeding sun
and then I fell from the sky

You never saw me again
not even when I returned
you never noticed my broken heart
or how my wings were burned

But if they tell you they saw me
do a swan dive off that bridge
Remember I've always been more afraid to die
than I ever was to live

And on the day I disappear
You'll all forget I was ever here
I'll float around from coast to coast
And sing about how you made me a ghost.

—Douglas J. Blackman, "The Day I Became a Ghost"

part one

Save the Savior

My oldest memory isn't one I *see* when I think back on the past, it's one I *hear*. I'm four years old, on my way home from a camping trip with my family. My eyes are shut tightly and I'm trying to sleep in the backseat of the car. My six-year-old brother, who is already asleep, keeps kicking me in the head, and I am about to kick him back when the song on the radio gets my attention. The smooth voice of a man is singing about a pony that ran away in the snow and died. Or maybe it was the girl chasing after the pony who died. Maybe nobody died. The girl and the pony might have just wanted to get off the farm. I was never really sure. All I remember is that before I knew it, I was sobbing so hard my dad had to stop the car so my mom could pull me into her lap and calm me down.

The song was senseless and sappy, but it made me feel something. And although I couldn't articulate it at that age, feeling something—anything—made me conscious that I was alive.

I would spend the rest of my childhood sitting beside radios, continually being transformed and exalted by a melody, a lyric, or a riff.

I would spend most of my adolescence in pieces on the floor, only to be picked up and put back together by the voice of one of my heroes.

It sounds silly, I know. But for me, the power of music

rests in its ability to reach inside and touch the places where the deepest cuts lie.

Like a benevolent god, a good song will never let you down.

And sometimes, when you're trying to find your way, one of those gods actually shows up and gives you directions.

Doug Blackman even walked like a god. I was standing near the elevator when I saw him enter the hotel. His arms moved back and forth as if set to a metronome, his torso stood erect and intimidating, and his eyes seemed a step ahead of his body, unblinking, taking in everything his peripheral vision had to offer.

He stopped at the front desk to drop off an envelope, and seconds later he was standing beside me, fishing through his breast pocket. He smelled like red wine and cigarettes, and his dark hair had wiry gray threads sewn all through it.

I told myself to stay cool. Don't stare. Act like the adult I was. But I had imagined Doug coming in with an entourage, had thought I'd have to fight just to catch a glimpse. And then he was beside me, our shoulders inches from touching—the radio prophet who had taught me almost everything I knew about life and love, politics and poetry, and was, in my opinion, the greatest singer/song-writer in the history of rock 'n' roll.

In person, Doug looked every bit his fifty-seven years. His face was like a mountain range: he had deep fissures in his cheeks chiseled from over three decades of life on the road; dark, sharp eyes that could have been cut from granite; a small chip in his top front tooth that he'd never bothered to fix; and his rumpled clothes looked like they'd been won from a vagabond during a street game of dice, which added a soft, modest charm to his otherwise unapproachable vibe.

I had a whole speech prepared, in case I got close enough

to talk. I was going to tell Doug that in my twenty-six years on the planet, nothing had inspired me or moved me like his music. I was going to tell him that for the past decade he had been both father and mother to me, and that "The Day I Became a Ghost" wasn't just a song, it was a friend who took my hand and kept me company whenever I felt alone.

Nothing he hadn't heard a thousand times, no doubt.

Before I could get a word out, Doug pulled a deck of cards from his pocket and said, "Pick one."

I turned and said, "*Huh?*"

It would go down in history as the worst opening line anyone had ever said to their god and hero. I wanted to take it back and say something profound. The man had given me the truth and all I could give back to him was a dimwitted interjection.

"Pick a card," Doug said again, holding the deck with both hands, the cards splayed out like a fan.

I was staring at him, wide-eyed, trying to will myself to speak. It should be noted here that I make my living talking to people. I'm a reporter. Evidently gods and heroes tongue-tie me.

"Go on," Doug said.

I chose a card out of the middle of the deck, quickly checked Doug's eyes for some kind of explanation he clearly didn't think he needed to offer, and then looked at the card—the three of clubs.

"This elevator takes forever," Doug grumbled. "Four hundred bucks a night and it takes the elevator ten minutes to get to the lobby. Now, here's what I want you to do. Write your name on the face of the card. It's okay if I see it. You got a pen? Write your name on it and then put it back in the deck."

I'm dreaming, I thought. It was the only explanation I could come up with to balance out the surreal experience of participating in a card trick with Doug Blackman.

"Do—you—have—a—pen?" Doug said again, as if he were speaking to a foreigner.

The only pen in my purse had purple ink. Purple seemed frivolous and gay and not nearly rock 'n' roll enough; I cursed myself for not buying black.

I put down my bag and began printing my name on the card. Doug was looking over my shoulder and I wondered if he could see my hand shaking.

"Eliza Caelum," he said. "You from around here, Eliza?"

I nodded.

"Put the card back in the deck."

I did.

"You know who I am," Doug said, not a question but a fact. He was shuffling the cards like a pro. "You were at the show?"

I nodded again. I was acting like an imbecile, and I knew I was never going to get anywhere if I didn't snap out of it.

"Okay, now pick the top card."

The top card was the ten of hearts, which devastated me. I thought Doug had messed up and I didn't want to have to tell him. Luckily he said, "Not yours, I know. Just hold it in your palm. Face down."

I held the card, and Doug made like he was sprinkling some kind of invisible dust over it. "My grandsons love this shit," he said. His hands were weathered and rugged and powdery-white. They looked like they'd feel cold to touch. "Okay. Take a look."

I flipped the card. It was the three of clubs with my name written in that gay purple ink. I could feel myself grinning, and for a second I forgot who the man beside me was. "Holy crap. How did you do that?"

Doug shrugged. "Magician, musician. Same thing. A little hocus-pocus and a whole lot of faith, right?"

My insides were swirling. I was spellbound.

As the elevator opened, Doug looked at me and said, "You wanna fuck? Is that what you're waiting for?"

He'd asked the question as if he were offering me a piece of gum or telling me to pick another card. And maybe it should have disappointed me a little. Okay, it did disappoint me a little. Doug is married, and barring the Greeks and Romans, gods and heroes aren't supposed to be philanderers. But I'm not that naïve. I've read *Hammer of the Gods* and *No One Here Gets Out Alive*. I know about life on the road. I also know that people like to pretend it's all about sex, when what it's really about is loneliness.

"Well?" Doug asked, stepping into the elevator.

I shook my head. I hadn't gone there for sex. What I wanted and needed was guidance. Besides, Doug was a father figure to me, and I couldn't have sex with any man who reminded me of my father.

I contemplated telling Doug I was a reporter, but I knew he didn't talk to reporters. And I guess you could say that what came out of my mouth next was the figurative, not literal explanation of why I had been waiting for him.

"My soul is withering," I said.

Doug's eyebrows rose and he actually chuckled. "Your *soul* is *withering*?"

Then I don't know what came over me, but I burst into tears.

Doug kept his finger on the button to hold the elevator open, and I laid it all out for him in rambling, weepy discourse. I either had to flee the suburbs of Cleveland or suffer the death of my soul. Those were the choices as I saw them. My parents had died when I was fourteen; I'd feebly tried to slit my wrist at sixteen; my brother had moved to Manhattan with his wife a few years back; Adam, my boyfriend of six years, had run off to Portland with his drum set and Kelly from Starbucks; writing for the entertainment section of the *Plain Dealer* wasn't exactly a dream job for an aspiring music journalist; and, to top it all off, I only had four hundred dollars in my bank account.

I was alone. In ways people aren't supposed to be alone.

And sure, I could've stayed where I was, continued working my nowhere job, living in my nowhere apartment, eventually marry some nowhere man, have a few kids and anesthetize myself with provincial monotony like most of my peers had done, and before I knew it I'd be six feet under.

I wanted more.

And I had hope.

"*I'm more afraid to die than I am to live,*" I told Doug, thinking that if I made my case using his prodigious lyrics, he'd be more apt to identify with my predicament.

The warning bell in the elevator was ringing but Doug didn't seem to care. He contemplated me for a long moment and then said, "How the hell am I supposed to say no to those eyes, huh?"

I lowered my gaze and tried to smile.

"All right," he sighed. "Get in, Eliza Caelum."

I took a deep breath, stepped inside the elevator, and focused on the numbers above the doors while Doug pushed the button for the eleventh floor.

I remember thinking it was the second time in a decade that Doug Blackman would change my life.

The day I got the job with *Sonica*—three months after Doug had granted me an interview, and the day I was certain I would be moving to Manhattan—I decided I was going to fly, not drive, to New York. When my brother, Michael, heard the news, he booked me a one-way ticket going non-stop from Hopkins International Airport to JFK. He also sent me a collection of audio tapes he'd found at a sidewalk sale entitled *Discover Your Wings*: *Overcoming the Fear of Flying*, which advocated the use of breathing techniques while visualizing run-of-the-mill takeoffs, uneventful in-air experiences, and smooth landings.

The meditations were painless enough when I practiced them on the couch, but I couldn't foresee them being any help during a hijacking, a wind shear, or a catastrophic engine failure.

"If I can fly, you can fly," Michael lectured me over the phone.

My sister-in-law, Vera, who was also on the phone, added: "It's the safest form of transportation in the world."

The day of my departure I awoke feeling like an inmate being paroled. I hadn't set foot in an airport in twelve years and I was afraid to look around, afraid I'd see something that would remind me.

Walking through the terminal, focusing on the ground

beneath my feet, I made it all the way to the gate, but then accidentally glanced out the window. As soon as I caught sight of the plane, my whole body began to shake, and the agony of memory bubbled and fizzed in my stomach like a box of antacid tablets in a glass of water—I was fourteen again, standing between Michael and our Aunt Karen, all of us waving goodbye to my parents, who were going to Daytona Beach for their seventeenth wedding anniversary.

I remember wanting to see their faces one more time, but not being able to find them in the tiny portals of the plane.

I remember being afraid I might never see them again.

The accident, we learned months later, was due to pilot error. A fan blade on the plane's number one engine had detached, causing the compressor to stall. According to the National Transportation Safety Board, shutting down that engine and descending immediately would have, in all probability, resulted in a safe landing. But the pilot had accidentally shut down the working number two engine instead of the failing number one. By the time he realized his mistake it was too late. The plane dove toward the ground and crashed into a field northeast of Akron.

There were no survivors.

The aircraft carrying me to JFK was supposed to have been a 777—a plane that, as of June 2000, had yet to be involved in a fatal accident. But there was a last-minute, unexplained equipment change, and the 777's understudy turned out to be a 737 that looked so old it probably made its inaugural flight when Jim Morrison was alive.

FYI: Jim Morrison died on July 3, 1971.

The plane also had filthy windows and needed a new paint job, and if the airline couldn't manage to clean the windows or update the paint, I figured there was no way they kept the hydraulics in working order.

More than anything, I wanted to get on the plane—if for no other reason than to prove I had at least infinitesimal courage—but I convinced myself there was a thin, fragile line between courage and stupidity, and no one in their right mind would trust the aeronautical competency of complete strangers when the future they'd been waiting so long for was a mere four-hundred and sixty-seven miles away.

I ripped my boarding pass in half and ran, stopping only to throw up on the feet of a dapper skycap standing near the curb.

"Mother-of-Pearl," Vera said when I called and broke the news. "You were *so* close."

"I'm taking the bus," I said. "I'll be there tomorrow night."

The bus left the station at 7:02 a.m. and stopped in half a dozen towns between Cleveland and New York City. I kept my forehead pressed to the window and felt like I was watching a slide show, one in which the projector was broken and the same two or three photos kept clicking onto the screen. All the places looked the same: the same fast-food restaurants, the same strip malls, the same Wal-Marts at every turn.

I imagined the towns were filled with people like me—lonely people who wanted to fly away, who wanted more from life than a dreary existence of one-stop shopping, but either didn't know what that meant, or didn't have the guts to go out and find it.

Doug Blackman had blamed my malaise, in part, on the homogenization of America.

"It's destroying our culture, it's destroying our individuality, and it makes us feel dead inside," he told me that night in Cleveland. "But we just keep letting it happen. And we don't think about it because thinking hurts too much."

I asked Doug if we could talk about music and he got even more wound up.

"I *am* talking about music," he said. "Popular music is a microcosm of the culture, Eliza. It reflects the mentality of the population. Tell me, when was the last time you heard a truly extraordinary new artist on the radio?"

Doug's impassioned sermon meant one of two things to me—either the mentality of the population was soulless, or its level of consciousness was on par with your average thirteen-year-old Wal-Mart rat.

I never did relax on the bus, and when it pulled in to Port Authority in Manhattan, an intimidating thought occurred to me: in a city of roughly eight million people, I really only knew two—Michael and Vera, who had moved to Manhattan two and a half years earlier, after Michael decided to give up his nascent career as a graphic artist to pursue his lifelong dream of becoming a rock star.

It had taken a lot of urging to get Michael to go. He'd been hesitant to leave me. But even Susan Cohen, the therapist I'd been seeing since my paltry suicide attempt at sixteen, thought it was a good idea for Michael to loosen the reigns. And I was okay when Michael left. I was okay until Adam ran off to Oregon with the girl who made us caramel macchiatos, and my head began to unravel like a ball of yarn tumbling down a staircase.

Despite struggling financially, Michael seemed happy in New York. He was playing guitar for a fledgling band called Bananafish and working part time as a waiter in a famous SoHo restaurant called Balthazar. He and Vera had been living on the Lower East Side, in a small two-bedroom apartment with a guy named Paul Hudson, Bananafish's lead singer and songwriter, but they had just relocated to a place of their own in a more affordable Brooklyn neighborhood, which allowed me to become the new tenant in their old room.

I exited the bus, lugging my overstuffed backpack across my shoulder, and the muggy July heat felt like a plastic bag wrapped around my head. I followed the signs to the subway, where everything was covered in a thin layer of grime and the pungent odor of pee and garbage permeated the air.

New York was not altogether foreign to me. Michael, Vera, and I had visited the city dozens of times as teenagers, when Michael would tell our Aunt Karen we were going on field trips with our school and we'd drive to Manhattan instead. At night we'd sleep in the car; during the day Michael would browse guitar shops and record stores while Vera—my friend before she became Michael's girlfriend— and I trudged around downtown looking for rock stars to stalk.

It was on those trips that I learned to respect and love the shortcomings of the city as one might respect and love a scar on the body of a loved one, especially the dingy East Village and Lower East Side neighborhoods where Vera and I used to loiter outside CBGB, well past the club's heyday, affecting British accents and claiming we were related to Joe Strummer so that all the punk rock boys would think we were cool.

"*This* is what I want to do with my life," I had decided back then.

"What?" Vera asked. "Sit on a dirty sidewalk and make out with juvenile delinquents?"

"No. Be a part of this. This *city*. This *life*. This *music*."

"Aim high," Vera said.

I'd squandered countless hours of my youth daydreaming about how happy I'd be if only I lived in Manhattan, but the realization that the dream of *someday* had just become *now* felt like crossing a bridge and then watching the bridge burn behind me. I could never go back. This was change and change was supposed to be good. But in my past, change and heartbreak were analogous, and as I made my way to the train I wasn't sure which one I was feeling.

One thing I never got a grip on during any prior visit to New York was how to navigate the subway. Michael is two years older than me. This made him the self-proclaimed leader. And I have what he calls an "inadequate sense of direction," which is why he'd given me explicit directions from the bus to the subway to the apartment on Ludlow, making me repeat them three times over the phone the day before.

"Michael, I'm twenty-six. Stop treating me like a child."

I made it from Port Authority to the A train without complication, which took me downtown to the West Fourth station. I was then supposed to transfer to the F and get off at Second Avenue. Michael had to work until midnight, and Vera was going to try to meet me at West Fourth, but to support herself and her husband's musical aspirations, she worked for a nonprofit cancer research organization that was having a fund-raising event at the Waldorf-Astoria and wasn't sure she'd get out in time.

"If you don't see me in the subway," she said, "I'll meet you at the apartment."

In the West Fourth Street station, Vera was nowhere in sight, and I had an anxious, fizzy feeling in my stomach while I waited for the train. But I could feel the energy of the city in the vibrations coming off the tracks, and the diversity of the faces I saw around me made me feel so alive, so much a part of something kinetic, I swore I could taste it like metallic electricity on my tongue.

The two most interesting people I noticed were waiting on the opposite side of the platform—an old man with a shaker of salt and a tomato he was eating like an apple, and another guy I guessed to be in his late twenties, fidgeting near the steps.

I watched the guy's head bob up and down while his leg bounced along with it, keeping the beat to a song only he could hear. His dark, stringy hair hung limp in his face, he had a strong Roman nose, and he was overdressed in an ill-fitted secondhand suit the color of split-pea soup.

I instantly thought the guy was cute, in that gaunt, never-sees-the-light-of-day, New York street urchin kind of way. And he never stood still for a second. From across the tracks I read his expression as *I have everything on my side except destiny*, only his expression clearly hadn't informed his head or heart yet.

The guy looked over and caught me staring, and once his eyes met mine they never deviated. He took several cautious steps forward, stopping abruptly at the thick yellow line you weren't supposed to cross. His arms dangled like a puppet and he seemed to skim the ground when he walked, as if suspended over the edge of the world by a hundred invisible strings.

I heard the train approaching, and the air that blew through the passageway was a fleeting reprieve from the heat. The guy in the green suit looked down into the tunnel, and then back at me with his head tipped to the left.

He eyed my backpack suspiciously and, in a low shout, said, "What's your name?"

His voice caught me by surprise. It was a confident voice pretending to be shy.

"What's your name?" he said again.

I remained mute, figuring it was dangerous to give personal information to a stranger in the subway. But even if he was a mugger, he was too far away to attack me. And let's not forget, he was cute. This was a new life. A new me. The chance to at least pretend to be the person I wanted to be. And I was never going to get over Adam if I didn't start paying attention to cute strangers.

"Come on," the guy said. "*Hurry.*"

"Eliza," I finally replied.

The guy smiled, and his face lit up radiantly, as if someone had poured gasoline on a pilot light inside his mind. Then he looked me up and down in a way that made me feel naked.

The train was seconds away from untying the curious knot that joined the two of us. "Eliza," the guy said, pointing at the approaching headlights, raising his voice. "Do *not* get on that train."

Then the train pulled in and I couldn't see him anymore. The new me was begging my legs not to move, but apparently the old me was still in charge of my motor functions because I stepped through the doors of the subway car, and the electricity that had been on my tongue surged down into my chest like a shot of adrenaline to the heart as the train began to pull me away.

Crossing the car, I looked out the window, hoping to catch one last glimpse of the guy in the green suit. He was still looking at me, smiling, and shaking his head.

I ended up on the wrong train. Turns out I'd been standing on the wrong side of the station and had been on my way uptown until I deciphered the word *Harlem* coming through the train's distorted loudspeaker.

It was after eight when I finally found my way to Second Avenue, walked the last few blocks down Houston Street, and then spotted the landmark telling me I had almost arrived at my destination—the *Wheel of Fortune*-like letterbox sign of Katz's deli on the corner of Houston and Ludlow.

From Katz's, I could see Vera standing halfway down the block. Vera had a cell phone to her ear, her lips were moving like mad, there was a tote bag over her shoulder, and she was wearing a plaid, below-the-knee wool skirt with socks and sneakers. Vera was the voice of reason in my life, but she dressed like a crazy Russian librarian, even when it was ninety degrees outside.

"*Yay*. You're *here*," she said when she saw me coming down the sidewalk.

Vera was a cute, brainy girl with dark hair and bright green eyes speckled with amethyst, though when she had her glasses on, which was almost always, it was hard to notice this feature.

She threw her arms around me. I hadn't seen her in months and her presence was a relief.

"Sorry I'm late," I said. "Have you been waiting long?"

She pulled a set of keys from her tote and shook her head. "I just got out of work. I left a message for your new roommate to meet you in the West Fourth Street station, but he has a bizarre subway phobia and rarely ventures underground. He never called me back."

Vera hugged me again and I could tell something was off. She'd squeezed too hard, and when she pulled back her chest looked inflated, as if she'd taken a deep breath and forgot to let it out.

"What's wrong?" I said.

"Long day."

It was a typical Vera answer. She was a whiz whenever I was in trouble—she'd wasted a week of her vacation time to come home and stay with me after Adam left—but she didn't like to burden anyone with her own problems.

"I don't believe you."

"You just got here, Eliza. Let's enjoy the moment."

She nodded up at the building, which was narrow, made of dirty beige bricks, had a four-tiered fire escape running down its face, and housed a tattoo parlor called Daredevil on its ground floor. "What do you think?"

"It looks like a tenement," I said.

Unlocking the door, Vera led me up an endless number of stairs. I could hear a television blaring in one of the second-floor apartments, and the whole place reeked of fried fish.

The hallways were dark and narrow, and all the doors were gray, except for the door of the corner apartment on the fourth floor, which was a deep scarlet color. "Paul painted ours," Vera said. "He wanted it to stand out. He also lost our security deposit."

It was an unusual paint job, as if someone had taken a bucket of color and, instead of brushing it on, had poured it and let it drip in thick lines from the top down. The door looked like it was bleeding.

Vera walked in first, turned on the light, and I followed. I was sure that if I spit from the entryway I could hit the back wall. The kitchen was the size of the trunk of a small car, and the bathroom had grimy tile that only went halfway up the wall and looked like it had been stolen from the subway.

"Nice, huh?" Vera said.

It was a dump. Possibly the worst apartment I'd ever seen. But it was all I could afford, and it was New York. I wasn't going to complain. Except to note that for two hundred dollars a month less, Adam and I had lived in a place with a dishwasher and a walk-in closet.

There was a cubicle to the left of the bathroom. I peeked my head in and Vera said, "That's Paul's disaster zone." A mattress rested on the floor, along with piles of books, tapes, and CDs stacked neatly in rows. But clothes were strewn all over, covering every inch of ground like a thick carpet of cotton and denim. An acoustic and an electric guitar sat on stands in the corner next to two milk crates. One crate had a small four-track recorder on top of it; the other held a plant that had seen better days.

The room's solitary window was small, and the only view it afforded was a brick wall that prohibited daylight from ever dawning on the space. There was an electric fan, a prehistoric laptop computer, and a dirty ashtray next to the bed.

"Paul won't bother you," Vera said. "He works during the day and he's at the rehearsal space most nights. Sometimes he sleeps there. You'll hardly ever see him."

All I knew about Paul was what Vera had already told me: "He's talented as hell. But he can be pretty…um…err*atic*."

"Is he cute?" I asked her.

"Cute? If you like the dysfunctional lunatic, male-slut vibe, sure."

I'd missed Vera. She had a way of delivering lines with a perfect ratio of sarcasm, syllable-stressing, and pausing that made everything she said sound either important or funny. And under different circumstances I'm sure I would have found Vera's description of Paul Hudson intriguing. Instead I took it as a warning sign. I didn't need to have my heart ripped out of my chest, pulverized, and then stepped on twice in one year.

The last room on the right was mine. It contained an old wooden bed, a lamp, a small bookcase, the three large boxes I'd mailed there earlier in the week representing all I had in life, a roach motel in the corner that, to sustain my composure I chose not to question, and, in what appeared to be a strange interior decorating choice, a large crucifix hanging on the wall across from the bed, complete with a bloody crown of thorns and bas-relief nails protruding from Christ's palms.

"That was here when we moved in," Vera said. "We thought it was weird and left it up. Feel free to toss it if you want."

I took a closer look. Jesus had piercing blue eyes, dark hair that hung in a flawless mess, his body was emaciated and taut, his hands and feet dripped with blood, and nothing but a gauzy loincloth hid what looked like a nice package underneath.

"Sexy," I said. "He looks like a rock star."

"Mother-of-Pearl," Vera sighed.

The room's saving grace was its window, and the tiny bench in front of the window, which was covered with an afghan I recognized as one of my Aunt Karen's creations.

After our parents died, Michael and I had moved in with our Aunt Karen—a history teacher with orange hair, skin that smelled like baby powder, and a penchant for knitting. She was a good-but-detached woman, more school marm than loved one. We stayed with her for two years—until Michael turned eighteen, and he and I relocated to an apartment with a dozen afghans in tow.

Aunt Karen stored her yarn in a cedar closet, and no matter how many times we cleaned the afghans they always smelled like mothballs. The smell of mothballs reminds me of death.

Outside the window I could see the iron bars of the fire escape. Across the street there was a crowded lounge, a small French restaurant, an organic market, and a thrift store called Las Venus.

"This room gets the best light," Vera said. She was showing me how to open the window when we heard what sounded like hammering on the stairs.

"Here comes Paul," she said. "You'll always know when he's on his way up because he never walks the steps, he *leaps* them."

Paul came in yelling, "Anyone home?"

"In here," Vera said.

My back was to the door when I heard a voice say, "I *told* you not to get on that goddamn train."

I turned around. The guy in the green suit was standing in front of me.

"Have a nice trip to Harlem?" he said.

I had to summon all my determination to hold his gaze. At the station, I'd been too far away to get a good look at his eyes. They were two crescent moons, small and lucent, the color of soft, perfectly faded denim.

Vera said, "Eliza, this is Paul Hudson. Paul, Eliza."

"We sort of met already," Paul said. "After forcing myself underground, I tried to tell her she was going the wrong way —but she didn't listen."

Paul Hudson was grinning at me. The same combustible grin he'd flashed in the station. He wasn't what I would call handsome, at least not conventionally. His face, when he wasn't smiling, had a pensive, ominous cast to it, but as soon as he grinned the severity melted into an airy radiance that made me want to touch his chest and feel his heartbeat.

"You guys eat yet?" he said. "I brought home one of those frozen pizza dough things."

He took off his jacket and added it to his bedroom floor. He had the most amazing tattoo I'd ever seen on the inside of his left forearm. It was a butterfly colored the deepest shades of autumn leaves, as if it were on fire. The insect's legs were disproportionately long, and holding fast to one of them was the figure of a scantily clothed creature that bore a striking, if not somewhat cherubic resemblance to Paul himself.

"I have to go," Vera said as Paul wandered into the kitchen. Then she turned to me. "Are you going to be all right?"

I nodded, but I felt dizzy when I thought about being alone with the strange stranger whistling "Kashmir" in the other room.

"What about you?" I asked Vera. "Everything okay?"

She gave me a scarcely discernible nod. "I'm really glad you're here."

Before Vera left the apartment, I heard her stop in front of Paul and say, "Remember what Michael said: Keep your hands to yourself."

I was arranging my clothes in garment-specific piles on the bookshelves when, through the corner of my eye, I saw Paul peek his head into my room and watch me for a good thirty seconds before he asked me if I was hungry.

"No. Thanks, though."

It was a lie. All I'd eaten on the bus was a bag of trail mix and an apple, but the lewd twinkle in Paul's eye made me nervous and I blurted it out.

He remained standing in the doorway. Another thirty seconds went by before he said, "Well, will you at least come and keep me company then?"

I had a notion he would have waited there all night had I not yielded to his request. I walked to the sofa, sat down, and felt one of its springs like a gun in my back.

"Weren't you supposed to be here yesterday?" Paul asked, puttering around the kitchen.

"I missed my flight," I said, picking at a small burn in the sofa's fabric. When I looked up, Paul was nodding slowly, like he knew the score, and he knew I knew, but he let it go.

He was smiling again. He had, I decided, a cocky-bastard smile.

"So," I said. "You're the singer, right?"

It was a stupid question. I knew he was the singer.

Preposterous, I told myself, that I could spend three hours in a hotel room with Doug Blackman and eventually

manage to stop crying and act normal, yet here was this little rocker wanna-be making my palms sweat.

"Yeah," Paul smirked. "I'm the singer."

He sprinkled a handful of black beans on the dough and
then set about opening a can of tuna while I tried to sneak
another look at his tattoo. He caught me and said, "You can
even come over and touch it if you want."

"Don't be gay," I mumbled, blushing.

"Don't be *gay*?" He howled. "Uh, I'm assuming you mean
that in the seventh grade, don't-be-an-idiot kind of way, as
opposed to calling me a homosexual, right?"

"Yes."

"All right. I won't be gay if you promise not to be a lesbo."

Laughing, I turned to look out the window and felt Paul's
eyes trained on me like flashlights. I could have sworn he was
looking at the scar on my wrist, and this made me feel self-
conscious. It also made me want to kick him.

"Do you mind?" I finally huffed.

He slid the pizza into the oven and said, "Hey, don't take
this the wrong way, but suffice it to say that if I'd seen you
in the subway station and not been there looking for you, I
would've wished I was."

I blushed again and wondered what the wrong way to
take that could possibly be. I couldn't tell if Paul was flirting, or he simply had no tact, but either way I was flattered,
namely because I'd been on the bus all day and was certain
I looked like a mess.

"*Oh*," he said next, squirting dishwashing liquid over a
pile of dirty dishes in the sink like he was practicing soap
calligraphy. "I read your Doug Blackman piece, the one in
Sonica. It was incredible."

"You like Doug Blackman?"

"*Like* him? He's my hero. I wouldn't be a musician if it
hadn't been for that man. He's the greatest songwriter *ever*.

I mean, it's Dylan, Lennon, and Blackman, right?"

I immediately wondered why neither Michael nor Vera bothered to inform me that I had a hero in common with my new roommate.

"How the hell did you get him to talk to you like that?" Paul said. "Supposedly Doug Blackman never talks to reporters."

I tucked my legs underneath my body, sat back down, and said, "It was his big farewell tour. He's officially retired from the road now. I guess he was feeling nostalgic. And, well, I think he felt sorry for me."

"I loved his theory that the state of music is a metaphor for America. My favorite line was: *Tell me what you listen to and I'll tell you who you are.*"

Paul was nodding as if he'd never heard anything more brilliant. In my mind, this elevated Paul to the status of friend, although I was first to admit I didn't have a lot of friends who made me dizzy and whose chests I longed to touch.

Adam, as irony would have it, hadn't been a Doug Blackman fan. When he'd wanted to piss me off he would call Doug pompous or overrated. Once he had even accused me of liking Doug more than I liked him, which was ridiculous. I had adored Adam. Everything he owned was blue: his car, his clothes, his drum set, his couch. At one point, even his hair. It sounds weird now, but at the time I found it endearing.

"So you sent the article to *Sonica*," Paul went on, "and they not only printed it, they hired you?"

I nodded.

Paul hopped over the back of the couch, sat down, and, with a gossipy zeal, said, "Just between you and me, did you fuck him?"

Paul said "fuck" the same way as Doug—as if it were equivalent to offering someone a piece of gum or asking them to pick a card. Maybe that was the key to getting rid of the loneliness, I thought. Treating love as entertainment, not as salvation.

"No."

"*No*? Come on, he must've at least *tried* to fuck you."

The way I saw it, Doug had made no real effort. He'd simply, matter-of-factly offered up the idea. My response hadn't seemed to matter to him either way.

"Actually, Doug talked a lot about his family. He's been married for thirty years, you know. And he has two sons. The youngest one's in film school. The older one, Loring, he's about your age. He just released his second record. His first one did pretty well but Doug thinks this one's going to be huge."

"I know Loring." Paul was fiddling with an unlit cigarette. "Well, sort of. I used to play at this place on Avenue A called Emperor's Lounge. They had an open-mike night where anyone could show up with their guitar, and the ones who showed up first got the gigs. Loring and I were always there by noon to make sure we got on. We'd wait around the bar watching talk shows until it was time to play. Back then he went by the name Sam Langhorne and no one knew who he was—even I didn't know until he signed with a major label and I saw his goddamn picture in the paper."

"He's talented, huh?"

"In a radio-friendly way," Paul said, which didn't sound like a compliment. "He's a decent songwriter. Honest, at least."

Paul got quiet as he tinkered around the kitchen, but I wanted to keep talking music with him. "Ever heard of a band called 66?"

He crinkled his nose and stuck out his tongue like he'd just swallowed cough medicine. "My manager works with them. Why?"

"I get to review their show at Irving Plaza tomorrow night," I said, thrilled about my first real assignment. But

Paul burst my bubble.

"I can write that review for you right now," he said. "They're a saccharin band. Sweet but artificial. Vocalist's name is Amanda Strunk. She's a media-hungry bitch and she can't carry a tune to save her life, but she bought herself a nice pair of tits and now she's famous. Actually, I went out with her a couple times, and I think she still has the hots for me, but even I have standards."

"Tell me how you really feel."

Paul shook his head. "We have this weekly gig over at Rings of Saturn—it's a small place, only holds about two hundred people, but it's the best thing that's happened for us yet. Not that it matters because who gets the record deals and the big marketing campaigns? Shitty bands like 66."

"So why do it, if you feel that way?"

Paul smiled faintly, but all of a sudden he looked sad. "If I could do something else besides make music, believe me, I would. I've been here for over eight years, playing in different bands, trying to put together the right bunch of guys, trying to make a living doing the only thing I care about. But I'm almost thirty and my day job is folding shirts at the Gap. Have you seen my room? I'm not messy. I'm rebelling against folding."

"Vera says you're talented."

"I am," he replied without modesty. "But sometimes talent isn't worth shit. There are tons of talentless people out there making zillions of dollars. And unfortunately, an equal number of brilliant artists whose names and voices you'll never hear."

The verity of Paul's statement, the idea that the world—that I—might miss out on the life-altering genius of an artist simply because the powers that be couldn't see the light caused my heart to feel stiff and heavy.

Paul pulled a lighter from his pocket and put the cigarette

he'd been fingering into his mouth. "I'm trying to quit," he said. "Just so you know."

He lit the cigarette and inhaled so long and so deep it sounded like air being let out of a tire. Then he walked to the window and blew the smoke toward the sky. He was half turned toward me and his eyes, at that angle, took on a fluorescent-white hue.

"It's not that I don't want to be successful," he said. "I do. But music's not a popularity contest to me. You either mean it or you don't. Fuck the ones who don't. I have no use for them. And I'd rather write some really good songs and sing them into my four-track, songs that no one will ever hear, than be some record executive's tool." He paused to take another thick hit, and then he put the cigarette out on the window sill, collected the residual ashes into a receptacle he made using the bottom of his shirt, and shook the debris into the night air. "Having said that, I can't deny that sometimes I wish I were smart enough to bite the Big One."

"Bite the Big One?"

"Sell out," he said. "Do you know how much I live on after I pay rent and the rest of my bills? Hell, when I splurge on a good cup of coffee I'm in the red for the week. I guess I need to find a happy medium, someplace between giving them what they want and ending up face-down in a pool of my own goddamn integrity."

I found myself suffering a considerable amount of admiration for what Paul made himself out to be—a spirited maverick who probably had a long, lonely road ahead of him.

"Then again, I shouldn't complain, considering what your brother's going through," he rambled. "Not that I have any intention of letting him quit the band, I'll tell you that. He's too good. And too organized. We'd fall apart without him."

Paul's words slapped me out of my quixotic musings. "*Huh?*"

"If I'm talking too much, just tell me to shut up," he said, clearly misinterpreting the look on my face. "I spent the day playing guitar in the rehearsal space. Haven't had a real conversation since breakfast."

"No, it's not that. What did you mean about Michael quitting?"

Paul's head tilted. "You don't know? I thought you and Vera were like, best friends or something."

"Vera thinks confiding in her friends is a burden."

"She never told you about the three-year plan?"

I did know about the three-year plan. Michael and Vera had made a pact before leaving Ohio. Michael got three years to get his music career off the ground, and then it was Vera's turn. For as long as I'd known her, Vera had wanted to go to law school, but in order to live in New York either she or Michael had to work full time. They couldn't afford to chase their respective dreams simultaneously.

"I didn't realize it had been three years already."

"It will be in November," Paul said.

"And Michael's okay with this?"

"No. Hence the problem." Paul put his hand up in the air like a traffic cop. "Can we not discuss this right now? It's throwing me off-rhythm."

He went to check on the pizza. Standing in front of the oven, he braced himself on the counter and began to moan like he'd just been stabbed.

"*See?*" He pointed to his right side. "As if being poor and desperate isn't enough," he said with his hand below his right hip, "I'm pretty sure I have some sort of growth on my pancreas. I'm probably going to die of cancer before I ever cut a record."

"FYI: Your pancreas is behind your stomach."

He moved his hand to his lower abdomen.

"Higher," I said.

He inched up a little more.

"Higher," I said again.

He waved the hand through the air. "What*ever*. The pain is migrant."

"Maybe it's an ulcer."

"I don't think so. Both of my parents died of cancer."

"*Pancreatic* cancer?"

"No. Breast and brain, but it's obviously in my genes. Hey, there's something else we have in common. We're both orphans."

As Paul walked by me, his pain inexplicably gone, the phone started ringing and he froze in place, wide-eyed and anxious.

"If it's for me," he said, nodding at the phone. "I'm not here."

I was hoping it would be Michael. I picked up the phone and said hello. Without saying hello back, the girl on the other end announced herself as Avril. She pronounced it with a French accent. Then, in what sounded like Long Island twang, she said, "Who are you and why are you answering Paul's phone?"

I wasn't the least bit surprised that Paul Hudson had intrusive girls with names like Avril calling him. I was, however, bothered by it. In my mind, Avril looked like Kelly: big-boned, thick-lipped, with one of those perpetually baffled expressions that bored men find so attractive.

"I'm Michael's sister," I told her.

"Michael who? Burke, Caelum, or Angelo?"

"What?"

At her wit's end, Avril said, "Bass player, guitarist, or drummer?"

"Guitarist." I covered the mouthpiece with my hand, turned to Paul and said, "Everyone in your band is named Michael?"

He nodded. "Weird, huh?"

"Put Paul on," Avril said.

Without thinking, I held the phone toward Paul, impelling him to throw his hands up in a silent, berserk protest as he took the call.

While Paul spoke to Avril, I took a shower. I couldn't get my mind off of Michael. I wanted to help him, but I had less money than he did. Still, I knew how much the band meant to him, and I didn't think I could watch him walk away from that. He'd spent years taking care of me. The least I could do, for once, was to take care of him.

I came out of the bathroom and the pizza, which smelled like dog food, was out of the oven. Paul was trying to slice it with a metal spatula. He told Avril to hold on and whispered, "You're not going to bed, are you?"

"I start work tomorrow. I have to get up early."

I closed my bedroom door but could still hear Paul talking. He was defensive with Avril, answering questions like a man being interrogated for a crime he had actually committed. After he hung up he went into his room and started talking again. Unless he'd snuck someone in through his window, which would have been impossible, he was talking to himself.

His solo conversation went on for about five minutes. Then there was a buzzing noise I guessed was someone trying to get into the building. I heard Paul walk to the door, followed soon thereafter by a flirtatious female voice in the living room.

I sat on the bench in front of my window while Paul and the girl whom I assumed was Avril retreated to his room.

Ludlow Street, as much as I could see of it, looked like it was lit from the inside out.

Across the hall, Paul was either fucking the girl or murdering her, I couldn't tell which.

I smelled mothballs.

The afghan was going to have to go.

Michael was seated, all six feet plus four lanky inches of him. His long, taffy legs were hanging over the arm of the couch, and he had a piece of pizza on a plate in his lap.

It was the morning after my arrival in New York. I was expected at work by ten, it wasn't even eight yet, and I'd just returned from a scorching run to Battery Park and back, trying not to get lost and hoping Avril would be gone when I got home.

Running was a hobby I'd picked up after Adam left. I'd read that it was a proven mood enhancer, and I had been trying to get it to enhance my mood ever since.

When I came in, Michael was picking beans off of his pizza, making a little pile of what looked like rabbit poop on the side of his plate. He had an impassive, stoic air about him, and as he put the plate down, stood up, and walked toward me, he moved with languid momentum that, coupled with his height, was more reminiscent of an old history professor than a prospective guitar god. He'd also been cursed with a head of hair that looked like a merkin sitting on top of his skull.

"Welcome to New York," he said.

Michael's embrace lifted me a foot off the ground. I pretended this was annoying every time he did it, but it secretly made me feel loved. His shirt smelled like parsley and garlic and I was sure he'd worn it to work the day before.

"Sorry I didn't stop by last night," he said. "It was late when I left work."

I didn't bother beating around the bush. "You're not really quitting the band, are you?"

Michael went back to picking at his pizza. "Not your problem," he said, his tone bordering on condescension.

He and Vera were made for each other, I swear. They both thought the person who cared about them the most was the one they should inconvenience the least. They had everything backwards.

"It's not fair for you to have to give up your dream," I said.

"It's not fair for Vera to have to give up hers either."

Michael was right. But he looked like our dad, and the resemblance alone gave his dream priority. For nearly twenty years, from the time he was eighteen until the day he died, our dad had worked on the assembly line at GM. His only hobby was playing an old Washburn guitar, and in the summertime, when Michael and I were still kids, he used to spend his Saturdays sitting on a plastic lawn chair in the yard, nursing a beer and singing "Born to Run."

Michael and I liked to scream the line *tramps like us* at the top of our lungs. At the end of the song we would applaud and beg him to do it again.

"See?" our mom would say to him, no doubt thinking she was making him feel good. "You could've been Bruce Springsteen."

"Right," he always replied. "And if my aunt had balls she'd be my uncle."

To this day I can't listen to "Born to Run" without feeling like I've been shot.

"You can't quit the band," I said again.

"Then you better start playing the lottery. Or better yet, get us a record deal."

Michael had been eyeing the door to Paul's room. As if

his gaze had willed it to life, it creaked open and Paul emerged looking like a hung-over somnambulist.

"This is disgusting," Michael told him, referring to the bean and tuna pie.

Paul lifted his head to see past the hair in his eyes. He squinted first at Michael and then at me, as if he didn't know who we were or what we were doing in his apartment.

"Mr. Winkle," Michael said. "Why aren't you ready?"

Paul shrugged and made no effort to get moving. He poured himself a glass of orange juice and paced the kitchen in a tiny circle.

"Who's Mr. Winkle?" I asked, trying to peek into Paul's room for evidence of Avril. All I could see was the foot of his bed and an empty liquor bottle on the floor.

Paul's flashlight eyes met mine and made a trail down to my toes and then back up again. "You're sweating," he said.

"I was running." I wiped my forehead and helped myself to a glass of juice. "Who were you talking to last night?"

"Huh?"

"After you got off the phone. It sounded like you were talking."

"Oh, nobody. I mean, I was talking to myself." Paul went into his room and came back with a microcassette recorder. "I decided to start chronicling my life. I've always wanted to keep a diary but I'm too lazy to write shit down so I bought this." He fiddled with the knobs. "Oh, but if you're referring to Beth, she's gone."

"*Beth*?" I practically shouted.

He put the machine in my face, flicked the RECORD button, and said, "Say hi."

I thought I'd be over the dizziness by morning, but there was no way around it: being near Paul Hudson made me feel like I'd just stepped off a fast-moving merry-go-round. It was either a good sign or a very bad one.

"Paul," Michael sighed, "we don't have time to socialize. Go get dressed."

Paul finished his juice and wandered into the bathroom while Michael carried his half-eaten piece of pizza to the garbage.

"Who's Mr. Winkle?" I asked him.

"Paul calls all record executives Mr. Winkle."

"Why?"

"I have no idea."

Then, trying to sound nonchalant, I said, "Who's Avril?"

Michael rolled his eyes. "Paul's girlfriend. But her name's not Avril, it's April. She's trying to break into modeling and decided she needed a classier name."

"How long have they been going out?"

He shrugged. "A month, maybe."

"Then who's Beth?"

Michael shrugged again. "Eliza, a piece of advice: don't try to make sense of Paul's love life."

Paul exited the bathroom shirtless, zipping up a pair of jeans. His chest was gaunt and hairless, his arms were sinewy like the Jesus on the cross above my bed, and he had another tattoo, a Chinese symbol, on his right shoulder. The tattoo occupied my attention for entirely too long.

"It's pronounced *wu*," Paul said, fingering the black ink.

"What does it mean?"

"To awaken to righteousness." He paused. I'm not sure what he saw in my eyes, but he said, "Yeah, I know. It's an ongoing process for me."

I glanced down into my glass and pretended to pick a piece of pulp from my juice. When Paul spun around, I watched him reach to the floor of his room, grab a random shirt, smell it, and then slip it over his head as smoothly as if carried by the wind.

It occurred to me then that I hadn't had sex in six months.

The last time was the day I found out Adam was sleeping with Kelly, when I'd come across a text message on his phone and realized he'd been with her less than an hour after he'd had his head between my legs.

Ballistic, I went straight to Starbucks, ordered my usual, and asked Kelly if she liked the way my pussy tasted. She threw the caramel macchiato at my head and called me a psycho.

"Why do you call record executives Mr. Winkle?" I asked Paul.

"Because that's what they do," he said. "They wink at you. Then they wipe their asses with their hands and shake yours, and they think you can't smell the shit."

Paul started pacing near the door. He wasn't wearing a watch but he glanced at his wrist, glanced at Michael, and said, "Let's go. We're late."

July 24, 2000

"This is a bad goddamn sign."

That's what I said to Michael when we arrived at the meeting spot designated by Mr. Winkle—a crowded, upscale microbrewery in Midtown, filled with the grown-up versions of the guys I went to high school with—the shitheads who scored touchdowns, got all the girls, and called me a fag.

The other two Michaels were already at a table. When Caelum and I sat down, Burke said, "Winkle's not here yet."

This is where I should probably describe the band. For—what do you call it when you want your kids and their kids to know? Posterity?

I'll start with Burke, our bass player. Burke's a tall, gangly guy with more rhythm than John Entwistle and John Paul Jones combined. He just turned twenty-five; he and his girlfriend Queenie live in a studio apartment below street level, and they have this big laundry sink in their kitchen where they make ice cream in their spare time. Burke is obsessed with ice cream. His dream is to own and operate a homemade ice cream shop someday—he's constantly talking about what kinds of "epicurean" flavors he'll serve, and how the secrets to a custardy consistency are the use of fresh ingredients and a perfect ratio of cream to butter fat.

People always ask if Burke and Caelum are brothers because they're both so tall, and neither Michael seems bothered by the question, but it drives me out of my mind because besides the height they look nothing alike. Burke's got blond hair and freckles. Caelum has a mass of dark pubic hair growing out of his head. Plus, how the hell could they be brothers when they have the same first name? That only works if your last one is Foreman.

Caelum—what can I say about Mikey C? He's the best friend I've ever had. A subtle but really innovative guitarist who lives and dies by this band. His dedication is inspiring, really. He makes fliers for all the shows, he designed us a website, and he's polite and friendly to Winkles, which is more than I can say for myself. I respect Caelum. He's a good guy and I hope we don't lose him.

Incidentally, Michael's sister just moved in with me. Eliza. More on Eliza later.

Angelo, our drummer, is the stereotypical rock star of the band. He drinks like a sailor on leave, has a penchant for well-endowed co-eds, and bears a strong resemblance to a serial killer named Richard Ramirez—you know, that goddamn Night Stalker guy. Believe it or not, this makes him a real hit with the ladies.

The Michaels and I, along with my manager, Tony Feldman, had met with the tardy Winkle twice before. The first time, he came to a show and made us a bunch of promises that got our hopes up. Second time he took us to a big industry party and got us drunk. But Winkle's eyebrows look like caterpillars trapped in cocoons, and I'm pretty sure someone catching bugs over their eyes can't be trusted.

Needless to say, the guy gives off a bad vibe. Being around him inflames my pancreas like nothing else. But the multimedia company that employs him happens to be the same company my favorite band, the Drones, signed to. The Drones are Winkle's big claim to fame. He discovered them in a garage in Fresno and a year later their first record went platinum. So did their next two. And they're no walk in the park. They're fuzzy guitars, feedback, and electronic experimentation, not the breezy pop music that's been saturating the airwaves, so their success is no small coup, believe me. Very little of the good shit ever makes its way into the mainstream.

When Winkle finally walked in, he craned around the restaurant like an ostrich until he found me. As he approached the table, I detected a look of surprise on his face. Standing above us, he eyed the Michaels like they were part of a police lineup and said he didn't realize we were all going to be there.

The waiter came over to take our order. I wanted chicken fingers but he said they were on the kids' menu and apparently you have to be twelve or under to eat strips of fried chicken. The guy even had the balls to ask me how old I was. Winkle slipped him two twenties and a ten and said: "He's fifty. Bring him his chicken."

After that, Winkle stood up and said—and this is his exact voice, like he has a dozen rocks in his throat—"Gentlemen, would you excuse me and Mr. Hudson for a few minutes?" He looked at me, and the little imprisoned caterpillars straightened into one long chrysalis. "Let's you and I go have a drink."

I gave the Michaels an iffy look and followed Winkle to the farthest corner of the bar.

"You've got an incredible voice," he said. "And some great songs. Really powerful stuff."

I thanked him and tried to convince myself the bad feeling I had was just nerves.

"I'm ready to offer you a deal," he said. "Right here, right now."

My heart pounded like a bongo drum, the kind of beat you can feel from your head to your toes, and strangely enough, the first thoughts that ran through my mind involved my new roommate. I imagined sprinting up the stairs, bursting into the apartment to tell her the band had just signed a record contract. Her cheeks would be flushed like they'd been this morning from running. Her skin would be warm and salty. She would throw her arms around me and kiss me and then she would drag me to the ground and we would do it like dogs on the kitchen floor.

"However," Winkle said, knocking me out of my little insta-fantasy as I began anticipating some sort of ludicrous stipulation I desperately hoped I could live with.

Then he goes: "We only want you."

My stare stayed totally fixed on that asshole's eyebrows. I told him I wasn't sure I understood what he meant, even though I had a pretty good idea.

He told me to can the band. He said, "You're better than they are."

According to Winkle, signing four guys to one contract is asking for trouble. And anyway, as far as he's concerned, Paul Hudson *is* Bananafish.

I didn't speak or move until Winkle looked like he was about to resume his discourse-o-shit, then I raised my hand to keep the silence in tact, and to halt the world as it spun around me.

"We're talking about the opportunity of a lifetime, Paul. Not to mention a lot of money."

Three hundred and fifty thousand dollars—that's the number he threw at me. Let me repeat: Three hundred and fifty thousand goddamn Gs.

I dropped my forehead to the bar, then I looked up at the table of Michaels across the room. I pointed their way and said, "Those guys are my friends."

Winkle said he'd make sure I had more friends than I knew what to do with, then he went on to outline the main points of the contract. I listened to all of it, feeling like the acid from the orange juice I'd had an hour earlier was eating away at my insides. Maybe it's killing the cancer, I thought hopefully.

With more desperation than I care to admit, I asked Winkle if we could work something out, if we could at least start with the band and see how it goes.

He said he sees me as a solo artist, plain and simple. But even a solo artist needs a band, right? The next twenty seconds went something like this:

"Paul, we've got the best studio musicians in the country lined up and waiting."

"I don't want a bunch of goddamn studio musicians. I want the Michaels."

"It's not open to negotiation."

I said I needed a minute to think. I hit the bathroom in a daze, locked myself in a stall, put the lid down on the toilet seat, and sat with my head in my hands, staring at the piss stains on the concrete, pondering the proposition that had just been laid before me, and also wondering why the idiots who used that stall couldn't aim their dicks into a bowl wider in circumference than my head and Winkle's ass put together.

A thick lump had formed in my throat, I wanted a cigarette, my pancreas hurt like hell, and for one pathetic instant I thought I was going to say yes.

I'm not sure if I spent five seconds or five hours like that, and I have no recollection of returning to the bar, but when I was back in front of Winkle I heard myself mumble, "I can't do it." I didn't even turn around when Winkle called my name because I was afraid he'd be able to change my mind.

My chicken fingers were waiting for me, with two little bowls next to the plate. One had ketchup in it; the other had some kind of creamy salad dressing shit. Normally I'd never in a zillion years put salad dressing on chicken, but I picked up a finger and dipped.

Burke asked me what happened and I said, "I'll tell you outside. Let's just go."

Angelo, who'd ordered a rib eye and the most expensive wine on the menu, said, "Can't we eat first?"

I dragged them outside. In the cab ride back downtown, I

told the disappointed Michaels that Winkle didn't understand the direction of the band. They asked a zillion questions and I repeated the same answer: "I don't want to talk about it."

The suckiest part was I felt almost as bad about lying as I did about the truth.

To be continued. I'm late for work.

Over.

The *Sonica* offices occupied the fifteenth floor of a tall, unremarkable building below Columbus Circle. Terry North, the editor in chief of the magazine, was on the phone when I walked in. He invited me into his cluttered office using a fly-swatting hand gesture and nodded for me to sit.

After finishing up his call, the first thing he said was that I looked just like his kid sister, Maggie, who had been killed by a drunk driver at the age of twenty.

I didn't know what to say to that. "Mr. North, I really want to thank—"

"Call me Terry. And don't thank me. I didn't hire you because Doug said you know your stuff, I hired you because your piece was smashing. I've known that guy since 1970 and I've never been able to get him to talk like that."

Terry was as an amiable but blunt man, mid-fifties, tall, with a head of bristly dark and tan hair like an Airedale.

From behind me, I heard a woman's voice, replete with sharp, hypercritical insinuation. "So, you're Doug Blackman's little *friend*."

Terry introduced me to Lucy Enfield. "If you want the good assignments you'll have to be nice to her," he said, "even if she isn't always nice to you."

Lucy Enfield was the creative director of the magazine. She had a reputation for being tough, and her obvious hauteur, combined with her sharp, uptown style, told me she thought she was better than all the music geeks who worked beneath her.

Lucy had long legs, tiny slits for eyes, and an ambushing smile. She made it a point to tell me she was *the* authority on the New York music scene and said, "If I don't know who they are, they're not worth listening to."

"Have you heard of Bananafish?" I asked, hoping my job would present me with an opportunity to help Michael.

"No," Lucy said. "But that's the dumbest name I've ever heard for a band. Who do they sound like?"

I found it revealing that Lucy said *who* instead of *what*. Furthermore, Bananafish was not a dumb name for a band. And even if it was, the greatest bands in the world have the dumbest names.

One glitch: I had no idea what Bananafish sounded like. I hadn't heard them yet.

"Radiohead," I told Lucy. To my knowledge, Bananafish sounded nothing like Radiohead, but this seemed to be the thing to say if you wanted to impress a critic.

Lucy looked momentarily intrigued. "Where do they play?"

"A place called Rings of Saturn, mostly."

As fast as I'd grabbed her, I lost her. "Eliza, Rings of Saturn is where bands go to die."

Terry told me to come back and see him at the end of the day, and from there I followed Lucy on a tour of the office, which could have been the headquarters of any generic business and wasn't nearly as hip as I had imagined.

Further dampening my mood, Lucy repeated her earlier dig, presenting me to one of the senior editors as "Doug Blackman's *friend*."

No matter that I'd only known the woman for fifteen minutes, I hated Lucy Enfield.

"I hope you weren't expecting a corner office with a view

of the park," she said, coming to a stop at a partitioned cubicle to the left of a large room.

My cubicle was identical to the ten or so other associate editors' cubicles surrounding it. It contained a desk and chair, a computer, and one encouraging sign—a coffee mug with a photo of U2 circa *The Joshua Tree* that the last occupant must've left behind—only there was a cautionary chip in the mug, right in the middle of the Edge's hat, like someone had pulled a William Tell on him.

Lucy pointed to a large stack of papers and two FOR PROMOTIONAL USE ONLY CDs on the desk. "Letters to the editor," she said. "Weed through them, see if there's anything worth printing. And the CDs need to be reviewed for the next issue."

I waited until Lucy walked away and then I sat down. It occurred to me that I might be in over my head, but I had to bury that, otherwise I would've started to cry. Or worse, run to Port Authority and hopped a bus back to deathland.

With nothing to put away, I opened and closed all the drawers in the desk, booted up the computer, and spent the rest of the day listening to one of the CDs I'd been given to review. The disc was called *Chocolate Starfish and the Hot Dog-Flavored Water*. In my humble opinion, it was crap, but I had to figure out how to say that using five hundred well-thought-out words.

At six o'clock I went back to see Terry.

"How's it going, Mags?" He tilted his neck from side to side and I heard his vertebrae release two loud cracks. "Mind if I call you Mags?"

"No," I said, even though it seemed creepy.

"Everything all right? You look a little gray."

I took a step forward and kept my voice down. "This might be out of line, but is Lucy always so curt, or did I do something to annoy her?"

"Both." Terry told me there was a hierarchy at *Sonica*. Lucy had started as an intern, putting in sixty-hour weeks to get to her high-ranking position; thus she had an aversion to any person who didn't start in the mailroom, especially if the person's employment could be construed as "carnal nepotism."

"But I swear, I never so much as—"

"Not my business." Terry waved me off. "Just expect the shitty assignments for a while. Hence the 66 gig."

Lucy came in shortly thereafter, handed me press credentials for the 66 show that night, then gave me a blue-lined copy of the September issue and explained that as an associate editor, I was required to read and copyedit the magazine before it went to print.

"You have until noon tomorrow," Lucy said.

It was going to be a long night.

"Only in America. This could only happen in America. Because America is in a tailspin from grace. What we invented—what our contribution to the world has been, the sonic representation of the freedom we as a country pride ourselves on—is rock 'n' roll music. But rock 'n' roll music is a dying man. No, not just a dying man. It's a man being crucified, Eliza. It's Jesus Christ. Our Savior. It's The Way, The Truth, and The Light bleeding down on us from the cross, and you know what? We're all just standing around watching the poor guy die."

That's the analogy that Doug Blackman had offered me over cheeseburgers and French fries in his hotel room in Cleveland.

Doug said radio was inundated with what he called "musical heathens and soulless pop pagans." For the most part, they don't write their own songs—and the ones who do can't seem to write good ones—but they dress in hip clothes, they dance and lip-sync like nothing else, they're skilled in the art of self-promotion, and, most notably, they play by the rules.

Doug picked up my tape recorder and spoke directly into the mike. "*Nobody*, and I mean *nobody*, ever started a revolution playing by the rules."

The man was cynical, to say the least. But he had come of age in the sixties—that mythical generation of turbulence and change, where new things were new and people had hope. Rock 'n' roll, civil rights, men walking on the moon. He'd protested wars and preached about a woman's right to choose. He'd earned his opinion.

Doug said the America he knew then was now the home of the lost, the confused, and the greedy. He said we live in a country that values commerce over art, a country that allows mediocre talents to thrive and breed and poison the airwaves, movie screens, television, and printed word like toxic chemicals in the water supply.

"Once in a while something pure slips through the cracks, but these days it's rare."

"Why do you think it's so rare?" I asked him.

By then he'd had half a bottle of wine. He was worked up. "I'll tell you one of the reasons why it's rare in music— because record companies have become little divisions of billion-dollar corporations, that's why. In some cases, record company CEOs are nothing more than middle-management kiss-asses. They don't know shit about music and don't care. Their job is to sell records. They don't need a good ear, they need good marketing skills. And that's only half of it. There's politics involved. *Politics*."

"How does that explain your success?"

Doug scratched his temple, which he had a habit of doing whenever he paused to think. "It was different when I started. We're talking 1966. What we were doing then was relatively novel. You had Dylan doing the folk-rock thing, you had the Beatles taking over the world, and I came from the blues camp—I was a white guy trying to make gospel music with a raspy voice and a guitar. But if I were twenty-four today and released the same record I put out then, how many copies do you think it would sell?"

"Blasphemy," I said. I couldn't imagine my world without the sound of Doug Blackman in it. "Your music changed my life."

I told Doug about my first concert experience: His 1990 *The Life You Save Could Be Your Own* tour at the Cleveland Coliseum. I was sixteen, and it was just a few weeks after my episode in the bathroom with the kitchen knife, so needless to say I was a little down on myself. Michael, Vera, and I sat in the fourth row—seats nine, ten, and eleven. And when Doug ambled onto the stage, red Gibson in hand, and belted out "The Day I Became a Ghost" with what looked like tears in his eyes, it was as if he were speaking directly to me.

"That song gave me courage," I said. "It reminded me of something I'd learned so many years before. That I could feel things. Even if it was pain."

"*That's* the magic," Doug said. "*That's* why you have to save the dying man. Because you want him around to keep saving you."

"Save the savior," I said.

"You dig, Eliza Caelum?"

"I dig, Mr. Blackman."

During the 66 show, Doug's words were all I could think about. 66 was one of the worst bands I had ever seen or heard. It was as if, instead of amps, the guitars were plugged into helium tanks. And all the girls in the audience were dressed exactly like Amanda Strunk, a peroxide blond with a trampy, been-around-the-block attractiveness, whose only real talent was the ability to say *fuck* and lift up her skirt at the same time.

The crowd screamed and applauded like they were watching the Beatles.

Following the show, I walked to Tompkins Square Park, where I sat on a bench, stared at the word HOPE carved into stone above the water-fountain gazebo, and jotted down notes about the concert as Doug's words echoed in my ears: *Tell me what you listen to and I'll tell you who you are.*

Musical heathens? Soulless pop pagans?

I recalled Paul saying he'd gone out with Amanda Strunk. I wrote *bitch* in parenthesis next to Amanda's name, questioned why I'd done it, and quickly scribbled it out until it became nothing but a rectangular window to the next page.

Most of the bars and cafes in the East Village were still bustling. There were cool people with cool hair and cool clothes everywhere. I saw a guy in a cobalt-colored shirt whose posture, from the back, reminded me of the way Adam used to stand, sort of off balance and tilted to the side. Adam was a blue, human Leaning Tower of Pisa.

I wondered how different New York would have felt if Adam had been there. Not that I wanted him there. I didn't miss him anymore. But I missed the idea of him. I missed having a hand to hold. I missed the illusion of safety.

Heading down Avenue A, I wondered how it was possible to be surrounded by so many people and still feel utterly alone. At Houston Street I came upon Rings of Saturn. The marquee said:

BANANAFISH UPSTRS EVRY THUR

I called Vera to see if she wanted to meet me at Rings of Saturn but she was already in bed. Then I tried Michael. He was still at practice, and I asked him if I could head down to the rehearsal space and hear the band.

"Not a good night for that," he said. "Some other time, though."

Inside Rings of Saturn, the main room was small, the ceiling was low enough that I could almost touch it, and everything—the walls, chairs, floor, tables, even the bar—was black. There was a staircase in the right-hand corner—also black—leading up to what I presumed was the stage.

The place was empty except for a young couple at a table in the back, and a burly bartender; I sat down and told the bartender that my brother was a member of Bananafish.

"Which one?" he said.

"Michael."

"Which one?"

"Oh, right." I laughed. "Caelum. The guitarist."

The bartender nodded as if he approved. He only had one working eyeball. The other was clearly made of glass and seemed ill-fitted, bulging so far out of its socket I was afraid it might pop into my lap if he got too excited.

He asked me what I wanted and I ordered the only thing I ever drank. "Water, please. But may I have it in a martini glass with an olive?"

As the bartender fixed my drink, he educated me on the proper way to hot-wire a car. He mentioned a red wire, and warned that if I didn't do it right there was a small chance I'd be electrocuted. He told me his name was John the Baptist, and when I expressed skepticism he admitted his real name was John Barnaby. The moniker had evolved from his chosen profession.

"Dispensing the blessed liquid," he said. "Why haven't I seen you at the shows?"

"I just moved here."

I asked him for a refill and he said, "Want me to throw in a little vodka?"

"No, just the water, please. And another olive, unless I have to pay for it."

"You a friend of Bill's?"

I didn't know what that meant. John explained it was a slang term for a member of Alcoholics Anonymous. He and Bill had been friends for twenty years.

"No," I said. "I just don't drink."

"Why not?"

I didn't feel like getting into the meat of it. That is, how the majority of my high school and college classmates got drunk every weekend, and how watching them throw up and pass out depressed me so I refrained from participating, even though this turned me into more of an outcast than I already was.

"It just seems like a bad idea," I said, "swallowing a liquid that can be set on fire."

Smiling, John refilled my glass. "Since you're new here, I'm going to give you some advice." John picked up a red plastic toothpick that had been designed to look like a teeny-tiny sword. He stabbed three green, pimento-stuffed olives with it, and slid the whole thing into my drink. "On the house," he said. "Now pay attention. If you're ever walking down the street and some psycho with a gun decides to open fire, here's what to do—don't make eye contact with him and keep walking. Do you hear me? Just pick up the pace and go in the opposite direction of the guy. Unless he's a trained assassin, in which case you're screwed. But if he's not, if he's just some postal worker or something, it's doubtful he'll be able to hit a moving target."

I wasn't sure if John the Baptist was an eccentric or a sociopath, but I liked him either way, and I left him the last two dollars in my wallet.

The question is one of faith. Faith in my talent. Faith in my decisions. And faith in the idea that the truth, even if it can't pay my bills, can still set me free.

I know. Funny. Ha. Ha.

Am I talking loud enough? I'm trying to be quiet because my new roommate is asleep across the hall, but I'll get to her in a few minutes.

First, faith—one of the many pancreas-burning issues I wrestle with every day. Trying to hold on to faith in this business is like trying to hold on to a rope while dangling off a cliff. And believe me, I'm not afraid I'm reaching the end of the rope as much as I'm afraid of letting go and having a long way to fall.

Rehearsal was supposed to run late tonight, but we were all down in the dumps over the Winkle fiasco and couldn't accomplish a thing. Then Feldman showed up, pissed as hell. He came in demanding to know what was wrong with me, and if I realized I'd alienated one of the biggest names in the industry, not to mention potentially throwing my career down the drain.

I dragged Feldman into the hallway, shut the door, and asked him if he'd sent me to the meeting knowing what Winkle was going to say. He told me I was supposed to go alone—his way of answering my question. I reminded him that I'm not a solo artist, and he goes, "Well, maybe you should be. You write the songs. You hold the crowds. You make the decisions."

I begged him to keep it down. He pointed to the door and said, "You didn't tell them?"

Hell, no, I didn't tell them. And I asked Feldman not to tell them either. They don't need to hear that kind of negative shit.

Feldman ranted until he ran out of rants. He thinks I purposely try to make everything harder than it has to be and said only a fool would turn down an opportunity to sign with one of the biggest record labels in the universe. But the thing is, it took me a long time to find three guys I click with—we're a band and we're staying a band, and if that means we play Rings of Saturn for the rest of our lives, so be it.

For what it's worth, I don't go out of my way to be difficult. I just want to sleep with a clear conscience and wake up with the ability to look at myself in the mirror. I also want my life to be my own. Even if it's a shitty goddamn life, it's still mine.

The night Feldman and I met, at the party of a mutual friend, Feldman hadn't impressed me in the least. And, well, actually, the so-called mutual friend wasn't much of a friend. She's what I like to call a fleeting lapse of judgment, but I don't really want to get into that. Anyway, she coaxed me into playing a few songs. Afterward, Feldman appeared out of nowhere and fed me one of those "you've got star written all over you" lines. I didn't fall for it right away. My goals have nothing to do with celestial bodies. But he was persistent. He showed an enthusiastic interest in my music, offered to manage me on the spot, paid for the rehearsal space, and even got me a social security card and driver's license—despite the fact that Hudson is my stage name.

All Feldman wants out of life—and he even admits this—is to be somebody's Brian Epstein—you know, the guy supposedly responsible for the Beatles. Feldman said he'd been searching for his McCartney or Lennon and he picked me. In the meantime, he works with 66 because they're actually making him money.

Feldman was also the one who got us the residency at Rings of Saturn. A few years ago I'd shamelessly begged for a chance to play there, but after doing a short set for the owner of the place, the guy said my music had "too much texture," whatever the hell that meant.

When I asked Feldman how he managed to change the guy's mind, he laughed and told me that as a young, struggling lawyer, he'd represented a number of New Jersey's finest organized crime families. "I have friends in low places and they all owe me favors," he said. "I just cashed one in."

I didn't ask.

After Feldman left rehearsal, we put our instruments aside in favor of getting stoned, and then spent half the night debating the most popular flavor of ice cream. Burke insisted it was chocolate, even though it's vanilla—I actually read this somewhere—but I was too distracted to argue about it. First, I couldn't stop thinking about Winkle. Then I couldn't stop thinking about Eliza, and I wondered what Michael would say if he knew I was letting my imagination run riot with his sister. He'd warned me before Eliza got to town: Hands off, he said. Keep an eye on her, be her friend if she'll let you, but no messing around.

When I asked Vera why Michael was so obstinate, she told me that some asshole had recently broken Eliza's heart. A drummer, no less. Hell, even I know girls should stay away from the goddamn drummers.

Speaking of, Angelo pointed a stick at my face and told me vanilla was boring, but the thing is, I never said it was the most fun, I said it was the most popular.

Caelum goes: "There have been studies done on this topic, gentlemen. You could wager a bet and look it up." Caelum always talks like someone's dad when he's high.

Angelo suggested bubble gum as a number one and I told him no one over the age of eight orders bubble gum ice cream. Then Burke raised his hand like he was in school and asked if maybe we could talk a little more about what happened with

Winkle. I immediately suggested we call it a night but Angelo wouldn't let the goddamn bubble gum issue die. He claims he orders bubble gum ice cream all the time.

Burke stood up and goes, "Maybe we should at least consider whatever Winkle suggested."

Angelo jumped on the bandwagon, yelling, "Yeah. It's better than nothing."

The rehearsal space is twelve by twelve, if that. There was no need to yell.

Caelum said yielding to Winkle would mean the end of folding shirts for me, not to mention it would keep him in the band. Or so he thought. The desperation in Michael's voice made me feel even guiltier, and for the zillionth time I said I didn't want to talk about it. My pancreas ached and I had to press on my side to ease the goddamn pain.

"Oh, here he goes," Angelo said. "Enough with the fucking pancreas."

"Is a little sympathy too much to ask?" I was looking to be coddled, not mocked.

"Here," Caelum said, passing me what was left of a joint. "Here's a little sympathy."

At that point I packed up my stuff and came home. This is where it gets interesting.

All the lights were off when I walked in. The windows were closed and it was so hot it felt like being inside a terrarium. I turned on the light, went to the bathroom to take a piss, and lit a cigarette. Then I went across the hall and knocked on Eliza's door. Nothing. No "Who is it?" or "Come in" from the other side. I just assumed she wasn't there and walked in.

She was there, all right. Sitting on her bed, reading. My fan was on her floor, positioned to blow directly on her face, and she was wearing a pink lace bra and matching pink lace underwear.

I said hi and then laughed while she scrambled for the sheet and covered herself up—bad idea. I took this as a sign of weak-

ness, and exhibiting signs of weakness in front of me, especially while in a state of near nakedness, was the wrong move. It
gave me an advantage.

I sat down on her bed, took off my shoes, and stubbed out
my cigarette using the bottom of my left sole. Then I hopped
over her, rolled her extra pillow into a ball, and lay down, completely ignoring her protests.

"Relax," I told her. "We're friends, right?"

She said, "We barely know each other."

"Irrelevant," I said. "I could really use a friend right now."

I made her swear a zillion times that what I was about to
say would never leave the room, then I told her the truth about
what happened with Winkle. I don't know why. I guess I
thought she might have some insight. I also wanted a reason
to stay in her room.

I told her how the worst part was I'd actually thought about
it before I said no. She said nobody would've blamed me if I'd
said yes, but holy Hell, I would've blamed me. I swear to God
I'd rather kill myself than give in to those cocksuckers.

I tried to play with the little pearl in her ear but she wasn't
having it. Then, just to get a reaction, I asked her if she always
wore bras that matched her underwear, and at first she got all
shy, but eventually she flipped her hair and said yes.

I asked her if yes meant unexceptionally always or once a
week. She said it meant every day. She also told me the reason—
because she doesn't have a lot of money to spend on clothes,
and this way, even if she has old jeans and a crummy T-shirt on,
she still feels like she looks nice. Like she's dressed up.

It probably goes without saying that from now on, every time
I see her, I'm going to wonder what color her underwear is.

I closed my eyes and moaned, trying to stymie the hard-on
I'd had since I walked in the room, and Eliza said: "What's
wrong? Your migrating pancreas acting up again?"

I told her it wasn't the pancreas this time and she called me a bastard, but she was kind of smiling when she said it. Honestly, it took all my strength not to lean over and kiss her right then. I would've done it, too, had I not been sort of distracted by the long, thin scar that slashed through the middle of her left wrist.

Without thinking, I reached out and took hold of her arm, and was immediately struck by how fragile it seemed. Then I ran my finger across the scar—it felt exactly like the hem on a pair of the boot-cut jeans I inventoried last Tuesday.

I knew all about the scar—Michael told me the whole story, how he'd found her bleeding on their bathroom floor when she was like, sixteen or something.

Eliza pulled her hand away and tucked it under her pillow. "I'm tired," she said. "Would you mind going to your room?"

Okay, so this is what I did next: I reached over and lifted a lock of her hair, one that had fallen across her eye. I moved it back off of her face, barely touching her skin, and my finger grazed the tiny pearl in her ear. I think we were having a moment but I'm not sure. By then I'd sort of lost myself in her face. No kidding, if you put me in a room with Eliza and a hundred beautiful girls, Eliza would be the one I'd walk over to. There's something magnetic about her. And sad. And she does this thing when she talks—she dips her chin and raises her eyes and looks right into you. It's a gift, really. I think she could make whoever she's talking to feel like the only person in the room— the only person in the universe, even. But then it switches— when she's not looking at you it's like her mind is in another world, miles away, and her dark, falcon eyes point upward, like she's in some kind of mesmerized state of flirtation with the sky.

Did I mention how much I wanted to kiss her? I wanted to kiss her lips and her eyelids and the curve in what I'm going to call "the transition area" where her hip flows into her waist. And my desire wasn't just confined to my dick. She made my whole goddamn body taut, like some invisible energy force was pulling me up by the skin.

I inched closer to her and she goes: "Don't even think about it."

I was starting to get the feeling she was trying not to like me, so I told her this story about how, when I was a kid, my mom made clam chowder for dinner one night. I think it was my birthday or something, and Mom thought it was a big deal to serve clam chowder but I refused to eat it. I told her I didn't like clams and she said, "You've never tasted a clam. How do you know you don't like them?" She said I had to taste it. If I didn't like it, she promised she'd make me a peanut butter sandwich, but I had to take at least one spoonful of the clam chowder first.

I paused to make sure Eliza was still listening. Then I said, "Needless to say, I didn't have peanut butter for dinner that night."

"That's a touching anecdote," Eliza said. "But I'm allergic to shellfish."

I told her she was missing the point and she started jabbering on about how she knew I had a girlfriend named Avril but was sleeping with this Beth chick, not to mention I was her brother's friend, not to mention the last thing she needed was to get involved with a guy like me, yada, yada, yada, I swear I thought she was going to start crying, and normally that would have sent me hauling ass in the other direction, but you know what? I had a bizarre urge to put my arms around her and hold her until she fell asleep.

Remember this moment, my friend the tape recorder. Lying next to Eliza, I had the feeling I'd just found something I didn't even know I'd lost. We hovered above the moment like two rain clouds, until I said: "Don't swear off all fruit just because you ate one bad apple."

She said, "Please go to your room."

I said, "If I go, I'm taking the fan with me."

She said, "Take the stupid fan."

I halted in front of the fan on my way out the door. I think I even touched the cord. But I left the room without it.

Over.

Prior to moving to New York, I had a lot of silly fantasies about what it was going to be like. Vera and I would hang out at quaint cafes by day, discussing life and how to live it; at night there would be cool lounges where she and Michael and I would see live music. But Michael and Vera were busy, and so was I. We hardly saw each other that first week.

And I couldn't get Paul out of my head. I kept thinking about what he'd told me the night he'd wandered into my room—about how he'd walked away from what might have been his only shot at a record deal because he didn't want to let my brother and the rest of the band down. There was a lot more to him, I guessed, than the flippant pretext and cocky-bastard smile he presented to the world.

But it was as though Paul didn't even live on Ludlow Street. More often than not, I had the place to myself and I didn't like it. I didn't like waking up and seeing the door to his room screaming-wide open, his bed in complete disarray but untouched from the day before. It made me feel like I was missing something.

Days went by before Paul ended our incommunicado, using a scrap of paper he stuck to my door while I was out running one morning, affixing it to the wood with a piece of gum.

Why didn't you come to the show on Thursday?

I get off work at 6 tonight. Meet me here. I've been thinking about you.

Potentially yours, WP Hudson.

I spent the entire morning obsessing over every word of
that note. I wanted to know what "I've been thinking about
you" *literally* meant. Thinking about me *how*? Did it mean
thinking: "I wonder how she is" or "I wonder if she likes Pink
Floyd" or "I wonder if she's good in bed" or what? There
were too many interpretations. And then the "potentially
yours" sign off. How was I supposed to decode that?

At any rate, I'd missed Bananafish at Rings of Saturn the
week before because I was busy trying to put the finishing
touches on my panning of the 66 show in the hopes of winning the respect of Lucy Enfield, only to have Lucy turn
around and assign me the job of fact-checking a feature on
a Brazilian fashion model, while Corbin, the guy in the cubicle beside me, got to interview Wayne Coyne.

I did my best to maintain the delusion that it wasn't
excruciating to be employed by the nation's paramount music
publication and have to research an article about a girl who
was quoted as saying: "It's like, such a drag when singers
whine about the world. I just want to say to them, you know,
like, shut up and dance."

"I hate my boss," I vented to Vera over lunch in Bryant
Park the day Paul left me the note. "Because of her, all my
coworkers think I'm a groupie."

We were sitting on a bench, and Vera scooted a few inches away so she could turn and face me. She split the cookie
she was eating in half and gave me a piece. "Why do your
coworkers think you're a groupie?"

"My boss told them I slept with Doug to get the job."

The tragedy of the situation escaped Vera. All she said was,

"I love how you're on a first-name basis with Doug Blackman."

I let it go. The November deadline was of supreme importance and I only had thirty minutes before I had to go back to work. "Don't make Michael quit the band."

Vera's breath blew a piece of hair off her face. "That's not fair, Eliza. I'm twenty-seven. If I don't start school soon, I'll be forty by the time I graduate."

"Marriage is about compromise," I said stupidly.

"Right. Except notice I'm the only one compromising," she sighed. "Do you know that almost every cent Michael makes at the restaurant goes into the band? We're living paycheck to paycheck. *My* paycheck. I can't do it anymore."

I couldn't argue with her. The situation was unfortunate for all involved. But someone had to feign hope and I decided that someone would be me. "I have a feeling things are going to start happening for Bananafish."

I crushed up my piece of cookie, tossed the crumbs onto the ground, and half a dozen pigeons swarmed the bench.

"E*li*za," Vera said. "If a rat scurried up to you right now, would you feed it?"

"No."

"Pigeons are rats with wings."

I wished she wouldn't have said that. I had enough to worry about and didn't need to add flying rats to the list.

Vera gazed over her shoulder at the New York Public Library. "I applied to Columbia," she said. "If I get in, I'll start in January. If the band isn't signed by then, Michael understands he has to quit." She looked directly at me. "This is what I want."

I had to laugh. The phrase *what I want* struck me. It contains so much entitlement, so many complications, but encompasses only what a person doesn't have.

It made me ponder what I wanted. I fingered the note in my pocket and felt emptiness in the pit of my stomach—

like I hadn't eaten for three years. Then I thought about Adam. I thought about all the things I'd wanted from him, things I knew he never could've given me, and I whittled all of them down to one juvenile, esoteric wish.

"A song," I said aloud.

"What?"

"The whole time Adam and I were together, he never wrote one song for me."

Vera looked like she was trying to think of an appropriate response to such a stupid desire. "He was a drummer. You hate it when drummers sing."

This is true. I say, down with the Romantics, Don Henley, Phil Collins! Down with songs like "Yellow Submarine" and "Love Stinks." Drummers have enough to do behind their equipment. Half the time nobody can see them. And fans should be able to make eye contact with singers. It's sexier that way. But Vera was missing the point.

"I'd be a sucker for a guy who wrote me a song," I said. "Like Beth or Rosanna or Sara. Or Sharona. Is that too much to ask? To be somebody's Sharona?"

"Aim high," Vera said.

I hadn't left the office before eight all week, but my conversation with Vera had left me feeling heavy, and I didn't want to spend all evening alone in the apartment, stuck under the burden that was my thousand-pound heart.

I snuck out of work early, went home, and had just gotten dressed when I heard Paul bounding up the stairs. A second later he was in my doorway.

"You're here." He grinned. "*Finally.*"

"*I'm* here? That's funny considering your bed hasn't been slept in for days."

Paul let out a laugh. "Oh, Eliza. Sweet Eliza. You do like me, don't you?"

Maybe I'm weak for music men. Maybe I'm weak, period. But I couldn't deny I was charmed by his arrogant, foolish guise. And since I hadn't been charmed by anyone in a long time, I couldn't just write that off.

Paul looked weird, collegiate. It took me a few seconds to figure out why. He was dressed, head to toe, in Gap clothes.

"I know," he said. "Let me change and then we'll go."

He reappeared in the hall a minute later, bright as a sunbeam, wearing the pants to his green suit and a yellow T-shirt that said: *My Jive Limo ~ A ride you'll never forget.*

"We match," he said, pointing first at his shirt and then at my chest.

"Excuse me?"

"Your bra," he said, which he could see through my dress. "Yellow. Nice."

I called him a bastard and he laughed with a sense of accomplishment, as if he'd been trying to get me to insult him. "Do you like to gamble?" he asked, furiously opening and closing drawers in the kitchen, a guitar pick sticking out the side of his mouth.

"Why?"

"Don't be so suspicious. Just answer the goddamn question."

"I've never really—"

"Score!" he said, discovering a five-dollar bill under a mess of pens, rubber bands, and plastic cutlery.

As soon as we were on the street, Paul prodded me to walk faster. "Kick it in the ass or we'll miss the first game."

"Why don't we take the subway?"

He came to a smashing halt in the middle of the sidewalk. "*Subway?*" he said, as if I'd invited him to walk through the gates of hell. "I don't ride anything that goes underground. I'll be subterranean enough when I'm dead."

Witnessing Paul exhibit vulnerability, even superciliously,

also made me want to touch his chest. I'd never had the urge to touch anybody's chest, but Paul was so animated and energetic, I imagined a metrical, pumping drum pounding in place of a heartbeat, and I wanted to feel the rhythm. I wanted to merge with it. I wanted to *be* it.

"That's the gayest thing I've ever heard," I said.

He laughed. "Warning: if you insult my heterosexual eminence one more time, I'm going to have to throw you down in the middle of the street and prove myself."

I almost said it again, just to test him.

Six months is a long time.

It was a thousand degrees outside.

"A-ha," Paul said. "Now I know how to shut you up."

In silence, we continued west halfway across town, eventually arriving at the door of a nondescript building with a green awning that said St. Vrain Senior Center.

"You said we were gambling."

"We are."

"This looks like a home for old people."

"What, old people can't gamble?"

"They better have air-conditioning."

Paul took me by the elbow and dragged me through the door, down a long hallway, and into a sad, spacious rec room with a low ceiling, a drab linoleum floor, and—thank the Lord—air-conditioning. The sour smell of urine and powdered mashed potatoes hung in the air.

A fleshy, middle-aged woman named Mary Lou waved at Paul. She called him Willie and told him to sit at table five. "Patty asked if you were coming," Mary Lou said. "She claims she never wins when you're not here."

"Patty is the most competitive player in this place," Mary Lou told me, her nose scrunching into a snout. "And she has a little crush on Willie."

Must be an infectious disease, I mused, following Paul to

a desk where another overweight woman sat with a box of *Hello, My Name Is* tags.

Paul picked up a black marker, wrote WILLIE in big, robotic letters, and stuck it on his shirt.

"What's with the name?"

"My alias," he whispered. "Don't blow my cover. I have a reputation to uphold. These people think I'm a goddamn kindergarten teacher."

I laughed. "Right. Because you look so much like a kindergarten teacher."

He filled out another tag and placed it above my heart, ostensibly trying to avoid making contact with anywhere I might construe as out-of-bounds. I kept my eyes locked on his as he pressed the paper into my chest, at which point I experienced a rush of blood to the inguinal region of my body.

"What?" he said, smirking.

"Nothing."

There were at least a dozen people at all ten tables. Paul and I approached number five and a frail woman with white hair, a ghoulish smile, and lines that ran down her face like the Manhattan bus map said, "Roger, move over. Willie likes to sit by me."

Roger, a toothless man who looked as old as a dinosaur, offered up his chair. "There's my girl," Paul said, giving Patty a big smooch on the cheek.

I looked around the room and noticed a number of people under the age of thirty. Some, I guessed, were family members. Others were obviously volunteers.

"Do you come here a lot?" I asked Paul.

"Once a month or so. I started coming after I moved to the city because someone told me volunteers got free meals."

Patty had four cards going at one time and never missed a beat. During the first game she was a B-17 away from BINGO and cursed out loud when an African American woman at table eight beat her.

"Betty has Alzheimer's. And she cheats," Patty said. "Willie, check her card."

A few minutes into the third game, Patty tugged on Paul's arm and yelled, "Tell Luka to pay attention."

Paul cleared his throat, prompting me to look at my name tag. "Very funny," I said. Then I inspected my card, stood up and shouted "BINGO!" as if I'd just hit the million-dollar jackpot at Caesar's.

Initially, I interpreted my win as a fortuitous event, but when I tried to claim my prize, Paul informed me that volunteers were not allowed to profit from the game. Not economically, anyway. Mary Lou did give me a keychain, and a calendar filled with photos of Weimaraner dogs all dressed up in silly outfits.

We left Bingo a little before dusk. Paul hustled me back to the Lower East Side where, if we hurried, he promised a spectacular urban sunset on the roof of the Pack-It-Away Mini Storage building that housed Bananafish's rehearsal space.

By the time we got there it was nearly dark, but the night was warm and clear, and we could see the East River, the Brooklyn Bridge, and the Manhattan Bridge. Paul quizzed me on what I was looking at and I scored a dismal one out of three. I got the Statue of Liberty right, but thought Brooklyn was Queens, and mistook Staten Island for New Jersey.

"I'm not very good with directions," I said.

"Not good?" Paul laughed hysterically. "You're geographically retarded."

I walked to the edge of the building and Paul followed. Although he could have stepped left to avoid touching me, he let our shoulders meet.

"I've been meaning to thank you," I said, shivering even though it was still so warm out.

"For what?"

"For not signing that deal. For not leaving Michael in the dust."

Paul shrugged, but his face softened and I could tell my words meant something to him. A while passed before he nodded toward my wrist.

"Why did you do it?" he said.

It wasn't a topic I was particularly keen on discussing, especially with someone I hardly knew. But the way Paul was watching me, with the utmost level of attention, and no trace of judgment, made me willing to offer him a response.

"I was depressed," I said, shrugging. "I was a stupid kid. I didn't mean it."

Paul stared at me like he wanted more.

"I couldn't feel anything," I finally told him. "I couldn't feel the truth. Does that make sense? Do you know what the truth feels like?"

"I know what it sounds like."

We both smiled, and a moment of complete understanding passed between us before I had to turn away.

Looking out over the city, I was certain there was nowhere else in the world I wanted to be than right there, with the blue-black sky above me, the aromas of Chinatown and Little Italy mingling below me, and the man beside me who, when standing on a dirty rooftop with a million twinkling lights behind him, looked a lot more like a lonely orphan than a cocky bastard.

I shifted to face uptown and tried to find Ludlow Street. All I saw were water tanks. I'd never noticed them before, these big wooden works of rustic, industrial art perched atop almost every building in the city like phallic offerings to the patron saint of metropolitan life.

"Do you think I'm a coward?" I said.

Paul lit a cigarette and backed up against the railing. There was a peculiar glint in his eyes as he watched me, and I swear he didn't blink for a full minute. Then he put his cigarette between his teeth and held it there while he reached down and flicked a chunk of tar off his shoe. After he took the cigarette from his mouth he said, "Why would you say that?"

"I know you know I was supposed to fly here, and that I chickened out. Now you know I've tried to chicken out of a lot of things."

Pointing at me, he said, "First of all, there's nothing cowardly about a person who has the guts to take a knife to their wrist. And there's also nothing noble about being fearless. How much do you wanna bet the last man standing in a battle is usually the biggest fool of all?"

Absorbing his words was like taking a drink of hot tea. They burned on the way down, but soothed my insides once they had time to cool off.

We were quiet for a while. Then Paul said, "I almost did it once."

"Did what?"

"Killed myself."

The confession alone was shocking enough. It was the stark, unapologetic fierceness of his tone that frightened me.

"*Why?*"

"I was depressed," he said with a smirk.

"Did you really want to die?"

"No one commits suicide because they want to die."

"Then why do they do it?"

"Because they want to stop the pain."

Once again, his lack of guile was unsettling. But his words resonated somewhere inside of me.

He took a drag off the cigarette, raised his mouth, and sent three smoke rings into the air. Watching them dissipate, he asked me if I was happy. But before I had a chance to respond, he said, "Don't answer that. It's a stupid question. I don't believe in the myth of happiness any more than you do."

This is where Paul had it wrong. I did believe in the myth. I had to. Otherwise I don't think I would have been there. Happiness is elusive, for sure. But like love, and music, I believed in it because I could *feel* it.

I told Paul this and he gazed off into space, his expression meditative. Then he said, "For what it's worth, I think happiness is a fleeting condition, not a permanent goddamn state of mind. I've learned that if you chase after moments of bliss here and there, sometimes those moments will sustain you through the shit." He paused to pick a piece of tobacco off his tongue. "Personally, I don't like inherently happy people. I don't trust them. I think there's something seriously wrong with anyone who isn't at least a little let down by the world."

Insisting we stop for a late-night snack of the liquid variety, Paul steered me to Rings of Saturn. As soon as we walked in, John the Baptist grabbed a bottle from behind the counter and said, "How's it hanging, Hudson?" Then he recognized me. "Uh-oh, what's a nice girl like you doing with this clown?"

Paul pointed back and forth between me and John. "You two know each other?"

"Sure," John said, winking in my direction. "Girl's got a penchant for green olives, martinis with no booze, and she tips, which is more than I can say for you."

"A martini with no booze?" Paul said, his face crooked. "What the hell is that?"

Without asking what we wanted, John went about serving up our respective drinks of choice. Evidently, Paul liked Captain Morgan's rum and ginger ale.

"It's a marvelous night for a moondance," Paul said to John.

John had a red bandanna around his forehead and a dishrag in his back pocket. He wiped his hands on the rag, then went to the stereo behind the cash register and put on the Van Morrison CD Paul had requested. Seconds later, a girl with long auburn hair parted in a perfectly straight line down the center of her scalp walked past the bar and drooled, "*Hi, Paul.*"

Paul mumbled, "Hey, Alicia," and turned his back to the girl so abruptly I was sure he'd slept with her. His indifference, coupled with my awkward jealousy, made me want to kick him.

"It's late," I said, getting up off my chair. "I should leave you to your *friends*."

I hated myself for saying *friends* the way Lucy Enfield did. But I felt stupid for being there, for being with Paul, and for thinking all the stupid things I almost allowed myself to think about him.

Paul touched my arm and, in an almost desperate voice, said, "Don't go. Please. I want to show you something."

He took his wallet from his pocket and pulled a small white feather out of the billfold. It was tattered from age, the ends looked like they'd been singed, and he held it as if it were a piece of broken glass. "I've never shown this to anyone."

I could hear my conscience chiding me to walk away. But Paul's eyes, at times, had an entirely different personality than the rest of his face. They were needy and they pleaded with me to stay.

"What is it?" I said.

"It's a feather."

"I know *that*. What's it for?"

"My grandmother sent it to me a long time ago."

I settled back in and began questioning Paul in the manner I would have used if I'd been interviewing him—probing but compassionate—and he proceeded to recount the facts of his life as if he were releasing toxins that had been in his bloodstream for years.

"I'm just going to start from the beginning," he said. "Late morning. December, 1972. Pittsburgh, PA. My mother, who will herein be referred to as Carol, goes into labor. So she gets dressed and asks her fiancé to drive her to the hospital."

"She wasn't married?"

Paul shook his head. "She was engaged. To this guy, Robert Davies, who, incidentally, is not the father of the child she's about to pop."

"Is Mr. Davies privy to this information?"

"Yeah, he knows. So he brings a radio to the hospital, per Carol's request, and they keep it on during the delivery. Six hours later I'm born, and the first voice I hear is Doug Blackman singing 'A Prayer for the Damned.'"

I was shaking my head. "You're telling me you remember that?"

"Like it was yesterday."

"Impossible."

"Do you talk to all your interviewees this way?"

"Not the important ones," I teased. "So, what's the story with Robert Davies?"

"Swear to God, I don't remember ever having a conversation with the guy. He was a man of few words and even fewer emotions. I grew up referring to him as Piece of Wood because he was stiff, void of personality, and spent most of his waking hours working. He spent the rest of his time planting flowers in our front yard. He might have been a walking log, but as a rose pruner he kicked ass."

"What did he do? For a living, I mean."

"He worked for a company that made and distributed electronics. His job was to make sure the various corporate branches around the country were being run as efficiently as possible. The company transferred him to a new city every few years to rework the offices, and he got to hire and fire as he saw fit. Besides the roses, hiring and firing people were the only things he ever got excited about."

"What was your mom like?"

"Bored," he said. "But she discovered ways of dealing with our transient existence and her emotionally absent husband. Bowling in the morning and a couple shots of scotch in the afternoon usually did the trick. I didn't have the same luxuries, at least not when I was a kid. All I had was a pile of old records to keep me company."

Sounds familiar, I thought. "Where does Grandma fit in?"

"Here's the thing…" Paul leaned in so close I could feel his warm, rum-flavored breath on my face. "I didn't know she existed until my thirteenth birthday, when I got a letter from her, and in it she said her son had been my father. She apologized for my not having met him, but something bad had grown in his brain and he'd died—her exact words. Later on, I learned he'd had a brain tumor. The feather was inside the envelope, and I've kept it with me ever since, a little talisman."

"Was her son really your father?"

He nodded. "When I showed Carol the letter she shrugged like it was no big deal and said, 'I don't know how that crazy woman found you.'"

Paul told me that after hounding his mother for days on the topic of his father's identity, Carol finally told him the truth.

"She said his name was William, he rode a motorcycle, and never had any money. He died before I was born, and Piece of Wood was kind enough to make an honest woman out of her. She never mentioned him again."

I scraped an olive from the toothpick in my glass and then sucked the little red pimento out of the middle. Seconds later John the Baptist dropped two more olives into my water.

"Why isn't your last name Davies?" I asked Paul.

"I went by Davies growing up, but it's not my legal name. It's not on my birth certificate."

"Hudson is your real father's name?"

He shook his head.

"What's your real name?"

"Can't tell you that."

"Why not?"

"No one knows my real name. Well, except for Feldman."

Paul looked like he was debating how much more information to divulge. He took a slow sip of his drink, went through a raise-your-right-hand, swear-over-your-life-you'll-never-ever-tell-a-soul rigmarole with me, and said, "When I moved here I wanted a clean slate. I felt like a new person and I wanted a new name. So, I made one up."

"Okay. Why Hudson?"

"The *river*." He said it like it should have been obvious. "I was living in this fleapit apartment in Hell's Kitchen, and when I say 'fleapit' I'm not utilizing a platitude for the sake of the story. My ankles used to itch every time I got out of bed. Even worse than that was the bathroom. The building had a serious plumbing problem, and there was never enough water at the bottom of the toilet, so you had to piss in it about five times before you could flush anything down." He stared into his drink. "This one night, middle of summer, it was a zillion degrees outside and the smell in my room was so bad I had to go up and sleep on the roof. It was the lowest I'd ever felt, and I remember laying there staring at the sky, feeling so fucking alone, and wondering what the hell was going to happen to me—if I was ever going to get any farther than that dump, if I belonged in New York, if I was going to be able to make a living making music, or if I should just chuck myself off the goddamn roof and be done with it." He paused to make sure I was getting the point. "The river was the first thing I saw when I woke up the next morning. Somehow I'd survived the night. And that's when Paul Hudson was born."

I felt the heat of Paul's gaze on my face. He was waiting for something from me. Acknowledgement. Validation. Commiseration, perhaps. I couldn't even look at him because I was afraid of feeling any more than I already did.

Focusing on the speakers above the bar, I listened to Van Morrison sing about souls and spirits flying into the mystic. Van was obviously trying to tell me something.

"I don't know why I just laid all that shit on you," Paul mumbled.

He finished his drink and sat quietly, stirring the ice in his glass. It took a while for me to think of something to say, and even then, all I could come up with was, "When did you start playing guitar?"

"We'd just moved to Rochester. I was sixteen." With his tongue, Paul dug out a piece of ice and crunched on it. "For me, moving was symbolized by the dreaded goddamn basement. I always had to clean and unpack the basement. One day I was digging through an old trunk and I found an acoustic guitar. It was dented and needed new strings, but I fell hopelessly in love with it. I had it tuned up, bought a box of picks and a used chord dictionary, and for a week I only put it down to sleep. When Carol tried to drag me out of the cellar, I made her bring Piece of Wood downstairs, and I played and sang an entire song for them. Ask me what song I played. Go on, ask."

"What song did you play?"

Paul was reanimated, his eyebrows dancing in chorus with his voice. "A little three-chord ditty called 'The Day I Became a Ghost' by Douglas J. Blackman. Needless to say, the boxes sat in the basement for a long time before anyone unpacked them. And the smell of damp cement still reminds me of the summer I discovered my calling."

"That's my favorite song," I confessed, which may have been the understatement of my life.

I toyed with the toothpick in my glass and tried not to be so drawn to the man beside me. But I couldn't deny the energy I felt being passed between us like the sonic waves traveling from the speakers above the bar to my ears. "How did you end up here?"

"After Rochester, we moved to Houston. Have you ever been to Houston?"

I shook my head. I'd never been anywhere.

"It sucks," he said. "The day I got there I started making plans to go off and earn my salt as a musician. I did construction, delivered food, worked at a record store, trying to save up enough money to get the hell out of Dodge. Then Carol got sick, Piece of Wood increased his working hours so he didn't have to deal with it, and I stuck around to take care of her. She went through chemo, lost both of her breasts, all of her hair, and died a year and a half later with a crew cut and a shitload of regret. A week later I packed my suitcase and boarded a plane for JFK."

I deemed Paul a hero because he mentioned flying as if it were incidental. "What airline did you take?"

He looked at me as if I'd just addressed him in Japanese. "I don't know. It was a long time ago. But I do remember the plane was painted like a dolphin."

My stomach did a somersault. "A *what*?"

"The company was doing a promotion with a movie studio and they'd painted the outside of the plane to look like the country's newest animated hero."

"And you got *on* it? Are you out of your *mind*? *Maybe* painting it to look like a bird might make sense. But a *sea* creature? That's a crash waiting to happen."

"Eliza," he said gently. "Do you have any idea what the odds are of being involved in a plane crash?"

"Depending on the circumstances, the odds of being in a plane crash are about 1 in 4.2 million, but tell that to my parents and the one hundred and seventy-eight other people who died with them."

Paul looked like he was about to offer a long, sappy apology, and I said, "No pity, please. Don't say you're sorry for something you played no part in."

"Fair enough."

I didn't like the direction the conversation had taken and wanted to turn it back around. "What ever happened to your grandmother? The one who sent the letter?"

"Pushing up daisies by the time I found her."

"And you have no other family?"

"Nope."

"What about Robert Davies?"

"He was transferred to Nashville not long after Carol died, but I haven't seen or talked to him since I left Texas." Without pause, Paul hopped off his chair, tugged on my arm, and said, "Dance with me."

I could think of very few things I wanted more than to stand as close to Paul Hudson as dancing would permit, which is precisely why I shook my head.

"Come on. One goddamn song."

"Has anyone ever told you how much you overuse that word?"

"What word?"

"Goddamn."

"I just spilled my guts all over your lap. It's the least you could do."

No one was dancing. There wasn't even a proper dance floor. And Alicia was still loitering. But Paul kept tugging until I stood up and followed him to the corner.

He put one arm on the small of my back and with the other he fiddled with the edge of the *Luka* sticker still stuck to my shirt.

"Is this okay?" he said.

I didn't know if he was referring to his hands, his dancing, or the ultraviolet warmth his body was emitting, but I nodded, moved in closer, and within seconds I let myself slip into a world where there were no sharp edges, where everything was curved and smooth and seamless, like Paul's voice as he hummed Van Morrison in my ear. I felt like I was being zapped between the legs with a stun gun.

Over Paul's shoulder, Alicia was glaring at me.

"Let's get out of here," Paul whispered.

We walked home in silence. When we got to our building, Paul said, "I'll race you," and went flying up the stairs.

I ran after him. On the fourth floor I found him standing in front of the bleeding door like a barricade, his arms in the shape of a V, the cocky-bastard smile plastered across his face.

"Eliza, do I make you nervous?"

"No."

He took a step forward. "Then why are you shaking?"

I lowered my chin, swallowed hard, but said nothing.

"Don't look at me like that," he said. "I can't be responsible for what happens in the next thirty seconds if you keep looking at me like that."

"Get out of the way."

"First you have to pay the toll."

Reaching around the back of my head, Paul leaned forward and planted his mouth on mine. He kissed me until he ran out of air, took a quick breath, kissed me again, and was grinning wildly when he finally set me free.

It occurred to me then that he kissed the same way he ran up the stairs—fiercely, passionately, and with complete commitment.

"I haven't had sex in six months," I said. Why I felt the need to blurt out that little tidbit of information, I'll never know.

"*Six months?*" Paul cried, as if it were impossible that I could still be alive after six months of celibacy. He leaned in and toyed with my earring. "Are you just making conversation, or was that an invite?"

"Phone's ringing," I mumbled, but I was only vaguely conscious of the sound coming from the apartment. I stood frozen while Paul spun around, opened the door, and went straight to it. "Hudson's house of ill-repute," he said into the receiver. Then he groaned. "It was a joke, Avril. Do you understand the meaning of that word?…I told you, we had practice tonight…" I walked into the room and Paul lowered his voice almost to a whisper. "Yeah, I miss you too. I'll see you tomorrow, okay?"

I kicked him in the shin as hard as I could. As he simultaneously doubled over in pain and laughed, I stormed off to my room, slammed the door, and bit the sides of my cheeks so that I didn't cry.

Paul entered my room without knocking. He sat down on my window ledge, rolled up his pant leg, and said, "My leg's turning black and blue."

"Why did you tell her you were at practice?"

"What was I supposed to say? That I was busy making out with my roommate?"

"Get out!" I yelled, tasting blood in my mouth, and christening myself the biggest fool in all of Manhattan.

He laughed again, limping over to me with his pant leg still rolled up to his knee. "Hey, no one said you had to kiss me back."

"I didn't kiss you back."

"You most certainly did. *Twice*." He clutched his side and moaned. "Ow. Shit. Now it's my leg *and* my pancreas."

I held the door open.

"Say you'll come to the show on Thursday."

"I mean it. *Out!*"

He stomped off to his room like a pouting child and then reappeared in the hall with his little tape recorder. "Thursday." He pointed at me. "Be there."

He left the apartment without another word, and from the window I watched him walk toward Houston Street. I stood there for a long time, even after he was gone, struggling to process the night, the last couple of weeks, my life, and where Paul Hudson might fit in to the equation.

I tried to tell myself he didn't fit in at all, but I had a sinking feeling that no matter how hard I tried to remain on the periphery of the country that was Paul Hudson, I had already willingly crossed the border.

Dreams can change histories and songs can alter destinies—two ideas that on good days I believe wholeheartedly and on bad days I denounce as a bunch of bull. It must be a stellar goddamn day because I was positive, as I wandered down Houston Street and away from the girl I knew was standing in the window watching me, that someday I'll look back on this night as a turning point. The convergence of my past and my future. History and destiny crashing together like the Big Bang.

I was having an epiphany. A moment of supreme clarity, leading to what I dubbed a "realization of solitude" that goes like this: I'm lonely.

I rarely notice it. The loneliness. I've learned that my mood remains steady when I'm completely oblivious to my isolation. But when I left that girl in the window I was sure I'd never felt more godforsaken in my life.

There's a big difference between being alone and being lonely. And I'm guessing that once you've discovered this distinction you can't go back to solitary confinement without serious emotional repercussions.

As I walked away trying not to limp, my shin still killing me from where Eliza had kicked me, all these ideas started coming in waves and I felt the kind of high I figure can only come from three sources: art, love, or narcotics. And that last one doesn't count because even I know it's a cop-out.

Is Eliza feeling even half of what I am? I don't know. What I do know is that she's searching for something too. It's in her eyes. It's in her scar. It's in her reverence for music, which I saw all over her face when she listened to that Van Morrison song in the bar. The girl is a real believer. That she doesn't yet believe in me is only a minor problem. If she's the kind of person I think she is, I'll win her over with one verse. One chorus. Maybe even one line. It'll be a goddamn test. I'll test her the same way she'll no doubt test me—with a song. Because believers know the truth when they hear it.

Epiphanic moment of supreme clarity number two came half a block later, after I caught a glimpse of my reflection in the window of Katz's. Circles under my eyes. Skin the color of a poached chicken breast. I look like a goddamn junkie and I swear over my life I've never touched that shit. Epiphanic moment of supreme clarity number two was this: Eliza makes me want to be a better person. And not for her sake either, but for my own, which seems pretty monumental considering I haven't even fucked her.

Eliza has the sky in her eyes and I've always wanted to touch the goddamn sky.

My supremacy of clarity was unprecedented and called for a lot of resolutions to be made, which I rattled off down the sidewalk. On my index finger I resolved to cut down on the smoking. On my middle finger I resolved to cut down on the weed—no, I resolved to cut out the weed. Well, I'll at least put in the effort.

And the shirt-folding. On my ring finger I resolved to be a better shirt-folder. The best goddamn shirt-folder the Gap has ever seen, because life is short and a man should take pride in his work, even if his work makes him feel like a total loser.

A kid went by me on a scooter and said, "Shut up, freak." He didn't even look old enough to drive, let alone old enough to be scooting Manhattan in the middle of the night, and I was going to tell him so, but right then a blast of hot, rank air shot up my legs and hit me in the face. I hadn't been paying attention to where I was going and shit if I wasn't standing on a subway grate.

My heart started pounding, and I experienced an admittedly irrational fear that I was about to be sucked underground—I'd never get to kiss Eliza again, or see her matching goddamn underwear, or run my goddamn tongue along the inside of her goddamn thigh.

A homeless guy pushing a shopping cart passed me, pointing and shouting, "There's a cyborg among us! There's a cyborg among us!"

Great, I thought. I'm morphing into something half human, half machine, and the magnetic suction of the underworld is trying to drag me down. The breath of Hades is deep, heavy, and rancid. One great inhale and I'll be a soggy piece of toast.

"There's nothing down there but cigarette butts."

That's what Eliza said to me when we were on our way to St. Vrain's. As soon as she figured out the grates creeped me out, she skipped and pranced over every one of them. I think I loved her for that. Especially when a train pulled in, her skirt did a Marilyn Monroe, and I almost saw her underwear.

"Take a look," she said, pointing into the ground. "Just for a second, you can still stand on the sidewalk. Just LOOK."

I peeked over the edge. It was six feet down, tops.

"Even if you fell through," she said, "it's not like you'd die or anything. You probably wouldn't even break your leg."

She pulled me over until I was on top of the grate and I stood there for like, fifteen whole seconds. I'd like to say it was an act of bravery, but I was only able to do it because she was holding my sleeve.

This is what I mean about epiphanies. With her, I'd had the strength to stand there. Without her, I would have run.

People who have something against cities, people who don't like New York, they're always whining that you can't see stars at night. This is no exaggeration—as I was having my epiphanies I counted thirty-three stars above the block I was on, and they seemed so bright and so close I was sure that if I held a match up as far as my arm could reach, it would have caught fire.

I looked down and realized I was back at Rings of Saturn. John the Baptist laughed when he saw me. He filled a glass with ice and lifted Captain Morgan from the shelf, but the last thing I wanted was a goddamn drink. I asked him for coffee and his operative eye glanced in the direction of a portable burner filled with something that looked like molasses. He said it'd been there since noon but I didn't care if it'd been there since the goddamn bicentennial.

He said, "Ever jumped out of an airplane, Hudson?"

I told him I had not.

"Take this to heart," he said. "If you're gonna jump out of a plane, remember you'll be falling at terminal velocity, and that's nothing to monkey around with. Check your gear and make sure your parachute is operational."

As usual, he was spewing a lot of crap, but I got the feeling he and I were on the same wavelength. I asked him if he'd noticed the way Eliza listened to the music, how she'd gazed at the speakers like God was talking to her.

He told me terminal velocity is about one hundred thirty miles per hour.

I could fall hard for a girl who listens to music like that.

"Sometimes when you open the chute at a high speed," John said, "the G force is so strong it breaks your arms. It's not common, but it's happened. Happened to a buddy of mine in 'Nam."

I asked John if it was a crime to want to live in a world where girls with falcon eyes and pretty underwear believe in the saving grace of rock 'n' roll and he said, "Just check your chute before you jump, that's all I'm saying."

Gotta get some sleep.

Over.

Vera gave me a sticker to put on my shirt. An all-access pass allowing me to roam Rings of Saturn as I wished. "Michael makes them," she said with pride.

The pass was electric yellow and shaped like a banana. But it was a suggestive, tongue-in-cheek banana. A penis disguised as a piece of fruit, to be exact. I stuck it to my chest and, in lieu of actually using it, e.g., possibly running into Paul in the dressing room, Vera and I made our way to a small table to the left of the stage.

"*Yay*. You're here," Vera said, patting me on the back. "Michael's nervous. He really wants you to be impressed."

I was nervous too, though surely not for the same reasons as Michael.

Minutes before the band was scheduled to go on, a girl dashed out from behind the curtain. She was striking in a brazen way, with dark, Cabernet-colored lips, Medusa hair, and she burned down the stairs in a violent flash.

"Oh, boy, *she* didn't look happy," Vera said. "Then again, would you be happy if you were dating Paul?"

I heard an involuntary noise escape my throat.

"Dear all Paul Hudson lovers," Vera said to no one in particular. "Give it up."

Most of the people who had been down at the bar were swarming up the stairs for the show, but the place was still only half full as the lights dimmed and Michael walked out.

He saw Vera and smiled, but it was quick and inadvertent, as if he had to maintain a level of coolness that showing affection for his wife did not allow. I stuck my tongue out at him and he gave me the finger.

"Doesn't he look sexy up there?" Vera said.

As Michael plugged his guitar into an amp and tinkered with the knobs, his presence conveyed a spartan detachment that was not at all what I would call sexy. Regardless, I was reassured Vera thought otherwise.

"Another reason why you can't let him quit," I said.

"Back off," she piped.

The drummer swaggered out next. Vera called him Angelo in a disapproving tone. Angelo was drinking a beer, mirrored sunglasses hid his eyes, and a small group of girls whistled at him. He reminded me of a serial killer, only I couldn't remember which one.

Burke, the blond, baby-faced bass player, was behind Angelo. "Oliver Twist," Vera whispered. "Doesn't he look like Oliver Twist?"

"I don't know what Oliver Twist looks like."

Paul walked out last, causing a downpour of rainy applause to sweep through the crowd. He was wearing the pants to his green suit, and a T-shirt on which he'd written: *Fuck you, Mr. Winkle.*

"I gotta hand it to him," Vera said. "The guy sure knows how to win friends and influence record execs."

Paul had a black Gibson around his neck and a bottle of water in his hand. He approached the microphone and adjusted it down toward his mouth. "Thanks for showing up," he said using his pretend bashful voice, greeting a group of fans up front, two guys and a girl who looked like runaways.

"They take the train in from Jersey every Thursday," Vera said. "Paul is their god."

Shielding his eyes from the light, Paul cleared his throat

and peered around the room until he found me. "This first song," he said, his eyes locked on mine. "We haven't really practiced it much but we're gonna play it anyway."

He winked, and Vera's chest inflated. "Did he just *wink* at you?"

I was able to disregard the question because the band had launched into a spacey, moving rendition of "The Day I Became a Ghost" that pricked open my ears and set me on the edge of my seat. But it was the next nine songs, the Paul Hudson originals, that raised me up and never set me back down until the band left the stage.

The music defied classification. If I had been writing a review of the show, I would have labeled it progressive, guitar-driven rock 'n' roll. But the guitars made sounds guitars didn't always make. Symphonic sounds. Sacred sounds. The music dug in so deep you didn't hear it so much as feel it, reminding me of a dream I used to have when I was a kid, where I would be standing on a street corner, I would jump into the air, flap my arms, and soar up into the sky.

That's the only way I could describe the music.

It was the sonic equivalent of flight.

And then there was the *voice*. I'd never heard anyone sing like Paul Hudson. Even Doug Blackman, master storyteller, whose passion and pain could be heard in every holy word he uttered, only wished for a voice like Paul's—a voice that swept up and down the scale and was, at times, filled with deep, lush, apocalyptic emotion, and at other times was a burning falsetto of hope and love and seemed too big to come from his throat, lungs, or diaphragm.

From his soul, I decided.

Before the last song, Vera leaned over and said, "Would you ever think such a little guy could make such a big sound?"

I couldn't even blink, let alone turn my head from the stage and respond to Vera. All of a sudden I was angry. It was incomprehensible to me that bands like 66 were play-ing to sold-out crowds, earning thousands of dollars a night, while Paul Hudson and probably so many other extraordi-nary artists were stuck in half-empty barrooms getting noth-ing but bogus attention from Winkles who wouldn't appreciate musical rectitude if it spit in their faces.

"Welcome to America," Doug would have said.

I set my martini glass down so hard its base cracked and water spilled over the sides, soaking my napkin. "I need air."

Outside, there was a deli next to Rings of Saturn. Through the window I watched a swarthy, heavily bearded man shoving a pastrami sandwich into his mouth, taking bite after bite before he finished swallowing what he was chewing. He had a glob of mustard on the tip of his nose and bits of meat stuck to the hair on his chin.

As the man washed down his food with gulps of soda, I knelt on the ground, let my head fall to my hands, and stayed like that until Vera found me ten minutes later.

"Hmm," she said. "Kneeling Mecca-style outside the club. *Not* a good sign."

I rose, brushing dirt from my skirt. "Why didn't you *tell* me?"

Vera looked cautious. "Tell you what? I said he was tal-ented."

"*Talent?* That's not *talent.* Talent is Liza Minnelli tap-dancing and singing at the same time. What I just saw was devastation. Dying man on the cross. Salvation in B minor. An ejaculation of truth."

"Oh, for Pete's sake, it's music. It's supposed to be fun, not devastating. Sex, drugs, and rock 'n' roll, remember? Whew-hoo. And don't get any crazy ideas about Paul. He's the last thing you need."

I followed Vera backstage, where Paul and the Michaels were huddled together in the corner, extolling each other's triumphs and picking apart their mistakes like a gang of school chums after a dodgeball game.

I avoided making eye contact with Paul. I wasn't ready for him. Not with so many people around. I waved to Michael and waited until he came to me.

"I'm going to try and get *Sonica* to let me write about you guys," I said. "If I have to sell my soul, I will." I eyed Vera and then refocused on my brother. "You are *not* quitting this band. No way. I'll get another job if I have to. *I'll* support you."

Vera was not happy with me. She left the room in a huff. But Michael's face, usually phlegmatic, had ignited. "*Sonica* would be *huge*."

A well-dressed man approached me. He had threadlike black hair, skin the color of a raw pork chop, and was a few pounds shy of being called stocky.

"Hey, Peepers," the man said, kissing the top of my hand. "How much do you want for your soul?"

I turned to Michael and said, "Did he just call me *Peepers*?"

"Watch it, Feldman," Michael said. "This is my sister."

"Sister?" Feldman said. "You never told me you had a ravishing sister with *Sonica* connections."

I immediately had misgivings about Feldman, as I would have misgivings about anyone who dubbed me Peepers. And something about the way his eyes spun around the room reminded me of a propeller. I'm terrified of propellers. If I'm watching a TV show and there's a helicopter in the scene, I have to change the channel.

"Peepers," Feldman said again, trying to hand me a wad of bills, "you would do us a big favor getting us mentioned in *Sonica*."

I gave Feldman a look and shoved the money back at him.

"Come with me." Michael took my arm. "I want you to

meet the band." We went into the dressing room. "You already know that guy," he said, pointing at Paul, who was slumped on a chair, wiping his face with his shirt, staring at the floor and looking spent.

Michael introduced me to Burke and Angelo, and Burke monopolized the conversation campaigning for basil as a tasty additive to ice cream.

"Think about it," he said. "It's an herb. And mint is an herb. And mint makes a hell of a combo with chocolate."

"Chocolate Pesto Chip," I said. "I think you might have something there."

"You've gotta meet my girlfriend," Burke said, galvanized.

Burke's girlfriend, Queenie, was a tiny, streetwise girl, with eyes that fluctuated from vigilantly independent to utterly vulnerable with every blink. She told me about her latest ice cream concoction, which she called The Movie Star, The Professor, and Mary Ann. "Ginger ice cream base," she explained, "with a shot of gingko biloba and chunks of coconut cream pie. Get it?"

I nodded. "*Gilligan's Island.*"

Over Queenie's shoulder, I watched a blond girl in black motorcycle boots loitering near Paul. Eventually the girl pulled up a chair beside him, leaned in close, and touched his knee, and I darted off to the bathroom because I couldn't bear to watch whatever was going to happen next.

Paul walked into the bathroom right behind me. "It's about goddamn time," he said, standing so close I could feel the dampness of his sweat-soaked shirt. "I've been sending you telepathic messages for ten minutes."

"I don't know if I can do this," I said.

"Do what? We're just hanging around a urinal."

"All the girls. I can't compete with that."

"I told Avril, it's done. With all of them. I'm over it."

I reached out and put my hand on his chest, but I didn't

find the drumbeat I'd expected. Instead I found a flutter. Paul, I swore, had a butterfly trying to break free from his rib cage.

He put his hand on top of mine and leaned in, but the door swung open and I quickly pulled away, pretending to be washing up as a guy Paul called Judo invaded the moment.

"Great show," Judo said, unzipping his pants and peeing into the urinal. "You guys were *en feugo* tonight."

I moved toward the door and Paul said, "Hey."

As I looked back, a pertinent soundtrack began playing, courtesy of John the Baptist, who had slapped Depeche Mode's *Violator* on the sound system downstairs.

Your own personal Jesus. Someone to hear your prayers. Someone who cares.

"Where are you going?" Paul said.

"Home."

"Wait up for me." His head was bobbing to the music. As I walked out I heard him chime, "*Reach out and touch faith.*"

I was sitting on my bed, feet flat on the covers, staring at Jesus on the wall, imagining that he and I were lovers, that we walked around New York holding hands, Jesus in a brown robe and sandals, and me with henna designs painted on my arms and feet like Barbara Hershey in *The Last Temptation of Christ*.

I made a gun with my fingers and pretended to shoot Jesus.

If Paul grew a goatee and got a tan, I thought, he'd look just like that guy.

Reach out and touch faith, all right.

Checking my watch for the umpteenth time, I wondered how long it took a bunch of guys to throw their equipment into the back of a van, haul it half a mile down to the rehearsal space, and unload it. After that I counted the myriad reasons why I would not be having sex with Paul when he got home: He was my roommate. He was my brother's friend. He probably had a sexually transmitted disease. I had no condoms. And last but not least, I hadn't had the time or money for a bikini wax.

I had just dozed off when I heard Paul's shoes colliding even quicker than usual with the stairs. Twenty-four steps until he hit the fourth-floor landing. There were twice as many stairs, but Paul usually took them two at a time.

He was humming when he came through the door. I listened as he went into his room, and then walked into mine carrying his acoustic guitar.

A voice inside my head whispered: No healthy, twenty-six-year-old woman should go six months without sex.

Paul folded his stringy bangs behind his ears, sat down and said, "I want you to hear something."

For the record, if I were Superman, a pale, scrawny guy holding a guitar would be Kryptonite. Just watching Paul tune the thing was rendering me powerless.

And there was something mesmerizing about his face. That's what I was thinking as I sat there waning. Especially his nose. Aside from his translucent eyes, his nose was his most arresting feature. It was conspicuous, a size too big, but all of his other features were so delicate, it added a marked quality of strength to his character.

"What are you looking at?" he asked in his pretend-bashful voice, his eyes still focused on the neck of the guitar.

"Your nose."

He ran his fingers down the bridge. "What about my nose?"

"It's sexy."

That's all it took. The bashful act vanished and everything about Paul's smirk told me he knew he'd won me over.

"Fuck, it's hot in here." He put the guitar down, stood up, whipped his shirt over his head and tossed it to the floor. Then he pulled off his belt like D'Artagnan drawing a sword and dropped it to the ground, causing his pants to slide down so low I could see the thin, glorious trail of dark hair that led to his groin.

Reach out and touch faith.

After kicking off his shoes, Paul repositioned himself on the bed with the guitar. I could smell rum and ginger ale and I wanted to lick his neck.

"The Michaels haven't even heard this yet," he said. "I want to know what you think."

After licking his neck, I wanted to dive into his throat and slide down his esophagus and swim around inside his hands while he strummed. Or maybe I just wanted to rest my head on his shoulder, close my eyes, and listen to him sing. I wondered if he was as nimble-fingered with a woman's body as he was with a guitar.

"Pay attention," he said.

I scooted closer. To hear better.

The song didn't have lyrics yet, didn't even have a title, but it was so haunting it almost put a damper on my mood.

I said almost.

"It sounds like a requiem."

Paul nodded. "It's about my mom dying."

He set the guitar down and we looked at each other, neither one of us moving nor speaking. But the hush carried the weight of words. In his face I saw the pain of memory—a pain he did a good job of hiding most of the time—as well as the lust of the present moment. I wondered if he could see the same in me.

Finally he leaned in, almost like he was falling, and kissed me. His tongue was a fire in my mouth.

We kissed for a long time. When we started undressing, Paul's hand stroked my thigh and I could feel the little guitar-playing calluses on his fingertips.

He kissed my chin, my nose, my eyelids as he unbuttoned my shirt. "Red," he said when he saw my bra. "Red is good."

I ran my tongue along his collarbone. He tasted the way Rings of Saturn smelled—like smoke and sweat and stale beer, which under normal conditions I would never find arousing, but I suppose there are exceptions to all rules.

"In my pocket," he whispered.

His pants were beside me. I reached into the right pocket and found a pack of condoms.

"I stopped at Duane Reade," he said. "Just in case."

I opened the box with all the right intentions. It never occurred to me that I wouldn't be able to do it. I *wanted* to do it. But somewhere between the kissing and having the condom in hand, my mind wandered off to the place where my past lived, where Adam lived, and I felt myself close down.

"I can't," I said.

Paul covered us in the sheet and cuddled up behind me. "It's okay. No big deal."

I wondered if he meant having sex, or not having sex.

He ran his fingers over my wrist. I could feel him breathing, and I could feel him hard against my leg.

"You know what I was thinking about on my way home?" he said quietly. "How different my life would be if you'd made that gash a little deeper. Or how different yours would be if I'd vaulted myself off a roof nine years ago. Do you ever think about things like that? Like, if either you or I wouldn't have made it, where would the other one be *right now*?"

It was something I thought about all the time: how death changes every remaining moment for those still living. "Are you glad you made it?"

"I'm glad you made it."

That's when I let go. I rolled over on top of him, reached for the condom I'd discarded minutes before, and put it on him as if it were an erotic sex act in and of itself. Then I slipped him inside of me and moved as slowly as I could above him. I wanted it to last as long as possible. Eventually every muscle in my body felt like it was tensed to its breaking point and Paul's eyes looked like they were upside down.

When Paul finally came, his back arched like a bow about to launch an arrow, and he exhaled a loud, melodious sound identical to one he'd made during the show, at the end of an intense, seven-minute-long song called "Never Prayed for Rain."

For me, the release was a spot in time with no past and

no future. Just the extraordinary simplicity of a moment—
the kind of moment that has a funny way of making a person believe that life and love can last forever.

The light coming through the window and the sounds
of the delivery trucks outside told me it was almost time to
get up, but I'd barely slept. Paul, on the other hand, looked
cataleptic. His hands were buried under his pillow, and his
face was so colorless that if it hadn't been for his nearly con-
cave ribcage moving up and down with his breath, I would've
thought he was dead.

I pushed his hair off his face and tried to will his eyes to
open. When that didn't work I kicked him in the foot and
pretended it was an accident. "You look like a corpse when
you sleep."

"You're weird," he said groggily.

"Tell me your real name."

He checked the clock and then rolled his eyes.

"Come on. We had sex. You have to."

He chuckled. "Eliza, if *that* were my only criteria, do you
know how many girls would know my real name?"

"Bastard."

That made him laugh even harder, which immediately set
off an alarm in my head. Maybe I was no different than
Avril or Beth or Alicia. Maybe Paul would turn his back to
me the next time he saw me in Rings of Saturn.

"Oh, God," I said in a panic. "Let's just lay this on the
table right now. Because I don't want to think this is one
thing and have it turn out to be the other. Is this real or is
it crap?"

"Jesus," he said. "The sun isn't even up yet."

"I mean it. I need proof. Tell me your real name."

"Proof?" He huffed. "You want proof? Give me your goddamn hand."

Skeptically, I did as he asked, and he proceeded to sing the chorus to one of 66's meaningless songs, mimicking Amanda Strunk's whiskey-flavored voice, pointing to my arm. Nothing had changed. Then he sang the last verse of "The Day I Became a Ghost" and every one of my hairs stood on end.

"See that?" Paul said. "Ten goddamn seconds."

"I don't get it."

"You didn't even have to hear the whole song, just a few lines, and you still got chills and that swirly, happy-sad feeling in your gut, didn't you?"

"So?"

"*So?*" he huffed. "That's the difference between the real stuff and the crap. I know which one you are and you know which one I am." He flipped over and buried his head in his pillow. "That's all the proof you need. Wake me up in an hour."

Lucy sounded like a mad donkey when she laughed, which is what she was doing as she browsed the makeshift press kit Michael had put together for me to show *Sonica* during the magazine's weekly pitch meeting.

There was a fact sheet inside the folder, containing information on each band member—their musical histories, what instruments they played; there were excerpts from two small local papers hyping Bananafish's live shows as "electric" and "intense"; and what Lucy seemed to find so hilarious, the group photo, which had been taken on Spring Street in SoHo by a friend of Michael's, a photographer who sets up shop on the sidewalk outside of Balthazar making washed out, vintage-looking Polaroid image transfers for tourists.

In front of the whole staff of associate editors seated around the oblong table, Lucy said, "Eliza, which one of these guys are you screwing?"

I felt my fingers tighten around my pen. I wanted to stab Lucy's eye with it.

Lucy made the donkey noise again. "I'm assuming that's the reason you're pushing so hard to get them mentioned in the magazine, no?"

After stabbing Lucy blind, I decided I would put my hands around her neck and shake until there was no air left in her lungs. Then I would write *Kick Me* on her forehead and leave her on the sidewalk in Times Square.

"Actually, the guitarist is my brother," I said, evading half the truth—half the truth being that I'd been sleeping with Paul for two weeks and hadn't told anyone yet, namely Michael and Vera. I wasn't ready for the lectures. The you-should-know-better lecture. The he's-going-to-break-your-heart lecture. The Mother-of-Pearl-are-you-out-of-your-mind lecture. Probably because on some level I thought Michael and Vera might be right, and I was in that highly romantic stage of denial.

Lucy scanned the fact sheet. Once she located Michael, she said, "I suppose it never occurred to you that having the same last name as the guitarist poses a major credibility problem."

"I don't have to be the one who writes it. The point is to get their name out there. One mention, that's all I ask." And then I expunged any headway I might have made in the respect department by begging. "If things don't start rolling for Bananafish, my brother is going to have to quit. Can we just do him this small favor? *Please*?"

Lucy stood up, poised herself behind her chair, and savored the moment. My weaknesses made her stronger. She took pleasure in zapping my energy and sucking on my life. "They're an unsigned band, Eliza. How many people outside of New York have ever heard of them? We aren't the *Village Voice*, we're a national magazine. Our job is to cover the artists people want to read about, not fill the pages with nobodies, even if you happen to be related to them."

I wished a long, painful death for Lucy. In the meantime, I suggested that perhaps she might like to come to a show and judge for herself, my thinking being that if Lucy saw Bananafish live, it would become less about my brother and more about the music. Then again, even if I did convince her to come to Rings of Saturn—a venue she considered beneath her—there was a good chance she would abominate the band out of spite.

Listen up, little tape recorder buddy. Things are finally starting to happen. Good things. Potentially great things. Exhibit A: Guess who called me this morning? Jack Stone.

Who is Jack Stone, you ask? Only the president and founder of Underdog records—a small but highly successful independent label known for quality over quantity. No kidding, there isn't a band on their roster that doesn't sing the truth and garner the respect of their peers.

I almost dropped the phone when he said his name. Then I covered the mouthpiece with my hand, grabbed Eliza before she ran off to work, and told her Jack Stone was on the phone. It was a curious thing. She didn't look surprised. But I'll come back to that.

Unbeknownst to me, Jack was at Rings of Saturn last Thursday. He raved about the show and wanted to know why he'd never heard of us, and I told him—because Feldman thinks I belong on a major label. Jack said that explained why he'd put in two calls to Feldman and hadn't heard back yet.

Note to self: Have a talk with Feldman regarding call-return etiquette.

Jack asked me if there were any Bananafish demos in existence, and let me say this on record: I'm highly opposed to passing out demos. They don't do our live shows justice. But I really wanted a shot with Underdog so I told Jack I could probably scrounge something up.

Jack said, "Drop off a tape sometime today, I'll run it by a couple of trusted ears, and you and I will get together next week." Then, before we say goodbye, he goes, "Oh, tell that roommate of yours I said hi."

Eliza denied any involvement until I threatened to call her brother and say, "Eliza sucks good dick," at which point she fessed up.

Turns out Jack is a good friend of Terry North's, and Eliza's been hounding *Sonica* about Bananafish—she wants to write an article, a little blurb, anything to help us out. But Lucy keeps shooting her down so Eliza had to go above Lucy's head. Unfortunately, Terry North agreed with Lucy that an unknown band wasn't going to sell magazines. But Terry also thinks Eliza looks like his dead sister so he let her tag along on a lunch meeting with Jack. A week later Jack showed up at Rings of Saturn.

Eliza and I called in sick for work and headed to Underdog, which is on Broadway, right between Washington and Waverly. Confession: I'd been to Underdog before. I stopped by once with my guitar, asking if I could play a song for Jack. Back then the girl behind the desk told me they didn't accept solicitors. Otherwise, she said, could I imagine how much "crapola" they'd have to listen to. That's what she called me. Crapola.

Today the same receptionist, the one with the Bettie Page bangs and polka-dot thrift-store dress, acted like she was expecting me, and she put my demo in a metal basket that had Jack's name on it.

After we left Underdog, I suggested we go chill out under a tree somewhere. Eliza wanted to go to Central Park, but I was sure a subway ride uptown would've killed me, and neither of us had money to waste on a cab so we stopped at some cheap NYU hangout for coffee and then walked to Washington Square.

In the middle of the park, near the old fountain, this guy was sitting with a guitar, singing that old Dobie Gray song "Drift

Away." A crowd had congregated around him. His pants were too tight and his shirt was only buttoned halfway up his chest—he was from Jersey, I suspected—but he had a pretty decent voice, and Eliza said he reminded her of her dad, so we walked over.

Eliza closed her eyes, swayed to the music, and I could tell she meant it when she sang, "Give me the beat, boys, and free my soul, I wanna get lost in your rock 'n' roll and drift away..."

I can say this because she's my girlfriend, even if, at the moment, she's only my girlfriend in secret—Eliza has one of the worst voices known to man. Swear to God, for someone so obsessed with music, she's borderline tone deaf. But trying to describe how I felt watching her dance around and sing would be like trying to build a skyscraper with my bare hands. It made me want to marry her. Made me want to buy her a magic airplane and fly her away to a place where nothing bad could ever happen. Made me want to pour rubber cement all over my chest and then lay down on top of her so that we'd be stuck together, and so it would hurt like hell if we ever tried to tear ourselves apart.

We sat under a tree with leaves that were beginning to turn the color of fire. Eliza picked one off the ground, examined it like a botanist, and said, "Isn't it funny to think that this magnificent piece of matter is in a state of decay? Really, can you think of any other living thing that looks this glorious as it's dying?"

This is what I mean. The shit that comes out of her mouth sends me to the goddamn moon.

Next I asked her if she wanted to hear something weird. When she gave me the go-ahead, I asked her if she knew her brother wasn't the original guitarist in Bananafish.

She said no, and her tone implied she was awaiting a good plot twist. So I told her how we had this other guy, Mike Barnes, and she stopped me right there. She didn't believe the guy's name was Mike.

A zillion times I swore over my life. Then I told her the whole story, how Barnes was very Molly Hatchet, and finally, when I couldn't take his goddamn "Flirtin' with Disaster" riffs a minute longer, I canned him, five days before our first gig. We had to replace him fast, so I hung flyers on every goddamn telephone pole and brick wall from the FDR to the Westside Highway. "But here's the weird part," I said, trying to really grip her. I told her how we'd scheduled auditions at the rehearsal space, and at the time, Michael was working as a peon for some advertising firm that had a storage unit across from ours, and he stopped by that day to pick something up. He had no idea we were having auditions, but he came in, played us a song, and got the job.

Eliza seemed to be grasping the significance of the story, but I spelled it out for her anyway: F-A-T-E. Michael and I meeting. She and I meeting. Our Doug Blackman connection.

"That's not fate," she said.

Well, if it wasn't fate, I asked her, what the hell did she call it?

She studied the scar on her wrist for a long time. Eventually she glanced up, but the sun was in my eyes and I couldn't tell if she was looking at me or the sky.

"Let me tell you a little something about fate," she said. "Fate is just another word for people's choices coming to a head. Destiny, coincidence, whatever you name it. It inevitably lies in our own hands."

This has been a presentation of Paul Hudson's diary.

Over and out.

It was true love. In the truest sense of the word. I was in love with Paul and, more importantly, I believed he was in love with me. It was in the way he had of calling me at work and saying things like, "Did you know nondairy creamer is flammable?" or "The dial tone of this phone is in the key of F," and for the rest of the day even Lucy Enfield would seem tolerable; it was in the way he had of ordering the spinach and ricotta pizza from Rosario's because it was my favorite, even though he would've rather had the pepperoni; it was in the way he set one of my favorite poems, "The Still Time," to music, and sang it to me when a plane would crash somewhere in the world or I would hear "Born to Run" on the radio or life would just feel heavy and I couldn't sleep with all that weight on top of me.

Sometimes I would open my eyes when we were kissing, I would watch him and I could see it. I could actually *see* LOVE—not words, not an emotion, not an abstract concept or a subjective state of mind, but a living, breathing thing. I'd known for a long time that LOVE had a sound, but after Adam left, I wasn't sure it had a face and body, too. Especially one that would show itself to me for the first time on a subway platform, fidgeting nervously, with pale, luminescent eyes, dark, limp hair, and a cocky-bastard smile that could boil water.

But I knew.

I could tell.

And I would've done anything for him.

I broke the news to Vera first, knowing she would then do my dirty work for me—that is, tell Michael. Her reaction left much to be desired. Mostly, it was the depth of my feelings for Paul that concerned her.

"Sleep with the guy, fine," she said. "But don't fall in *love* with him. Geesh. I certainly hope you've been putting a cap over that been-there-done-that dick of his."

Vera and I were watching Bananafish do their sound-check at a small club in Brooklyn called Warsaw, where, with Terry North's help, I had booked the band a gig opening for a popular space-rock band from Scotland.

The Warsaw was actually the Polish National Home, but when there were no Polkas to draw a crowd, rock bands played there. The show that night was sold out.

"I've never felt like this before," I told Vera. "Not even with Adam."

Vera cocked her head. "Don't get me wrong; I like Paul. *As a person.* But I can't fathom any girl thinking he's boyfriend material. He's a rock star, for Pete's sake."

"I think you need more than ten fans to be a rock star."

"That's not what I mean. It's the attitude. Asking Paul not to fool around is like asking the Pope not to pray."

"People change," I said wistfully. "Don't you think people can change?"

We both looked over at Paul. He was in the process of trying to hock up a lugie and spit it on Angelo, prompting Vera to put on a piteous smile that told me she loved me, but also told me she thought I was being naïve. "Do *you* think people can change?"

I nodded, refusing to consider the possibility that any of us are doomed to die the same sorry people we sometimes become.

Paul began an impromptu rendering of the Cure's "Just Like Heaven," and Vera put her arm through mine. "Remember when I said I applied to Columbia? Well, I not only applied, I got in. I start in January."

I was trying to listen to the song but Vera was ruining it. She was ruining everything.

"If the band isn't signed by Christmas," she went on, squeezing my elbow, "Michael understands it's over. I hope you can, too."

I should have congratulated Vera. I should have said something nice to her. I could tell this is what she wanted from me. But all I did was take my arm away.

In the background, Paul was singing about a raging sea.

Soft and only.

Lost and lonely.

When Paul finished the song, he walked over to Michael and they started writing up the night's set list. They looked like comrades. Brothers in arms. Potential energy waiting to be set in motion.

"They'll be signed by Christmas," I said.

September 26, 2000

After news of my burgeoning relationship with Eliza got out, Angelo made a joke about how my new girlfriend was liable to be the Yoko Ono of Bananafish. I swear I almost bashed him over the head with my guitar case when he said it. Holy Hell, Yoko gets a bad rap. John loved that woman. And we should never ever blame a guy for love.

But Michael's reaction hit me the hardest. Sunday night, during practice, his face was like a goddamn rubber band about to snap and finally, after he barked at me for accidentally unplugging his amp, I told him we needed to go somewhere and talk.

I steered him down the street and into a pool hall, and once we both had beers in our hands I told him that until he set me straight, I would be assuming he didn't approve of me as an acceptable suitor for his sister, and he goes, "If I were you and you were me, would you want me dating YOUR sister?"

While I tried to work through the linguistics of that question, Michael turned his attention to some crazy cab driver who burst through the door yelling about an emergency outside. The guy seemed upset, but this is New York. Hardly anyone looked over, so the cabbie went around asking random people if they were veterinarians. He asked Michael first. Then he asked a woman in a short black skirt.

Outside, horns were beeping like crazy. I leaned back to look out the window. The cabbie had left his car in the middle of the street and traffic was stopped dead.

I asked the guy what happened and he told me he hit a pigeon. The bird was apparently in pretty bad shape, but not dead yet. When the guy started walking away I stopped him. I wanted to know why he didn't wonder if I was a vet. Trust me, I look more like a vet than the chick in the black skirt. But he never answered me because a cop came in and took him back to his car.

"Listen, it's a free country," Michael said.

I cracked a peanut out of its shell and set it aside, then strategically positioned mine and Michael's bottles as a sort of goal line and flicked the peanut around, playing finger hockey.

Michael said, "I know I can't tell you or Eliza what to do, but she's been through a lot in the last year and I don't want her to have to go through it again. I don't want her to get hurt."

Michael loves his sister. He worries a lot about her. This I know. But the thing is, sometimes people can have so much love between them, they end up treating each other like retards.

"I'm not going to hurt her," I said.

I aimed and shot the peanut-puck through the middle of the bottles. It bounced off the wall behind the bar and landed mere inches away from its point of departure.

This is where Michael started lecturing me about how Eliza wasn't like most girls I know. He said she wasn't Avril or Beth or Amanda, "or any of the random floozies who follow you around like flies on shit."

First of all, I know this. Second, I didn't need Michael reminding me of my numerous lapses of judgment.

"I'm in love with her," I announced at double speed, hoping that saying it quickly might lessen the weight of its impact.

He looked at me with doom in his eyes and goes, "Jesus Christ, Paul."

I said, "I mean it. Like deep crazy soul love."

Michael almost choked. "Deep WHAT?"

I laid it all out for him: Eliza believes in me, she moves me, and she's moved BY me. She makes me happy, she makes me sad, she makes me try harder, she makes me laugh, and she makes me feel like I can fly. Isn't that the goddamn definition of love?

I was trying to appeal to Michael's romantic side but all he said was, "This is a joke, right?"

I cracked open another peanut and sulked. "Thanks a lot," I said. "That's real nice. See if I ever spill my guts to you again."

Michael apologized and said it was just that he'd never heard me use the word love unless it was in reference to a song. Again, not the vote of confidence I was looking for.

To help my argument, I pointed out how much I've changed since I met Eliza: I'm down to half a pack of cigarettes a day, I haven't smoked pot in weeks, and my pancreatic cancer has miraculously gone into remission.

Michael started shaking his head. Nothing seemed to be sinking in. That's when I knew there was something else going on. Something he wasn't telling me. He seemed more on edge than I'd ever seen him. And when I asked him to give it to me straight, he told me Vera got into Columbia. This means barring a record deal falling from the sky in the next two months, I'll be looking for a new guitarist come December.

Michael said he was sorry at least ten times. He sounded devastated.

"Things are progressing with Stone," I told him. "There's plenty of time for a deal to come together."

I think I said that because I needed to believe it just as much as Michael did.

Then I told Michael I had to go because Eliza was making dinner, and he said, "My sister's cooking? Jesus, she must be in love."

Outside, Michael and I walked down the middle of the

street looking for the pigeon. We found it near the curb, all dis-combobulated. There was no blood on it anywhere, but it wasn't moving so I bent down and poked at it with my finger.

Michael told me not to touch it. He said it probably had germs galore, but I kept poking at it anyway to make sure it couldn't be saved.

Nothing. Nada. It was dead as a goddamn doornail.

Over.

Sorry it's been so long. I've had a crazy month and a half. Let me back up to where I think I left off.

Jack Stone. Jack Stone. Jack Stone. Try saying that fast about ten times.

Not long after my first meeting with Jack, back in September, a chivalrous courtship began. It was nothing like being preyed upon by Winkle. Au contraire, my dear diary, it was polite and respectful and made me feel more like one of Vesta's sacred virgins than some cheap Eighth Avenue whore.

But it was crunch time. Time was running out for Michael and as a result, he, Eliza, and I began doing some serious Bananafish campaigning. Eliza got the *Village Voice* to do a small article on me, she got *Time Out* to feature the band, and after the three of us made a zillion calls to the local public radio station, she got us booked on one of their most popular music shows—something even Feldman hadn't been able to do. Michael and I did an hour-long acoustic set on the air, and since then Rings of Saturn has been standing room only on Thursday nights.

Jack Stone was extra impressed with our growing fan base and promised that if I signed with him, Bananafish would become the biggest fish in his little Underdog pond. Here's what Jack said to me and Feldman, more or less verbatim, at our last meeting, in Feldman's office:

"You need to understand the way we work. We don't sign

an artist simply because we think he or she can make us a lot of money. We sign them because we like their music. As with anything, there are pros and cons to this. Because we like the music, we trust you, which means we give you complete creative control."

I whistled at the prospect and Feldman gave me a gothic look of scorn.

Jack added, with a quick nod to Feldman, that what he couldn't offer Bananafish was a big advance, a glitzy advertising campaign, and all the promotional brouhaha—yes, he actually said brouhaha. The deal was: keep the costs low and the aim simple. The music's the priority. We make it, Underdog distributes it. That's about it. Although Jack did say Underdog has relationships with a lot of the college stations, as well as a few music publications and the best independent record stores in the country. There would be some initial press, but they couldn't promise much more than that, not that they wouldn't try.

He said what it all came down to, really, was where I saw myself in the big picture. I assured Jack I have a very realistic idea of where I might fit into the big picture. I don't expect to play football stadiums with a laser light show behind me. I just want to be able to quit my day job, keep Michael in the band, buy my girlfriend some sexy lingerie once in a while, and maybe support a family someday.

Note to self: Discuss the possibility of kids with Eliza.

I felt Feldman's dissatisfaction. Apparently Jack felt it too. He tried to offer my manager some consolation. He said that unlike the major labels, Underdog actually pays its artists for every unit sold. Then he went on to elaborate on major-label accounting, claiming that since the dawn of the recording industry, the big companies have managed to come up with incredibly ingenious ways of bookkeeping, ensuring that they always get the lion's share of the profits.

"We don't shell out hundreds of thousands of dollars on

extraneous costs," Jack said, "so we don't have to screw you."

Feldman informed Jack that he didn't need a lesson in Music Biz 101. That's when Jack asked Feldman if he was against me making a deal with Underdog. Feldman admitted that in the last few months there had been major-label interest and, as my manager, he had to consider what was best for my career.

Jack turned to me and said, "Is that what you want, major-label support?"

I told him the money would be nice. But like I explained to Jack, I don't know why the majors want me. I don't have many songs under five minutes, I never play anything the same way twice, and Michael and I are known to indulge in epic-long guitar drones on stage. You put all that together and you're not looking at major-label material, at least not in this decade.

Before Jack left, he pulled me aside and told me that I should get myself a lawyer, someone with an objective opinion on contracts and careers.

Feldman didn't even get up when Jack left. Then he roared at me from behind his desk. "You most certainly ARE major-label material!" He was pounding on the sides of his chair but the cushy leather on the armrests muted the sound. He wanted to know why I would say a thing like that to Jack, and I told him it was because I like Jack and he said if I like Jack so much I should fuck him, not sign with him. He kept saying, "Your potential is endless. Blah, blah."

He was having one of his Brian Epstein moments.

Like I told Feldman, I appreciate the faith he has in me, and I owe him a hell of a lot, but I suspect his expectations for my career, and maybe his own, might be a little high. I mean holy Hell, even if he is the twenty-first-century's answer to Brian Epstein, no one can recreate the Beatles. That was a once-in-a-lifetime thing. And sure, it was talent, but it was also timing. No band will ever be bigger than Jesus again.

Feldman accused me of underestimating myself, but that's

not really the problem. I just happen to comprehend the low standards of the majority of the music-buying public, and I don't care how condescending that sounds, it's true. They always go for the shiny gimmicks. Always.

All of a sudden Feldman was smiling like a freak. He got up and stood really close to my face like he was going to kiss me. Then he hands me this huge stack of papers and goes, "I didn't want to say anything in front of Stone, but as far as I'm concerned, Underdog was nothing more than a stepping stone for this."

I asked him what it was and he goes, "Your ticket outta Liverpool, kid." The document was so heavy I had to sit down and rest it on my lap.

Feldman asked me if I knew Jack Stone used to work for my favorite record exec—old caterpillar eyebrows. I did not. Apparently the two didn't part on good terms and now everything's a fucking contest.

"No kidding," Feldman said. "When Winkle got wind that Underdog was after you, he called me in a panic. This morning he sent over that bible you're holding."

Feldman pointed to the advance. The number had doubled to seven hundred grand. It stopped my heart for a second.

"And don't forget," Feldman said. "That doesn't include a publishing deal. When all is said and done, we're talking well over a million dollars."

See, the way it works is you sign a record deal, and then the songwriting, a.k.a. the publishing, is separate. Numbers-wise, a good publishing deal can be as much as the recording advance—there are megabucks to be made selling songs.

According to Feldman, Winkle has also developed a new-found appreciation for the Michaels. He won't sign them, but he'll let me keep them on salary.

Translation: Michael could pay his wife's tuition AND stay in the band AND quit his day job.

Feldman said, "Winkle wants to talk to you ASAP." So I sat

there like an idiot, paging through the contract, while Feldman's secretary got Winkle on the line, and over Feldman's speakerphone Winkle not only claimed he'd been wrong about the Michaels, he also claimed he was prepared to nurture Bananafish, to allow me to develop and grow into one of the label's more respectable "career artists."

The next thing he said was, "I see you along the lines of the Drones."

The guy knows how to get my attention, I'll give him that. Before we hung up, I promised Winkle I'd seriously consider the offer, but I should point out that as soon as I said it my pancreas started to throb.

Feldman said, "This is a no-brainer, Paul. And it's not just the monetary difference between Jack and Winkle you need to consider, it's the amount of exposure the band will get. Underdog admittedly provides little promotion for their artists, and Winkle's got a major PR machine behind him."

I made Feldman promise not to let me turn into a musical heathen or soulless pop pagan, and he goes: "That's Peepers talking."

They were Doug Blackman's words, actually. Eliza just borrowed them. But I didn't feel like getting into that with Feldman. I don't think he likes Eliza. Not since she so eloquently denounced 66 in *Sonica*. And even though she's really helped us out a lot, Feldman's nose is a little out of joint about it. It's an ego thing. He wants us to be successful, but only if he's responsible for the success.

In all fairness, Eliza doesn't like Feldman either. She thinks he's creepy and always says, "Paul, if I live to be a hundred I'll never understand what you see in that guy."

But my point to Feldman was this: I don't want to sell out to some corporate goddamn executive who doesn't know his ass from an amplifier. Of course, Feldman was quick to remind me that we were talking about the man who discovered the

Drones. Winkle might be an asshole but he has a good track record.

If I sound like I'm trying to convince myself, it's because I am.

Then, without an announcement or a knock, the door to Feldman's office flew open and I turned around to see Amanda Strunk standing in the doorway. She was the last person in the world I felt like chatting with. I grabbed my coat and tried to make a quick getaway, but she stretched her leg out to block my exit, fiddled with the top button of my shirt, and said, "Wanna go have a drink with me, pussycat?"

These goddamn people, I swear.

I snatched her hand off of my chest, and the disdain I felt in that moment for Amanda Strunk, for what she represented, and for the advantage that people like she and Winkle had over me, made me want to snap her wrist in two. I envied their emptiness. I envied the simplicity of their goals. I envied how little it took to make them happy. I almost envied their greed.

"Let's go wet our whistles," Amanda said. "I promise not to tell your girlfriend."

I stepped over her foot and told her to go to hell.

"Two words," Feldman clamored after me. "The Drones, Paul. The Drones."

I'm going to take Jack's advice and consult a lawyer, and I assured Feldman he'd have an answer by the end of the week.

A no-brainer, right?

Over.

Before Paul gave Feldman the go-ahead, he and I met the band, along with Paul's new lawyer, Damien Weiss, at the rehearsal space for one last powwow.

"What's Yoko doing here?" Angelo said when he saw me. He was only teasing and I laughed. But Paul stared him down for what felt like an hour, until Angelo said, "Jeeze. It was a joke. Fucking lighten up."

I hated the rehearsal space. It was a dark, cramped unit with cinderblock walls, no windows, and a stifling lack of fresh air. The furnishings consisted of a ratty futon, carpet remnants scattered here and there, and mounds of instruments, cords, and amps taking up every inch of space. There was barely room for the band, let alone guests, and I had to lean against the door.

Unsurprisingly, the vote among the Michaels was unanimous in favor of Winkle, and when Damien Weiss arrived bearing gifts of admonition, Paul was the only one pendulous about the deal.

Damien Weiss bugged me, too. He was a tall, starched shirt, he spoke with a deep, condescending tone, and his Adam's apple was so big he looked like he'd swallowed a golf ball. And do I need to add that I saw *The Omen* when I was a kid? All I'm saying is, Damien was the name of the devil child.

Damien was trying to find someplace to stand, and he had a copy of Paul's eighty-seven-page contract in his hands.

He asked if Paul had read the document.

"Not word for word. Some of the sentences are ten paragraphs long."

Paul assured Damien that Feldman had explained it in great detail, and Damien set the document down on the table so that Paul could see it. Then he spoke as if he were teaching a class of first graders. "Has anyone ever heard the word *recoupment*?"

Paul pushed his bangs behind his ears and nodded. "It's the amount of money the record company has to make back before I get any royalties."

Damien nodded with him. "And did Mr. Feldman explain just how much your recoupment costs are going to be if you sign this?" He turned to a section he'd highlighted in yellow and pointed to the math he'd done in the margin. "I calculated a number of your definite expenses—the advance, the recording budget, band salaries, and promotion. Now, look at this." He flipped a few more pages. "*This* is the percentage you receive from record sales—*before* taxes." He flipped back to the original number and then turned the page over, where there were half a dozen more equations, plus another seven-digit number that had a * by it.

"What's that?" Paul asked.

"*That*," Damien said, "is the staggering number of records you'll have to sell before you see *one cent* of your royalties."

Paul's face wilted first. The Michaels followed like Dominos.

Damien Weiss was on my last nerve. I set my hands on my hips, jutted my pelvis out to the side like Daphne from *Scooby Doo,* and said, "Who are you to say they can't sell that many records?"

"Listen," devil man said. "I'm not saying they *can't* sell that many records. But let's just say they *don't*. Then what?"

Being an artist in the music industry is a lot like being a gay man in the army. A thousand-to-one, the guy's not welcome. Which is not to say he can't sneak in unnoticed and, by sheer luck and a bit of self-control, have a long and successful career, but let General Winkle catch Private Hudson with a dick in his mouth and trust me, things could get ugly.

It's not like I don't understand the nature of the business. But the whole process is a dichotomy to me...Hold on...What the hell was I going to talk about? Oh, yeah. Recoupment. Before I made my final decision, Eliza and I went to Feldman's office and had one last discussion on recoupment.

"Contrary to what anyone tells you," Feldman said. "Recoupment is essentially a nonissue."

Eliza nodded in agreement. I can't tell you how weird it was to see Eliza and Feldman in harmony against me.

Feldman went on to outline his reasoning in two parts—the upside and the downside. The upside was to assume we'd sell enough records to pay back the initial costs. "Which I believe you will," he said. "Eventually. And when that happens, you'll start seeing more money."

As a sidebar, I should probably add that Feldman gets seventeen cents of every dollar I make.

The downside was to assume that, worst case scenario, we didn't sell any records—in this instance Bananafish flounders and dies and I get screwed, but the record company gets screwed harder because they haven't seen a return on their investment, whereas I get to keep the advance, which whether the record fails or not is a pretty goddamn significant amount of money—more than I ever imagined I'd see in my life, that's for sure. And certainly enough to live on if Winkle sells me down the river.

"See? Problem solved," Eliza said.

Feldman told me my girlfriend was smart and I should listen to her. He even called her Eliza. He'd obviously put his contempt on hold. Matter of fact, he suddenly looked like he wanted to stick his head between her legs.

One final snag came when a timeframe was presented. The company, which I have dubbed Winkle Records, wanted us to go into the studio right away. They were going to give us six weeks to make the first of five records I would be under contract to deliver. Winkle hoped to have the first CD in stores by spring.

Feldman and Eliza both begged me not to start another pissing match, but I had one more point of contention. I've been writing songs a long time. I'm not bragging about how prolific I am, but I have close to sixty songs to sort through. I need time to do nothing but rehearse and work on the arrangements. And I want to make the record without a clock ticking.

No one was more surprised than I was when my demands were met. Still, I held out until one last carrot was dangled—

The Drones. They're tentatively scheduled to launch a big American tour about a year from now. Winkle said their audience is my future audience and he promised to do everything in his power to get Bananafish the opening slot.

These clever goddamn people. They really know how to play a guy. But holy Hell, their biggest skill is raping you, all the while making you think you're having consensual sex.

My gut and pancreas were screaming Underdog—Jack and I understand each other, and I trust Jack. But it's not that simple.

A year ago, it would have been, but not anymore. I have people besides myself to think about. And for the first time I see something on the road up ahead that I've never noticed. Something I'm looking forward to: the future.

Ultimately, I don't want to be one of those assholes who make decisions based on money, but I'm not stupid either. Here I am, twenty-eight and still folding shirts to pay my rent. I've never had more than a couple hundred dollars in my bank account at one time and, frankly, I've never given much thought to the day after tomorrow, let alone all the days following all the tomorrows.

I want more. I want a life that extends beyond retail sales, a crappy apartment, and cheap coffee. And I know that doesn't make me a bad person, just more honest than I've ever been. I also know my dream goddamn future will look a lot brighter if I let Winkle fuck me in the ass.

And so I did. This morning, a frigid but perfectly clear December day, the kind of day that feels like a snow cone in your lungs, after weeks of negotiations, doubts, and deliberation, I traipsed like a soldier into a gleaming high-rise not far from Rockefeller Center and signed a deal with one of the largest, most powerful multimedia conglomerates in the world.

Facing caterpillar eyebrows, you know what I did? I picked up the pen, scribbled my name as fast as I could, and rallied the nerve to do something I've always wanted to do—I winked at Winkle.

Immediately after leaving Winkle's office with a big-ass check in my hand, I headed down Sixth Ave with my heart aching and my pancreas burning.

I walked forty-plus blocks, all the way to the Gap, and resigned. Then I went to the bank. Needless to say, it was turning into a major goddamn day and it wasn't over yet. I was contemplating one more big move; I just needed someplace meditational to think it over.

I was right near St. Joseph's in the Village. I'm not a religious guy but I decided there were worse places to ruminate. Unbeknownst to me, the church had a daily mass that I'd inconveniently shown up in the middle of. Quickly taking a seat in the second-to-last pew, I felt like an imposter, like anyone who turned around and looked at me would know I didn't belong.

When the priest asked the congregation to kneel, I knelt too. Then I bowed my head and tried to think about what it all meant—the contract, the band, the money, my goddamn career. I hate the connotation of the word "career." It doesn't seem to truly account for the way I spend my time. It embodies all the direct opposites of my hows and whys and most of all it implies a choice, and I've never felt like I had any choice. I do what I do out of need and necessity, and because it's the only thing I've ever been good at, not as a means to an end, not even for money or the adulation of the world, but for my own measly survival.

Not that I won't welcome all that if it comes my way, right? Let me tell you, depositing a check for seven hundred grand did not suck.

The priest said, "Peace be with you."

"And also with you," everyone responded.

Then the guy suggested we all make peace with each other, and the whole place started shaking hands with whoever they could reach. Something about the scene made my heartache go away. I wanted to hug every person in that church, but I was the only one in my row. I had no one to touch so I got back down on my knees and picked up where I'd left off.

It's like this: I feel almost cursed by the overwhelming and admittedly self-induced pressure I've placed on my shoulders. On the other hand, I feel like if I stay focused I'll find value in the journey. And the bottom line is I want Eliza along for the ride.

I am of the theory that all of our transcendental connections, anything we're drawn to, be it a person, a song, a painting on a wall—they're magnetic. The art is the alloy, so to speak. And our souls are equipped with whatever properties are required to attract that alloy. I'm no scientist so I don't really know what the hell these properties are, but my point is we're drawn to stuff that we've already got a connection to. Part of the thing is already inside of us.

That's what I mean when I say fate. Fate is the magnetic pull of our souls toward the people, places, and things we belong with.

After leaving the church, I kept heading south down Sixth Ave., turned left on Grand, and went into a shop I'd gone into a dozen times in the past two weeks, where I had a long talk with Harry, the man behind the counter. Harry called me Mr. Hudson no matter how many times I told him Paul was fine.

"All right," I said. "Let's do it."

Now I'm back at home, waiting. I killed some time folding and putting away all the clothes on my floor. Following that task I chewed up a piece of gum and used it to paste a note to the door that said: ON THE ROOF. Then I climbed up the fire escape with a pen and an envelope full of index cards.

It's been almost an hour. I'm still up here waiting for her. I'm cold and nervous as shit.

Over.

According to the weatherman, the day's high was thirty-three degrees. I guessed it hadn't reached that number, but when I found Paul on the roof he was perched near the edge wearing a black hooded sweatshirt and a pair of jeans. No hat, no gloves, no coat. He looked like a refugee from an Eastern Bloc country. And there was something about the way he was standing with his shoulders slumped, together with the bleak expression on his face, that caused me pain.

I couldn't make out what he was doing. All I saw were index cards that he seemed to be ripping up and tossing off the side of the building.

"Hey, rock star," I said, hoping to generate some enthusiasm.

He looked back, smiled tensely, and called me over. As I approached, I noticed he was watching shards of paper dance to the sidewalk. And each of his index cards had different words written on them, things like:

FEAR
COMPROMISE
LONELINESS
ANGST

"What are you doing?"

"Getting rid of all the goddamn negativity in my life."

I looked down at the mess he was making.

"I know," he said, his lips moving in frozen slow motion.

"I'm going to clean it when I'm done."

After ripping up the last of his cards, he sat down on the ledge and pulled me in so that I was between his legs. He put his hands inside my coat, rested his head on my chest and squeezed. His whole body was shivering.

"I talked to Michael. He said everything went well. He's euphoric." I lifted Paul's chin. "Why aren't you?"

He sighed. "My name is Linus Van Pelt. It's dawn, I'm standing in the pumpkin patch, I've been here all night, I skipped trick-or-treating for this shit and what do I get? Nothing. Nada. The Great Pumpkin never showed up. The Great Pumpkin doesn't exist."

Paul's uncharacteristic frailty was melting me. "Hey. Do you realize what you accomplished today? You're supposed to be happy right now."

"I am. That's the most fucked-up part," he said. "I've never been happier in my life. But when dreams come true in reality they never feel the same as when you imagine them, and you know what that means? It means that no matter how good things are, maybe they'll never be good enough, and there's something seriously wrong with that."

I kissed him and tried to warm his ears with my mitten-covered hands. "All your cocky-bastard nonsense, it's an act, isn't it?"

"If I said yes, would you love me less?"

"I'd probably love you more."

"I'm *so* glad you said that." He began to pace back and forth in a line, speaking to my feet. "Eliza, I need to ask you something. And all I want is an answer. Not an answer in the form of a question, not a goddamn soliloquy on my future as the savior of the heathens and pagans, just what's in your heart, all right? I need to know that wherever I end up, in the stars or in the gutter, you're along for the ride."

It felt like a trick question. "What do you mean?"

He actually stomped his feet. "What did I just say about answering a question with a question?" He spun me around and made me sit in the spot he'd just vacated while he resumed his pacing. "It's like this: What if I decided to pump gas for the rest of my life? Would you stick around?"

If I'd had a hammer I would've nailed his feet to the ground. "Are you a gas pumper who plays guitar and sings, or are you a gas pumper who sits around smoking pot and drinking beer in his spare time?"

"I'm the first guy, mostly." There was an innocence and sincerity on his face that made me ache. "Bottom line, Eliza—you're my home and my family, and I don't want to lose you. I could lose everything else, and as long as I still had you and a guitar I know I'd be all right. Do you get what I'm saying?"

In the six years Adam and I were together, he'd never said anything so important to me. I'd only known Paul for five months and already I was sure I never wanted to spend a night without him.

"Yeah," I said. "I'm all yours."

"Good. Okay. Perfect." Paul began trying to remove the mitten from my left hand, but the shaking of his own was making that difficult. Once he managed to get the mitten off, he reached into his pocket and pulled out a ring that looked as if it had been made a hundred years ago. There was a pearl in the center, surrounded by eight tiny diamonds cut into triangles, set to form the shape of a flower.

"If you don't like it, Harry said you could come in and pick out another one."

Before I knew it, Paul had slipped the ring on my finger, and my mouth fell open as if the hinges to my jaw were loose.

"I know what you're going to say." He put his hand up to keep me quiet. "This is the last thing I should be thinking about now, right? It's supposed to be all about my career, the band. But one thing I've realized is that my life in its entirety is more important than any one aspect of it. And the sad truth is that until I met you I didn't *have* anything else. So, if you love me and want to be with me…Well…What do you say?"

I was a second away from jumping into his arms and screaming *Yes!* But a wave of anxiety stopped me, and threatened to split my chest in two.

Paul must have sensed my apprehension. He backed up and shoved his hands into the pockets of his sweatshirt, then jammed his fists together, stretching the cotton tightly across his shoulders. He looked like he was trying to hug something that wasn't there.

"Silence," he said. "*Not* a good sign."

It was my turn to pace. I walked in a four-by-four square pattern, turning the corners at sharp, ninety-degree angles. Inside my coat I was sweating.

"Shit, Eliza, don't do this to me."

I covered my face with my hands, which felt weird because I was only wearing one mitten. Closing my eyes, I bit my cheeks and tried to imagine all our possible futures, but I couldn't escape a shattering hunch that Paul's future, as I suddenly foresaw it—the fame, the women, and most daunting of all, the traveling—made little room for me.

"Here's a bonus," Paul said. "If you marry me, I'll have to tell you my last name."

In his eyes I saw all the other possibilities. The dreamworld possibilities. The fairytale possibilities. The seemingly impossible possibilities. Maybe Bananafish's record would go platinum; Paul and I would buy a townhouse in the West Village, one with a stoop out front where Paul could sit and strum on his guitar and write songs; I'd be doing cover stories for *Sonica*, and we'd have a kid or two—boys with shaggy hair and cool rock 'n' roll names like Rex and Spike; Vera and Michael would live next door, and everything Paul and

I needed, wanted, and loved would be within a five-block radius. We would never have to leave the neighborhood, let alone leave New York, let alone leave the ground.

"Eliza, say something."

Over the ledge I could see the little bits of index cards pirouetting in the wind like tiny ballerinas on the sidewalk.

"I'm scared, Paul."

"Look at me," he said.

I shook my head, and an army of tears made its way down my cheeks. A stronger breeze scattered the papers into the street. Paul was never going to be able to clean them up now.

He held me against his chest and said, "Tell me what you're scared of."

"Getting left behind."

"I'm not going to leave you behind."

I stepped back far enough to look Paul in the eyes. The longer I looked, the more the tension drained, first from my face and then down my body, and I began to nod.

"Is that a yes?" he said.

"Yes."

He put his hands on the sides of my face and kissed me like a drowning man gasping for air.

We celebrated at Balthazar that night. The Michaels were all there, along with Vera, Queenie, Feldman, and the woman known only as "Feldman's wife" because Feldman hardly ever brought her around, and when he did he never introduced her to us.

"Her name begins with an M," Vera said.

"Cheryl." I was sure her name was Cheryl.

"In what language does Cheryl begin with an M?"

Paul and I often visited Michael at Balthazar for free coffee and croissants, but we'd never been able to afford a meal there. The restaurant was large, crowded, and noisy, but with its red leather upholstery and Parisian-brasserie decor, it reminded me of the places Hemingway wrote about in a book Paul had given me, *A Moveable Feast*.

When Paul and I arrived, the champagne was flowing; there was a plate of raw oysters in the middle of the table and two dishes of fried calamari at each end.

I took the seat next to Vera while Paul tapped Michael on the shoulder and said, "Need to talk to you for a sec. In private." He wanted to be the one to tell Michael. He thought it was more chivalrous that way.

Grabbing a tentacle, Paul dipped a piece of calamari in marinara sauce, tossed it into his mouth, and then dragged Michael around the corner. They were out of sight for no more than a minute. When they walked back to the table Michael had a blithe, if not surprised smirk on his face.

"I hope you know what you're getting into," my brother said, kissing the top of my head. Then he looked at Paul. "Maybe I should be saying that to you; I'm not really sure anymore."

Everyone bellowed to know what was going on. Michael pointed at Paul and said, "Ask my future brother-in-law."

The table fell silent as Paul slid in next to me, plucked an oyster from the platter, sucked the meat from its shell, and then lifted my ring finger. "Jesus, do we have to write it out on a goddamn chalkboard?"

Vera caught on first. She eyed me with apprehension, and then she surrendered, cheering, and the rest of the party followed suit.

For the first time in my life, everything felt like it was in its right place. Paul and I were in love, my brother had a career to look forward to, and Vera would be starting law school in another month.

It was a good night.

Even Feldman looked hopeful.

July 28, 2001

I'm a man of principles. A decent-enough guy. And confrontation, believe it or not, does not come easy to me.

Is this goddamn thing working? Check, one, two, three. It's been like, six zillion months since I've used it. Okay, it's moving. Shit, where was I?

Getting my ass kicked.

No kidding, I probably would have received less of an ass-kicking squaring off with Mike Tyson than I did when we finally headed into the studio in February. And just to make myself feel better, I'm going to blame everything on Winkle. I'm going to say he instigated all the conflicts, because who the hell likes to admit they should've watched where they were walking when they find themselves sinking in quicksand?

The problem with Winkle, he has this phony-sycophantic, leader-of-the-pack mentality that irks my last nerve. His modus operandi while we were recording went something like this: He'd start off by telling me how great a song was, going on and on until he'd used every thesaurus entry for the word "incredible," then five minutes later he would give me a dozen reasons why that very same remarkable fabulous awesome amazing astounding song couldn't go on the record. But his reasons could always be whittled down to one—it doesn't sound like the shit that's selling now.

I've come to a conclusion though. This is all just a game to

Winkle, a game he has to win or else he's out of a job, and he resents me because I won't play along.

Our first big run-in happened when I came up with the idea to record the entire album on eight tracks with a twenty-five-thousand-dollar budget. I'd read that the Drones debut had been made for less, so I knew it could be done well. And as I'm still conscious of the recoupment factor, I wanted to be efficient. To my genuine surprise, this plan didn't sit well with Winkle. I guess he wanted me to waste as much money as possible.

"Eight tracks?" he spouted, his eyebrows ready to burst forth from his forehead. "We're offering you a state-of-the-art studio and you want eight tracks?"

I told him I was pretty sure *Abbey Road* was recorded on eight tracks. So were Doug Blackman's first two records. He said I had a better chance of being struck by lightning. He also laughed at what he called my naïve budget plan.

"Paul," he said. "The Sykes Brothers alone are going to cost that much."

Welcome to blowout number two. Winkle had hired the hit-making team known as the Sykes Brothers to produce the record. Listen, the Sykes boys are nice and all, but they have serious pop-pagan tendencies. They also put their stamp on everything—in other words, they go into a project intending to make a Sykes Brothers record, not an insert-band-name-here record.

Winkle wanted to know who I thought should produce the record and I proposed myself. Again, it would have saved a lot of cash. Again, I got nothing but a laugh in the face.

"What's the last hit record you produced, Paul?"

I stared him down, hoping he didn't notice my hand on my pancreas. He said if I wanted a career I better quit pouting, get my ass in the studio, and make it work with the Sykes Bros. Actually, what he said was: "Show up and shut up, or get the fuck off this cloud."

So I did. I showed up, shut up, and made it work. But it felt like compromise. And if you ask me, compromise feels like amputation.

Winkle was beginning to hate me. I could see it in his eyebrows and I could smell it on his breath, which called to mind the warm air that shoots up from the subway grates and smacks of a slow, steely death.

The Michaels and I spent four months in the studio with Sykes and Sykes—three weeks longer than our allotted time. We recorded fourteen songs, twelve of which were slated for the album, two that will be saved for B-sides and the like. After finishing what the brothers considered to be the final song, they decided their work was done, packed their bags, and moved on to the next bunch of heathens, even though I was still unhappy with the half the tracks.

Their departure turned out to be the best thing that could have happened. It gave me a chance to fiddle with all the moments on the record that didn't feel right. After a couple more weeks working out the kinks, I was satisfied we'd made the best record possible under the circumstances.

That's when I finally let Eliza listen to it. I'd been holding out on her. I wanted it to be a big deal, you know? I wanted her to get the whole package in one dose.

She cried and told me I was a genius.

Note to self: Always remember how lucky you are to wake up next to someone who thinks you're the shit.

Next step, the finished product got messengered over to Winkle for approval, but before he'll sign-off on it, he's sending us to Los Angeles to meet with "a few key marketing and promotional people."

Sounds fun, huh?

Michael and Vera have never been to California, and Vera is out of school for the summer so Michael's going to bring her along, maybe stay a few extra days and hang out on the beach.

Here's how stupid I am. I had this notion that I'd tell Eliza about the trip, the prospect of a few weeks frolicking on the beach would inspire her, and she would agree to come.

As soon as I broached the subject, Eliza's expression darkened, like it does every time we talk about travel requiring flight. Man, the amount of pain that history, fear, and irrationality can dredge up is mind-blowing.

I played like I assumed she would be tagging along, and mentioned that we'd be leaving on the twelfth. So she turns to me in all seriousness and goes, "Can we drive?"

I had to make a conscious effort to keep my eyes from expanding. First off, we don't have a goddamn car. A train would take, like, a week. And a bus, a zillion years. Eliza kept repeating the date and I sensed a fit of hysterics coming.

"Paul," she said, practically hyperventilating, "don't you know that more planes have crashed on August twelfth than on any other day in the history of aviation?"

Believe it or not, I was completely unaware of this fact. Something like fourteen accidents so far. She made me promise I wouldn't go anywhere near a plane on August twelfth.

I sat her down on the couch and told her the same shit I always tell her: flying is no big deal. I said I'd sit right next to her and talk to her the whole time. I tried to convince her how much fun we could have eating crappy food, watching a stupid movie, and having cramped sex in the bathroom. After five minutes she wouldn't even know she was in the air.

First she used work as an excuse, claiming Lucy would never let her go. Then I made the case that it could be a working vacation. She screamed, "I CAN'T!" and locked herself in the bathroom.

I hate that word, CAN'T. I wish it had never been dreamed up, spoken, or defined. I wish the concept of CAN'T could be eradicated not only from language, but more importantly from the psyche of a girl who I know is filled with so much CAN it seeps out of her pores and scents the air.

I told her I could change the date. We could leave on the eleventh. She kept screaming "No!" and then I sort of lost it. I pounded on the door and started screaming back at her. I told her she was a baby and that she couldn't stay in New York for the rest of her life. I told her that someday—hopefully—I'll be going on a world tour, probably be gone for months, and if she cares enough to see me she's going to have to get her ass on a plane.

She stayed in the bathroom and cried. After I calmed down I told her I was sorry, but she sniffled and said SHE was the one who should be sorry.

I sat against the wall trying to get her to come out, trying to reason with her, but if there's one thing I've learned from Eliza, it's that there's no reasoning with fear.

I'm off to the City of Lost Angels.

Let the odyssey begin.

Over.

"Armageddon," Paul said when he called from Los Angeles. "I mean it, Eliza. The end of the goddamn world." He'd only been gone for three days and already he was having a breakdown. "Do you have any idea how this company made most of their money, before they acquired a record label, a movie studio, and half of the Internet? Cigarettes and processed dairy products. 'If our goddamn tobacco doesn't kill you, try the mayonnaise!'"

Apparently Paul had been doing research on the corporation that now "owned his ass," as he phrased it. "Technically, the Gap was a better gig. At least they gave me health insurance."

According to Paul, the corporate structure was a hierarchy of separate companies, with the most profitable division—its Internet server—the apex. Music was third on the ladder, and probably did little more than provide a nice tax write-off every year.

"I'm still working for the man and he's still got me by the balls."

By the end of the first week, Paul's resentment had evolved into doomsday pessimism as he gave me blow-by-blow accounts of the budding compromises he was being faced with on a round-the-clock basis.

"Day one," he said. "This guy, Clint, a.k.a. Winkle Junior, tells us that although he *likes* the songs we've recorded, he's sorry to inform us that he doesn't hear a single, and in accordance with a stipulation in our contract that says we have to deliver recordings the company deems *commercially satisfactory*, I have to write one. Or else."

"Or else what?"

"Or else *everything*. If Clint doesn't get his single, Clint can make it so our record never sees the light of day. He told me I *had* to write a single. He said: 'Go write a single, Paul. You're not leaving here until we've got a single.' That began World War III."

I'd never heard Paul sound so upset. "What are your options?"

"Options?" He took a long hit off of a cigarette—a habit he admitted had returned with a vengeance during the week. "I wouldn't exactly call them options. I either give them their radio song or, according to Feldman *and* Damien Weiss, they can terminate my contract on the grounds that I'm in breach of the deal."

"Jesus…"

"Wait. It gets worse. Meredith from—I don't know what department—art or marketing or something—Meredith is concerned about the Bananafish image. She wants to take us shopping and buy us some new clothes. She's convinced I need a new hip-ass hairdo to go with said clothes. *And* she informed me, after a day-long photo shoot, they were planning on putting my goddamn face on the cover of the album. *Me*. Not some cool graphic, not the whole band, just *me*. World War IV."

I wondered if Meredith was pretty. "I thought you had approval over that stuff."

"It's all bullshit. Our contract says we have to be *consulted* on the artwork. It says nothing about them having to listen to the opinions expressed during that consultation. The only good news is I think I won that battle. Unfortunately, it didn't come cheap. I give them their goddamn single and they keep my face off the cover."

As much as I loved Paul, his ambivalence toward success made me want to kick him. "Explain to me why you don't want your face on the cover."

"Eliza, my pancreas."

"You're cute. And cute sells records."

"Holy Hell, I don't want anyone buying my record because they think I'm cute." He coughed and cleared his throat. "Day three, Clint's back. And Clint has developed an annoying habit of ending every goddamn sentence with my name. First thing he says to me: 'How you coming on that new *song*, Paul? You're going into the studio in three *days*, Paul. You're not leaving California until you record a *single*, Paul. We can't make plans for the *video* if we don't have the *song*, Paul.'"

I visualized Paul's hand roaming his lower abdomen, searching for that infernal gland of his.

"I miss you," I said.

"Yeah. Me too." He coughed again. It sounded like bark scraping his esophagus. "Nobody's on my side with this video thing. Even your brother wants to make a video."

Paul was out of his mind. That's what I decided. "You're kidding right? You *have* to make a video."

"Music is not a visual medium."

"How do you expect to sell any records if you don't make a video?"

"Music is *not* a visual medium."

"Yes, it is. Music became a visual medium on August 1, 1981, the day MTV was born. I don't like it any more than you do, but—"

"Music is *not*—"

"All right, I get it. We'll talk about it when you get home. In the meantime, hang in there. It's only a few more days."

"I don't know if I'm going to make it. My pancreas is killing me and I can't breathe. Will you meet me at the airport on Friday?"

It sounded like the choice between life and death.

"Just say you'll try."

"I'll try."

I didn't make it to the airport. Instead I spent the five and a half hours Paul was on the plane calling the airline's automated flight arrival and departure information number every fifteen minutes to check on the status of his trip just like I'd done when he'd left.

When I heard Paul's feet ricocheting off the stairs, I ran to the landing and leaned over the railing just far enough to get a peek at him. He was lugging his duffel bag over his shoulder, and his face looked jet-lagged and freakishly pale for someone who'd just spent the better part of the month in Southern California.

Without a word, he took me by the arm, dragged me into his room, and made me sit on the bed. At first I thought he was mad that I hadn't shown up to meet the plane, but he didn't look mad. He looked single-mindedly preoccupied.

"Nice to see you too," I said.

Dropping his bag to the floor, he said, "Close your eyes," and then picked up his guitar.

"What kind of hello is that?"

He leaned over, gave me a quick peck on the cheek, and then proceeded to tune the guitar. "Close your eyes."

"Are you high?"

"Don't be ridiculous. I have a surprise for you. Now close your *goddamn* eyes."

Once I complied, he said, "Okay. This is the sound of Paul Hudson making Clint happy. And the only reason I don't consider it selling out is...well, just listen..."

He did a vocal dance to find the right key, and then strummed a slow, melodic, dare I say "radio-friendly" tune and sang:

She is a dolphin. She is a keyhole.
She is a candle but the wind still blows.
She is a lover. She is a dance.
She is an angel but only at a glance.

The days before her never were
Nights alone now only a blur
I just want to go home to her

She is a choir. She is a hurricane.
She is the sun when it looks like rain.
She is granite. She is sand.
She won't tell me the way but she'll take my hand.

She is a virgin. She is a whore.
She gives it all and I beg for more.
With lace under her clothes she drinks my soul.
She opens up and swallows me whole.

Not only was it the most commercially viable song Paul had ever written, with a running time of less than four minutes, it was romantic, sexy, and remarkably close to being a ballad.

"It's about you," he said.

This incited an emotional riot in me, and for a brief, irrational moment I didn't want anyone else to ever hear the song. I no longer wanted to share Paul with the world. I wanted to lock him up in that room and keep him there like a songbird in a cage. I wanted him to belong to me and only me. I didn't want his talent or his soul to be picked apart and trampled underfoot by Winkles and critics and all the potentially insensitive music listeners who might never dig deep enough to find a place for him.

He set the guitar on the floor and scooted toward me.

"It's beautiful," I said. "What's it called?"

"Originally, 'The Goddamn Single,' but Clint is forcing me to rethink that. I might name it after you just for shits and giggles."

I flopped backward onto the bed, pulled Paul on top of me, and for the rest of the night, at least, he did belong to me and only me.

Some people believe in a master plan, that there's no such thing as free will, and humans are nothing but pawns in the chess game of the gods who sit up in the sky on their white fluffy clouds lavishing good fortune on a select few and conspiring against the rest.

I know better. Namely, I know that if I ever have the audacity to blame fate or God for holding a gun to my temple, I also have the wherewithal to remind myself that if I end up with a hole in my head, I was the one who pulled the trigger.

Those were the thoughts running through my mind after Paul turned to look out the window of the limousine and said, "Someone shoot me now. Please. Just put me out of my misery."

"Gimme a gun," Angelo grumbled.

"Chump," Queenie said.

Vera threw ice at Paul's head. I rubbed his arm and said, "Don't be gay. This is going to be fun."

We were on our way to a Labor Day picnic at Mr. Winkle's East Hampton compound. Winkle had called Feldman personally to make sure the band would make an appearance. He even sent the limo to pick them up. Although according to Paul, Winkle made it sound like a job requirement, not an invitation, emphasizing that there would be press there.

"Basically, the guy ordered us to come," Paul said. "Who

does that? Who *orders* people to a party?"

Feldman didn't agree. He considered the attention monumental. "Winkle's putting a lot of eggs in the Bananafish basket."

"Mother-of-Pearl," Vera said when we arrived at the gated entrance and started up the long, paved driveway to the stately Georgian mansion.

"I've died and gone to hell," Paul said.

Before we got out of the car, Burke commented that the driveway looked like the yellow brick road to Oz.

"Yeah," Paul said. "Oz in Hell."

Paul stepped onto the lawn and looked around in disgust. "It's a goddamn heathen-and-pagan festival."

There were at least three hundred people at the party, including numerous famous "heathens and pagans" I recognized right away, along with what Vera described as "the typical Hamptons crowd"—people who looked like they were about to either play or watch Polo.

"These are the same boneheads who used to come to all my events," Vera said, referring to her former job in the nonprofit world. She pointed to a bejeweled woman slipping forks into her handbag. "See? All the money in the world and they *steal* things. Winkle should have a guard checking bags on the way out."

Winkle's backyard was huge. There was a tennis court to the right of the patio, adjacent to the spot where a white, Barnum & Bailey-sized tent was set up, under which numerous buffets sat. And the lawn was overpopulated by round tables decorated with crisp linens and floral arrangements filled with voluptuous purple flowers. It looked more like a debutante's wedding reception than the Labor Day festivities of a music mogul.

Despite copious bars set up at various strategic locations

inside and out, a perky waitress popped up to take drink orders the minute we stepped foot on the grass.

"Shit," Paul said, squeezing my hand. "Here comes Winkle."

I watched the man move across the lawn at a perfectly calculated, I-Am-the-Boss speed, as if he were on a public relations conveyor belt. His appearance surprised me. The way Paul talked about the guy, I'd expected a gargoyle. But Winkle had a friendly, working-class face. He looked like the lead singer of Styx during the *Kilroy Was Here* phase. And even though his eyebrows were white and bushy, he was younger than I'd imagined. Forty-five, tops.

Mrs. Winkle, donning a hat that seemed to have been designed to match the centerpieces on the tables, fell in line beside her husband and feigned knowing who the band was when Feldman announced them as Bananafish.

"Follow me," Winkle told Paul and the Michaels. "There are people here you need to meet."

In my ear, Paul whispered, "If we're not back by dark, call in the National Guard."

The band trailed Winkle into the house a moment before the perky waitress returned with all the drinks. She appeared unglued about what to do with the orphaned glasses on her tray.

"Give them to me," Queenie said, lifting the tray right off the waitress's arm.

I took my water-filled martini goblet, and as Queenie went to distribute libations to Paul and the Michaels, Vera and I made our way to the food tent, stopping at the end of the shortest line, behind a couple of men who were having an amicable dispute about which Doug Blackman record contained a song called "The Landscape You Made Me."

"It's on *Speaking Without Words*," a guy with thinning hair and a bulbous chin said as he scooped a heap of gourmet potato salad onto his plate.

The other guy, who was tall, had thick, shiny hair the color of bronze in the sun, and whose back was to me, mumbled, "*Lay This Burden Down*."

The shiny-haired guy was right. As sure as I know my name, I know "The Landscape You Made Me" is the third track on *Lay This Burden Down*.

"I don't care who you are, you're wrong," the big-chinned guy said. "While you were off in your oblivious little Brit-punk world, jacking off to the Clash, I was living and breathing Doug Blackman."

"I'll bet you a grand," the shiny-haired guy said to his friend.

"Make it two and it's a deal."

They sealed the pact by setting down their plates, maneuvering their drinks into their left hands, and then shaking with their rights.

Vera nudged me. She wanted me to set the guys straight. Shrugging, I tapped Mr. Shiny Hair on the shoulder and said, "If you promise to split half the cash with me, I can settle—"

"Whoa. *Hi* there," Vera said as soon as the guy turned around.

Like Vera, I recognized Loring Blackman immediately. Not just as Doug's oldest son, but as the man whose most recent record, *Rusted*—a gut-wrenching rhapsody about the breakup of his five-year marriage—happened to have been one of the biggest success stories of the last year, making its way into the number one album slot amidst the heathens and pagans, where it remained for four weeks straight.

It was hard not to notice Loring Blackman. His features were flawlessly proportioned and made complete aesthetic sense, as if a sculptor had used mathematical equations to calculate the ideal placement of eyes, nose, and mouth. He was the kind of man I would have normally referred to derogatorily as "clinically good-looking," but there was something about him that enabled me to see beyond his handsomeness—he seemed to wear it like a burden; it often overshadowed his music, garnered him just as much attention as his famous father, and I could tell by the mortified expression on his face after Vera's greeting that he considered it to be nothing short of a curse.

The blond guy stepped in front of Loring. "What do you two know about Doug Blackman? You're girls."

"Thanks for noticing," Vera said.

"I have to pee," I whispered to her.

Shaking his head, Loring turned toward me and muttered, "Don't pay attention to Tab. He just spent the better part of the year on the road and what few social graces he had are long gone."

Loring's voice was deep and he spoke so quietly I had to take a step forward to hear him.

"What are you implying?" Vera asked Tab, helping herself to two slices of watermelon, handing one to me. "Girls aren't allowed to like Doug Blackman?"

"Call me sexist," Tab said. "But Doug's a man's man. Women just don't understand that kind of pain."

"*Ha*," I said.

Loring smiled at me. Tab said, "Are you a musician? If not, then you don't know what you're talking about."

"She *writes* about music," Vera announced.

Loring asked me who I wrote for but I just shrugged. I knew *Sonica* was on his shit list. The needle dick who wrote the review of Loring's record tore it apart by comparing every one of his songs to one of his father's, proclaiming that he was nothing but a poor imitation of the master. Then Lucy Enfield added insult to injury by having the nerve to bombard Loring with numerous requests for a cover story once he hit number one. After enduring months of her begging, he wrote her a wry letter declaring, in no uncertain terms, that he wouldn't grant an interview to *Sonica* if his life depended on it.

Tab lurched toward me and began playing with the fringe on the scarf I had around my neck. "Who are you, the president of the Doug Blackman fan club?"

Tab's chin had a deep cleft, reminding me of a butt, and I had to make an effort not to laugh at it.

"Trust me," I said, yanking the scarf out of his hand and then looking at Loring, thinking he might back me up while I sparred with his friend. But as soon as our eyes met, Loring glanced down at the untouched tomato, basil, and mozzarella salad on his plate, and I categorized him as shy to the point of being backward.

"You gotta give me better proof than that," Tab said.

Vera picked up a cube of cheese, plopped it in her mouth, and said, "Hmm. Coke? Pepsi? Oh, sorry, *Tab*—I happen to know that my friend here was listening to that record the first time she had sex. Trust me, a girl's not going to forget a thing like that."

"*Vera.*"

Tab bit the side of his cheek, causing his butt-chin to shoot out even farther as he nodded with a newfound affection for his adversary. "You know," he told Vera, "if you ix-naed the glasses, you'd be hot. In a math teacher sorta way. And I think you've convinced me." He elbowed Loring. "She convince you, Lori?"

Loring was still staring at his tomato. "I didn't need convincing."

I was about to pee my pants. As gracefully as possible, I spit two watermelon seeds onto the lawn and started dragging Vera away.

"Mother-of-Pearl," Vera said as we entered the house. "What a face on that guy. Whew. Can you say *hottie*?"

After I peed, it took me five minutes to find Paul in the crowd. When I spotted him he was making his way to the gazebo, shouting: "Samuel goddamn Langhorne!"

He was addressing Loring, who looked up and squinted, visibly trying to place the face in front of him.

"Hudson?" Loring finally said, wiping off his hand and extending it out to Paul. "I'll be damned."

The two men greeted each other like long lost war buddies. Paul congratulated Loring on his recent success and Loring dismissed the applause, seemingly more interested in what was happening with Paul's career.

"*You're* Bananafish?" Loring said. "No kidding, there's a serious buzz about you guys. The next Drones, right?"

Paul rolled his eyes and invited Loring to stop by Rings of Saturn on Saturday to judge for himself. "We're kicking off a two-week club tour around the East Coast. It's our last New York show until the record's released."

I stepped up beside Paul and he said, "Ah. Here's my betrothed."

With a weak smile, Loring looked up and said, "Hi again."

"You two met already?" Paul said.

"Not officially." Loring extended his hand and introduced himself to me in a way that was humble and self-effacing.

"Eliza Caelum," I said, straightening the bra strap that kept falling out from under my T-shirt. "FYI, you might want to put a leash on your friend. He tried to follow my sister-in-law into the bathroom."

"Tab's not my friend, he's my drummer," Loring teased. Then his eyes spun. "Wait a second. *What* did you say your name was?"

Shit, I thought. He couldn't possibly know.

"You work for *Sonica*, don't you?"

I shook my head and Loring nodded, laughing. "Yes, you do. I know who you are. You're the girl who stalked my dad in Cleveland."

"Busted," Paul quipped.

With his thumb, Loring pointed toward the food tent. "Why didn't you say anything over there?"

"I know you're not a big *Sonica* fan."

"Forget *Sonica*," Loring said. "My dad told me so much about you, I feel like I know you."

I found that virtually impossible to believe. "Can I just say, for the record, I didn't *stalk* him. I—"

But then Mrs. Winkle came rushing over to tell Loring that her sixteen-year-old daughter wanted to have her picture taken with him. As the woman dragged the hapless rock star away, Paul yelled, "See ya 'round, Sam!"

"Same time, next year, this could be you," Loring said, waving as if he were going off to war.

part two

Everything
Is a Complete
Disappointment

Loring was in trouble and he knew it. He heard the warning bells and a voice in his head telling him that if he were smart, he would walk back out the door and disappear into the crowd on Houston Street.

The voice said *flee*.

It said *fool*.

Unfortunately, Tab's voice was louder: "There she is. At the bar."

Loring saw no point in denying the reason he'd come to Rings of Saturn. For the last hour—hell, for the last four days—he'd been telling himself it was to see the band. But when he saw the girl slouching over the bar, her chin in her palm, with a tropical flower tucked haphazardly behind her ear, he knew it had nothing to do with the band.

She hadn't spotted him yet. The bartender, who looked like a one-eyed Hell's Angel, had her undivided attention, and was in the middle of an exhaustive explanation on the science of how one could ascertain the distance of a storm in miles simply by counting the number of seconds between thunder and lightning.

"Some people think the lightning can happen without the thunder," the bartender said. "Not possible. Just because you can't hear it, doesn't mean it's not rumbling out there somewhere."

Loring didn't want to interrupt what looked like a

profound, if not one-sided conversation on the wonders of meteorological phenomena. But if he'd been hoping to remain unobtrusive, bringing Tab along had been the wrong move.

"Don't just stand there, you shithead. Stop gawking and say hello."

"I'm not gawking."

"You're a rock star, for fuck's sake. At least get her phone number."

"Tab, she's engaged."

That's when she looked over and waved.

"Eliza Caelum," Loring muttered, as if he'd happened upon her by chance.

After asking the bartender to excuse her, she rotated her barstool in Loring's direction and said, "Paul didn't think you were going to show up," at which point Loring decided he was obligated to stay. For Paul.

Tab took Eliza's hand, kissed the top of it, and then said he was going upstairs to get a table.

Without Tab acting as wingman, Loring couldn't think of anything to say except, "Can I get you another drink?"

"Sure," she said. "Martini. Hold everything but the water and the olives."

He must've looked confounded because a second later she said, "Tell John the Baptist it's for me. He'll know."

"Who?"

She shot him a smile that could have charmed a wall. "The bartender."

"Two martinis," Loring told the bartender, whose name, apparently, was John the Baptist. "The way she likes them."

As soon as the band began clanging around the stage, Eliza touched Loring's arm and said, "Come on, you can't miss the first song."

Following her up the stairs, Loring was more than a little disconcerted by the thoughts in his head, yet still unable to take his eyes off the way she moved. Like gossamer lace in the wind, he thought. The girl doesn't walk, she breezes.

Eliza walked to a corner table where Tab was already sitting beside a girl Loring remembered from the picnic.

"I found the math teacher," Tab said. "Vera. She's married to Eliza's brother." Tab looked at Vera. "Did I get that right?"

"Well done, Pepsi." Vera turned to Eliza and said, "Wow. You went for a glass of water and came back with *him*. How did *that* happen?"

Loring sat to Eliza's right and took surreptitious glances at her while she watched Paul approach the stage. She looked like someone under hypnosis and he told himself, for the tenth time, he shouldn't have come.

The first song was an intense listening experience, like riding the world's highest roller coaster. The second song was even better—a slower, evocative tune that communicated so perfectly what Loring was feeling in that moment, it caused him physical pain, particularly when he conceded that his feelings were for the girl about whom the song was surely written.

Loring recalled Paul as a gifted singer and songwriter, but he and Paul had been young and inexperienced back in the Emperor's Lounge days. And those shows were always acoustic. Loring had only seen the "unplugged" version of Paul. With electricity, a little maturity, and a driving rhythm section behind him, the guy belonged to a realm of manifest talent that was visionary and yet completely accessible.

It's that "it" people always talk about. Whatever "it" is, Paul Hudson had it in spades.

During the encore break, Tab leaned over and said, "Hey, Lori, I think you have some admirers."

To his right, Loring saw three girls staring at him. He bowed his head and focused on the table, wondering if it was made of pine or maple. Soon thereafter he felt a tap on the shoulder.

Girl number one requested an autograph, which he gave her. Girl number two suggested he might like to buy her a drink, which he declined. Girl number three, who seemed higher than the moon and couldn't have been a day over seventeen, put her hand in his pocket and tried to grab his dick.

He felt like a deer in headlights, probably looked like one too, judging from the way Eliza stood up and said, "Let's get you out of here," just as Bananafish commenced their last song.

Backstage, there was an elfin girl on the floor painting her toenails. Eliza called her Queenie, and Loring shook her hand.

"Wow. You *are* a hottie," Queenie said.

Ordinarily, a comment like that would have sent Loring running for the nearest exit, but Queenie had an irreverent, ironic tone that told him she was not only innocuous, she might very well be mocking him. What's more, Queenie's statement implied that she'd been *told* he was, to use her word, a hottie. Loring hoped but doubted it had been Eliza who had given Queenie the report.

Loring sat on the edge of the couch and tuned in to Paul's voice as it bled through the walls. "Damn, he's good, isn't he?"

Eliza nodded in a way that would indicate, even to the most insensitive person, how much she adored the guy. She plopped down sideways beside Loring, her knee touching his leg, and said, "You knew him before I did. Give me some dirt."

Laughing, Loring said, "I'll tell you a story that sticks in my mind. Right before I got married, Paul was the one who warned me—and I quote—marriage is an institution best suited for morons and eunuchs. You've obviously been a positive influence."

"Oh, I can't wait to throw that one back at him."

"Throw what back at me?" Paul had just sauntered in and wrapped a sweaty towel around Eliza's neck.

"A plus B equals C," she said, her hand reaching behind her, looking to touch any place on Paul's body that she could find. "If marriage is for morons and eunuchs, and I know you're not a eunuch, ergo you must be a moron."

"Hold it." Paul sat down on the arm of the couch. "The waitresses at Emperor's Lounge *paid* me to say that. They all had crushes on Sam here, and there was a hundred bucks in it for me if I put a stop to his goddamn wedding."

The room began to fill, and Paul was summoned by one of the record company reps to brownnose a local concert promoter. He thanked Loring for showing up and suggested they all get together for dinner sometime.

"Yeah, let's do that," Loring said.

Toying with Eliza's necklace, Paul murmured, "In two minutes, come over and pretend you need me for some kind of emergency."

After Paul walked away, Eliza leaned in and said, "Did your dad *really* use the word *stalk*?"

Loring decided it was this way Eliza had of looking and listening that made her so attractive. The girl really knew how to focus her attention on the person with whom she was engaged in conversation. It was no wonder his dad had spilled his guts to her.

"Well, *did* he?"

"Yes," Loring teased. "But he meant it in a good way. He was very impressed with you."

Now she was glowing. She was one of *them*. One of those Doug Blackman worshippers.

"You know, I was there that night, in Cleveland," Loring said. "I'd done a show in St. Louis a few hours earlier, and I had the next two days off so I flew in to spend the weekend with my dad. He'd left me a message telling me to stop by his room. He wanted me to meet you."

"Why didn't you?"

Loring had been asking himself the same question all week. "It was late. I was tired, I guess. I went to bed."

"Wow. So we missed crossing paths by *that* much." She held her thumb and index finger a centimeter apart. Sadly, she didn't seem to find the brush with destiny as catastrophic as he did.

"I think it's been two minutes," Loring said.

Eliza told Loring to have a drink, that she and Paul would be right back. But after trying unsuccessfully to locate Tab, and after watching the way Eliza and Paul fooled around in the corner, Loring put his hat on, snuck out the back door, and decided it would be in his best interest if he and Eliza Caelum did not cross paths again.

Monday morning, Terry North called me into his office. He had a headset on like an operator, and he waved his hands when he saw me.

"Mags!" he said. "Sit. *Sit!*"

Lucy was standing behind Terry, a little off to the side. Her arms were crossed, and her lips were bent into a bitter pucker that made her look like she was holding a tablespoon of vinegar in her mouth.

If Terry hadn't looked so excited I would have assumed I was in trouble.

"Do you want to tell her or should I?" Terry asked Lucy.

"First Daddy and now Junior," Lucy said, barely moving her lips. "You must give one hell of a blow job."

I had no idea what was going on, but I'd had it with Lucy treating me like a whore. I glared at her and then shifted to Terry. "What is she talking about?"

"The guy's been blowing us off for a whole year," Terry said. "He even took the time to write a letter to get us off his back. Then all of a sudden his manager calls up and says he'll let us do the story, but on one condition—Eliza Caelum has to write it."

"*What?*" I said.

"Cheers, Mags." Terry handed me a note with a date, time, and address on it. "You just scored your first cover piece. And you're getting a raise."

September 18, 2001

Last Tuesday, I woke up with the most intense goddamn hard-on. The clock went off early and I'd been in the middle of a dream where I was back at the Gap thanklessly folding mass-produced American classics dyed the color of dead tree trunks. I would set out a pair of pants and a customer would come in and mess them up, and I'd straighten them and another customer would come in and mess them again. After about ten messy customers, Eliza walked in and coaxed me into a dressing room.

Just as the dream was getting good, the clock radio began blaring the sax intro to "Baker Street" at a volume designed to get my betrothed out of bed for her morning run.

I rolled over, pressed my dick into her leg and begged her to pretend it was Monday. She doesn't run on Mondays. On Mondays she stays in bed and tends to my needs.

She kissed me on the shoulder and whispered, "It's Tuesday," using a voice that was way too seductive for someone about to get out of bed. But then she said, "Hold that thought. The minute I get home I promise it'll be Monday."

I went back to sleep. Less than an hour later the front door slammed open and I heard Eliza screaming my name all frantic, with the one syllable lasting for too many seconds. The clock radio had been off for a while but Gerry Rafferty was still in my head: "Another year and then you'd be happy. Just one more year and then you'll be happy…"

I was already sitting up when Eliza collapsed into the room. Her eyes were wet and her chest was going in and out like mad. I immediately felt her head, her face, her arms. Even though I was still in that purgatory between sleep and wakefulness, she seemed to be all in one piece, but her shirt was blotchy with what looked like puke.

"What happened?" I said. "Are you sick?"

She tried to explain but she was talking too fast. Something about running down Broadway, about how she stopped and watched because she knew, even before it happened. I couldn't make sense out of it. And you know what's kind of twisted? I remember thinking how beautiful she looked. Her eyelashes were all shiny from her tears, each of them individually defined like they'd been combed.

I asked her to slow down, take a deep breath, and start at the beginning, and I managed to pick out a few key phrases. Things like "too low" and "too fast," but her voice was doing that stuttering, hiccupy thing kids' voices do when they've been crying really hard and it was impossible to put everything together.

Finally she swallowed and said, "A plane."

She swore she'd seen a plane crash.

Sensing my doubt, she squeezed my shoulders and shook me, rambling about how she really and truly saw it, and how she thought to herself: That plane looks like it's going to crash. "And then it did!" she screamed. "It did!"

I still wasn't taking her seriously. Whenever she sees a plane above her she stops and stares at it, and she *always* thinks it's is about to drop out of the sky and onto her head.

"I saw it," she said for the zillionth time. I'd never seen anyone so terrified in my whole goddamn life. She told me I didn't understand, that it "hit one of those big buildings." She said she thought it was a 757 but couldn't tell for sure because it was going too fast, and it crashed straight-on like it was aiming.

She was starting to freak me out. She seemed so in shock I wondered if I was going to have to take her to a doctor or something. But before I could get any more information from her, she bolted from the room.

I threw on some pants and ran after her. By that time she was already on the floor, inches from the TV. Not a good idea. About a year ago, when a DC-10 went down off the coast of California, she'd watched the coverage of the accident for hours and didn't sleep for days. There was no way I was going to allow a replay of that.

I was about to turn the TV off when I looked at the screen. I guess it goes without saying I wasn't prepared for what I saw. I knelt down next to her and tried to process what even at the time I knew was some pretty bad shit going down.

That's when I noticed the sirens. The city was screaming outside our window, and you wanna know my first thought? I needed a cigarette. How pitiful is that? Manhattan was under attack and all I could think about was nicotine—I'd smoked my last one the night before, figured I'd buy some in the morning, and was screwed.

I remember blinking to make sure I was seeing things right. And I remember pulling Eliza's head down and covering her eyes right before a second plane smashed like a rocket-shaped wrecking ball into the tower next to the one already on fire.

Inside our little room, with the window open and the TV on, we thought we heard screams in stereo. We felt it. Then we watched the nightmare unfold. We saw fire, smoke. We saw people falling out of sky-high windows. And some of them fell like they were already dead. But some of them flapped their arms, you could tell they wanted to live, and there was a weird reverence in Eliza's voice when she said, "They're trying to fly, Paul."

I was crying by then. My tears were dripping into Eliza's hair. Her head was soaked.

At some point during all this drama she screamed her

brother's name, dove on top of the phone, dialed Michael and Vera in Brooklyn, and then freaked out because no one answered right away. When Michael finally picked up, Eliza yelled something like how could he sleep at a time like this. But once she confirmed that Michael and Vera were nowhere near lower Manhattan, she threw the phone in my lap.

"What the hell is wrong with her?" Michael said.

I told him to put on his television. Michael made me promise not to leave Eliza alone, not even for a second, and I swore she wouldn't piss without my hand in hers.

After the second tower collapsed, Eliza and I could taste the dust and smoke in our apartment. Even after we shut the windows, the place was asphyxiating. And the whole building was silent. Like either everyone had fled or they'd been scared into seclusion too.

We didn't leave the apartment for three days. We sat in front of the TV, ate in front of the TV, slept in front of the TV, made love with a be-all, end-all frenzy in front of the TV, we cried in front of the TV, and we wondered, in front of the goddamn TV, if the world was about to end.

It was the longest I'd gone without a cigarette in eight years. By the second day I had the shakes and a headache that wouldn't go away no matter how many Advil I popped, but Eliza was still too terrified to go out, and I couldn't leave her like that.

We spent a lot of time pondering the meanings of all the things we hold sacred. The record, the single, all my self-righteous integrity. It suddenly feels so stupid to me.

Only time will tell, I guess.

One thing's for sure: the events of last week did not bode well for Eliza as a future airline passenger of the world.

This is Paul saying goodbye. And God bless.

Over.

The streets were practically deserted when I left for Loring Blackman's apartment. A few merchants were hosing down their storefront sidewalks, a couple dour-faced people were walking dogs, but there wasn't a soul on the subway car that took me uptown.

The city was always quiet on Sunday morning, and normally this had a calming effect, but I didn't feel safe outside yet. I didn't feel safe anywhere except in the apartment with Paul. The hush of the city was still too dark, the air still smelled like a funeral pyre, and every sound made me jump.

For the last two weeks I had gone to work, hurried home, and made few additional excursions beyond Ludlow Street. Going any farther downtown was out of the question, as Ground Zero was maybe two miles southwest of where we lived.

It was supposed to be a big deal. A cover story. I'd been waiting over a year for an assignment that would promote me to feature-writer status and potentially garner me some respect with Lucy. But there I was, on my way to the interview, and it didn't seem to matter. Regardless of how badly I wanted it to matter.

The inimitable characteristics of New York City—the skyscrapers, the subways, the people, the barrage of art and culture—had all been turned into memento mori. Excitement had been replaced with fear, certainty replaced with doubt. Hopes and dreams replaced with a basic instinct to survive.

I studied the few faces I passed near the park. They were sallow and afraid. They were the faces of orphans. There were orphans all over the city, just like Paul and I were orphans.

Loring lived on 77th between Central Park West and Columbus Avenue, on the top floor of a charming prewar building across from the Museum of Natural History. The bald, droopy-eyed doorman knew who I was as soon as I walked in. He greeted me by name and escorted me to the elevator, where the press of a button and the turn of a key took us directly into Loring's living room, the backdrop of which was two walls of windows affording views of the museum and the park.

"Mr. Blackman will be back in a few minutes," the doorman, a spitting image of Uncle Fester from *The Addams Family*, told me. "He says make yourself at home."

The first thing I noticed was the central air-conditioning. After walking in the warm sun, Loring's apartment felt like December in Cleveland.

Uncle Fester left, and I wandered around the apartment. Despite being furnished in shades of blue and gray, the place was luminescent with natural light. And it had a comfortable, lived-in feel, due in part to the occasional presence of kids—Loring had twin sons, evidence of which was scattered around in the form of toys and the cutest little pair of Doc Martens.

Making my way into the master bedroom, I was sure Loring had a housekeeper. His bed had been made in that plush, perfectly neat, five-star-hotel style that looks inviting and untouchable at the same time.

I played detective in Loring's bathroom: gray slate floor, ecru marble sink, beige towels, and a three-headed shower. The only drugs I could find were Ibuprofen and children's chewable vitamins. Loring wore alluring cologne that smelled green and peppery, used waxed dental floss, a Gillette razor, cheap drugstore shampoo, and had Mark Twain's *Roughing It* next to the toilet.

The room across the hall from Loring's was a sparsely furnished guestroom that also served as a storage space for platinum records, instruments, and other various music-related paraphernalia. The other bedroom had a set of bunk beds, two small desks, two high-end desktop computers, and a glow-in-the-dark solar system on the ceiling.

A large sectional sofa took up most of the main room, and on the floor in the middle of the couch there was a disassembled tent, pillows, and a box of Legos.

When Loring showed up he was dressed like he'd been running, and he greeted me by apologizing for half a dozen things all in one breath—being late, not having any food ready, making me work on Sunday, the mess on the floor. He seemed uneasy, as if he'd walked into my apartment, not his own, and in so doing he'd made me nervous.

I only seemed to make things worse by hugging him, which I considered common courtesy since we knew each other, and because 9/11 inspired a we're-all-in-this-together mentality. But Loring returned the gesture awkwardly, and I hoped his reserve wasn't going to carry over into the interview, otherwise it was going to be a long day.

"The boys slept here last night," he said, nodding toward the middle of the couch. "They wanted to go camping. We compromised." He had a bag of bagels and muffins under his arm. "Does this seem stupid to you? An interview, I mean. In lieu of what's going on in the world."

"I was thinking the same thing on the way here. But Rudy wants us to try and get back to normal, right? So, let's do it for the mayor."

I forced a smiled and he smiled back. It was as if we'd made a pact.

"For the mayor," Loring said.

I followed him into the galley-like kitchen, where everything was made of stainless steel. Opposite the refrigerator, there was a small breakfast bar with four stools that backed up into the living room. Loring filled a teakettle with water and explained his reasons for being late—he'd taken his sons for pancakes, gone for "a quick run," which turned out to be eight miles, and then stopped for groceries. "I'm sure you have better things to do than wait around for me all morning, but do you mind if I take a shower?"

I wondered if he would use all three shower heads.

Before Loring sped away, I asked him if I could borrow a sweater.

"Are you cold?" he said.

"I'm about three degrees away from being cryogenically frozen."

Laughing, he fiddled with the thermostat in the hallway and then disappeared. While he was squandering the city's water supply, I took a plate from one of the cupboards, arranged the bagels and muffins, and finished making the tea.

Loring reappeared in less than five minutes, bringing the scent of his cologne with him, which smelled even better on him than it did in the bottle—like sex on freshly cut grass after a summer rain. He handed me a gray cashmere pullover and I slipped it on. The sleeves hung inches below my fingertips.

Loring, barefoot, wore a chocolate-colored T-shirt and navy blue pinstriped slacks. His skin was still dewy from his run, and just tan enough to highlight his soft brown eyes.

The guy was stunning. Really. I didn't think there was any harm in admitting this, at least to myself, and most likely to Vera later on. His face was so perfect I felt inadequate, as if I needed to be cool and beautiful to be in the room with him.

"Are these your kids?" I asked, referring to the numerous photographs on the refrigerator.

"Yeah." Loring stepped behind me and pointed over my shoulder. "That's Sean, and that's Walker. They just turned five."

Undoubtedly identical twins, both boys had cute, mischievous smiles and floppy hair that touched their shoulders, much like Rex and Spike, the sons I imagined Paul and I would have some day.

"Your wife?" I asked, alluding to the woman in one of the photos.

"Ex-wife," he said.

The woman's face was vibrant and approachable. "She's pretty."

Loring nodded with no semblance of malice or regret and explained that his ex-wife, Justine, lived three floors down. She and Loring had lived there together, and when they divorced he bought the penthouse so he could stay close to the kids.

"Doesn't that get weird? What if you bring a girl home and you're in the elevator, then it stops on her floor and there's the ex?"

He chuckled. "Unfortunately, I haven't had to worry about that lately, but Justine and I are good friends. We get along really well."

Loring picked up the tray I'd prepared and headed to the living room. I followed close behind, to ride the wave of his cologne.

"Right," I said. "If you get along so well, why did you get divorced?"

He set the tray down on the coffee table and tried to kick the collapsed tent out of the way. "Can't you beat around the bush before you hit me with the personal stuff?"

"Sorry. I'd rather not pry into your personal life, believe me. But considering every song on *Rusted* seems to address the topic of crumbling love, it's a pretty unavoidable topic.

In other words, you either resign yourself to talking about it, or send me home without a story. And please don't do that because my boss lives to see me fail."

"Lucy Enfield?" Loring's tone was subtle but managed to convey his negative feelings toward the woman.

I nodded. "The day I got this assignment she was so mad she sent me to Office Depot to buy her a stapler, just to remind me who was in charge."

"In that case, I'll talk."

I moved from the couch to the floor, impelled by a nostalgic yearning to be closer to the Legos. Loring followed me to the carpet, attached two blue plastic squares together, and then continued adding pieces while I prodded him about his marriage.

His responses were reticent at first, but eventually he got sidetracked by his project and started rambling about college. I couldn't remember where he'd gone and when I asked him, he muttered "Yale" as if it were the local vocational school.

"What did you study?"

"Art history," he said, digging through the Lego box. "Well, specifically, it was humanism in renaissance art and architecture, but don't you dare print that."

"Is that where you met your wife?"

"Ex-wife," he said again. "And no. I spent my junior year studying in Florence. I met her at the Uffizi. We fell in love staring at Botticelli paintings."

"Is she Italian?"

"Uptowner," he said, pointing in a direction that must have been north. "She actually grew up eight blocks from here. She was supposed to be backpacking around Europe and ended up staying with me the whole time." He fixed two yellow Legos together to form what looked like an arm. "I know the media wrote a lot of crap after we split. They said Justine was seeing someone else and then I was seeing someone else. None of it was true. There were no third parties involved. Nor did I say I hated being married like the *Daily News* alleged." Loring's intonation conveyed how important it was to him that I understand this. "Hell, I want to be in love just as much as the next guy."

I checked to make sure my tape recorder was running. "I can't believe you just said that."

He didn't raise his head, just his eyes.

"No joke, Lucy gets orgasmic over statements like that. She might even be nice to me for a day. And I'm warning you now, she'll probably put it on the cover."

"Can I take it back?"

"Not a chance." I laughed. "So, where did it go wrong? Your marriage, I mean."

I was trying to construct a multilayered Lego building in which every floor was a different color. The level currently under construction was red. As Loring responded to my question, he passed me half a dozen red rectangles. His hands were distracting. They were lean and strong and perfectly symmetrical to the rest of him.

"Nothing ever really went wrong per se. There was just stuff that was never going to work. Stuff we never discussed until it was too late."

"What kind of stuff?" I pressed, and when he looked flustered, I said, "May I remind you this was your idea?"

He yielded with a smirk. "The life of a musician, mainly. Justine had no idea what she was in for, like breast-feeding in the back of a tour bus. She wanted a nine-to-five husband whose travel schedule consisted of a Christmas timeshare in Vail." Loring was searching for a specific Lego. "Eventually she just started staying home, and we grew apart—Justine learned how to say that in therapy—*we grew apart*. The thing is, we loved each other, and on some level we always will, but when you're twenty-three and you fall in love, you tend to think that love will supercede any problems. That's what *Rusted* is about. Realizing that no matter how much you love somebody, no matter how desperately you want a relationship to work, life can act as an oxidizer and corrode it to pieces."

I was saddened by Loring's sentiments, mainly because what happened to him and his wife was exactly what I was afraid was going to happen to me and Paul.

"Can I ask you something? Why did you agree to do this interview?"

He put his Lego creation on hold to slice a bagel and smear it with a thick layer of cream cheese. "My manager had been bugging me to do it forever. Then I met you and, I don't know, I figured you could be trusted. Doug was the one who actually suggested it. He said you were worth talking to. Even if you are a stalker."

"Don't start that again," I said, laughing. "Or I'll write that you were rude and difficult, and you waste water with your three-headed shower."

He cleared his throat and a smile completely devoid of offense appeared on his face. "Someone's been snooping."

"Uncle Fester told me to make myself at home. Do you always refer to your father by his first name?" I said quickly.

"When I'm talking to a reporter I do."

"Ugh. Don't think of me as a reporter. Think of me as an old friend."

Loring nodded, and I launched into a tirade of questions about his childhood. He told me many things I already knew, like how he'd grown up in a townhouse on West Twelfth Street, but that his family also had a farm in Vermont, in the same town where his mother, Lily, was born. She raised horses there. And Loring had a younger brother, Leith, a film editor who lived in TriBeCa.

"When I met your dad he told me you were the last person

in the world he thought would end up in this business," I said, carefully tearing off the top of an elephantine blueberry muffin. "He thinks you're too smart to be a rock star."

My nerves were gone by now. I felt comfortable talking to Loring. Despite his background and his success, I found him to be disarming, bright, and not the least bit jaded. He was also the only musician I'd ever met who wasn't completely self-absorbed. Hell, even Paul was completely self-absorbed, in his own heartfelt way.

Loring scratched his temple and said, "Can we not talk about me for like, five minutes? I'm boring myself. Besides, it's hardly fair that you know everything about me and I don't know anything about you."

"There's nothing to know."

"I don't believe that," Loring said.

I saw him glance down at my wrist, and that's when I knew that Doug had already told him my whole life story. I flipped my wrist for Loring's inspection. "Paul wants to get a tattoo just like it. Instead of wedding rings, we'll have matching scars."

"How romantic," Loring said, but he sounded facetious. And he sounded like he was trying to change the subject. "When are you getting married, anyway?"

"Soon. But Paul's got a lot on his plate right now."

Loring took a bite of his bagel. There was a warm, sad smile on his face, one that I chalked up to disappointment over his own failed relationship.

I mined around the body of my muffin, trying to locate a blueberry, my thoughts now on Paul. He'd been gone for almost a week, riding around with the Michaels, playing shows on college campuses along the East Coast. I imagined him, that very minute, curled up on the floor of the van in some deserted rest stop, hungover and hungry for a cigarette.

"Loring, can I ask you something? How do you handle

all the bullshit that comes along with what you do?"

"Are you asking as a reporter, or as the concerned friend of a potential rock star?"

"Concerned friend," I said. "Paul is so obsessed—with not selling out, with not compromising, with being unable to maintain his integrity. Every step forward is a battle for him." I shrugged. "I don't really know what I'm asking, I just worry."

"I remember one night at Emperor's Lounge, a girl came up to Paul raving about one of his songs. But she was wearing an Aerosmith T-shirt and he freaked out. He said Aerosmith was one of the biggest sellout bands in the world and he couldn't reconcile that someone could like his music *and* Aerosmith's."

"That's exactly what I mean. It took me a month to convince him to make a video. And even then, he only agreed to let them film a live performance of the song."

"Maybe it's just easier for me because I grew up around it, but I think Paul takes his job too seriously. We're not curing cancer. We're not negotiating peace in the Middle East, right? Hell, it's only rock 'n' roll."

I felt my jaw drop.

"Uh-oh," Loring said. "She's lost all respect for me."

"Are you *sure* you're related to Doug Blackman? Because I don't think he would *ever* raise his son to say something as stupid as *It's only rock 'n' roll.*"

Loring laughed. "You think I'm wrong?"

"What I think is that you can't trivialize art. 'The Day I Became a Ghost' changed my life. Do you understand how *big* that is? That a silly little song can alter the course of a person's destiny? My life would be remarkably different, remarkably less extraordinary, less *everything*, if it weren't for the mystical force that a second ago you pitifully reduced to *only* rock 'n' roll."

He was still laughing at me.

"Answer me something," I said, fired up. "Don't you think what you do has immense, ineffable value?"

"Maybe. But maybe not. All I'm saying is that making a video isn't the end of the world. And the truth is I want my songs played on the radio, I want my videos on TV, I want to sell records. And I don't think there's anything wrong with that."

"Paul wants that, too. Just not at the expense of his self-respect."

"He's a lot like my dad that way. Fortunately, Doug's got his own history to back him up. Paul doesn't have the same luxury. Not yet, anyway. I'm sure I don't have to tell you this, but I think Paul could be huge if he would just give in a little."

"Giving in is against his religion."

We were both quiet while Loring finished his bagel and I scanned my notes. "Question," I said, getting back to the interview. "Have you ever had a real job?"

"As opposed to my fake one?"

I chuckled. "Sorry. I just mean, did you ever have to really struggle?"

"I never had to struggle financially, if that's what you're asking. But I did have to clean the horse barn when I was a kid." His answer came out sheepish and I wondered why he sometimes seemed embarrassed by who he was.

"Can I ask you something?" I said.

"Why do you keep asking me that?"

"It's my way of warning you that my next question could be construed as invasive."

"You already searched my house. How much more invasive can you get?"

"Why are you so self-conscious about who you are?"

There was a long pause. "I guess one of the reasons is

because I've taken a lot of flack for my last name—case in point being the record review in the magazine you work for. Don't get me wrong, I'm proud of my dad. But I never feel like people see me as separate from him. His name is always mentioned when my career is being discussed, yet notice how he has complete autonomy from my shadow. The irony is I don't think I'm a musician because of Doug Blackman."

He held up his finished product for inspection. It was a robot and it looked like it came straight from a toy store.

"You've obviously had a lot of practice," I said, comparing it to my structure, which was nothing but a rainbow-colored box. "So, if not for Doug, then why?"

"October, 1982. The Clash and the Who at Shea Stadium. Imagine the impact on a nine-year-old."

"*See*? You just proved my point! *That's* the power of music!"

He acquiesced with a shy smile that called to mind Vera's word *hottie*.

"Don't you think your dad's proud of you?"

"Off the record?" Loring said. "I think he's completely disappointed in my chosen career. He used to give me that old 'you're too smart to be a musician' line, but sometimes I think what he really meant was 'you don't have it in you.'"

"Have what in you?"

"That *thing*. Like he has, and Paul has. That overwhelming life-or-death *need* to make music."

"He sure went on about you when I met him."

Loring looked surprised by that. "Here's a perfect example of what I mean—I was on the track team in high school. Junior year I could run a mile faster than anyone in the district and my dad bragged about that like it was the greatest accomplishment in the world. But he's never once patted me on the back and said, 'Congratulations on those number one records, kid.'"

"How fast?"

"What?"

"How fast could you run a mile?"

"I don't know."

"Yes you do. Tell me."

"I think my best time was four minutes eleven."

"*Four eleven?* Are you kidding? I run six days a week and can't break nine minutes. What about now? If you're sprinting?"

"I could probably manage a four fifty-five, but it would kick my ass."

"So what's next on your schedule? Writing? Recording? The Olympics?"

"I have two weeks of shows in January—makeup dates we cancelled after September 11. I might record a song for a movie soundtrack next year. Other than that, I plan on taking a lot of time off. I'm going to hang out with my kids and try to cultivate some kind of personal life."

I began putting the used dishes and napkins back onto the tray and Loring said, "Are we done?" He almost sounded disappointed.

I took off the sweater, folded it like Paul had taught me, and set it on the couch. "Is there anything else you want to say? Any censorship you wish to impart?"

He thought it over. "Actually, I've never understood why what I'm wearing or what I look like is relevant. It would be really cool if someone wrote an article that didn't include that stuff. Oh, and the three-headed shower—that was here when I moved in."

The cover of the January issue of *Sonica*, which hit news-stands in early December, featured a photograph of Loring Blackman posed on top of a bed, his back against the head-board, a blond-and-black Telecaster in his lap, and a dash-ing, well-lit look of self-consciousness on his face. To his right, the headline read: *Rock's Most Eligible Bachelor: "I want to be in love just as much as the next guy."*

The article itself was a miscellany of quotes taken out of context that painted Loring as an achingly handsome, surly, broken-hearted whiner with an Oedipus complex.

In my original draft, the article made no mention of Loring's clothing, his empirically good looks, or his famous father. Immediately noting that Doug had been overlooked as a topic, Lucy called me into her office and said, "What is this kiss-ass crap?"

I wanted to blink myself invisible. Better yet, I wanted to blink Lucy into oblivion.

"I beg your pardon?" I said.

"You expect me to believe you didn't talk about Doug during the interview?"

"We did, but—"

"Then *write* about it. His father is the king. You can't write about the prince without mentioning the king. If you were any kind of journalist you would know this. And peo-ple will want to know what the guy was wearing."

I couldn't get *no* out of my mouth, let alone *fuck off and die*. But I did manage to shake my head. "Writing about Doug would completely vitiate the dignity of the piece."

Lucy scoffed. "What do you think this is, the *Wall Street Journal*?"

I prayed to God, my dead parents, and the late Jim Morrison that I didn't start crying in front of Lucy—I would be back at square one if I let the bitch see me cry.

"Loring trusted me," I said. "And do you really think there's a person out there who'll pick up this magazine and not already know who his father is? For once, why not let the guy stand on his own? Considering the completely erroneous record review *Sonica* gave him last year, it's the least we could do."

"It's not our job to do these people favors, Eliza."

Lucy told me that if I didn't make the changes I would have to hand over my notes, and she would write the article herself. "I know he's cute, but is Loring Blackman worth losing your job over?"

I walked to my desk, collected my notes, and took them back to Lucy's office.

"Just keep my name off of it," I said.

Loring dialed the number three times before he pushed "send." And even though he was well-aware of whose number he was calling, it startled him when he heard Eliza's voice.

"Hi." He paused. "It's Loring."

Sonica had hit the newsstands days earlier, but judging from the silence on the other end of the line, Loring guessed one of two things: either Eliza had no idea when *Sonica* hit the newsstands, or through the static of his cell phone and the noise of the traffic behind him, she had no idea what he'd said.

"It's Loring," he repeated.

"I know who it is." Her voice was murky. "Why does it sound like you're in the middle of Times Square?"

Actually, he was standing outside a coffee shop on Columbus Avenue. He'd just walked the boys to school, stopped to get a scone and, he told her, someone had left the magazine on the counter.

"You read it?" she sighed.

"Yes."

"Are you calling to tell me how much you hate me?"

"No."

Loring quickly confessed that he'd run into Terry North at a party a few days back. He refrained from confessing that he'd only gone to the party because it was *Sonica*-sponsored and he thought she might be there.

At the party, Terry had told Loring all about the squabble Eliza and Lucy had over what Lucy mockingly described as "the fucking dignity of the piece." Terry said Eliza had almost lost her job, and that Lucy tried to rile Eliza even more by assigning her the task of digging up rock stars' high school yearbook photos for an upcoming fluff piece.

"I was going to call you," Eliza said. "I just didn't know what to say. Not that it's any consolation, but I actually enjoyed talking to you, and I was really proud of the first draft."

"I enjoyed talking to you, too."

Loring focused on a long crack in the sidewalk that was shaped like the Mississippi River on a map of the United States. He was standing off to the east, near Atlanta, trying to find a hidden message in Eliza's words.

"How about we just laugh it off?" he finally mumbled, watching a bug crawl towards St. Louis. "That's not even why I'm calling."

"Why are you calling?"

"My parents are coming over for dinner Saturday. I'm sure Paul would love to meet my dad, and I've been meaning to invite you guys over for a while…"

Paul was standing at the foot of his bed, staring blankly into his closet as if none of the clothes in it belonged to him, searching for the perfect outfit in which to meet Doug Blackman. He was trying to decide on a shirt to wear with his green suit and had already changed three times.

"Do I look all right?" he said, turning to face me in a red, long-sleeved shirt. "Or do I look like a *fan*? I don't want to look like a goddamn *fan*."

"You are a goddamn fan."

"I know, but I don't want to *look* like one."

"What do you want to look like?"

"A *peer*. I want Doug to see me as a fellow musician. A kindred soul. Not some freak who knows every word and every riff to every song he's ever recorded."

"If the shoe fits."

He pointed at his chest. "Yes or no?"

I liked Paul in red. It made his skin look like perfect alabaster and, in combination with his dark hair, made his eyes sparkle. But red worn in conjunction with the green suit gave me pause. "To be honest, you look a little like a Christmas tree. I'd opt for black or white under that silly suit."

"Silly?" He ran his hands down the jacket's lapels. "You think my suit is silly?"

"The color's a little silly," I said gently.

I could make fun of him until my eyes turned blue, but I

was just as excited to see Doug again as Paul was to meet him.

Paul kept the red shirt on, but dumped the suit in favor of black trousers and a black belt studded with silver grommets. He spent another five minutes trying to get his hair to stay out of his eyes enough to see clearly, but not so far that he looked like what he called "a goddamn cracker."

On the way uptown, Paul insisted we stop for flowers, but he was completely dissatisfied with the bouquets he found in the neighborhood markets.

"Weeds," he said, pointing at wilted daisies. "We can't bring the greatest songwriter in the world a bunch of weeds."

"Maybe you should get him a nice corsage."

"Funny. Ha-ha." He held a cluster of maroon and yellow orchids in my face. "What do you think of these?"

"They look like scabs."

After a detour into a gourmet market, Paul scrapped the flower idea, opting instead for a bottle of wine and an Oreo-cookie-crusted cheesecake.

As highly strung as he'd been throughout the day, as nervous as he'd been all the way uptown, and insomuch as he was possessed by a strong desire to make a good impression on his hero, when the elevator door opened into Loring's apartment and Paul found himself face-to-face with Doug Blackman, I watched him behave as if he'd just walked onto a stage and was the superlative star of an already-in-progress performance, remarkably transformed from a goddamn fan to a composed equal, respectful and gracious, yet acting as if he were unfazed by the legendary figure standing before him.

"Eliza Caelum," Doug said, pointing at me. "I had a sinking suspicion I was going to run into you again someday." He crushed me with the kind of bear hug that made me wish I still had a dad. Then he stepped back, visibly scrutinizing Paul. "You the fiancé?"

"Paul Hudson," Paul said, catching Doug's hand as if drawn to it by a powerful magnet. "It's an honor to meet you, sir."

I laughed out loud. I'd never heard Paul call anyone sir, and I basked in the glory of the moment. Paul's face was aglow and I celebrated the scene as one of those rare instances when you actually catch sight of happiness in motion. Happiness made everything soft and shiny like Vaseline on a camera lens.

I leaned in toward Doug and whispered, "Save the savior."

"Hear that?" Doug elbowed Paul. "She thinks you're the Second Coming."

"Yeah, well," Paul said, still beaming, "she also thinks Brooklyn is on the way to Jersey."

Behind Doug, Loring appeared with one of his sons thrown over his shoulder, the other one running in circles behind him. Loring was wearing jeans and the gray sweater I'd borrowed the last time I was there, but no shoes or socks. I thought it was sexy, the way he walked around his apartment barefoot.

Paul put his hand on the little boy's head and asked his name.

"This is Sean." Loring flipped the kid around to face the guests. "Sean, say hi to Paul and Eliza."

"I'm not Sean, I'm Walker," the boy said.

"No, you're not. You're Sean." Loring shook his head. "They just discovered they can fool people and they're relentless."

Loring herded us into the living room and introduced us to his mother, Lily, an attractive, elegantly dressed woman in her late fifties, busy in the kitchen getting dinner together. Paul offered to help but she said, "Mr. Chow already took care of the cooking. All I have to do is empty it into serving bowls."

Twin number two tried to get the room's attention by sounding the alarm on the large toy fire truck under his arm.

He told Paul his name was Sean.

"Walker," Loring said. "Quit it."

Paul crouched down to match the boy's eye level and egged him on. "Nice truck you've got there, Sean. My name's Eliza." He pointed at me. "That's my friend Paul."

Walker giggled, rolling his truck back and forth across the arm of the couch, leaving wheel marks in the velvety fabric. "Is her name *really* Paul?" the boy said. Then he tossed the toy aside as if it meant nothing to him. He was staring, riveted, at the studs on Paul's belt. "You wanna play Sega with me? I have *Sonic the Hedgehog*."

"Are you kidding? I love *Sonic the Hedgehog*," Paul said.

I was sure Paul had never played this game. He was going to be a good dad someday, and for an instant I wished he and I could trade lives with Loring. I wished Paul was my humble, Grammy-winning rock star husband with a legendary father, an apartment on Central Park West, and these two lovable, rambunctious boys who, in our alternative universe, would be called Rex and Spike.

"No Sega until after dinner," Loring said. "Walker, please go wash your hands."

Walker stomped away and Paul shifted his attention back to Doug, who wanted to give his account of the day he and I met. Not surprisingly, he skipped the part about asking me if I wanted to fuck.

"She cried," Doug said. "And then she refused to leave my room until I granted her an interview."

Paul laughed. "Funny, that's not how she tells it."

"That's a *huge* exaggeration," I said.

"Put it this way," Doug continued, "I didn't think I was going to get rid of her, so I figured I might as well talk to her." He leaned back and crossed his arms, examining me as if I were a painting on the wall. "How do you say no to those eyes, huh?"

"If you figure it out, let me know," Paul said.

"Papa," Sean yelled, yanking on Doug's sleeve, "show them how you make the cards fly."

Doug whipped a deck of cards from his pocket, much like he'd done with me in front of the elevator. The child watched intently.

"Pick one," Doug told the boy. "Show it to Paul and Eliza, and then put it back."

"I *know* how to do it," Sean said. He picked the jack of hearts, made sure Paul and I got a twenty-second-long glance at it, and then slid it into the middle of the deck with his little hands cupped around the edges so Doug couldn't see it. As Doug shuffled the cards, the boy bounced back and forth on the couch from one foot to the other.

"Here we go," Doug said. He spread the cards on the coffee table, snapped his fingers, and the jack of hearts leapt from the deck to the floor, where it landed face-up.

"Wow. You've progressed," I said.

Sean jumped and cheered and begged to see the trick again. But Paul's reaction was even more priceless—his jaw dropped and he said, "Jesus," as if Doug had just made it rain inside the apartment.

Lily announced it was time for dinner, and as we congregated around the table, Paul took the seat next to Doug, and he kept trying to steer the conversation toward music, but all Doug wanted to discuss was the Yankees who, back in October, had lost the World Series to the Arizona Diamondbacks.

"An *expansion* team, for Christ's sake." Doug thought the team's pitching had been inconsistent the entire first half of the season, but that by June things had finally come together. He wanted to know who Paul thought was a better hitter, O'Neill or Jeter.

"I have no idea who those men are," Paul said.

"One time I saw Jeter steal a base!" Walker exclaimed.

Paul admitted he wasn't much of a sports fan, he had never even seen a live baseball game, and Doug spent the next five minutes lecturing Paul about broadening his horizons. "There's more to life than your guitar, and you'll be a better songwriter, a better person, if you get a few extracurricular activities that have nothing to do with music."

"Eliza's my extracurricular activity," Paul said.

At this point, Paul looked so in love with Doug I thought he was liable to lean over and plant a big wet kiss on the man's cheek.

Eventually Doug got around to asking Paul about Bananafish. He wanted to know what the band's tour plans were, and he told Paul that the only way he'd make a respectable name for himself was to get his ass out on the road and play until his fingers were about to fall off.

"It's up in the air," Paul said, explaining the red tape he'd been dealing with. "The record was supposed to be released in October, then they pushed it back to January. There's been talk of opening for the Drones, but that's not until March."

"The Drones," Doug said, pointing into the air like Einstein. "The only reason to listen to the radio in the last five years."

"Thanks, Dad," Loring said, spooning a small serving of rice onto Sean's plate and sounding more amused than offended.

"Wait until you hear Bananafish," I told Doug.

One of the twins repeated the word Bananafish, the other twin chimed in, and for a full minute they tossed the word back and forth like they were playing tennis with it.

"Boys," Loring said. "Settle."

They did, for half a second. Then Walker tapped on Paul's arm and said, "Can you do this?" He let a string of milk-thickened spit run from his lips all the way past his chin before he quickly slurped it back into his mouth.

Loring pointed at his son. "I'm not going to tell you again."

"Can I have a sip of your milk?" Paul whispered to Walker.

After the boy nodded maniacally, Paul took a large gulp of the milk, swished it around in his mouth, and then tried Walker's trick, only the milk hadn't had time to thicken his trail of saliva and instead of being able to suck it back into his mouth, it dropped into his lap.

"It's okay," Walker said, sliding his glass back to Paul. "Just drink some more."

Feigning authority, Loring told Paul he couldn't have any dessert unless he behaved. Then he said, "Walker, eat, please."

Walker shoved a handful of a fried seaweed-like substance into his mouth, turned to Paul with strings of the green stuff spilling down the sides of his face and said, "You wanna see my room?"

"Sean, I would love to see your room," Paul responded, knowing full well he was speaking to Walker. Then the other twin said, "Hey, what's *my* name?"

Paul studied Sean. "You're Walker, right?"

"Walker Black Man," he said as if he were Native American. "I'm five."

Justine joined us for dessert. She was wholesomely pretty, like a model on a soap commercial, and she told Paul she remembered meeting him at Emperor's Lounge.

"Uh-oh," Paul said. "I never hit on you, did I?"

"No," Justine assured him. "Although I did hear a rumor you were involved in a plot to sabotage my wedding."

"Nothing personal. I only did it for the money."

Later on, Lily and Justine took the boys downstairs to give them their baths. As soon as they were gone Doug pulled a bag of marijuana from his breast pocket.

"Take it outside," Loring sighed.

Doug made a bid for company and Paul jumped on the invitation, while Loring and I went back to the table, took turns picking at the cheesecake, and watched the two grown men pass a joint back and forth on the terrace like a couple of teenage stoners.

"You don't smoke?" Loring asked.

"Only when set on fire."

After discussing the merits of any dessert containing Oreo cookies, I said, "Paul's life is complete now, just so you know." I turned my chair to face Loring. "Thanks so much for doing this. For everything. I still feel horrible about the article."

"Forget it." Loring put his fork down and pushed the dessert closer to me.

"This is my last bite," I said, digging into the underside of the crust so as to come away with an Oreo-covered forkful.

Loring kept pressing on his teaspoon as if trying to flatten it.

"Hey," I said. "Aren't you leaving town soon? Your make-up shows, I mean?"

His nod conveyed a less-than-tepid interest in the upcoming mini-tour. "I was just getting used to being off the road. The last thing I feel like doing right now is going back on tour. Plus, we're leaving right after New Year's and we just lost our opening act."

Apparently the drummer for Dogwalker, Loring's scheduled warm-up band, had broken his wrist in a snowboarding accident three days earlier. I contemplated Loring's predicament and came up with what I thought was the greatest idea of my life.

"Ever heard of this band called Bananafish? I'm pretty sure they're available."

It took Loring a few seconds to catch on. When he did,

he looked ready to make a comment—his mouth was open, the tip of his tongue was touching the roof of his mouth, but no sound came.

"Just *consider* it. *Please*," I said, getting more excited by the second. "I know it's asking a lot, but the record comes out the same week, and the Drones tour, if it even happens, isn't until March. You'd be doing them a *huge* favor, and—"

"Eliza." Loring scratched his temple and sat back in his chair. "Let's discuss this rationally. Even if I *did* say yes, and I'm *not*, but if I *did*, don't you think Paul would consider it below him to open for a mainstream success like me?"

He had a valid point. But, one step at a time. "I'll handle Paul. First things first."

Loring went silent, and I figured it was best to let him ruminate without interruption. I picked an Oreo from the cake, split it in half, and scraped out the filling with my teeth.

"What about you?" Loring said a few seconds later, as if speaking to his spoon. "Do you really want me to take Paul away for two weeks, or would you, you know, would you come along?"

I paused. "Are there any flying machines involved in this tour?"

"No. Buses."

Paul had wanted me to tag along on the last Bananafish outing, but traveling in a van with four men who only showered every couple days was not high on my list of glamorous vacations. On the other hand, I'd been dreaming for eons about what life on a real tour bus would be like.

"If I can get the time off work," I said, "I'd *love* to come along."

"Tell you what," Loring murmured, his eyes and fingers still preoccupied with the spoon. "You work on Paul, and I'll see what I can do on my end."

"Over my dead goddamn body," Paul said in the cab on the way home.

"Just *think* about it. Doug said it himself, going on the road is the best thing you could do right now."

"Watch it, Peepers. You're starting to sound like Feldman."

I tried to kick him but couldn't get a good angle. "Don't be gay. This is an *arena* tour. We're talking at least twelve-thousand people a night. You'd be crazy not to go."

"Eliza, half of Loring's audience is made up of sorority girls who have the hots for him. That's not the crowd I want to attract. Not that they'd appreciate me anyway. My fans are the lunatic fringe. The fallen souls and suicidal freaks."

"I beg your pardon," I said. "Besides, winning over the heathens and pagans should be your top priority. And I've never been to Toronto or Chicago."

Slowly, Paul pulled back, his glow-in-the-dark eyes spinning so fast I could practically see the synapses flashing like lightening in his brain. "All right," he said, the cocky-bastard grin in full force. "I've got a proposition for you."

I rested my hand firmly between his legs, certain he was on some carnal wavelength. "Name your price, sailor."

"I'll do the tour if you agree to two conditions." He shook his head. "I never in my life thought I'd say this, but get your hand out of my crotch. I need paper."

I quickly obliged his request, even handed him a pen. And he wrote out a contract stating that in signing my name, I would be agreeing to the unnamed conditions. In counter-signing, he would be agreeing to do the tour.

I scribbled my name and tried to guess the outlandish demands he might have in store for me. "Sex in the stairway? A ménage à trois?"

He made a funny gesture with his hand, a conductor

leading an orchestra, only his baton was a black Bic. "You just agreed to marry me."

I laughed. "Haven't I already agreed to do that?"

"I don't mean someday. I mean ASAP. As soon as we get back from the tour."

"Done," I said, thinking I was getting off easy.

"Hold on. There's more. We're going on a honeymoon after the wedding."

Again, painless. I was about to acquiesce when Paul narrowed his eyes and said, "And we're going to *fly* there."

I instantly felt nauseous. "Paul…"

"That's the deal. Take it or leave it."

I leaned my head back against the seat, forced a long breath down into my lungs, and left it there. In reality, the events of 9/11 had delivered a mortal blow to my already weak will, and I had sensed then that any chance I had of ever getting on a plane had vanished. I just hadn't yet shared this information with Paul.

"Yes or no?" Paul said.

Without exhaling, I nodded. But only because Paul was talking about the future, and it's easy to think of the future as being so far away, there's a good chance it will never arrive.

Paul was bleeding.

It happened the second night of the tour, during the show in Toronto, after he cut his pinkie on a broken guitar string. Neither the cut nor the missing D string interfered with his ability to finish the song, but when the blood began dripping down the front of his guitar, I imagined a holy weeping wound and wanted him so badly I had to sit down.

Standing off to the side, stage left, I backed up, parked myself on a crate, and squeezed my knees together. The louder the music got, the harder the crate vibrated. It was like having sex with Paul's spirit until his body could step in and finish the job.

He had his beloved ES-335 around his neck and was in the middle of "Charlie Bucket," one of my favorites, when it happened. The song was a complex tune with a tribal rhythm, and Paul sang it with understated longing right up until the end, when he would let loose and wail like someone had just plunged a stake through his heart.

There were two common reactions to this song: terror and captivation. In Toronto, the majority of the crowd looked captivated. And when they saw the blood, the first few rows cheered with a perverse satisfaction rivaled only by my own wanton response.

Paul had been right about Loring's audience. They were

mostly college kids, with an 80-20 female-to-male ratio. The night before, in Montreal, I'd found them to be less than enthusiastic. But one thing that impressed me about Loring's fans—they were kind. Despite appearing almost frightened by Paul's intensity, despite the glazed looks on their faces when he screamed, they clapped politely like people who didn't want to hurt the poor lunatic's feelings.

I did, however, notice a handful of people up front who were moved. They were easy to spot: eyes the size of balloons, stupefied smiles, heads bobbing in a trance.

They'd been converted.

Loring stepped up from the darkness behind me, temporarily disrupting my concentration. He had to cup his hands around his mouth and yell to be heard above the music. "Think he knows he's bleeding?"

I shrugged and yelled back. "Paul could catch on fire during this song and he wouldn't notice."

Then I started imagining Paul's finger in my mouth, imagined I could taste the sharp, metallic flavor of his blood on my tongue. I was also getting whiffs of Loring's cologne, and before the song was over I had to pretend to sneeze to disguise my uncontrollable shudders.

The date of the Toronto show coincided with the twenty-seventh birthday of Loring's rambunctious drummer, Tab. He decided there was going to be a party in his honor and he invited everyone to Loring's suite to celebrate. He put me in charge of ordering food, and Vera, who had flown in for the weekend before she had to go back to school, went to get a cake, hats, and balloons.

Loring's room was exponentially larger than the one Michael, Vera, Paul, and I were sharing. It had a king-size bed, a living room with a dining table that sat six, a couch, a bar, and a video game system hooked up to the TV.

While we were setting up, I told Vera what had happened during the show. "Mother-of-Pearl," she said. "You had sex with a guitar crate?"

The party commenced soon after the show ended. In addition to both bands, Tab had invited half a dozen young ladies he'd met backstage. Supposedly they'd hitchhiked up from Detroit to see the show and had no way of getting home. He promised them a ride back on the bus the next day.

One of the guests, Brandy, a towering, masculine girl with eggplant-colored hair and wearing so much make-up I could have carved my initials into her cheek, questioned Tab in a cutthroat voice about who Vera and I were.

"They're our merch girls," Tab said. "Among other things."

"What's a merch girl?" a ditzy blonde who introduced herself as "Star-with-two-Rs" asked.

Tab said, "Basically, they sell our T-shirts and other merchandise, and they suck our dicks whenever we tell them to."

Brandy's eyes widened; Vera, who'd already had three vodka tonics, quickly sat down and signaled me to play along. "It pays well," she said with a shrug. Her hair was in pigtails and she was wearing one of her long plaid skirts, making her look more like the band's tutor than their on-call "merch" girl.

Star-with-two-Rs looked like she was ready to apply for the job. "What's Loring like in bed?" she asked Vera, as if they were suddenly best friends.

"A tiger."

Loring and Paul were in the midst of a video baseball game across the room. Since meeting Doug, Paul had taken an avid interest in baseball. Burke and Michael were also in front of the TV waiting their turns, and they all appeared to be listening at least intermittently to our conversation because every so often I heard them chuckling.

Brandy had huge hands and a five o'clock shadow on her upper lip, and for a while I considered the possibility that she might be a transvestite, but according to Vera the girl didn't have enough cleavage. Brandy was also drunk, and she kept leaning in close to my ear when she talked. "So, you've pretty much slept with *all* of them?"

I could tell Brandy thought she was being quiet, but being quiet to a drunk, mannish groupie equaled loud to the whole room.

Tab said, "They'll tell you I'm the best, aren't I, love?"

"By far," Vera said, her pigtails moving to and fro, her eyes glassy. "The things you can do with that chin. *Whoa.*"

"What about *him*?" Star-with-two-Rs asked, salivating in Paul's direction. "He's kind of cute. Even with that nose."

I whispered, "Just between you and me, he's gay."

Brandy nodded at Starr. "See? I told you he looked a little femme."

Vera scribbled something on a napkin and slid it toward me. It said *She wouldn't know "femme" if it sat on her face.*

There was another girl sitting with us at the table, a pretty redhead whose name I didn't catch. She was reading a book and didn't get up when Brandy and Starr disappeared into the bedroom with Angelo and Loring's keyboard player, Juan.

"The Yankees win the title for the second time this hour!" Paul cheered, waving a hundred-dollar bill in the air. Then he said something about David Justice being named MVP as if he knew what being named MVP meant.

I lowered my chin and stared at him. "Who are you and what have you done with Paul Hudson?"

The redhead looked up. "You're not really a merch girl, are you?"

"Worse. I'm with the gay one."

The girl laughed. "I'm Anna," she said.

I took notice of Anna's book. The cover was a picture of

the Sistine Chapel, the Creation of Adam segment where God and Adam are touching fingers.

"It's a biographical novel about Michelangelo," Anna said. She told me she was a painter studying at an art school in Toronto, and then excused herself to go to the bathroom.

Michael replaced Loring as Paul's new opponent, and Loring took a seat beside Vera. He looked glum and I asked him what was wrong.

"I'm tired," he said unconvincingly.

Vera leaned in toward his ear. "Know what you need? A tension breaker."

"Excuse me?"

"S-E-X," Vera said. "You look like someone who hasn't had it in a *long* time."

Loring glanced my way, like he expected me to rescue him from my inebriated friend, but all I did was offer him a baited smile and nod at Anna's vacated seat. "How about that one? She seems sweet."

He shook his head. "I don't do groupies."

"She's not a groupie, she's a painter." I pointed to Anna's book. "Renaissance, right? You have something in common."

Loring picked up the book, paged through it too fast to have taken in a word, and put it back down.

Vera sniffed his neck. "Wow. You smell yummy. Eliza, come over here and smell him."

"I know what he smells like," I said without thinking.

The comment went unnoticed by Vera, whose nose was still stuck on Loring's neck, but Loring raised his eyes for a fraction of a second and I looked away as fast as I could. I felt guilty, though I wasn't sure why.

"When was the last time you had sex?" Vera said, distracting Loring.

He rested his chin on his palm. "Why is this pertinent to your life?"

"Vicarious living. Come on, we'll tell you if you tell us."

"You first," he said.

"This morning, in the shower," Vera answered.

"You did it in our shower?" I whined.

"It's our shower, too." Then Vera laughed, yelling, "Hey, Paul. Can you guess when the last time Eliza had an orgasm was?"

"Yesterday," Paul yelled without turning his head from the screen. He nudged Michael. "You were at lunch."

"That's what *you* think," Vera chimed. "She cheated on you with a guitar crate."

"She *what?*" the whole room practically said in unison.

I covered my face and took Vera's drink away from her.

"You were bleeding," Vera explained to Paul, imitating the inflections in my voice when I'd told her the story. "And those crates vibrate when the music gets loud."

To get the most out of his laugh, Paul rolled onto his back, but he composed himself quickly because his team was about to head into the outfield. He nudged Michael again. "Doesn't she make you proud?"

"I stopped listening at *yesterday*," Michael said.

"Hold it." Loring leaned forward. "You mean, when I was standing there, you were—"

"Can we just drop it?" I sighed, morbidly embarrassed.

Tab walked over wearing a cone-shaped hat that said *My First Birthday*. His shirt was unbuttoned and he was smoking a cigar. "What am I missing in here?"

"My betrothed had sex with a guitar crate," Paul said proudly.

"She *what?*"

"*Forget* it!" I cried.

Vera yanked on Tab's sleeve. "When was the last time Loring got some?"

Tab sat down on the table, excited by the topic. "Alone

or with someone else?"

"Either or."

"I'll tell you a little secret about Lori." Tab's head rotated back and forth between Vera and me. "He's a speed-showerer. Normally it takes him three minutes from the time he turns on the water until the time he turns it off. When he's in there longer than that, I know something's up, no pun intended. In Montreal he broke nine minutes."

I could feel Loring's discomfort as Vera grabbed Tab's elbow. "There are over half a dozen girls in here," she said. "You mean to tell me there's not one he'd be willing to at least make out with?"

As if he knew something she didn't, Tab said, "I'm *sure* there's at least *one*."

At that, Loring shot up out of his chair. "Put a lid on it," he said to Tab. Then he asked Brandy, Starr, and Angelo to vacate his bedroom, and after lingering outside the door while they presumably dressed themselves, he locked himself in and the festivities continued without him.

It was almost noon by the time I woke up. I had no idea how long the party had gone on after Paul and I left, but I'd made plans to run with Loring so I stopped by his suite to see if he still wanted to go.

Tab answered the door with a beer in one hand and a piece of cake in the other.

"Is that breakfast or a late-night snack?" I asked.

"Both." He jutted the cake towards me. "Want some?"

"No, thanks. I'm going running. Is Loring up?"

Tab beckoned me in by opening the door as wide as it would go. "Lori," he yodeled. "A Thousand Ways is looking for you."

"What did you call me?"

Tab laughed. "Nothing. Come in."

Inside, Starr was making Bloody Marys over the sink. A girl I didn't remember meeting was watching TV. Anna was asleep on the floor, and Brandy, who had taken a liking to Angelo hours ago, was nowhere in sight.

Loring was on the couch, knees pulled up into his chest, his face bent over a steaming mug of tea as if it were a fire keeping him warm.

"Morning," I said penitently, playfully kicking the bottom of his foot.

He raised his eyes and gave me a weak smile.

"Are you mad?" I said.

"No."

"You seemed kind of mad last night."

"I wasn't."

"In that case," I nodded in Anna's direction, "you get any?"

At least I'd made him smile. "You think you're so funny," he said. "Right. We'll see who's laughing when I channel all my pent up sexual energy into my run and dust you."

January 14, 2002

The concept of time, as it's commonly understood by normal people with normal jobs and normal goddamn lives, doesn't exist on the road. The nights spread out like the dark, godforsaken highways that distinguish them, and the days run together like Thanksgiving dinner smothered in gravy. You never really know where you are or what time it is, and the outside world starts to fade away.

It's cool.

And sure, an extended period of said lifestyle would no doubt have major drawbacks, my biggest complaint so far being the food—it's next to impossible to avoid shitty food. But two weeks isn't nearly enough time to suffer the disadvantages common to life on the road. Hell, I like riding around on the bus. I like waking up in a different city every day. Playing for thousands of people night after night is the high of all highs and right now, sitting in my bunk in a parking lot in our nation's capital, I feel like being on this tour is a glimpse of the band's goddamn yellow-brick future. Not to mention that Loring had to go and tell me stories about how, on his first big tour, he and his wife set up cribs in the back of the bus, and how his kids had been to almost every state in the country before they were a year old. Loring's wife thought being on tour was like living in hell, though. She eventually went home and that's when things started getting "rusted."

Since Eliza doesn't fly but longs to travel all the same, this is a dream come true for her. Unfortunately I never get to bed before the middle of the night, so I sleep half the day, but my betrothed is always up at the butt crack of dawn to run. She usually sleeps while the bus is moving, then she hangs out with Loring—this was part of the deal with *Sonica*. Lucy let her have the two weeks, but only if Eliza agreed to do a daily online diary of life on the road with Loring Blackman. Basically, Eliza follows Loring to soundchecks, hangs out with him backstage, compiles set lists, takes a few candid digital photos, then hooks into the *Sonica* website and posts it all.

It's not like I mind—theoretically—but Eliza and Loring have been spending a lot of time together, and there was this one incident a few days back...probably not even worth mentioning, but it's on my mind so I'm going to document it.

We had a day off in Chicago, and Eliza and I had been sharing a room with Michael all week, so I forked over cash out-of-pocket and got us our own one bedroom suite. As soon as she got back from a run with Loring, which has become a daily event, she and I were going to do some sightseeing and then go shopping for wedding rings. I was expecting her back by eleven. At noon I heard a commotion in the hallway, and when I looked out the peephole, Loring was standing in front of the door, carrying Eliza on his back and trying to get the card key in the slot without dropping her. They were laughing in this relaxed, familiar way that seemed, I don't know, way too relaxed and familiar. Her arms were holding his shoulders, his furled like a pair of goddamn wings around her legs.

I didn't know what to do so I went back into the bedroom and waited. There was a half wall dividing the sitting room and bedroom, and I was pretty sure they wouldn't be able to see me when they came in.

I watched Loring set Eliza on the couch like she was breakable. "RICE," he said. "Rest, ice, compression, elevation."

Whatever the fuck that is.

She took off her shoe and propped her foot on the arm of the couch while Loring grabbed a towel and filled it with ice. Then he cradled her ankle like Prince Charming testing the goddamn glass slipper and set the ice pack on top if it.

I kept watching Loring watching Eliza and a disturbing thought came to me. But it wasn't a strike of lightning or anything. More like a subtle tap on the shoulder, which is why I didn't go ballistic. Besides, I trust my betrothed.

This is not to say I wasn't put off by the way Loring's eyes darted around Eliza's face when she wasn't paying attention to him. And by the way they both laughed when the towel slipped and ice spilled all over the floor.

I got up and made like I'd been sleeping, and both of their heads spun in my direction. Eliza seemed genuinely happy to see me, which made me feel better, but Loring acted like a teenager who'd been caught screwing in his parent's bed.

I asked Eliza if she was okay. She laughed and looked at Loring and said she thought her ankle was broken, giving me the impression "broken" was some kind of inside joke told for Loring's benefit because he laughed right back at her and said, "It's not broken. She just twisted it. It'll be fine in a few days."

I looked at her ankle. It was definitely swollen, and there was a bruise forming on the left side. When I asked her what happened she started telling me Loring had tripped her. Then he raised his hand and cut her off, claiming she'd wanted to race, and because he's considerably faster than she is—his exact words—she purposely stepped on his heel and then fell.

I'd never heard Loring talk so goddamn fast, so loudly, or so clearly.

Eliza started moaning, and right away Loring volunteered to go get her some Advil. I told him not to bother, I had some, and I might have sounded rude. Actually, I'm sure I did, because

Loring gathered up all the spilt ice, dumped it into the sink, and said he'd see us later.

Eliza thanked him a zillion times and he gave her one of those charming, humble smiles that make the sorority girls swoon. When the door shut behind him, Eliza looked up at me and said, "You're in a lousy mood today."

Lousy mood? I wasn't in a lousy mood. It was just that, as I pointed out, I blew the whole goddamn morning waiting for her while she was gallivanting around Chicago with Loring.

Using her pissed-off, I'm-about-to-kick-you voice, she huffed and told me she hadn't been gallivanting. She said when you can barely walk, gallivanting is literally impossible.

I wanted to come right out and say what was on my mind, but I didn't want to spend the day in a big goddamn fight. Still, I knew I'd feel better if I threw my worries up in the air and watched to see where they bounced so I asked Eliza, very calmly, if it had escaped her attention that she'd spent more time with Loring in the last week than she had with me.

She goes: "You exaggerate, Paul."

Next I asked her if she and Loring were like, best friends now or something, and she said, "Well, we're friends, I guess. Does that bother you?"

I asked her if it should.

A honey-sweetened smile crossed her face, her head tilted down, her eyes blinked toward the sky, and all the doubts plaguing my feeble fucking mind dissipated into the air.

Jesus, she would kick my ass if she knew I'd just recounted that story. This one's between you and me. Thanks for listening.

Over.

The band got the news before the show in D.C., when Feldman showed up unexpectedly, flying into the dressing room like a bomber ready to drop its payload, swooping down on Paul who, along with the Michaels, sat huddled around an advanced copy of *Sonica*, which had a review of Bananafish's just-released, eponymously titled record.

"Swear over your life you didn't tell him what to write," Paul yelled at me over his shoulder.

I was on the floor near a phone jack, computer on my lap, sending in a diary entry. "I swear," I said. I'd made no secret of tirelessly pleading with Lucy to assign someone to review the record, but beyond that it was out of my hands. Lucy's position on Bananafish was still critical at best. Although she did admit, after I miraculously convinced her to attend Bananafish's last Ring of Saturn show, that Paul had an incredible voice, she also couldn't help but throw in a typically negative *but*—

"He looks like a junkie."

And when Lucy heard Bananafish would be replacing Dogwalker for the two-week tour with Loring, she said, "Eliza, does your fiancé know you've screwed half the Blackman family?"

Sonica called *Bananafish* "a promising, intense debut," and said Paul was a songwriter possessing "the heart of a madman, the soul of a hopeful romantic, and the voice of a god. Definitely worth a listen."

Time Out also did a piece on the band, heralding them as "light at the end of a long, dark, pop-music tunnel. A post-rock, rock 'n' roll tour de force."

Not everyone liked it. *Rolling Stone* only gave it two stars, equating the songs to "self-indulgent Hallmark cards." Oddly enough, this review pleased Paul, as *Rolling Stone* had recently given three-and-a-half stars to a famous dancer-slash-actress-slash-singer whose musical success, Paul claimed, was proof of the decline of civilization.

Feldman grabbed Paul's arm. "We gotta talk. It's about the Drones tour."

The whole band had been in the clouds for months over the possibility of a tour with the Drones. Their faces shriveled instantly. But I could tell Feldman was hiding something. His cheeks were like pomegranates, round and pink and ready to burst with juicy little seeds of pleasure.

Feldman made a fist and shadowboxed a one-two punch. "Pack your bags," he said. "You're in."

I stood to the side and watched one Paul and three Michaels go slack-jaw, their tongues lying motionless like dead fish in their mouths. Then wild revelry broke out among them, complete with high-fives and cries for alcohol. Michael borrowed Paul's phone to call Vera. And when Paul dove to embrace me, the look on his face was one of absolute, perfect joy—the kind of joy that can't be reproached, stolen, or marred—the kind that only the innocent or the ignorant are capable of experiencing.

I wanted to freeze the moment. Freeze it and jump inside of it and stay there until it melted into the warm, swishy liquid of happy memories.

Feldman threw his arm across Paul's back and said, "I'm really proud of you," and I found myself filled with momentary affection for Feldman. I thanked him and even kissed his pinguid cheek. But as I continued to watch the celebration, my feelings got more and more convoluted. I was thrilled for Paul, for Michael, and the rest of the band—I wanted nothing more for them than this—but there was a prickling underneath my skin that felt like a portent to heartbreak.

My own, not theirs.

I was scared.

I already felt left behind.

Once everyone calmed down and Michael got off the phone, Feldman expanded on the details of the tour: The band would be flown to San Francisco the first week of March to meet up with the Drones. They would travel down the coast, through most of the Western states, the Midwest, Texas, the East Coast, Florida, and then culminate with a show at Madison Square Garden in early July.

"Madison Square Garden," Paul mumbled in disbelief.

"And this isn't your average sideshow carnival," Feldman said. "We're talking first class all the way. The Drones are gonna cart your asses around in a 737, for Christ's sake. Boys, we ain't in Kansas anymore."

Feldman had said: "*737.*"

I had heard: "*Potential rudder reversal problem.*"

Vivid images came slashing through my head like a machete, hacking away at my tenuous, oscillating bliss: March, 1991. *Slash.* I skipped school to watch the news after United flight #585—a 737-200—crashed in Colorado Springs, killing all twenty-five people on board. *Slash.* The USAir flight that went down outside of Pittsburgh in 1994. Again, a 737.

Judo, Bananafish's tour manager, told the band it was time to hit the stage, and Paul gripped the sides of my face. "Can you believe this?" he said. "We'll go a few days early. San Francisco can be our honeymoon."

"Let's go," Judo yelled.

Paul moved in to kiss me but I couldn't seem to kiss him back.

"What's wrong?" he said. "You haven't changed your mind about the honeymoon, have you?"

I shook my head.

It was supposed to be a love scene of sorts.

It wasn't the time or the place to say anything else.

The show that night was so spectacular I couldn't watch it. I felt like a hanger-on. No better than Starr or Brandy or any nameless fan who wanted to be a part of the Bananafish world, but in reality would never be anything more than an interloper.

I asked Feldman to tell Paul I was tired, and I headed back to the bus. In the parking lot I thought I saw Loring walking towards me, carrying a pizza.

"Shouldn't you be inside?" I said. The guy looked up and I chuckled. "Sorry. I thought you were Loring." I stepped back and surveyed the guy's face. "Anyone ever say you look like him? In the dark, anyway."

"They usually say he's better looking."

Whoever *they* are, they're right, I thought. The guy was a mutant Loring. His features were the same shape, but the sizes were off. Smaller eyes. Bigger teeth. Fifteen extra pounds. And his hair was a drab version of Loring's thick, shiny-bronze locks.

I started walking away, and mutant Loring, who was eying the laminated pass around my neck, said, "Ten bucks says your name's Eliza."

I froze, not sure whether to be amused or spooked.

Mutant Loring extended his hand. "Leith Blackman."

"Oh." I nodded. "The only Blackman I haven't met yet."

Leith and I chatted outside the bus for a few minutes. Or rather, Loring's brother chatted and I listened while he filled me in on all the details of his life. He was four years younger than Loring, single, and in town cutting a documentary on the Smithsonian.

Leith may not have had Loring's looks, but he certainly annunciated better. "By the way," he said. "I caught some of your boyfriend's show. Impressive." He opened the pizza box and offered me a slice.

"No, thanks. I was just on my way to back to the bus. It was nice meeting you."

"You, too," Leith said. "I'm sure I'll see you around."

"Paul, I threw up on a skycap's shoes! Just *thinking* about a forty-five-minute flight from Cleveland to New York and I spilled my cookies all over the man's loafers. Imagine what would happen if I had to fly every day. I'd have a heart attack. I'd *die*."

"Holy Hell, you won't die."

Paul was sitting on the bus, in Angelo's bunk, his hands tearing through his hair. Standing above him, I could see his white-blue eyes pointing up at me, reminding me, as they often did, of flashlights. Aligned with the severe angle of his nose, the effect was one of a man possessed.

"You *promised*," he said with the crushed disappointment of a child.

I hadn't wanted to have this conversation until we got back to New York, but my brother had to offer his unwelcome opinion. "Dream on," I'd heard Michael say as he and Paul boarded the bus. "There's no way you'll get my sister on that plane."

Angelo had run off with a leggy brunette he'd met backstage, and Michael and Burke were waiting for Paul to finish up with me so we could all go celebrate. I shut the curtain that separated the bus's living quarters from its sleeping quarters and said, "We'll be home tomorrow. Can we talk about this when we have more privacy?"

"I don't care who hears me," Paul shouted. "I have no intention of spending the first half of my year as a newly-wed away from my wife. What's the point of being togeth-er if we're going to live separate lives? You know what Loring told me? He told me it's impossible to maintain a relation-ship like that. You *have* to get on the plane."

"You can't make me get on a plane. Besides, I have a job, remember? I can't just take off for four months."

Paul said, "This has nothing to do with your job and you know it."

I knelt down and rested my chin on his lap. "You won't be leaving for almost six weeks. We'll spend every second together until then, I promise."

"Not acceptable." He stood up, looking like he wanted to pace, but there was no room. "Eliza, you can't go through life like this. Do you know that on an annual basis, donkeys kill more people than planes?"

"Oh, yeah? Well, do you know that between 1975 and 1981, more than ten percent of the toxicological tests on pilots were positive for alcohol?"

He rolled his head in a circle. "Jesus, *where* do you get this shit?" He made a growling noise that meant his patience was shot. "Listen, I don't want to demean what happened to your parents, and I know I could never begin to imagine what it was like to lose them like that, but Michael still flies. He's okay, right?"

It wasn't just my parents' ill-fated flight holding me back. What was also swirling through my mind was the terror I'd felt standing on the corner of Broadway and Houston Street watching American Airlines flight 11 aim for the World Trade Center.

Both horrifying events pointed to an unpredictable world where terrible things are completely out of a person's control, and I didn't know how to surrender to that.

Paul must have seen what the conversation was doing to the little equanimity I had. He pulled me up from the floor, held me, and said, "I'm sorry, I'm sorry, I'm sorry," kissing the crown of my head in between each apology. "I just want us to be together. You know that, right?"

Sure, I knew. But I didn't think Paul understood fear. Fear, to Paul, was an occasional lapse of cocky-bastard confidence—it was subway grates and selling out. For me, fear was fettering, but it also afforded a strange, almost placid consolation, and a belief that the trauma was too deep to ever have to be faced, which, at times, created a zone of comfort around me, one I obviously didn't have the power or the guts to relinquish.

"Drugs!" Paul cried. "Just this once, Eliza. A couple of pills and a Bloody Mary and I swear to God you won't know the difference between flying on a plane and riding the merry-go-round in Central Park."

I felt trapped by the bus, by Paul, and by my anxiety. I couldn't catch a good breath and was afraid that if I didn't get outside I was going to start hyperventilating.

This is what it would feel like to be inside a 737, I thought. My hands were shaking as I hurried to put on my shoes.

"Where do you think you're going?" Paul snapped.

I grabbed my coat and Paul, in turn, pushed past me as if we were in a race to see who could get off the bus the quickest. He split the curtain in half and made his way down the aisle, muttering, "goddamn this" and "goddamn that" and "goddamn" something about his pancreas.

"Let's go celebrate," he barked at the Michaels, both of whom got up and followed him like disciples. By the time I limped down the steps on my still-sore ankle, the three of them were halfway across the parking lot.

Outside, the cold air was a relief. Thinking I should stay close to the bus, I sat about ten yards away, on the hood of a dirty Camaro, and watched a man in the window of the hotel across the street. For distraction I invented a life for the stranger: He worked in banking, had a wife and two kids at home, drank scotch, liked to watch dirty movies when he was out of town but lied and told his wife he didn't, and he'd read every book Tom Clancy had ever written.

Eventually the man's failure to do anything but remove his tie caused me to lose interest, and for diversion I turned to the soggy Chinese takeout menu someone had left on the Camaro's windshield, but that only made me hungry, so I closed my eyes, bowed my head, and prayed for strength and courage and some kind of baffling *Star Trek* miracle of flight that would allow me to move quickly through space and time without having to put all my faith in a five-hundred-thousand-pound hunk of metal.

Loring didn't know if he should approach her. Her eyes were closed, her head was down, and she didn't look like she wanted company. But he had to walk past her to get to the bus. It would be rude not to say hello. And he questioned her safety, sitting alone in the middle of an empty parking lot.

He stepped closer and she looked up. Her dark eyes were tired and watery, and she only pretended to smile.

"Everything all right?" Loring said.

She nodded, using the edge of her sleeve to wipe her cheek.

"I heard about the Drones gig," he said. "Paul must be ecstatic."

"Oh, he's ecstatic all right." Her voice was a double layer of caustic overtones and discordant tumult.

"This probably isn't the safest place for you to be hanging out." Loring looked at his watch and then pointed to the hotel. "I'm meeting my brother in the coffee shop…"

"I met your brother."

"I know, he told me." Loring scratched his temple. "Why don't you come and eat with us?"

She started to shake her head, but then dropped her chin and bit her lip—a gesture that struck Loring as saturnine. "Actually, I am hungry."

On their way to the hotel, Eliza held onto Loring's arm; he felt a rising tension in his jeans and began trying to recite

America's capital cities to himself, listing them in alphabet-
ical order by state, hoping it would help move the blood
back up to his brain.

Alabama, Montgomery. Arizona, Phoenix. Arkansas,
Little Rock.

They walked through the lobby of the hotel and straight
into the almost-empty restaurant, where everything was a
different, depressing shade of orange: carotene seat cush-
ions, pumpkin wallpaper, apricot-and-bile menus.

Leith was seated at a table in the farthest corner of the
room. He stood up and put on his coat when he saw Eliza.

"Was it something I said?" she joked.

"I already ate. The pizza, remember? I only agreed to come
over here so *he*," Leith jerked his head at Loring, "didn't have
to eat alone. I'll catch you guys later."

A young waitress dropped off menus and Eliza said,
"What are the chances you have anything Chinese? Sweet
and sour chicken? Fried rice?"

The waitress, whose hair color came close to matching
the walls, seemed to think she was being gibed at. "We have
regular rice. Like, the *white* kind. And I can bring you some
soy sauce." But then she recognized Loring and her attitude
did an about-face. "Actually, I could ask the cook and
maybe—"

"Forget it," Eliza said. "What's the soup of the day?"

"Corn chowder."

She settled on the Roman omelet with rye toast and no
butter. Loring ordered a club sandwich and a bowl of the
soup, and no sooner did the waitress bring the chowder than
a pretty girl and her not-nearly-as-attractive friend appeared.
They told Loring they'd driven in from Richmond to see his
show and were staying the night in the hotel. They wanted
him to sign their shirts.

"Right here," the pretty girl said, pointing to a spot that

was probably her nipple.

Eliza exhaled loudly and with contempt, and Loring tried not to laugh as he reluctantly obliged the girl's request, only he scribbled his signature on her sleeve, hoping she and her friend would then have the decency to go away. He resented the discontinuity brought on by the girls' arrival. The tour ended in a day and who knew when or if he'd see Eliza again. All he wanted was to sit across from her without interruption. They didn't even have to talk. He just wanted to *be* with her.

The girls lingered at the table, the pretty one doing a lot of chattering. She told Loring that her sister's boyfriend had been a junior at Yale when he was a freshman, as if this somehow formed a bond between them.

"Brady Meltzer. He says he knew you."

Loring shrugged. The name didn't ring a bell.

The girl slid a small piece of paper under the salt shaker, prompting Eliza to sit up and lean across the table. And then she did exactly what Loring had a feeling she was going to do—she reached down and seized the note.

"Christy and Janis," Eliza read aloud. "Room 271. Is this a take-your-pick kind of offer or a two-for-one special?"

Loring buried his mouth in his fist; Christy's face went ashen. She grabbed the note out of Eliza's hand and stormed away, her friend following like a puppy behind her.

"Sorry," Eliza said. "I hope you didn't want that. I'm not in a very patient mood."

Loring shook his head, wishing he could have attributed her umbrage to a secret crush, rather than what was clearly repulsion with those less reverent than she.

"That happens a lot, doesn't it? Girls offering themselves to you?" She waited for Loring to nod. "I mean really, you could be sitting here trying to have a nice, quiet meal with your girlfriend, and they still have the nerve to proposition you like that. Are they stupid or just downright mean?"

Loring decided that for the remainder of the meal he was going to pretend Eliza was his girlfriend.

"Dover," he said, although he hadn't meant to say it out loud.

"What are you talking about?"

"Nothing. Delaware."

She set her elbow on the table, rested her chin on top of her fist, and stared at his bowl of soup while he ate. It was the kind of look that, had he taken the bowl away and asked her to describe what the soup looked like, she never could have done it. He knew she was thinking about Paul and for the first time in his life he experienced a malignant envy that felt like a saber-tooth tiger gnawing on the inside of his torso and was so intense, malice seemed like the only conceivable relief.

Back in the Stone Age, Loring could have instigated some kind of Darwinian, alpha-male showdown with Paul. He was older, taller, stronger, and survival of the fittest might have given him the advantage. But here, in the middle of D.C., he was powerless against his unwitting opponent. That he actually liked Paul only made it worse.

Loring needed to get Eliza Caelum out of his system. He needed to throw in the towel, step out of the ring, and accept defeat. This meal is a farewell dinner, he told himself. A Last Supper in this rotting tangerine of a room. Enjoy it now because after tomorrow it's all over. After tomorrow you will never contact her again.

"Loring?" she said quietly, knocking him out of his internal diatribe. "Have you ever said yes to any of those girls?"

The question seemed to contain a subtext Loring couldn't decipher. He shook his head. "You know what I call that? Herpes on a stick."

"Did you ever cheat on Justine?"

He set his spoon down and wiped his mouth with his napkin. "Do you ask everyone such personal questions, or do you just like to pick on me?"

She gave him a coy smile that disappeared as fast as it came. "Are you going to answer me?"

Of course he was going to answer her. He would have given her his ATM code if she'd asked for it. "No. I never cheated on Justine."

"Not even a little kiss?"

He put his right hand on his heart. "Swear over my kids."

"Did you ever want to?"

He thought it over for a moment. "I don't know," he said in all honesty. "I guess I'd be lying if I said some of the opportunities that presented themselves weren't a little enticing. Sometimes you meet people who are actually interesting, and obviously attractive. But there's a gigantic difference between thinking about it and doing it. You have to cross a line to get to that point, and that line, for me, is not drawn in sand."

"Justine was out of her mind to let you get away."

Again, her frankness was too sad and blatant to hold any cryptic messages of love. Had Loring been a braver man, or maybe a duplicitous one, he would have seized the moment and owned up to his infatuation, promising to be everything Paul was and more, if only she'd give him a chance.

"What about you?" he asked. "Ever mess around on Paul?"

"*No,*" she said, the thought apparently too outlandish to consider.

The waitress brought Eliza her omelet, along with Loring's humongous, four-decker club, and he pushed his soup aside to make room for the new plate.

Loring adjusted the toothpick in his sandwich, moving it toward the corner so he didn't bite into it. Minutes went by and they ate in silence. Eventually Eliza looked up and said, "Do you think Paul would?"

He watched her take a French fry off his plate. He loved that she took it without asking and that she dipped it in his ketchup and for the life of him he couldn't remember if the capital of Oklahoma was Tulsa or Oklahoma City.

"Do I think Paul would what?"

"He's in a hotel in Seattle two months from now, and some Christy comes by and whispers her room number into his ear. Does he drop by for a visit?"

Loring guessed this is what had been bothering her all night. "Eliza, I can't answer that."

She bit the fry in half. "He wants me to go on the tour but I can't. I want to. More than anything. But there's no way I can fly all the way to California, then fly from city to city every few days. *Especially* on a 737. That's why he got mad and stormed off." She picked a rye seed out of her toast and somehow managed to eat it in three pieces. "I don't know what to do."

Loring thought she was going to cry. He almost wished for it. Tears would have given him an excuse to put his arms around her and touch her hair.

"I know you can't answer it for certain," she said, "but come on, you went to Yale. Make an educated guess."

"Should I remind you that our half-wit, sub-literate president also went to Yale?"

"Just tell me what you think. Please?"

He took a drink of water and debated what to say. He'd known Paul pre-Eliza and back then he would've had a cynical answer. Paul was different now. Still, Loring considered this his great Machiavellian opportunity. He could plant a seed in her head. He could tell her how hard it is for someone who isn't used to all the attention to say no.

He couldn't do it. Not only would it have been unkind,

it would have been a lie. Based on his own feelings, Loring believed he understood how much the woman sitting across from him meant to Paul Hudson.

"My opinion?" he said. "I wouldn't worry about it."

The bus was supposed to leave Boston as soon as Bananafish finished their set. It was the last show of the tour and the drive home would take a little over five hours. As long as it didn't start snowing, we would be back in Manhattan before the sun came up.

Paul was hung-over and choleric, and with the exception of grilling me about where I'd been when I returned from dinner with Loring, he'd barely spoken to me since our argument. He walked into the dressing room, sweat still dripping from his hair, and I watched him make a willful effort to avoid me.

"All right, let's go," he said, craning around the room. "Where's Angelo?"

Burke said, "He was right behind me a second ago."

We waited for twenty minutes. Everyone sensed Paul's agitation and tried to stay out of his way. I even offered to go find Angelo, just to get out of the room, but Judo told me to stay put while he tried to locate the missing Michael.

Loring was in the middle of his show by the time Judo returned. "Bus driver saw Angelo wander into the parking lot with that brunette from D.C."

"Fuck Angelo," Paul snapped. "The brunette can drive his ass home."

"Paul," I sighed. "We can't leave without him."

"Whatever. I'm going to watch the rest of the set," Paul said to no one in particular, before leaving the room.

Over the course of the tour, Paul had developed a genuine appreciation for Loring's music. Although Loring's mid-tempo sound and straightforward style was diametrically opposed to Bananafish's intensity, and Paul still categorized Loring's songs as too radio-friendly, Paul had a habit of saying that what Loring lacked in originality, he made up for in sincerity.

As soon as Paul was out of sight, Michael turned to me and said, "Go with him, please. We don't need to misplace two band members."

Loring was in the middle of the title track from *Rusted* when I caught up to Paul on the side of the stage. I reached for his hand and was surprised when he let me take it.

I don't have the strength to pick up the pieces.
Or to walk away and say that maybe I was wrong.

Loring didn't have Paul's pipes, he didn't have the range or power Paul had, but there was an understated drawl to his voice that was sexy and pleasing to the ear.

If Paul's music was like flying, Loring's was an afternoon drive along a rural highway—sunny, romantic, but with an undertone of prosaic sadness that pulled on the heartstrings.

I felt a tap on my shoulder, turned to see Leith beside me, and grabbed Paul, yelling, "Loring's brother," repeating it three times before Paul understood. Leith went on to tell Paul how much he liked Bananafish's show the night before.

"I hope you missed tonight's show," Paul shouted. "It sucked my ass."

For the remainder of the song, the two men had a conversation by screaming into each others ears.

"This next one's new," Loring said a minute later, futzing with the tuning on his black Stratocaster. "No one's heard it yet, so let me know what you think."

I looked down at the set list. Between "Rusted" and the encore break, it said "A Thousand Ways."

The phrase struck me as uncomfortably familiar. Like déjà vu had just punched me in the stomach.

Loring counted backward from four and then started strumming a catchy chord progression. Right before he began to sing, I remembered why the title sounded so familiar. The morning in Toronto, I'd walked into Loring's suite and that's what Tab had called me.

It didn't take long for the whole dreadful scene to unfold in front of my eyes in much the same way watching a car drive off a cliff might. For a fleeting moment I was able to convince myself it was my imagination playing a not-so-funny joke, but that hope vanished when I started to feel guilty for things I knew I hadn't done. And Loring's words struck me as so undeniably intimate, had he been whispering them in my ear he couldn't have been speaking more clearly to me.

If I had the guts I'd ask you to be free
I'd ask you to roam the universe in search of me
I'd ask you to love me the way that you love him
And always hold me, always near
I swear I would ask you this
If only you were here

I remember how you wore my sweater like moonlight
and how it smelled like heaven for days
And maybe I'll never get that close to you again
but I've dreamt of it a thousand ways

If I had the guts I'd ask you to dance
I'd get down on my knees, beg you for a chance
I'd shed my blood to touch the pearls that kiss your ears

I'd wipe away your every tear
I'd sell my soul to see you fly
I'd chase away your fear

Paul had seemed only marginally suspicious until the blather about the pearls and the flying, at which point an apocalyptic scowl unfolded across his face.

"I knew it!" he shouted toward the stage as if Loring could hear him. Then he spun to face Leith. "Who does he think he is, Eric fucking Clapton?"

Leith stood with his arms glued to his sides, rigid and helpless, a child taking the rap for something he didn't do.

Next, Paul turned on me. His teeth were clenched and I saw a pulse beating in his jaw as he searched my face for the answer to a question he was too afraid to ask.

He jumped down off the stage and fled, and I chased after him as best I could, but I was still moving like a gimp. Making my way toward the dressing room, I came face-to-face with Loring, who had just exited the stage and was being led down the hall by a bald man with a flashlight.

Paul and I had said our respective goodbyes to Loring earlier that afternoon, explaining that we were leaving right after Bananafish's show. Judging from the look on Loring's face, it was clear he had no idea we were still there.

He froze when he saw me, our eyes locked, and we remained like that until Loring opened his mouth like he was going to speak, and I, conflictingly in shock, overwhelmed, and ill-equipped to deal with whatever Loring wanted to say, ran.

On my way out I saw Michael. "Where's Paul?" I said, digging my nails into my palm to balance out the pain shooting through my foot.

"He just stormed out to the bus. Eliza, what's going on?"

"Nothing," I said, hobbling as fast as I could toward the exit.

Angelo was standing in front of the bus. "I wouldn't go in there if I were you."

"Where have you been?" I screamed, deciding the whole mess was Angelo's fault. "Everyone's looking for you! Go tell Michael you're here! Do *not* pass Go! Do *not* collect two hundred dollars! Just find Michael!"

"Jeeze. Take a chill pill."

Angelo headed in the direction of the arena, and I pounded on the bus's door until Paul swung it open so fast it almost whacked me in the face.

I walked cagily up the steps, sat sideways on the couch, exhaled toward the window and watched my breath turn into a thin circle of moisture on the glass. "I don't think we were supposed to hear that song."

"Oh, you don't, huh?" Paul crashed down beside me. "You know what *I* think? I think *I* wasn't supposed to hear it. *You*, on the other hand…" The hand went to the pancreas. "*You* spent a hell of a lot of time with him in the last two weeks, running and piggyback riding and wherever the hell you were last night—"

"Hold it—"

"No, *you* hold it. I'd like to know when you had the opportunity to wear his clothes. What did you do, play dress-up during all those long runs?"

"What?"

"His goddamn sweater. Don't tell me you didn't hear the lyrics because I saw your face. When did you scent his goddamn sweater? And more importantly, what did you scent it with?"

My head fell forward. "The day I interviewed him. I was cold and I borrowed a sweater. That's all."

"What about last night?"

"What *about* last night?"

"Where were you?"

"We went to eat. I already told you."

"In a *hotel*? What did you order?"

"You've got to be kidding," I said. But Paul didn't look like he was kidding. "I had an omelet with artichoke hearts, sun-dried tomatoes, and mozzarella cheese. Loring had soup and a sandwich. Our waitress's uniform was the color of throw-up and there's no Chinese food on the menu. Call the restaurant right now if you don't believe me."

"What kind of goddamn soup?"

"Don't be gay."

He moved in so he was practically in my lap. "I'm only going to ask you this once," he said, his eyes glistening with panic. "And I swear over my life I'm going to believe whatever you say. Do you understand? With my whole goddamn heart and soul I'm going to believe you so please don't lie to me because I would never get over it."

"No," I said before he even asked the question. "Nothing happened between me and Loring. Not last night, not ever."

"Look me in the eyes and tell me he never made one pass at you, never tried to kiss you or told you shit like, 'I only invited your goddamn fool of a fiancé on this tour because I'm fucking in love with you and I want to kiss your earrings and fuck your goddamn brains out.'"

I took his face in my hands and said, "I mean it. I had no idea."

Paul's jaw was still pulsing. "Well, what if he had? What if he walked on this bus right now and begged you to run off with him? What would you do?"

"Paul, I'm not interested in Loring."

"You expect me to believe you're not attracted to him?"

This required tact. The honest reply was that only a blind woman wouldn't be attracted to him—a blind woman who couldn't get close enough to smell his green, peppery, sex-on-the-grass cologne.

And then there was the matter of the song. I was touched and flattered by the song, and for a moment, at least, I would have to *consider* that. I would discard it, for sure. But a swift, internal maelstrom of contemplation would come first.

"Eliza, please answer me."

"What are you asking? If I think he's cute? He's a very good-looking guy. So what?"

"He's more than just a good-looking guy and you know it."

But, I thought, he doesn't have flashlight eyes or a cocky-bastard smile that can boil water or a voice from the heavens and most of all he says things like, *It's only rock 'n' roll*.

"Corn chowder," I said.

"What?"

"The soup of the day."

Paul kissed my palm and then pressed it against his heart. "Please come on the tour with me. Come to San Francisco. At least say you'll try."

"I'll try," I said. And I meant it. I always meant it. But deep down I knew I was never going to get on that plane.

We sat like that for a while, until Michael boarded the bus with Angelo, Burke, and the rest of the crew behind him.

"All right," Judo said. "Everybody present and accounted for?"

Michael approached the couch. He was looking at me suspiciously. "Loring wants to know if he can have a word with you before we leave."

Paul shot up out of his seat. "I think she's heard enough of his goddamn words." He rushed to the front of the bus, looked at the driver, and said, "*Go*."

The voice on the other end of the line said, "Meet me at Kiev in an hour."

I was filled with instant dread. "Feldman?"

"Just be there."

"I don't have time."

"Make time."

It had already been a bad week. Loring kept leaving messages for me, asking for a chance to explain. Paul was fighting the inclination to call Loring back and tell him off, and I was working hard to convince my fiancé that the prudent course of action was to just drop it. I was uncomfortable enough, and the last thing I wanted was to have to face the guy.

When I called Vera to discuss the whole fiasco, she said, "I *knew* he liked you. I knew it in Toronto. I didn't say anything then, but now—Jesus, Eliza, how do you feel about him?"

"What is this, psychotherapy all of a sudden?"

"It was obvious you guys were getting along. I *saw* it."

"Saw what? Vera, I'm going to tell you the same thing I told Paul—I'm not interested in Loring Blackman. That's it. End of discussion."

On top of everything else, Paul was acting weird. He was unduly cheerful, despite wanting to confront Loring. And he hadn't said a word about the Drones tour since that night on the bus. I didn't know if this meant he was resigned to the fact that I wouldn't be joining him, or he just assumed

I would be, but every time I tried to bring it up he said, "We'll talk about it after the wedding."

The wedding was another predicament. Paul and I wanted to get married ASAP, but the city of New York and Lucy Enfield were refusing to cooperate.

"You just missed two weeks," Lucy said. "You can't skip any more days."

"But I'm getting married."

"I don't care if you're being canonized. Work it out on your own time."

This meant all the preparations had to be made after seven, but the clerk's office closed at five, it was the only place to get a marriage license, and both the bride and groom had to be present.

I hated going above Lucy's head. It made me feel like the loser on the playground who needed her big brother to fight her battles, but in a way that's exactly what I was at *Sonica*. And I considered marrying Paul a noble enough cause so I took the matter to Terry. He congratulated me and gave me Friday off. Paul and I would get the license then, there would be a twenty-four-hour waiting period, and on Saturday we would be married by a municipal judge in City Hall, with Vera and Michael as our witnesses, and Loring's silly love song nothing more than a story to tell Rex and Spike someday.

"This better be good." I startled Feldman by tossing my purse into the booth a moment before my butt hit the seat. "I only have half an hour."

Kiev was a nondescript Eastern European diner in the East Village offering a three course meal for twelve dollars. When I arrived, Feldman already had a cup of coffee in his hand and a large order of potato latkes on a plate in front of him. It was rude, I thought, inviting someone to a restaurant and ordering before they got there.

The waitress walked over and I asked for the first thing I saw on the menu. "A Coke," I said. I was pretty sure I'd never in my life ordered a Coke, but the frown on Feldman's face and the waitress's eager smile made me act on impulse.

Feldman waited until the waitress brought me my soda, then he let out a rhonchus snort and said, "He told me to turn it down."

"Who?"

"*Who*? That asshole you're marrying. Who do you think I'm talking about?"

Chewing on my straw, I said, "He told you to turn what down?"

Feldman smeared sour cream over a latke and then took a bite. It was hard to watch him consume food. He ate like a giant two-year-old.

"The *tour*," he said, as if he couldn't understand how I could be so dense. "The fucking Drones?"

A sharp pain throbbed in my head like an aneurysm about to explode.

Feldman took hold of my wrist. His fingers were sticky, as if he'd dipped them in syrup. "It's because of you. He doesn't want to leave *you*."

I pulled free and let my face fall into my hands so that I didn't have to look at Feldman's pink cheeks.

"You can't let him do it," Feldman said, much louder than necessary. "Are you listening to me? I've put a lot of time, effort, and money into his fucking career, and if you care one iota for him you won't let him throw it down the drain."

I hated Feldman. Hated him with a fear. Hated him almost as much as I hated visions of single-engine prop planes on stormy nights. But I lifted my head and nodded because I knew he was right.

"Radio's not playing the single," he said. "No surprise there. The video was in moderate rotation for about a minute, the marketing campaign has been minimal at best. And I'll tell you something, Paul's attitude has a lot to do with it—Winkle's not trying to ruin his *life*, Eliza. He's not trying to *exploit* Paul Hudson. He just wants to sell music." Feldman exhaled like an exploding balloon. "Do you have an idea how many records they've sold? I'll tell you—about nine thousand, which is a small but respectable amount under the circumstances. But I'd bet my ass ninety-eight percent of the people who bought it are either relatives of the Michaels *or*—and this is a big *or*—they saw the Blackman tour. Am I making sense or do you think this is a game? 'Cause for all I know you might like stringing him around by his dick. Maybe you want him to fall flat on his face, but I'm not going to let some—"

"*Stop!*"

I started rubbing a pressure point in my palm, a spot someone once told me made headaches go away. It didn't work.

"Why didn't he tell me?" I said, blinking rapidly.

"The asshole thinks you won't marry him if you know, that's why."

"Please stop calling Paul an asshole."

"He made me promise not to say anything until after the wedding."

"Well it's nice to see you're a man of your word."

"Don't give me that high-horse shit now. Just tell me what you're going to do."

"I don't know what I *can* do. When Paul makes up his mind—"

Feldman grabbed my arm again, squeezing so hard I felt like I was having my blood pressure taken. "Do you know what Winkle went through to get him on this tour? The promises, the wheeling-and-dealing, the ass-kissing? Do you know what will happen if Paul Hudson just up and decides

he wants to stay home with his *wife*? It's career fucking suicide. They're already booked. The contracts have been
signed, reservations have been made. Paul's relationship with
Winkle, what's left of it, and with the agents and promot-
ers, it would all be caput. So unless you want to be personally responsible for destroying his life, you better think of
something in the next forty-eight hours. After that it'll be
too late. Do you get what I'm saying, Peepers?"

I got it, all right. In ways Feldman would never understand. And it wasn't just about Paul. There was Michael to
think about, too.

In an odd way, knowing all this calmed me down.

There was something reassuring about knowing things.

Knowing things allowed me to feel like the one in control.

It would be the last time I would wake up next to Paul in the apartment. I didn't know it then, otherwise I would have sat on the window ledge a little longer, gazing at his face while the advent of daylight played tricks with his hair. I would have tried to take mental photos of the way he lay with the sheet covering his naked body from the ilium down, his arms splayed out to the sides, his head tilted to the left.

A very crucifixian pose.

I would have remembered the good stuff.

Nobody ever remembers the good stuff.

The night before, we'd gone to bed a little after midnight and had intense, quiet sex lying on our sides like two spoons in a drawer. Then I'd asked Paul if we could talk, he said he was tired and went to sleep, and I stared at the ceiling for the rest of the night.

The situation was simple, really. I loved Paul, I loved my brother, and I understood in a very rational way that I had to do whatever it took to make sure they were on that plane to San Francisco in March.

Paul was scheduled to do a live performance on a local public radio show that morning, and I asked him to come home as soon as he finished. I told him there was something we needed to discuss before we went to get the marriage license.

"I'm going to see Winkle at ten," he said. "How about we meet for coffee near the clerk's office around eleven?"

I couldn't let him see Winkle. That much I knew. "Can you stop back here first?"

Paul was in the doorway. He cocked his head to the side, suggesting he found my request fishy, and I considered having it out with him then, but he was already running late, and I could barely keep my eyes open. I needed to get some rest, and I needed to collect a decent amount of ammo before I would be armed enough to win this battle.

"You're not getting cold feet, are you?"

I assured him that was not the problem. "Just promise you'll come here before you see Winkle."

He agreed. After he left I took a long shower, wrapped myself in my robe, and curled up on the couch. Maybe a minute later, maybe an hour, the buzz of the door shook me back to consciousness.

"Who is it?" I said into the intercom, and immediately recognized the low-pitched mumble on the other end.

"Eliza," Loring said. "Can I come up?"

"It's not a good time."

I took my hand off the button so that I couldn't hear his retort, but in the time it took me to brush my teeth and splash my face with water there was a knock on the door.

I opened it and barked, "How did you get in here?" But I knew how he got in. He was Loring Blackman and virtually any of the budding artists, students, and junkies in the building would recognize him and gladly let him walk right on through.

"Five minutes," he said, his hands in the air as if I were holding him at gunpoint.

I stepped back and Loring entered the apartment apprehensively. Either he couldn't believe the squalor Paul and I lived in, or he could sense something was amiss, something that had nothing to do with his arrival.

"Eliza, are you all right?"

He wasn't just asking to ask. He was genuinely worried about me and that made me feel terrible for being rude. "I'm sorry, Loring. I have a lot going on right now. Please say what you have to say and then we can get on with our lives and pretend this never happened."

He chuckled like he wished it could be that easy. "First," he said, leaning against the back of the couch, kicking at the floor. "I didn't think it was going to be so obvious. The song, I mean. Not to mention I didn't even know you were still there."

I felt my face flush. "This is really uncomfortable."

"How do you think I feel?"

"For what it's worth, it's a beautiful song, I mean it. I'd be lying if I said I wasn't *extremely* touched, but—"

"*Don't.*"

"No, look, Loring, if I did anything at all that made you think—"

"You didn't do anything, Eliza. That's one of the things I came here to say. Not just to you, but probably even more so to Paul. I want to make this clear to both of you—I didn't write that song to try and win you over, or to steal you away from him. I wrote it because I knew I never could."

I didn't want to listen to any more, but I didn't have the heart to kick Loring out after a statement like that.

"There's something I need to ask you." He scratched his temple, and it occurred to me that the only time he ever resembled Doug was when he scratched his temple. "Say we'd met that night in Cleveland…If I'd come to my dad's room instead of going to sleep…" He hesitated. "I guess what I really want to know is, under different circumstances, would I have had a chance?"

I sighed. "Why does that matter?"

"It just does," he said. "Think of it as a period at the end of a sentence. Necessary to move on and start a new paragraph."

So much of love is in the timing, I thought. And back then the possible existence of Paul Hudson was nothing more than wishful thinking. Loring probably would have swept me off my feet.

"Without a doubt," I said, because it was the truth, and because Loring deserved to hear it. But I could tell he didn't know whether to be pleased or pained by the hypothetical nature of what would go down in the history books under the chapter titled "What Might Have Been."

"Eliza, are you sure you're okay?"

Loring had the most sympathetic eyes—soft, brown, velvet havens where you could stash secrets and know they'd be safe, and I was a moment away from unloading the whole Drones dilemma into them. I even thought about asking Loring to call Doug. If anyone could talk some sense into Paul, it would be Doug.

Then I heard the sounds.

Like punches.

Fists colliding with jaws.

And that's when I decided, or, more precisely, it was the moment I chose not to decide, to just act. Because in that split second it seemed like the only for-sure solution.

"Kiss me," I said.

Loring's eyes widened.

"*Kiss* me," I said again, with more urgency.

He wasn't cooperating. He remained motionless, still leaning against the back of the couch and clearly confused beyond all reason.

I reached out and caught my finger in the top buttonhole of his jacket. Dragging myself in, I stepped between his legs and pressed my lips to his.

It only took a moment for Loring to open his mouth to

me. A second later his hands found the sides of my face and I felt the tips of his fingers in my hair.

I was hyper-aware of every detail: Loring's height, the softness of his tongue in my mouth, the warmth of his palms on my cheeks, the metal rivets on his jacket pressing against my chest, the sexy green smell.

And above it all, the punches.

I counted them down like a song about to begin.

Four—

Three—

Two—

Paul didn't make a sound upon entering the room. Or, if he had, I never heard it. I never heard a thing until he whispered my name with a question mark chasing after the last vowel, as if holding on to the possibility that he'd walked into the wrong apartment.

"Liar," he spat. "Fucking whore."

But I could forget that. I could put all words out of my mind. It was the expression on his face that threatened to crush me. The look in his eyes that would remain.

This is for your own good, I wanted to tell him.

In the instantaneous daydream I'd had, the one that had compelled me to kiss Loring, I had imagined our lips touching, and then the movie in my head cut directly to Paul and the band en route to San Francisco. I had failed to consider all the scenes that might happen in between—the way Paul's face turned from enchanted to fossilized in a second, or the way his white-blue eyes became the color of dirty dishwater and echoed with the ancient history of his soul—a soul that suddenly seemed resigned to the fact that what it had been searching for, what it believed it had found, was impossible to find.

It was the same look that caught my eye that day on the

subway, the one that said: *I have everything on my side except destiny.*

"Get out," Paul said. "Both of you."

Loring took a step forward like he wanted to say something to Paul. I had no idea what he could have said, but I shot him a look and he kept quiet.

Paul spoke again. This time he raised his voice, but only on selective words. "Get *out* of my *god* damn *house.*"

He went into his room and closed the door. I'd expected a slam, had yearned for it even. But Paul shut it so gently it hardly made any noise at all.

I walked to the door and leaned my forehead on the splintery wood, picturing Paul in the same position on the other side. When I reached down and touched the knob, he said, "Don't you dare."

I heard him flip the lock and walk across the room. Then I heard the sound of something, possibly a guitar, crash against the wall.

"Go," he said. "*Now.*"

I went into my room, sat down on my bed, and pondered, just for a moment, the absurdity of sacrifice.

I stuffed a duffel bag full of clothes and shoes and whatever else I thought I might need. Then Loring and I walked out of the apartment, down the stairs, and got in a cab.

In the impatient tone of a native New Yorker, the cab driver asked his two dazed passengers where we were going. I almost told him to take us to Coney Island, for lack of any better idea, but I wasn't sure where or what Coney Island was, and at the last minute I decided I wanted to cross the Hudson River.

"Jersey," I said.

Loring looked at me sideways, as if the possibility I was out of my mind had just dawned on him. He leaned forward so that his head was past the Plexiglas partition that divided the front seat from the back and said, "Seventy-seventh and Central Park West."

I was shivering, only partially from the cold, and when I reached across my chest to bundle up I realized I was still wearing my robe. I slipped on a pair of jeans and a sweater while Loring stared out the window and the cabbie tried to sneak a peek.

"What just happened back there?" Loring said once I was dressed. "It was like you knew he was coming. Like you did it on purpose."

There was a penny on the floor next to my left foot. I picked it up and said, "My mom used to tell me pennies were from heaven."

"What?"

It was weird mentioning my mom. I did it so rarely. But once in a while a memory would surprise me, and I would feel the need to let it out. "My mom said if you found a penny on the ground, or somewhere it was unusual for a penny to be, like the floor of a cab, you're supposed to check the date on it because someone who was born or died in that year sent the penny to you as a message of love."

Loring asked me what year was stamped on the penny but I slipped it into my pocket without looking because I had no desire to know who was trying to communicate a message of love at such an inconvenient time.

"Are you going to tell me what's going on?" Loring mumbled.

I fingered the penny, trying to guess which side was heads and which was tails.

"Eliza, you kissed me. Don't you think you owe me an explanation?"

"Stop the cab!" I screamed, even though traffic was at a standstill and the cab hadn't moved in a minute.

I jumped out and trudged in slow motion down the

sidewalk, wanting to run but feeling like I was underwater. Glancing back, I saw Loring get out after me. He accidentally knocked my robe to the pavement, picked it up, and tossed it back into the car. I heard him tell the driver not to go anywhere, and then he was calling my name, asking me to wait.

I stopped at the corner of Houston and Broadway, covered my face with my hands and began to sob.

Loring put his arms around me, pulled my head into his chest, and told me everything was going to be all right. And I believed him, one-hundred percent, until some jackass in a tie-dyed shirt interrupted the safety of the moment by tapping Loring on the shoulder and asking him if his old man was ever going to put out another freakin' record.

Loring made the best milkshake in the world. So good I told him he could win an award. So good it would have made Burke and Queenie pee their pants.

"I make them for the boys when they have boo-boos," he said. But he wouldn't tell me what was in it. "Secret recipe I'll take to my grave."

I saw him add milk, chocolate ice cream, and a thick glob of peanut butter to the blender, but after that he pulled a couple of tin cans off his spice rack, covertly threw in a pinch of this and a pinch of that and then *presto!*—the best milkshake in the world.

While I drank my milkshake, I talked and Loring listened. I started at the beginning, with Doug's dying-man-on-the-cross analogy, his "save the savior" advice, in case Loring had forgotten my *Sonica* treatise on the subject, and so it looked like I had at least peripherally sane justification for my behavior. Then I told Loring about Feldman, about the latkes and the sticky fingers, about Paul intending to turn down the tour, and about how I refused to be responsible for ruining the lives and careers of the two men whose happiness meant more to me than my own simply because I was too chickenshit to fly.

After I finished the milkshake and the explanation, Loring said, "So, technically, this is my dad's fault?"

I had to laugh, even if it was a weak laugh that made my

eyes water again.

"Dying man on the cross, my ass." Loring's face was sardonic. "He was probably high when he said that."

Loring didn't get it. His approach to his work was too effortless, too practical. Not life-or-death like it was for Paul and Doug. Neither did Loring grasp the significance of his vocation, nor the mediocrity of the industry with which he had to contend.

I gazed up from my glass and noticed Loring gazing at me in a way that filled me with remorse. "I can't believe you're still speaking to me," I said. I reached out to touch his hand, but then decided against it. "I'm *so* sorry, Loring. For not having the decency to talk to you last week, for not calling you back, and for kissing you like that."

He picked up my glass and began rinsing it out.

"You think I need a lobotomy, don't you?"

He shut off the tap but kept his hand on the faucet as if he needed it to lean on. "What I think is that you're being incredibly unfair to Paul. You do realize he thinks there's something going on between us now? Way more than that kiss, no doubt."

"That's the whole point. Come on, even you have to admit only a fool would turn down an opportunity to tour with the Drones."

"Has it ever occurred to you that maybe Paul doesn't want what you think he wants?"

"He doesn't know what he wants."

"Yes, he does. And more than anything, it seems he wants you."

"Then he's a bigger fool than I give him credit for."

While Loring continued to clean up the kitchen, I forced myself to do what I'd been dreading since the whole incident went down. I had to call Michael and Vera.

Vera answered, and her tone was disparaging, to say the least. "Mother-of-Pearl, Eliza, Paul is *freak*ing out. What in the name of God are you doing?"

"Can I crash with you for a few days?"

"Can you *crash* with us? That's all you have to say? I'm your friend, remember? Two days ago you told me you weren't interested in Loring."

"Can I or can I not stay with you?"

Vera put her hand over the mouthpiece, garbled something I couldn't hear, then got back on and said, "Michael said we don't have room."

Their couch converted into a bed. They had room.

"Forget it."

I hung up and Loring said, "You can stay here, you know."

"Thanks, but I don't think that's a good idea."

"For the record, I don't agree with what you're doing. But if you're hell-bent on making Paul think we're having some sort of torrid affair, moving in with your brother isn't going to convince him."

He was right. In any case, I didn't have a choice. Burke and Queenie's apartment wasn't much bigger than a station wagon, and when I tried to reach Michael again later, Vera said the reason he couldn't talk was because he was with Paul.

The bed in Loring's guest room was made as nicely as his had been the day I interviewed him, and I considered sleeping on top of it instead of getting underneath the covers so I didn't mess it up.

Loring gave me an extra blanket in case I got cold, and told me if I needed anything else, or if I just wanted to talk, all I had to do was knock on his door. He said goodnight, and then hesitated before leaving the room. "I know it's none of my business, but I'm going to say it anyway: He deserves to know the truth."

"Promise me you won't say anything to him."

"Eliza—"

"Please, Loring. You have to promise."

He scratched his temple. "I promise."

The next morning Loring woke me up with a sequence of quiet knocks, then leaned his head into the room. "Your brother's here."

I sat up, pushing my hair off my face. "You didn't tell him anything, did you?"

"No. And I can tell by the way he's looking at me I've become the devil incarnate. He thinks this is my fault."

Michael met me wearing a mask of confusion, narrowing his eyes every time Loring moved. It was unusual for Michael to display so much blatant hostility and it immediately put me on edge.

Loring excused himself, saying he'd promised Sean and Walker a soccer game in the park even though it was January. Before he left he took me aside and said, "Think about what you're doing before you do it."

Michael gazed out the wall of windows and kept his back to the elevator until Loring was gone, and then he turned around with his hands deep in the pockets of his coat. "I'm only here because Paul asked me to come. I have no idea what to say." He wandered over to the table behind the couch and picked up a photograph of Doug and Lily with the twins between them. "Any minute now," he sighed, setting the photo back down, "feel free to tell me what's going on."

I bit the sides of my cheeks. "It's complicated."

"Complicated? *I'll* say. I thought you and Paul were in love. I thought you were *moved* by each other. Do you have any idea what he's going through right now?"

I didn't want to know, and I was sure I would disintegrate if Michael told me. If I was going to pull off the farce I'd started, I needed to imagine Paul in a state of perpetual bliss, the cocky-bastard grin plastered across his face. "I wish I could explain but I can't."

"Can you *try*?" Michael didn't raise his voice but he didn't have to. His aggravation manifested itself in every gesture, and something about his stoicism, in combination with his height and hair, made me want to run and hide. It felt like being reproached by Abraham Lincoln.

"You know," Michael huffed, "when you and Paul got together, I lost a lot of sleep worrying he was going to break *your* heart. Never in a million years did I think you'd be the one out fucking around."

If Michael was trying to make me feel as small as possible, it was working. The irony was that he should've been thanking me, not chastising me.

"Eliza, I heard that song in Boston—"

"Listen, I really don't need you to judge me right now. You have no idea what I'm doing or why I'm doing it."

"Are you or are you not sleeping with Loring?"

I knew it wasn't Michael posing the question. He would never want to know a thing like that. "Did Paul send you here to ask me that?"

"Why do you make it sound like that's relevant to your answer?"

My ensuing silence only angered Michael more. He marched to the elevator and pushed the call button.

Approaching him with caution, I said, "What about the tour?"

"The *tour*? What *about* the tour?"

The elevator arrived, and Michael couldn't get in fast enough, but I stood in the way of the doors. "Has Paul said anything about the tour in the last twenty-four hours?"

"Let me put it this way, due to recent developments he's looking forward to getting away for awhile."

I took a step back, watched the elevator close, and actually thought I heard the sound of my heart crack in two.

Every day before the band left for San Francisco was a pin prick in my chest. Not since Adam left had I felt so lost. Somehow Loring managed to keep me from completely falling apart. As a friend, his attention to detail was flawless. He went running with me, checked up on me at work, made sure I ate, and on weekends he would eclipse the bounds of compassion and pathos by inviting me to Vermont with his family.

I never went to Vermont. Between Loring's explanation to his relatives and my own evasiveness, what the Blackmans knew of the situation was highly skewed and, I figured, would only produce *Three's Company*-like confusion.

Everyone knew Loring had feelings for me. They knew Paul and I had split up. And they knew Loring was the supposed catalyst for the split—a rumor he was under strict orders not to deny. Lastly, they knew I was bunking at Loring's apartment. But the situation was incomprehensible to all except Sean and Walker. They were the only ones who got straight answers.

"Daddy," Sean said, "does Eliza live here now?"

"She's staying for a while."

"Why?"

"Because she's a friend and she needs a place to live. And that's what friends do, they help each other out."

"She doesn't have a house?"

"Not right now."

"What happened to it?"

"Someone else is living there."

"Who?" Walker asked, suddenly interested in the conversation. "The boy with the shiny belt?"

It's amazing what kids remember, I thought.

"That boy's name is Paul," Loring told his son.

"Paul!" Walker yelled the name with a series of energetic nods.

"Where's Paul?" Sean said.

Loring picked Sean up and kissed his head. "Paul's getting ready to go on tour."

I waited for Loring to explain what "going on tour" meant. Then I realized Sean and Walker already knew. They'd spent half their little lives on tour.

The Friday before Bananafish was scheduled to depart for San Francisco, Vera called me at work and asked me to meet her for lunch.

I'd been avoiding Vera. I was afraid of all the questions. But I missed her. And earlier that day Lucy had gotten wind of my new living situation. She'd stopped me in the hall and said, "I heard you and Junior finally came out of the closet," and I knew if I didn't take time to see my friend, I was apt to murder Lucy before the clock struck twelve.

Putting on a happy face, I met Vera at a diner on Ninth Avenue that smelled like retro coffee—what coffee used to smell like before it got hip.

"This place stinks like Folgers," Vera said when she walked in.

The next three words out of her mouth were: "So, how's Lori?"

"Fine. Good. Great." I tried to sound normal, and I was obscuring my face with the menu so Vera wouldn't be able to read my expressions. "I mean, well, he's going to Vermont tonight. With the boys. But he's great."

While we waited for a server, Vera pulled a package of peanut M&Ms from her purse, poured half the bag into her palm and offered me the rest.

"Start talking," she said.

I turned down the candy and went on about work. "I'm finally getting some good assignments. Lucy still hates me, of course. But Terry thinks I've got a voice. That's what he said. He likes my voice. I might get to interview David Bowie in April."

I thought that would distract Vera. David Bowie was one of her favorites. Or maybe I was trying to spark my own interest. A year earlier I would've been doing cartwheels over the chance to interview David Bowie. But, talking about it with Vera, I felt nothing.

Maybe it was true what Paul said about dreams. When they come true in reality, they never feel the same as they do when you imagine them.

"I don't mean *work*," Vera said.

Telling Vera what she wanted to hear turned out to be easier than I'd anticipated. I made up an elaborate, off-the-cuff story about how I'd been confused, that between the wedding, the tour, and then Loring's wooing, it was all too much and I just cracked.

Two at a time, Vera ate her peanut M&Ms. Except for the red ones. These, she alleged, were made from the guts of dead bugs. She put the red ones in a pile next to the salt shaker. "I'm not here to judge you, you know that. I love you no matter what happens. I just want to make sure you're making the right decision." Vera accidentally put a red candy in her mouth. She didn't notice and I didn't know whether to tell her.

"I am," I said. "Anyway, all is fair in love and war, right?"

It was, by far, the dumbest cliché I had ever uttered. It was an insult to love and an inadmissible exoneration of war. And certainly history proves that there's nothing fair about either one.

Sliding my hand across the table, I squeezed Vera's hand. I wanted Vera to know things she couldn't know. I wanted her to know the truth.

"What?" she said.

"Nothing. Just thanks, that's all."

I tried to arrange Vera's red M&Ms into the shape of a P but there weren't enough. The closest I could get was a lowercase l, or maybe it was a capital I. Either way I took it as a devastating omen.

"Have you seen him?" I asked.

"Paul? I saw him last night. I see him every night."

"Is he all right?"

Vera laughed glibly. "Hmm. *No.*"

Forget that stupid saying about it being better to have loved and lost than never to have loved at all. Letting Paul go felt like the end of the world, and there were nights when I wished I'd never met him.

The day my twenty-eighth birthday rolled around, I would have been content to let it slip by in abeyance, but Michael and Vera insisted I celebrate with them, and the three of us met at a Mexican restaurant on Amsterdam Avenue for an agonizing meal.

Because Michael was getting ready to leave, he and Vera were in a lovey-dovey mood, holding hands and feeding each other tastes of this and that, sharing margaritas. I wanted to push them both into a deep manhole and close the lid.

And Michael had taken to pretending Paul didn't exist. All he talked about was how he and Vera were going to get a dog as soon as he got back from the tour, and how they couldn't decide what kind to get, as Michael wanted something small, conducive to apartment living, whereas Vera wanted a "real" dog.

"If it's less than twenty pounds, it's a rodent," she said.

Vera talked about the weather in Brooklyn as if it were a continent away, and then spent the remainder of dinner telling me about a corporate law test she'd been studying for all week.

I asked the waitress for a box of crayons and tried to do

the maze on the back of the children's menu, but I kept hitting dead ends.

Dinner ended without one mention of Paul or Loring.

Later that night, while I was trying to beat Walker's high score on *Sonic the Hedgehog*, Loring called from Vermont.

"The boys want to tell you something," he said.

Walker got on first and sang a mangled version of "Happy Birthday" while Sean mumbled in the background, sounding just like his father. After Walker gave his brother the phone, Sean told me about the walkie-talkies he got for his last birthday. Then he said, "We're making popcorn. Here's my dad okay bye."

"How did you know it was my birthday?"

"I have my ways," Loring said. "Hey, would you mind looking up a phone number for me? My book is in the nightstand, left side of my bed."

The nightstands on either side of Loring's bed were two square cubes made of burnished oak, with little mesh doors that opened in front.

I checked the first cube. "It's empty," I said, staring at a bare shelf.

"Are you sure you're on the left side of the bed?"

"Well, it's the left side if you're in the bed. You know, facing the TV."

He laughed. "Try the other left side."

Instead of crawling across the mattress and messing it up, I walked around. There were a few books inside the cube, along with a pair of broken glasses, a toy car, and a notebook-sized box wrapped in white tissue paper.

"Happy Birthday," he said.

I shook my head even though no one could see me. "Loring, I can't."

"You have to. It took me hours to find it. You'll hurt my

feelings if you don't at least open it."

I sat down on the floor, turned the gift over a few times, and shook it. Nothing rattled. "What is it?"

"*Open* it."

The extent to which I was touched by Loring's gesture surprised me. I tore the paper along the seam where it had been taped together. Underneath the wrapping I felt glass, and I could see the back of a frame on the other side. I lifted it up and turned it around. A tear fell down my cheek and splashed over the word *sky*.

In my hands, under the glass, was a piece of paper containing the handwritten words to "The Day I Became a Ghost." The paper had been torn out of a spiral notebook and still had the frayed ends on the left side. Phrases had been crossed out here and there, new ones written on top of old ones, and there were thin lines drawn through a never-before-seen verse that hadn't made the final cut.

"I know that's your favorite song," Loring said. "Those are the original lyrics."

I sniffled.

"Eliza, are you crying?"

"No."

"Yes, you are. Shit, I'm sorry. I was only trying to cheer you up."

"You did. It's just that, well, sometimes happiness hurts."

A little before midnight the doorman buzzed me. "There's a Mr. Hudson looking for you."

"*What?*" I said. "He's *here?*"

"Should I send him up?"

"No! Tell him I'm not answering."

But I heard Paul shout, "I'm not leaving until I see her!" Then, sounding like he'd set his lips right on top of the mouthpiece: "Tell your fucking boyfriend to call the goddamn police if he wants! They'll have to drag me out kicking and screaming!"

He was obviously drunk, and bordering on disorderly.

"I'll be right down."

Paul was standing near the reception desk, examining the doorman's pen as if he'd never seen a writing instrument. As soon as he heard the elevator he turned around. He was glassy-eyed and off-balance, and all I wanted to do was put my hand on his heart, drag him upstairs, and show him that the original opening line to "The Day I Became a Ghost" wasn't *I was only a child when I learned how to fly* but the more applicable *All I ever wanted was to be able to fly*.

I led Paul out the door, and neither of us said a word while we crossed the street. Once we made it to the other side, Paul stopped to stare at the building. He was babbling incoherently. The only words I caught were "fucking uptown" and "pancreas." He still had the doorman's pen in his hand.

"Are you in *love* with him?" he said, his head lifted to the sky, his pronunciation of the word *love* like a tennis ball he'd just lobbed into the air.

I bit the sides of my cheeks and kept walking until we were at the entrance to the park. Paul stopped when I did, landing under a street lamp that cast a heavenly yellow nimbus around his head. The pen was gone. He'd either put it in his pocket or dropped it.

"How long this has been going on?" he said. "Since the tour? The interview?" He tried to kick a garbage can but missed by a foot. "When did you start *fucking* him, Eliza?" I didn't reply, and he seized me, not roughly, but desperately. "How about showing a little remorse then, huh? How about pretending that at some point over the last year and a half you actually gave a damn about me?"

I could smell something hot and cinnamony on his breath. Big Red. He was chewing gum and I wanted to open his mouth and take the gum and keep it under my tongue until he got back from the tour.

He grabbed my hand and slammed it palm-down into his chest. "*Can you feel that?*"

I didn't know what he was alluding to, but I couldn't feel anything through his coat—it was as though his heart had stopped—and it threatened to break me down while I twisted out of his arms.

"Don't do this to me, Eliza. Please. I *need* you."

I looked at Paul. He was crying.

"You don't need me," I said, wondering whether or not I believed it.

He gripped my face and kissed me. But it was a hard, painful kiss. A severe and bitter kiss. A kiss that seemed so black, so final, it was like death.

"Happy fucking Birthday."

He spit his Big Red into the trash and then disappeared into the park. As soon as he was out of sight I tried to find the gum but it was too dark, there were too many liquids spilling out over the garbage, and as usual I just gave up.

I convinced myself it was a victory. But Loring called it a pyrrhic victory, won at too great a cost.

"They teach you that word at Yale?" I said during what had become our nightly chess game.

"Whether or not your sacrifice is worth the price remains to be seen. And unless you tell him the truth now, you could be waiting a long time to find out."

"You act like I have a choice."

"Do you really think you don't?"

What I had was hope and denial, and sustaining just the right amount of these devices is what had enabled me to endure the days leading up to Bananafish's departure. "Once Paul is gone," I said, "it'll get easier."

Loring took one of my knights. "How long do you plan on keeping up this charade?"

"Just until July."

"July," he said. "*July*?"

Deciding whether to move my rook to take one of his pawns, or to sacrifice my knight to take his bishop, I explained my plan: I would wait until Paul returned in July, tell him everything then, and hope for the best. Although, according to Vera, there was talk of a European tour in the fall, which could complicate things all over again.

"Eliza," Loring sighed, "don't you see how ridiculous this is?"

"You don't understand," I said, choosing to eliminate the

bishop. "Someday Paul will thank me for saving him."

"That's pathetic. Not to mention self-righteous."

"There's nothing self-righteous about offering up my happiness so that Paul can realize his dreams."

"That's even more pathetic," he said. "Besides, are they his dreams or yours?"

"I like you better when you mumble inaudibly. But if you have an alternative idea, I'm listening."

"Think about it," Loring said. "They're leaving in three days—even Paul knows he can't back out of the tour now. Why not let him go knowing the truth? That way you can work it out before it's too late."

"Why is it so important to you that Paul and I make up?"

His eyes were locked on the chessboard, and he might as well have been speaking to his queen when he said, "Surprise, I care about you, okay? I just think you'll be sorry if you don't tell him."

"I plan on moving back to the apartment as soon as he's gone."

"You can stay here as long as you want. That's not the point. July is four months away. A *lot* can happen in four months. A *lot*."

Loring's words really hit me. I imagined myself old and gray and alone, staring out a window in a dank apartment on Delancey Street, a soft-rock station on the radio. The DJ would play "Wildfire," "Seasons in the Sun," and "Superstar," and I would be haunted by lingering thoughts of Paul Hudson, wondering where he was and telling myself everything could have been different if only I hadn't been such a coward.

I moved one of my pawns forward two spaces, and Loring positioned his queen to trap my king.

"Checkmate," he said.

The next morning I called the apartment at an hour Paul often termed "the butt crack of dawn." His voice was groggy and hostile. "What do you want?"

"I need to talk to you. Can I stop by after work?"

"I'd rather you didn't."

"It's important."

I could hear him breathing. Finally he said, "Come by around seven" and then hung up.

As usual, the F train took forever. I decided F stood for fucking-slow-ass-crowded-fucking chug-a-lug train. I got to the apartment a little after seven and ran up the steps wondering if Paul could hear me coming the way I used to be able to hear him.

At the fourth floor landing I froze, struck by how strange and baleful the bleeding door looked.

Paul was standing in the kitchen when I walked in. He was shirtless, his hair looked greasy, and there was something gangrenous in his eyes as he picked up a pack of American Spirits off the counter—not his standard brand—and smacked the bottom until a few popped up.

He grabbed a cigarette with his teeth and lit it. As I approached him, he blew a mouthful of smoke in my face.

"Well?" he said. "What's so goddamn important you had to come all the way down from your penthouse to talk to me?"

His animosity was thicker than the smoke but I let it go. I deserved it. "Obviously you're upset, and I don't blame you." I fanned the air. "Loring was right, I should have been honest with you right from the beginning and—"

"*Don't* utter that name in my house."

But I never got the opportunity to utter Loring's name, or anything else after that. Time stopped, and the last year and a half of my life became a blur as I watched the topless figure of Amanda Strunk strut like a proud peacock out of

Paul's bedroom.

"As you can see, I have company," Paul said. "Can you make this snappy?"

For a second I thought I saw something in Paul's eyes that said: *This hurts me more than it hurts you.* But when Amanda sidled up to him, ran her hands down his chest and drawled, "Where were we before we were so rudely interrupted?" he flashed his cocky-bastard grin and followed her to the bedroom without ever looking back.

When Loring came home I was on my bed, wrapped in a thick blanket, trying to picture what happiness might look like if it could be contained in a piece of matter. After careful consideration, I decided happiness would be an unwieldy, odd-shaped object, like a big lava rock or a chunk of ore. Undoubtedly, it would have to be an object that, because of its properties, because of its very essence, would sink in any substance whose molecules flowed freely. This I knew for sure: Happiness would never, ever, under any circumstance, have the ability to float.

I listened to Loring putter around the kitchen and put the water on for tea. Then he must have noticed the light in my room. He shut it off as he walked by, but a second later he reappeared in the doorway and flicked it back on.

"Sorry," he said. "I didn't think you'd be here."

I tried to hide my face. Loring knew I'd arranged to see Paul. He'd be able to take one look at me and guess something had gone awry.

He sat down on the edge of the bed and cocked his head so that our eyes were on the same plane. "Did you tell him?"

"I didn't get a chance," I said, picking at the ratty tissue in my hand.

"Why not?"

"Let's just say he's moved on."

Loring reached down and lifted a piece of lint from my pillow. Then he dropped it and it sailed to the floor. "Is that what he said, that he's moved on?"

"He didn't really *say* anything. He didn't have to. The half-naked woman who came out of his bedroom kind of tipped me off."

Loring scratched his temple and said, "Shit."

"Wait, it gets better. It was Amanda Strunk."

"*Amanda Strunk?*" Loring shook his head and mumbled something about Paul being an idiot, but after gauging my reaction to that, he said, "Sorry. It's just that Amanda Strunk is the bottom of the barrel."

The clamor of a harmonica began blaring through the apartment. Loring had the silliest teakettle I'd ever heard—when the water reached its boiling point, it didn't whistle, instead it sounded like Bob Dylan warming up in the next room.

"Hold on," Loring said, and when he got to the kitchen he must have turned Bob off because he was back, tea-less, within seconds.

"You should've seen the way he looked at me, Loring. He hates me."

Loring sat on the floor next to the bed. "He doesn't hate you. He knew you were coming over, right? He was just trying to hurt you."

I shook my head. There was so much more to it. I likened it to the intimate version of Doug's *Tell me what you listen to and I'll tell you what you are* theory. This was: *Tell me who you fuck and I'll tell you what you are.*

Spiritual duplicity.

"Choice betrays character," I said.

"That's not true." Loring moved his finger along the sheet as if writing his name in cursive. "Eliza, you can't judge a man solely on his actions. Sometimes actions are nothing more than *reactions.*"

What Loring meant, but was too nice to say, was that he thought I had no one to blame but myself.

And I couldn't get the images of Amanda out of my head: The way her surgically perfected breasts defied gravity as she strutted across the room, the way her dark pink lipstick looked permanently smeared around her mouth, the way she stood behind Paul and made nail marks in his chest.

I blinked hard to make it all disappear. When that didn't do the trick I tried to create a diversion, focusing at length on Loring's warm, sympathetic eyes. I wished I could curl up inside one of Loring's eyes and hide. And I thought maybe, just maybe, Loring's eyes could make Amanda go away.

Loring swallowed, noticeably uncomfortable, but he didn't look away, and I leaned toward his face like a baby bird reaching for food from its mother's beak. The tip of my nose brushed his and I turned my head a fraction, but when our lips were about to touch, Loring flinched and made a face like he'd just smashed his finger with a hammer.

"What's wrong?" I said. "I thought it's what you wanted."

His body twisted. "Eliza, I like you. A lot. But I can't be the puppet in some two-can-play-at-that game between you and Paul." He got up and kissed my forehead. "Try and get some sleep."

I closed my eyes and listened to the carpet crunch and flex below Loring's feet as he left the room. And he never did finish making tea.

He went across the hall and took an eight-minute-long shower.

Paul was gone. And not just physically. What he'd personified, the potential that his life, talent, and love held for me was now as far away as he was.

Making matters worse, without consultation, Paul had decided to sublet the apartment on Ludlow until he returned in July. For all intents and purposes, I was not only heartbroken, I was also homeless.

Vera and I saw each other often after the band left, and she was quick to offer me ebullient accounts of Michael's news from the road: what his days were like, the cities, the weather, the people, the shows. But never a word of Paul.

According to Vera, Michael was living his life's dream. In my mind this meant Paul was too, and with pitiful profundity, this made my pain worth the consequences it was yielding.

Michael kept me updated via the occasional email. He was happy to report that the audiences were responding well to Bananafish. The problem, he explained, was that only ten percent of the ticket holders showed up for an opening act they'd never heard of.

Michael also let it slip that Ian Lessing, the Drones's singer, was an alcoholic egomaniac and "dumb as a doornail." I knew this must have disappointed Paul. Ian was one of his heroes. But when I asked Michael how Paul was doing, he ignored me.

I couldn't take it anymore. I needed answers. Closure. Proof that Paul had indeed moved on. And finally, before the band left Portland, I broke down and called his cell phone.

He didn't answer, and I left a message asking him to call me, but it was Michael who I heard from that night. At first all he talked about was Oregon, and about how he and "some of the guys" had driven to Hood River and gone windsurfing on their day off.

"Did your lead singer go?" I said. In a million years I couldn't imagine Paul windsurfing.

"Yeah. And Eliza, the reason I'm calling…" Michael's voice was dull and careful. "Paul's really trying to get on with his life, and you calling up, leaving him messages isn't going to help him do that."

"What are you trying to say?"

"I think it's best if you live your life and let Paul live his."

"Is he sleeping around?" I asked. I kept imagining the Oregonian versions of Christy and Janis slipping their room numbers under the salt shakers, with Paul and Angelo tossing coins and calling heads to see who got which girl.

Michael refused to say another word on the subject, and the next morning I called Vera and demanded to be told the truth.

"You must know what's going on."

"You mean with Jilly Bean?" Vera sighed.

"*Jilly Bean*? What the hell is *Jilly Bean*?"

I was sitting at the kitchen counter pretending to read the previous day's *Times* when Loring came home from walking the boys to school during a freakish spring snow storm. His cheeks were pink from the cold, his long eyelashes had tiny icicles on them, and the hat he wore was dusted with snow.

"Morning," he said, whipping his hat off in a quick swoop, causing little flurries to sprinkle to the floor. He put the water on and asked me if I wanted any tea.

"Paul has a new girlfriend," I said.

Loring spun around. "How is that possible? He's only been gone a month."

"Four weeks and two days, actually." I shut the paper. "Her name's Jill Bishop. Michael told Vera she leaves notes for Paul all over the place, signs them *Love, Jilly Bean*. Apparently they're inseparable."

"*Jilly* Bean?" Loring said, the inflection falling hard on the J. "Paul's new girlfriend is *Jilly* Bean?"

"Don't tell me you know her."

He pulled off his wet shoes, dropping hunks of slushy dirt onto the floor. "Eliza, everybody knows her."

"She's a groupie?"

"Tab coined the term *leechie*. She has a tendency to leech onto budding rock stars. Picks a new one every year. She just hasn't been able to pick a winner yet."

I ordered Loring to tell me everything he knew about the girl. He wiped melting snow from his face, and the two little lines in his brow appeared as he tried to conjure up images of Jilly Bean. "I only met her once, at a show in San Francisco last year."

I let my head drop to the counter with a thud, and then lifted it back up to say: "Paul's not supposed to fall in love with a leechie. Jesus, at least tell me she's mean and dumb and looks like the Elephant Man."

"I shook her hand and said hello. That was the extent of my interaction." Loring shrugged apologetically. "Tab slept with her, though. He thought she was nice."

"*Nice*? Warm, sunny weather is *nice*. You need to be more precise than that." I raced into the kitchen and hopped up on the counter. "Let's start with the obvious: what does she look like?"

He made a quick check to see if his water was boiling.

"She has a small head."

"A small head?"

"I remember Tab saying that. He thought her head was completely out of proportion to the rest of her body."

"She's cute, isn't she?"

"She's all right."

Loring's responses were entirely too evasive and for this reason I tried to boot him in the leg, but he was quick—he put his hand down and blocked me.

"Careful where you aim," he said. "I might want more kids someday."

"Yes or no. Is she cute?"

He ran his hand through his hair and sighed. "Yeah. She's kind of cute." He was surveying his vast array of teas, deliberating between Royal Yunnan and Jasmine Pearl. "But she's just, you know, she's just a girl."

"Translation?"

"There's nothing special about her."

I got the impression Loring was censoring himself, but apparently he chose to override that, probably because he knew my need to hear what he had to say was greater than his inclination to keep it inside.

"Compared to you, I mean," Loring said. "I can assure you it's blatantly obvious to Paul, of all people, that Jilly Bean Bishop doesn't hold a candle to you."

Loring was a good friend. He always knew the right thing to say. And if he'd been standing a foot closer I might have kissed him.

"Anyway," he mumbled, turning nervously toward the stove as if he could read my mind, "I thought you didn't care about Paul anymore. I thought he was a big fake."

"He is. And I don't. The bastard."

I made a resolution to banish Paul from my mind. Paul was the past and evoking the past was a worthless human ability that had evolved for the sole purpose of reminding mortals of their mistakes. Forget the noose. Forget the Iron Maiden. Forget the electric chair or the guillotine. The mind was mankind's most painful torture chamber, the blessed liberty to cogitate offering either doom or salvation, depending on one's disposition.

Even in my feeble mental state, I knew that any hope for survival hinged upon my ability to break free from the windowless cubicle inside my head. But breaking free meant letting go—a skill that required guts—and guts were visceral assets of which I believed I was 99 percent void.

For this reason, exactly two weeks after I learned of Jilly Bean's existence, when Loring asked me to reserve a couple hours of my Saturday afternoon so he could take me somewhere, my only question was, "Where are we going?"

"It's a surprise."

Loring was in the middle of recording a song for the soundtrack of an upcoming feature film. He was on his way to the studio when he scribbled an address on a piece of paper and handed it to me. "Come by around four, and we'll go from there."

Loring wrote like a scientist, with tiny lines and quick strokes all slanted to the left. It looked like he'd drawn a fence, not an address.

"Am I supposed to be able to read this?"

He rolled his eyes and reprinted it more carefully.

"Can you give me a hint?" I asked.

"A hint?" He thought about it, then said, "Don't eat beforehand."

At four o'clock I was standing in Chinatown with nary a cab in sight and only a vague idea of the quickest way to get to the Chelsea studio where Loring was waiting for me. I called him, not only to ask for directions, but to apologize for my tardiness.

"Don't laugh. I'm sort of lost."

He laughed anyway. "Where are you?"

"On the corner of Mott and Bayard."

"I thought you were going to look at apartments today."

"I did."

"Eliza, in Chinatown?"

I'd visited eight apartments in three hours, and every one was a step farther into hell. The vacancies in my ideal neighborhoods were too expensive, too dark and depressing, or, worst of all, would have to be shared with a roommate, and there was no way I was going to welcome someone new into my life. Besides, Paul had started out as a roommate, and look where that ended up.

Loring wanted to know which side of the street I was on and I said, "Left side."

"I mean north, south, east, or west?"

"If I knew that I probably wouldn't be lost."

He laughed again. "Tell me what you're standing near."

"A restaurant. Mr. Tang's. There's roasted animals hanging in the window, you can't miss it."

He told me not to move and arrived twenty minutes later in the chauffeured sedan he'd reserved for wherever he was taking me. When I got in the car I asked him for the second time that day where we were going, but he acted like he hadn't heard the question. He took a drink of water from the bottle in his lap, looked out the window, and mumbled, "You're not moving to this neighborhood. I'll call Vera. We'll have an intervention."

I told him about the last apartment I'd seen. "It was four-hundred square feet, the Bunsen burner from my high school science class was bigger than the stove, the water that came out of the tap was brown, and the whole building smelled like the inside of an egg roll. But hey, it's affordable."

"Eliza, imagine the mice in a place like that. And take a look at this street. All the people, the cars, the tchotchkes, and the noise. You can't live here. You'd go insane."

"Easy for you to say, money bags."

"Seriously, I don't want you to move into some shithole just because you think you've worn out your welcome with me."

"I can't stay with you forever. It's not right."

"Just don't rush into anything, okay? At least, not on my account." With obvious reluctance he added, "I like having you around."

We drove across town, went north for a bit, and headed into the Lincoln tunnel.

"Okay, please tell me where we're going."

He rotated his whole body to face me and said, "Promise you'll keep an open mind."

I had no clue how to interpret that, but Loring's winsome smile deluded me into thinking we were going someplace fun, so I took the vow.

"Think of this as the first step in a long line of steps," he said. "You only have to go as far as you can. But it's time you start trying, otherwise you're going to be trapped for the rest of your life."

That made me slightly uneasy. But it wasn't until we passed Giants Stadium and I saw a sign for Teterboro

Airport that I unbuckled my seatbelt and tried to climb into the shelf below the rear window. "Turn this car around or I'm jumping out!"

Loring locked the doors and pulled me back down. "Relax. My dad just leased a Lear jet from this airport, and he wants me to see it. I thought maybe it would be good for you to come along."

"And do what?"

"Visit the plane."

"I don't want to visit a plane!"

"It's all locked up in the hanger. It won't even be turned on. We'll just sit in it, that's all."

"You don't understand," I whimpered. "I *can't.*"

Loring took my hands and said, "Eliza, yes you can."

My body trembled as the car arrived at the gated entrance to the small New Jersey airport and I listened as the driver rattled off a tail number into a call box.

The gate opened and we drove until we were directly in front of what looked like a giant turtle shell made of metal; I wondered if Loring could feel me shaking.

"You're going to be fine," he said. "I'll be right beside you the whole time."

He practically lifted me out of the car and tugged me gently toward the hanger, where we were greeted at the door by a husky man who introduced himself as "Tom Martsch, the plane's captain."

I liked that the man said captain instead of pilot. Captain sounded nautical and boats didn't frighten me at all. I shook Tom's hand.

"If you have any questions about the aircraft, just ask," Tom said. He led us inside the hanger and I was glad Loring had told me not to eat.

"You're safe," Loring assured me. "None of theses planes are going anywhere."

There were three planes inside the hanger. One was a tiny deathtrap of a machine, painted taxicab yellow, and looked like the stunt planes that flew above state fairs in the Midwest. It had a big propeller on its nose, a glass roof, and held only two people, one directly in front of the other. The second plane was what Tom called a "Falcon," which I thought was a comforting name for a machine that had to propel itself through air. He told me it was "a hell of a bird," sat twelve people, had satellite television, two bathrooms, and belonged to a billionaire hotel baron who only used it on holidays.

The plane we were supposed to board, the Lear, was smaller than the Falcon. It sat six and was white with a silver and black stripe down the side. Tom said the Lear had powerful engines, climbed fast, and that under the right conditions could even break the speed of sound.

I told myself I was all right. But when Tom opened the jet's door I stopped walking, pulled on Loring's arm, and sobbed, "Please don't make me do this."

Loring took me aside and put his hands on my shoulders. "I'm not making you do anything. Just say the word and we'll turn around and walk out of here right now."

Staring at the aircraft made me want to bolt. It was Loring's compassion, coupled with the colossal silence inside the building that enabled me to stay. The hanger looked big enough to fit a whole city block, but it was completely quiet, making it seem as though all the planes were fast asleep.

Loring said, "Walk on board for a minute. Walk on, sit down, and then we'll go."

I stared at the plane, and Loring said, "It's just a tour bus with wings."

"Tell him to keep the door open."

"You have my word."

"Can I close my eyes?"

"You can do whatever you want."

My mouth felt like it was filled with breadcrumbs, my palms were damp and cold. "You go first," I said. "And please don't let go of me, not for one second, or I'll kick you so hard you'll never walk again."

He looked more amused than threatened. "I'm not going to let go."

Loring walked slowly up the steps of the plane, crouching down so as not to break contact with me. I squeezed my eyes shut, began to ascend, and he guided me up the steps, making sure I didn't bump my head on the low ceiling.

"Okay," he finally said. "You're in."

It was stuffy inside the plane, and I didn't like the way it smelled—like stale air—but Loring continued to navigate me, he kept telling me everything was fine and I managed—albeit barely—to hold it together.

He turned me around. "You can sit now, if you want."

The seats were made of leather. I imagined they were beige. Right after I sat, Loring sat. The left side of his body was touching mine, like we were on a couch.

"What color are the chairs?" I whispered.

"Gray," he whispered back.

I was having a hard time comprehending the fact that I was sitting on an airplane, but I figured this was a good thing. I reached my hand up and touched the ceiling. It felt like a firm pillow upholstered in suede. Then I reached around and tapped on the oval-shaped window. "Plastic," I said, horrified. My heart was beating so fast I thought it might pop. "I'm going to try and look."

Loring squeezed my hand and I lifted my left lid a fraction, but the shadowy images I glimpsed with half an eye open seemed creepier than if I opened it all the way, and so I did.

Tom Martsch was squatting in front of me, blocking much of my view. He scooted back into a chair and smiled. His face was too round and corpulent, like an over-stuffed jelly donut, and his teeth had a yellowish, caffeinated cast to them.

I cracked open the other eye and saw that the carpet was gray too, with little maroon and black specks forming a haphazard pattern, like a handful of confetti had been thrown into the air and left to freckle the floor. I noticed a red emergency exit sign next to Tom Martsch's head.

"You okay?" Loring asked.

I nodded, but my eyes veered toward the cockpit—the gages, controls, and the throttle were all visible from my vantage point.

I had visions of my parents, of what their last moments must have been like. The fear. The helplessness. It was too much.

I tore out of my seat, down the steps, and out of the hanger. The chilly April wind was like a splash of ice water in my face and I was certain it's what saved me from throwing up.

Hands on my knees, head down, and breathing heavily, I felt Loring's arm reach across my back.

"I'm sorry, Loring. I tried."

But when I stood up I saw that he was smiling.

"You did great," he said.

"I did?"

He nodded. "Truthfully, I didn't think I was going to get you out of the car."

On our way back to the city, Loring asked me if I felt like stopping to eat. He said he knew a great Middle Eastern place on MacDougal where, for $3, we could get the best falafels in town.

"I can't," I said, actually disappointed that I wouldn't be spending the rest of the day with him. "Vera and I are going to Queenie's to make ice cream tonight."

He told me he'd drop me off at Queenie's, then he shifted toward the window, and while he watched New Jersey turn back into New York, I studied his face in profile—the sculptural line of his nose, the way his eyelashes looked as if they'd been curled, the tawny-rose color of his lips.

I reached up, ran my fingers through the shiny locks that hung behind his ear, and saw goose bumps rise up on his neck.

"Why are you so nice to me?" I said.

It had been a rhetorical question. I couldn't understand how or why a man like Loring would have so much patience for a girl like me. But Loring set out to answer me anyway, wheeling his head slowly to look my way, seemingly torn between giving me a candid answer or a self-depreciating one and, in my estimation, decided on the only response that fit into both categories.

"I'm a fool."

I pelted him with a quick but potent kiss on the mouth. Then I turned to look out the window, and for the rest of the drive neither of us said another word.

The ice cream was dripping all over everything. My fingers were covered in chocolaty, milky goo, and the first thing I did when I got back to Loring's was put the container in the freezer before it got too soupy to eat.

I washed my hands and then tip-toed down the hall. Loring had to be back in the studio early and I didn't want to wake him if he was already asleep. As I got closer to his room, I could see the greenish glow of the TV emanating from his slightly ajar door, and I heard him talking on the phone.

Peeking in, I caught a glimpse of him lying on the bed wearing nothing but a pair of faded sweat pants with YALE written on the left thigh. One hand held the phone to his ear, the other rested on his stomach.

I stepped into the room just far enough for Loring to notice me.

"Leith," he said into the phone. "Hold on." He covered the mouthpiece and sat up a little. "I didn't hear you come in." His voice was awkward, like he didn't know how to act after what had happened in the car.

"I made you some ice cream."

Scratching his temple, he smiled and told me he'd meet me in the kitchen in five minutes, and then he picked up where he'd left off with Leith. But I didn't want to meet him in the kitchen, nor did I want to wait five minutes. I wanted to curl up next to him and fall asleep on his chest. And the ice cream needed to stay in the freezer for at least an hour.

I took off my shoes, set them next to the chair in the corner, and walked to the edge of the bed. I stood there as if I were looking into the deep end of a cold pool, trying to muster the nerve to dive in.

Loring continued to chat with his brother like nothing out of the ordinary was going on, but he never took his eyes off of me while I moved about the room.

Sometimes, to chase away thoughts of Paul, I picked a song title and tried to make an anagram out of it. Perched above Loring, I considered Doug Blackman's "Soul in the Wall," but all I could come up with was "Lost in Hell," and I ended up with a W, an A, and a U I didn't know what to do with.

I needed a distraction stronger than word games.

"Scoot over," I whispered.

Loring made a place for me, and I nuzzled in close to him. He was warm, and smelled like he'd just taken a shower.

"Leith," Loring said. "I gotta go."

I took the phone, set it on the table behind me, and maneuvered my lower body so that Loring's thigh rested between my legs. His eyes were darting all around my face.

"How about I give you two options?" I said, pausing for a breath. "Option number one: tell me this isn't a good idea and I'll get out of your bed, no questions asked."

He was already hard. I could see it under his sweats, the cotton fabric like a faded baldachin draped over his erection.

"Option number two," I said, my finger tracing the Y in YALE. "Spend the rest of the night making love to me."

He turned onto his side, put his hand on my hip, and moved it slowly up my body until it was in my hair. Then he pulled my face closer and let his lips touch the pearl in my ear. "Let's go with number two."

"For the record," I said, "this has nothing to do with two-can-play-at-that-game." Not that I was so sure.

"For the record," Loring said, "right now I don't think I'd care if it did."

I ran my thumb over his eyebrow, down his cheekbone, and kissed him, tentatively at first. But as soon as he rolled over and I felt the weight of his body on top of mine, I buried all nonphysical sensations and raced to get undressed before I changed my mind.

"Not so fast," Loring said. He downshifted to a more leisurely speed, unwrapping me like a gift, tracing me from head to toe with lips and hands and tongue, which, I had to admit, was pretty incredible, but gave me too much time to come up with more anagrams.

"Enough of the soundcheck," I whispered. "It's time for the show."

"So," I said, lying in Loring's arms after the fact. "You want some ice cream?"

He laughed. "Actually, I would love some."

I sat up on my elbow so that I could watch him walk naked into the bathroom, come back, and slip his sweats back on. It occurred to me then that Loring and Paul had very little in common, and nowhere was that more evident than physically. Paul's body was vulnerable and fragile, like if you dropped it, it would shatter into a thousands pieces. Loring was athletic and majestic. A sanctuary.

I tried hard to convince myself that having sex with Loring was a progressive achievement on my part. I was one step closer to getting over Paul. Then I remembered I wasn't supposed to be thinking about Paul and I tried to make an anagram out of Bananafish's "Avalanche," but gave up because by making an anagram out of one of Paul's songs, indirectly I was still thinking about the bastard.

"What kind is it?" Loring said. He'd briefly disappeared from the room and had returned with my robe in his hands.

"What?"

"The ice cream."

"Oh. It's a surprise."

I took the pint from the freezer and hopped onto the counter while Loring grabbed two spoons from the drawer underneath my legs. He handed me a spoon, then opened the container and smelled it. "You really made this?"

"Well, Queenie *really* made it. She figured it out. But Vera and I helped mix."

Loring said the color bore a strong resemblance to the East River after a sewage spill, but the consistency was perfect. It couldn't have been any creamier.

"Ready?" I put a giant spoonful in my mouth, wrapped my legs around Loring, and kissed him, letting the ice cream flow from my tongue to his.

At first he moaned. Then he coughed. "Hold it!" he said, catching ice cream in his palm as it dripped down his chin. "This is my milkshake! You stole my milkshake!"

"Secret recipe no more!" I threw my arms into the air. "It only took Queenie three tries to figure out your so-called *mystery* ingredients. Cinnamon and co—"

"Don't say it!" He put his hand over my mouth, inadvertently smearing ice cream on my face. He was laughing, I was laughing, and it was fun. Like a slumber party with a close friend. And it might have been a record—at least two whole minutes went by without one thought of Paul. But there he was again, popping in unwelcome in the middle of a fine, otherwise enjoyable stretch of time.

Take this, you bastard.

I scooted to the edge of the counter, slid open my robe, and pulled Loring back into me.

Loring had to be at the studio early the next morning, but he was so quiet upon waking I never heard him leave. The phone woke me a little before eleven.

"There was an angel in my bed this morning."

I rolled onto my side and hugged a pillow to my chest. "Hi," I said, conscious that I was smiling. "What are you doing?"

"Working. And thinking about you."

I took a deep breath through my nose. "The bed smells like sex and chocolate."

He moaned. "Don't tell me that while I'm stuck in a room with six men."

Behind Loring, I could hear those men, immediately recognizing Tab's voice above the din, clamoring to know who was on the phone.

"Hold on, I need to change rooms." It got quiet and Loring said, "What are you doing tonight?"

"Interviewing some band from Omaha at four. After that, nothing."

"Will you have dinner with me?"

"I have dinner with you at least three times a week. You think now that you've licked ice cream from my belly button that's going to stop?"

"I mean out. Someplace nice."

"Like a date?"

"Yeah." Loring paused. "A date."

I heard Tab again. Wherever Loring had relocated, and I guessed the hallway, Tab had followed, shouting, "Who the hell are you dating?"

Loring ignored Tab, but I said, "Let me talk to him." After audibly expressing his reluctance, Loring handed the phone over.

"Tab, does Loring look any different today? Does he seem more relaxed?"

"Eliza? Is that you?"

"You mean to tell me we finally do it and he doesn't even *tell* anyone?"

Tab dropped the phone, and at the top of his lungs he began announcing to whoever was within earshot that in the last twenty-four hours a bonafide miracle had occurred—Loring had finally made his way into my pants.

"Thanks a lot," Loring said after he got back on the phone.

"Pick me up at eight."

The first line of the first song on Bananafish's first record goes like this: "If condemned to burn for the rest of my days I still couldn't feel the fire of this much pain."

I wrote that when I was nineteen, sitting in a hospital watching my mom die. But the lyric, and the song "Death as a Spectator Sport," took on a whole new meaning the day Eliza dumped me for Loring Blackman.

Usually, the power of a song to transcend its own boundaries and communicate a completely new meaning, even to its creator, awes me. In this particular case, however, the sensation is more like nightly impalement. That song is even harder to sing than the goddamn single, because the single is about the contradictions that make Eliza who she is. It's her lightness but it's also her darkness, and something about that makes it cathartic to play. Especially when I focus on the negative.

Performing "Spectator" is like stepping into someone else's shoes, taking on the whole of their angst, and then realizing you're standing in your own worn-out boots.

It's all been so exhausting. The break-up. The tour. The pressure to sell a zillion goddamn records. Never in my life did I think I'd be concerned with how many records I was selling. But these people, they make me care. They call me up and give me numbers and figures and advice on what I have to do to earn more money than God, and suddenly it's all so complicated, when all I really want to do is play music.

Everything—and I mean everything—is a complete disappointment.

I know, I know. I'm the jackass who thought he wanted to be a fucking rock star. And sure, at times it's been fun, but if all I wanted out of life was fun I would've become a juggler or a candy maker or one of those boy band singers who dance like puppets.

These last few months on tour, I've been keenly aware that my situation is the opportunity of a lifetime, and there have been short-lived moments here and there when I've been on top of the world. Holy Hell, who wouldn't want a small entourage catering to their needs, women throwing themselves at their feet, and the chance to play for thousands of people on a nightly basis? It's a goddamn dream come true. I've made it to a place so many of my peers long for and will never even get close to. But no matter how hard I try, I can't get myself to truly appreciate my position in relation to my life as a whole.

All the perks I just mentioned, they're minor distractions. They can make the bad feelings go away, but only temporarily. And even then, there's always something lingering above it all, something ungodly and lonely that I just can't shake.

The very first day of the tour, I knew. I walked up to that prick Ian Lessing at the Hyatt in San Francisco, and I knew. It was mid-afternoon, day of the show, and Ian was so out of it he spoke to my left shoulder instead of my face. He acted like he'd never heard of the band. After I explained who I was, how much I admired his work, and what I was doing there, he said, "Right. Charlie Bucket." He was referring to one of our songs. He's called me "Bucket" ever since.

I guess I'm supposed to admit to being guilty of under-the-influence behavior similar to Ian's at least once or twice in my life, but that was back when I had nothing to look forward to except folding shirts and eating a can of baked beans for dinner. And not before a show. After, maybe, but never before.

It seems irresponsible, stereotypical, and just plain sad to act like such a goddamn rock star. No kidding, these guys are walking caricatures of the myth, and they're constantly being egged on by everyone around them. I guess they're easier to control that way, but I'm not falling for it. And part of me thinks I'm toeing the line just to spite the motherfuckers.

Irrespective of all that, I think I would be okay if the Winkles would show some respect. And I don't mean for me. They could stick me in a crate with two air holes and I wouldn't complain. I want respect for the music. It's not about the music for them. No matter how hard I try to convince myself they care. THEY DON'T FUCKING CARE.

About a month into the tour, Winkle called to tell me I needed to start being more forthcoming in interviews. He said I'd been described as "terse" and "petulant." Well, you know what? I don't like answering the same stupid questions every goddamn day, and I don't think my personal life is anybody's business, especially when the name Loring Blackman comes up.

Winkle's next demand: add a cover song to the set so the audience has something to sing along to. Something popular, he said, like maybe one of those big power ballads from the eighties.

"'Faithfully!'" I said. "Journey, 1983."

Okay, I was so fucking kidding. But Winkle was like, "Yeah, yeah. Great, Paul. Great." It was the most genuine sentence he'd ever said to me.

Before he got too excited, I told him he'd have to peel all my skin off with a paring knife before I'd agree to that. Not that I can't ape Steve Perry note for note, but our set is short enough. We fit in about six songs if we speed things up, which we rarely do. And let's not forget, most of the people who come to the shows have never heard of us. Last thing I want is for them to associate Bananafish with someone else's hit.

If Winkle and I had been in the same room during this

conversation, there's no doubt in my mind he would've beat the shit out of me.

Last but not least, Winkle asked me to cut down on my guitar playing on stage. "Let that other guy do it," he said, as if it's so hard to remember the names of my band mates.

His reason? Girls prefer their singers hands-free. That's what he said. And, well, I laughed. Because I honestly thought he was joking. I mean, that sounds like a joke, right?

Anyway, he's wrong. Eliza used to cream her pants whenever I got within two feet of a guitar.

Winkle called me a moron, which I granted him, but then he had the nerve to accuse me of having no ambition and that's when I lost it. Hell, I've been working my ass off for a decade. I sleep what I do, I eat what I do, I dream what I do, I live what I do.

I told Winkle what he didn't understand was that my ambition, I've come to realize, doesn't go beyond the music, and he said: "Well, it *has* to. This is a *business*, Paul. Not a *hobby*. Not a *religion*. It's a fucking *industry*."

Know what? For the first time I actually saw where Winkle was coming from. But he and I live on separate islands, there's a stormy sea between us, and we have no boats to get us across.

A call from Feldman followed shortly after my conversation with Winkle ended. Feldman tried to convince me that the debate between art versus commerce is archaic and stupid. He said the key is to learn how to bend but not to break. Good advice if you're Stretch Armstrong, but I've always been more of a Humpty-Dumpty kind of guy—hard shell, soft and mushy on the inside, liable to roll off the wall and crack into a zillion pieces beyond repair.

And let's face it: this mess goes way beyond Paul Hudson and Bananafish. Way beyond art versus commerce. A guy doesn't need Loring Blackman's magna goddamn cum laude Ivy League degree to understand that what most people call capitalism is actually greed, and the whole country is going to hell because of it. I've seen it with my own goddamn eyes. No kidding, it's spawned something of a cultural awareness in me. Or lack thereof, as the case may be. I've spent the last three and a half months traveling across America with my eyes pricked open, looking for a goddamn culture, looking for some meaning. But all I see are truck stops and golden arches and Big Gulps and a lot of little dreams crushed by big powerful men behind big desks.

Maybe that is the culture. Maybe it's supposed to make me proud to be an American, but all it makes me feel is positive we're doing something wrong.

Doug Blackman said it best—all that shit about America being homogenized. He's right. Sacramento is San Diego without the beach. San Antonio is Tampa without the palm trees. Miami is the Art Deco version of L.A. and Denver is Pittsburgh plus the Rocky Mountains. The suburbs are even worse. Apparently sometime in the last ten years every suburb in America has mutated into an exit off the Jersey turnpike.

But you know what? Forget it. Forget everything I just said. I'm no political scientist, I'm no sociologist, and I'm not smart enough to figure out who or what is to blame. Us lazy consumers? Washington and Jefferson? George Bush and his goddamn cronies? Sam Walton and that guy who played Moses? Maybe the guy who signed Shitney Spears had a hand in it. I just don't know.

What I do know is that I'm no threat. I'm a little Dixie cup floating in an ocean of molten lava. To Winkle and all his minions, I'm nothing, and sooner or later I know they'll see to it that me and my big mouth are six feet under where we belong, and when that day comes I expect the heathens and pagans to break out their expertly choreographed hip-shaking asses and boogie all over my goddamn grave.

One more thing I should mention—the girl. I met the perfect girl. So perfect she could have been manufactured at a sweatshop in Malaysia and purchased during a blue-light special at K-Mart. Her name's Jill Bishop and she is completely devoid of any principles. She thinks life is too short not to smoke. She thinks the reason music exists is solely for entertainment. She thinks Starbucks invented coffee. She thinks only nerds read books. She doesn't know the words to any song released prior to 1980—incidentally, the year of her birth. And her mismatched bras and underwear look like they came from the goddamn lost-and-found.

I don't feel much of anything at all for Jill Bishop, except maybe a little loathing. But that's why I let her in.

Listen, I know I've been slacking here with the goddamn audio diary. I just tried to cram a lot of information into a little bit of tape and now the tape is running out so to sum it up, let me just say that the last few months have been horrible, amazing, and surreal, but most of all they've been disappointing, and I'm glad the tour is coming to an end.

I'll check back in once I get home.

This is Paul Hudson reporting from the penitentiary of his mind.

Over and out.

A lot can happen in four months.
—*Loring Blackman, March 2002*

The summer had started off relatively mild, but by the end of June the meteorologist on Channel Seven's morning newscast warned that a suffocating July 4 was around the corner. I elected not to believe a word of it. I had no intention of acknowledging the imminence of Independence Day, hot or cold, because acknowledging Independence Day meant acknowledging the day Paul was scheduled to board a Boeing 737 at Miami International and, a few short hours later, God-willing, touch down at JFK.

As it turned out, Loring's warning had been an understatement. A little over three months had passed and he and I were now sharing meals, recreational activities, as well as a bed every night except for Fridays and Saturdays when the twins slept over and I hung out in Brooklyn with Vera.

"We need to talk," Loring said that same June morning immediately following the newscast. He'd just returned from a five-day video-filming trip to Los Angeles and was unpacking. There were clothes all over the bed.

"You wore short sleeves?" I said, partly to change the subject, which sounded deeply important, and partly because I was concerned for his safety. I tugged on his shirt. "Please tell me you didn't wear this on the plane."

The two little lines creased in his forehead.

"For someone so smart, you can be a scatterbrain. Never wear short sleeves on a plane. In the event of a fire, your arms would be pizza crust."

"In the event of a fire, my arms would be the least of my problems."

I grabbed the shirt's tag. "Synthetic. This is nothing but ground-up plastic. It would melt right into your skin."

"My Kevlar shirt was at the cleaners," he said.

"Joke all you want. If I were you I'd wear a race car driver's suit. Leather is your best bet. After that, pure wool, then untreated cotton."

Loring kissed the top of my head and laughed. "Can you imagine the field day the press would have if I walked through JFK in a racing suit?"

I wished he hadn't mentioned JFK. JFK reminded me of Paul.

"Eliza, can we talk seriously for a minute?"

I felt my face twist into a grimace. Talking seriously, to Loring, meant asking questions that seldom provided him with the answers he wanted. And it was too late to start lying to him, he knew too much.

"Why are you looking at me like that?" he said.

"Like what?"

"Like you just bit into a lemon."

I was sitting on the bed with my back against the headboard, hoping Independence Day would never come, and trying to adjust my sour face so as to appear normal. "You've been gone almost a week. Can't we just fool around?"

He finished separating his dirty clothes from his clean ones, dropped what needed to be washed into a big ball on the floor, and then sat down. "What is it we're doing?"

The question suffused me with inexplicable sorrow.

And Loring was slouching. Usually he had excellent posture, but he suddenly seemed depleted of all upper-body strength. "I found myself talking about you a lot while I was gone. Of course it never failed that someone would ask who you were and I didn't know what to say—she's my friend, she's my roommate, she's the girl I'm sleeping with? What am I supposed to call you?"

"Last weekend, Vera and I met a guy in Prospect Park who, for a dollar, made up a rap using our names. He told us to call him Yo-Yo. Why don't you call me Yo-Yo?"

Loring neither smiled nor laughed. "Help me out here, please."

"Sorry. What do you want to call me?"

"Mine."

I sighed, and Loring's expression grew even more staid. "At least tell me this," he said. "Tell me what's going to happen on the fourth."

"I'm not going to the show, if that's what you mean."

"That's the least of it. Eliza, I need to know if it's really over between you and Paul, or if I should be prepared to watch you pack your bags, hail you a cab, and wave good-bye while you drive back to your own personal Jesus down on Ludlow Street and out of my life for good."

In a million years Loring could not have realized the significance of his word choice. If he had, there's no way he would have said it.

"*Reach out and touch faith*," I mumbled.

But Jesus didn't live on Ludlow Street. The following night I rode the train down to Second Avenue and walked by my old apartment, and it looked so completely Jesus-less I couldn't believe I'd ever been fool enough to think otherwise.

For at least ten minutes I stood outside the building. And then, more or less unconsciously, I headed in the direction of Rings of Saturn, jaywalking at the intersection, almost wishing a car would turn without looking and flatten me.

John the Baptist stopped what he was doing. "Well, if it isn't Miss American Pie."

His eye was disconcerting. I couldn't tell, from where I was standing, if he was looking in my direction. "Are you talking to me?"

"Yeah, I'm talking to you. Who else would I be talking to?" He fixed me a drink and said he'd missed me. "So, how's our boy? He enjoying the life of a rock star?"

I knew, by way of Vera, that Paul had spent a lot of time drowning his sorrows in Rings of Saturn after our breakup. There was no doubt in my mind John knew the score.

"Don't be gay," I said.

"Whatever you say, Miss American Pie."

"Why do you keep calling me that?"

"It's a good name for you. Know where Don McLean got the title for that song?"

"No."

"Supposedly, American Pie was the name of the plane that crashed and killed Buddy Holly."

If John was trying to be funny, he was failing. "That's a *horrible* name for me. And anyway, what kind of idiot gets on a plane named after a pastry? He should've known better."

"We should all know better, Miss American Pie."

Leith was having a wrap party for the cast and crew of an indie film he'd just cut, and I'd promised to meet Loring there at ten, but it was after eleven when I left Rings of Saturn and started walking toward Leith's place on Leonard Street. Halfway there, I took out my phone intending to call Loring, to tell him I was on my way, but when I passed a wall of fliers advertising the upcoming Drones show at Madison Square Garden, something possessed me to call Paul instead.

I loitered on the corner of Canal and Broadway looking at the posters, looking at my phone, trying to work up the courage to send the call, and reasoning that it came down to one basic fact: Loring deserved an answer to his question, but I couldn't be Yo-Yo or anything else to Loring until I learned where I stood with Paul.

At the last second I almost abandoned the cause, but then I realized I had nothing to lose that wasn't already gone and I pushed "send."

Paul picked up on the third ring. The sound of his voice was like a defibrillator to my chest. I wanted so badly to hate him, but his voice had the power to flood all my enmity and water it down to nothing but a steady stream of longing. Despite everything, I swore I could still hear a burning supernova of hope and truth and love inside that voice.

It wasn't until his third "Hello" that I finally spoke.

"Please don't hang up."

He cleared his throat. Behind him, a girl's voice said, "Baby, who is it?"

Paul told the girl to go back to sleep. Into the phone he said, "You still there?"

"I'm here."

"Hold on."

I listened to what might have been a sliding-glass door open and close. I pictured Paul shirtless, a sheet wrapped around his lower body like a holy shroud, leaning over a hotel balcony.

It was beyond heartache, imagining Paul like that. It was heart obliteration.

"What do you want?" he growled.

"I'm not sure. I was just walking down the street, I saw posters for the show, and thought I'd call and see how things were going."

I heard him drag a lengthy stretch of smoke into his

lungs. "I'll ask one more time. What the hell do you want?"

I stifled the urge to call him a bastard, and another one to cry *I love you*. My eyes were fixed on a water tank atop the building across the street. "I need to know what I am to you."

He laughed, but the sound translated into contempt. "What's the matter, you and The Thief have a spat?" I heard him take another drag. "By the way, you're affectionately known as The Liar."

His voice was sharp as spit and every word that came out of his mouth was thicker and more venomous than the last.

"Can you be civil for a minute?" I pleaded. "We used to be friends, remember?"

"Friends don't lie and cheat."

"What if I told you the truth is a lot more convoluted than you think?"

"Is it true you lied to me?"

"Yes, but—"

"Can you take it back?"

"No, but I can almost explain it away, if you'd give me a chance."

"How about how you're fucking someone else? Can you explain *that* away?"

He kind of had me in the corner there. Nevertheless, I found his position staggeringly hypocritical. "Can *you*?"

"We're not talking about me. The question is: can you or can you not change the fact that you suck Loring Blackman's dick?" He waited, and when I didn't respond he said, "*Answer me*."

I sighed. "No."

There was a loud bang in my ear, like Paul had taken the phone and hit the wall with it. "I can't do this, Eliza. I can't talk to you."

"I answered your question. At least answer mine."

"Fine. You want to know what you *are* to me? You're my guitarist's sister. My old roommate. After that, you're nothing. Zero. Naught. Nil. Zip. Zilch. Don't call me again."

"I won't, you—"

He hung up before I could get the rest out.

In mutiny, I dialed Leith's apartment.

A male voice answered, party static behind him, and I asked to speak with Loring. I heard the voice yell something about Loring being wanted on the phone. A second later the voice got back on the line and said, "Who can I say is calling?"

"Tell him it's his girlfriend."

Because of the security measures implemented after 9/11, we arrived for our flight out of Miami ridiculously early, but the weather was shitty, there were thunderstorms and hurricane-force winds all over Southern Florida, and they told us it would be at least an hour before we'd take off.

I didn't feel like sitting around the lounge so I hit the sundry shop. I got a bag of pistachios and a carton of cigarettes for myself, and a bottle of perfume for Jill—she went back to San Francisco to restock her suitcase and is planning on meeting up with me before the show at the Garden.

At the newsstand, I stopped for some reading material. I picked up a novel called *Hallelujah*, written by some guy who, according to the inside flap, had died in a drowning accident before the book's publication. I opened the book to a random page and read the first sentence my eyes landed on:

"I couldn't give in to them because I knew that if I did, I'd be giving away the part of me that belonged to her."

I bought the book. I also bought a few magazines: *Sonica, Time,* and with the acme of reluctance, *GQ.*

"*GQ*?" Burke laughed as we boarded the plane. "Since when do you read *GQ*?"

I'd tried to hide that one, but Burke grabbed it from under my stack. And when he saw Loring on the cover next to the headline: *Life, Love, and the Pursuit of Happiness—Blackman*

Speaks Candidly, he put it back and said, "Ah, man, why do you have to torture yourself like that?"

Now I understand what Eliza meant when she complained about pity. Burke's face was a goddamn symphony of the stuff.

Less than five minutes after we took off, the first officer announced they were expecting moderate to severe turbulence for the next half hour. He asked everyone to stay in their seats with their seatbelts fastened until he shut off the sign.

I didn't think it was any big deal, but most of the tour personnel, who were seated toward the back, acted like they'd just been told the plane was going down. They all started rustling in their seats, their lips formed little Os of worry, and they talked in these hushed tones that sounded like a bunch of elves behind me.

But the real ruckus was coming from the front of the plane, where Ian was laughing and singing a drunken medley that included the best of Jim Croce, Pasty Cline, Harold "Hawkshaw" Hawkins, Rick Nelson, and every other music-related plane-crash fatality that popped into his blueberry-sized brain.

Eliza would have hated that. With a passion only she would have been capable of exhibiting.

Burke put on his earphones and fidgeted. Angelo bounced his way up to the galley and armed himself with a can of tomato juice and a mini bottle of Smirnoff. I asked him to grab me a soda and he told me to fuck off. Angelo and I haven't been getting along. He keeps accusing me of undermining my success and I keep lecturing him about falling prey to the trappings of the rock 'n' roll lifestyle. Another week on the road and I'm sure it would've come to blows.

The flight got bumpy, worse than I'd ever experienced. But what can you do? It's not like they could pull over and let us out. I tightened my seatbelt and stared out the window. And maybe Burke was right. Maybe I do like to torture myself. Because I kept trying to picture all the things Eliza would have been doing if she'd been there. I knew exactly what she would have wanted to do—walk up to Ian and kick him, only she would have been too afraid to get out of her seat.

"Turbulence is like driving on a worn-out road," I would have explained to her. "Just a couple potholes. Nothing to worry about." Then I would have pulled down the shades, held both of her hands and sang "To Sir with Love" or something by Jeff Buckley until the bumps went away.

The plane flew into a thicker, darker cloud, and we all shook like little bits on the inside of a rattle. That's when Burke tapped me on the shoulder and asked me if I was scared. I wasn't. "Not with that guy around," I said, pointing at Caelum asleep across the aisle. "He's a guardian angel for the whole rotten bunch of us."

According to my calculations, the law of probability was on our side, as the likelihood of Michael being in a plane crash after losing his parents in one seemed nonexistent. No exaggeration, the plane could've run out of fuel or flown into a wind shear and I still would've expected to walk away unscathed. Had Eliza been with us we'd have been doubly blessed.

"Bring on the hurricane!" I shouted. "Fate is on our side!"

Burke said if I didn't shut up I was going to jinx the flight, but I assured him that the jerk-off up front singing "Crazy Train" at the top of his lungs was the real bad luck charm.

Just between me and you, tape recorder, the reason Burke was such a basket case was because he'd had a little incident in Austin where he'd gotten drunk and ended up fooling around with some chubby blond who worked for the caterer. Only Burke. There are supermodel-caliber groupies everywhere and he ends up with the caterer. Anyway, to say he felt guilty is an understatement. He was positive the flight was the wrath of God raining down on him. And he swore he was going to confess to Queenie as soon as he got home. Then he said, "Do you think I should tell her? Paul? I should tell her, right?"

Thinking about Eliza had put me in a crappy mood. Burke's

my friend, he needed my shoulder to lean on, but you know how I answered him? I told him it didn't matter. I reminded him that Eliza and Queenie were friends, and that meant Queenie had probably been screwing the mailman while Burke was gone.

Burke called me an asshole and turned the movie up so loud I heard voices coming out of his ears.

I spent the rest of the trip dwelling on how Eliza should have been sitting next to me on that plane, and how she should have been my goddamn wife. And what did I get in her place? Loring Blackman's perfect *GQ* face staring out from the seat pocket in front of me. Even if I was wrong about fate, losing an engine or flying directly into the eye of the storm couldn't have been much worse than that.

With Burke distracted, I pulled out the magazine. One more look at the cover and I decided the whole thing was part of a plot to destroy me. Loring had allowed his face to grace the pages simply to crush yours truly. Loring had "Eliza Is Mine" written all over him. Loring had "I'm head over heels" in his smile. He had "too bad, Paul" in his eyes.

But you know what hurts the most? In so many ways Loring is everything I'm not, everything I'll never be, and honestly, part of me doesn't blame Eliza for choosing him.

Let Loring be her goddamn messiah. Let Loring save the world with his sappy goddamn radio songs. I'm not trying to save the world, I'm just trying to save myself. And hell, I can't even do that.

All his humble-ass bullshit was bad enough. I certainly didn't need to see the two of them together like that. But there they were—The Thief and The Liar in a candid, picture-perfect love embrace.

Life, Love, and the Goddamn Pursuit of Happiness.

Funny. Ha Ha.

I call it highway robbery.

Overoveroveroverover.

All I wanted was a Snickers. I was in the 59th Street station, standing in a zigzag of strangers, trying to forget the words to that old Tom Waits song about riding the train with girls from Brooklyn, the one about being lonely, when the craving hit. Before that I'd been musing over the likelihood that one of the strangers would turn around and be Paul. Almost eight million to one, I figured. I had a better chance of getting hit by the subway than I did of running into Paul while I was riding it.

It was a brilliant idea, pretending pain was hunger. I walked to the newsstand for a candy bar and the first thing I saw was Loring on the cover of *GQ*. Compared to my plummeting blood sugar—i.e., self-induced, world-weary malaise—he was nothing more than a random face on a magazine.

A few bites into the Snickers, I regained my equilibrium enough to admit that Loring looked quite handsome in the photo. And yet the idea that his face was *right there* gave me a headache. Or maybe that was the chocolate. Something felt inappropriate. Loring seemed vulnerable and manipulated. A Winkle's pawn.

I realized how hypocritical my sentiments were considering I'd encouraged Paul to become the sacrificial lamb of rock 'n' roll, and I immediately questioned the rightness of my decisions, but the idea that I might have been pursuing a selfish, erroneous goal was too hard a pill to swallow, and so I spit it out.

Paul had gotten what he'd wanted. He was content. I had to believe that.

With no sign of the train, I picked Loring up off the rack and read for distraction:

...Blackman lights up at the mention of her name, and when pressed for details about his new girlfriend (Eliza Caelum, a journalist), all he'll say at first is, "She's an amazing girl and I'm really happy."

Slowly, Blackman opens up and tells me the story of how the two met.

"I was standing in a buffet line at a party when someone tapped me on the shoulder. I turned around and almost dropped my plate."

Rumor has it Blackman romanced his new live-in love right out from under the nose of Paul Hudson, lead vocalist for Bananafish, the band Loring toured with earlier this year. It's a rumor he adamantly denies.

"That's not how it happened at all," he says.

Blackman speaks with a shy taciturnity that makes me believe his declaration. He goes on to say that they live a pretty ordinary existence and spend most of their time with his two sons from a previous marriage, or...

And then there was the shot of us standing at the top of a knoll in Central Park: My arms were thrown around Loring's neck, and I was reaching up so far my T-shirt was rising, exposing my navel. Loring's arms were clasped at the small of my back.

We looked happy.

We looked like two people in love.

I remembered exactly when the photograph had been taken. Right before Loring left for the video shoot, Sean and Walker had wanted to go to the park, and while the boys stood in line for ice cream sandwiches, Loring and I waited on the grass. We'd been about to kiss when Loring covered my face, put his head down and said, "Someone just took our picture."

I bought the magazine, exited the subway station, and ran ten blocks down Broadway, toward Doug's manager's office, where Loring was in the process of planning an upcoming Doug Blackman tribute concert that would coincide with the legendary singer's sixtieth birthday in October.

The reception area of the management company looked like a nursery school. Every piece of furniture was a different primary color, and there were framed chalkboards on the walls where visitors had signed their names and sketched drawings.

The receptionist, an exotic, attractive woman—Persian maybe—with dark skin, bright green eyes, and voluptuous lips, greeted me.

"I need to see Loring. Could you please tell him Eliza's here?"

The receptionist disappeared and I doodled on one of the chalkboards. I drew a banana, but then realized what I'd done and erased it with my palm. I was rubbing my hands together, trying to rid them of white dust, when a door to the right of the desk opened and Loring walked out.

I dragged Loring into the hallway, leaving chalky finger-prints on the arm of his navy blue shirt, and held the *GQ* in front of his face. Only then did I realize how heavily I was breathing. I must've sprinted the whole way there. "Have you seen this?"

He scratched his temple and looked at me sideways.

I opened the magazine and pointed to the parts where I was mentioned. "I never said you could make my life public knowledge!"

A blond, disheveled guy, who probably spent the major-ity of his workday fantasizing about the receptionist, stuck his head around the corner. Loring said, "Hey, Lou. How's it going?"

Lou apparently sensed something unpleasant going down. He waved and then ducked back into his office.

Loring glanced at the paragraph in the magazine. "I was just making conversation." But then his focus became critical, his expression sullen. "Oh," he said. "I get it. This is about *him*, isn't it? You don't want Paul to see this."

It probably would have behooved me to utter loud, thrashing words of denial, but I didn't see the point.

Loring handed the magazine back to me. "I'm sorry, Eliza. Really." He was already walking away. "I promise I'll never again tell anyone how happy you make me."

I spent the next hour walking around the park, trying to figure out why I still cared what that bastard thought. No matter how hard I tried, I couldn't formulate an explanation that fit into my life as I currently knew it.

When I got back to the apartment I waited for Loring on the couch. The minute he walked off the elevator he announced he was going for a run. He came back an hour later, took a three-minute-long shower, made tea, and went out to the terrace with a Taiwanese Oolong that smelled like lilacs.

Watching him from behind the glass, he looked like a suddenly sentient specimen in one of the dioramas at the Museum of Natural History across the street.

I slid open the door and tried to act like an oblivious housewife. "Want me to order some dinner?"

"No. Thanks, though."

Few things were more aggravating to me than someone who was clearly mad as hell but still being polite. I wished Loring would scream at me or put his fist through the door or toss that cup of lilac-flavored tea in my face.

Loring scraped chipped paint from the iron railing. Then he turned around and said, "Eliza, do I have a birthmark?"

I stopped short of answering him.

"Yes or no?" he said. "It's not a trick question."

"Um, yes?"

"Good guess. Where is it?"

I perused his body top to bottom and had a vague notion there might be something over his right shoulder, but I was terribly unsure, and I guessed that making an inconclusive statement would have been much worse than verbalizing nothing at all.

"You don't have a clue," he said.

He lifted his left foot and pointed to a tan-colored, amoeba-shaped splotch at least an inch in diameter, right at the top of his ankle. He made sure I got a good look at it, and then he put his foot back down.

"You have one on your right wrist and one under your left arm," he said. "And something tells me that if Paul Hudson has one, you not only know where it is, you'd probably be able to find it with your eyes closed."

Paul's birthmark was on the left side of his forehead, right beyond his hair line. It was the size of a pea, the color of a weak latte, and I used to kiss it sometimes before we went to sleep. With my eyes closed.

"You were right," I sighed. "About the article. About Paul."

He stared at me for a long moment. "You're still in love with him, aren't you?"

"It's over between me and Paul. We're beyond repair. He's made that crystal clear."

"See, why do you say it that way? As if it's all up to Paul? I thought you deemed him a fake and a bastard? Choice betrays character, isn't that what you said? So which is it? Do you or do you not still love the guy?"

"I just don't want to hurt him any more than I already have. I don't think he needs his nose rubbed in it."

"Now that he's home, are you going to see him?"

"No."

"Just tell me if you are. That's all I ask."

"I'm not."

Loring turned back around, leaned on the railing and mumbled, "Go back inside. Please. I want to be alone."

The housekeeper had been there that afternoon. I could always tell because the sheets on the bed would be tucked in so tight, trying to get them out was like wrestling an alligator. I fought until every inch of Egyptian cotton had been freed from the mattress and then I collapsed, muffling my tears by feeding them to the pillow.

Why couldn't I just fall in love with Loring and be done with it?

When Loring finally came to bed he took off his shirt and got in behind me, but his chest felt cautious against my back.

"I'm sorry," I whispered. And I was. For so many things. But I knew that no matter how remorseful I felt, my repentance would only toss a blanket over the truth, and all the contrition in the world wasn't going to change that.

"Eliza, how would you feel about maybe going away for a while?" Loring adjusted his pillow and put his arm above my head. "We could drive up to Vermont, just the two of us, forget about everyone else and see what happens."

I wondered if he really wanted to get away, or if he just wanted to keep me from Paul. I also wondered how someone who could explain the chaos theory, identify every work of art painted between 1420–1600, and had four top-ten singles to his name could be so dippy when it came to love.

"I'm not clueless, Loring. I know what you want. I'm just not sure I can ever give it to you."

"I know. But I'm not willing to throw in the towel yet."

"A friend once told me that the last man standing in a battle is usually the biggest fool of all. Everyone has to know when to say when."

"I'll take that under advisement when your friend does."

An MD-80 was flying nearby. I didn't have to see the aircraft, I was able to identify it as an MD-80 by the noise it made. The engines on that particular plane had a specific tenor. They seemed quieter to me. I figured the flight had probably just taken off, and I wondered how many of its passengers feared for their lives and how many were either too smart or too stupid to be scared. Then I wondered how many of them would curse fate if the plane started hurtling toward the ground at five hundred miles an hour.

"Okay," I whispered.

"Okay, what?"

"Let's go to Vermont."

Loring eased me onto my back, put his hand on my cheek, and I closed my eyes, but when I did that I saw Paul's face above me. And when Loring kissed me, I felt Paul's lips. And when Loring moved inside of me, I felt Paul moving inside of me. And when Loring called my name I heard Paul's voice call my name. And then Loring came and I came, and I didn't open my eyes again until the morning sun told me to.

Michael and Vera lived on the fringes of an area in Brooklyn known as Park Slope, though not the hip, gentrified section with the renovated, million-dollar brownstones. Their apartment was in the basement of an aluminum-siding duplex, with a tiny cement porch covered by a green plastic awning that made even the slightest sprinkle of rain sound like hail.

Before Loring and I left for Vermont, Vera invited us over for a barbeque. Burke and Queenie were there too, and everyone sat in front of the house listening to Michael and Burke tell stories from the road while I played with the dog Michael and Vera had just adopted, a fragile Italian greyhound they'd named Fender.

I wanted to go home as soon as we finished eating. I'd been uneasy about bringing Loring over and didn't want to be there any longer than necessary. Queenie made me sit back down, insisting that everyone play the board game she'd brought with her, a game which required its players to split into teams of two and do things like spell words backward, hum songs, make sculptures out of lemon-scented clay, and draw pictures with their eyes closed.

During the first round, it was clear that Michael's hostility toward Loring had waned, especially when the two of them unilaterally declared me the worst player the game had ever seen. This came after Loring picked a card, drew what looked to me like a striped cat and a bunch of trees, and expected me to guess what it was.

"Frosted Flakes," I said, thinking the cat might be Tony the Tiger.

Laughing, Loring said, "Remember, it's a person."

"If it's a person, why did you draw a cat?"

Loring just kept tapping the cat with his pencil and adding more trees.

"Forrest Whitaker," I said.

"Come *on*," Michael teased. "He can't make it any clearer."

I tried to kick Michael but he grabbed my foot and cracked the knuckles in my toes.

Time was running out and Loring quickly drew what I thought looked like a golf club. He pointed at the cat again, drew an arrow from the cat's paw to the golf club, and another arrow from the golf club back to the cat's paw.

Certain I'd figured it out, I yelled, "*Caddyshack!*"

Everyone roared with laughter. And when the last grain of sand had emptied from the hourglass timer, they all chanted, "*Tiger Woods!*"

And then it happened. With everybody watching, Loring bent over and kissed the top of my head. And no one in the room batted an eye at the profanity of the action. It was as though an induction had taken place. Loring was now part of the landscape my friends saw when they looked at me. They accepted him, which meant they'd officially disassociated me from Paul, and as much as I wanted this to be a good thing, it felt like they'd taken a chisel to my heart and carved out all the sacred parts.

It was an awful moment, and if anyone thought I hadn't noticed that Paul's name hadn't been mentioned once all night, not even by accident, they were wrong. I'd been counting on a slip or two here and there, to feel his presence, no matter how vague. Apparently everyone else had made a conscious effort to leave him at the door, but I could hear him lingering like the footsteps of a ghost in a dark, empty attic.

I learned later that week, through Vera, that Paul had indeed seen the article in *GQ*. Michael told his wife that on the plane ride back to New York, Paul had ripped the photograph of Loring and me out of the magazine, blackened our eyes, wrote *Ain't love grand?* above our heads, and taped it to the back of the seat in front of him with a piece of gum, where it remained until they started their decent into JFK, when Michael saw Paul staring at it and tore it down.

Dead.

That's what old caterpillar eyebrows said.

The conference room he had me and Feldman holed up in felt as big as a football field. If I'd been sitting at the other end of the table instead of two seats away from the guy I would have been too far to make out his face, let alone study the rotting cocoons above his eyes.

Feldman repeated the word. Dead. Then Winkle said it again. They were like two parrots vying for the next seed. But unlike Feldman, there was a pejorative echo in Winkle's voice. And an utter lack of sympathy. "As far as I'm concerned," he said, "the record is D-E-A-D."

It's almost comical, really. I said *almost*. Because debacles are nearly always funny, unless they happen to you.

Our record was released Tuesday, January 8, 2002. I could be wrong, but I'm pretty sure almost everyone in the music industry would agree there isn't a worse time to release a record. Who in their right mind, right after the holidays? Especially by a band no one's ever heard of. And when there's something of a recession going on. And when the number one record in the country that week is by a band of musical heathens who pass themselves off as believers, but whose sole talent consists of being able to flex their biceps and plagiarize their infinitely more-talented contemporaries.

There's no way in hell I can compete with that.

As much as I hate to admit it, the gigs with Loring helped us. There had been a small but promising flux of album sales during those two weeks. After we started the Drones tour, a couple of fan sites popped up on the net, and a couple magazines even touted Bananafish as a band to watch, but neither radio nor video know where to put us, which has led to a kind of commercial oblivion that's only exacerbated our already shaky position with the record company.

I have a new theory on the situation. I call it "the Catch" and it goes like this: Had we signed with Underdog, we'd be considered "indie," we'd be considered "cool," we'd be considered superior to the mainstream simply because Underdog conjures up that kind of bullshit aura. Furthermore, our music would have been initially "marketed" toward, and/or stumbled upon by the proper audience—namely, the kind of people who might recognize and appreciate what we do. Pay attention, my obsolete little recording buddy, because here comes the actual "catch" part: I signed with Winkle and Co. in order to reach a larger audience, but Winkle's measly publicity plan was aimed at the soulless pop pagan crowd—the crowd that demands handsomeness, a nice wardrobe, or, at the very least, a certain amount of self-serving ego from their icons. I guess "barking up the wrong tree" is an appropriate cliché to insert here.

In continually trying to pass Bananafish off as part of the pagans and heathens, the Winkles are succeeding in ostracizing most of the true believers—that is, they're shunning the very audience our music is meant for—the fairly smart, predominantly liberal, dare I say misfits who probably take one look at the poseur shot of me on the cover of the record—the very shot Winkle and Clint and Meredith promised not to use—judge me to be nothing but a no-good wanker and put the disc back in the Bananafish bin.

Who am I kidding? We don't have our own goddamn bin.

We're thrown in with the other random Bs.

I will now read a few lines from a review of our show in Austin:

"In a parallel universe," wrote a guy named Daniel J. Pierson, "one in which talent counts for something, a band like Bananafish would have ignited an inferno of excitement in music. The song 'Pale Blue Jeaner' could have done for the new millennium what 'Smells Like Teen Spirit' did for the end of the last one."

Yeah. And how does that saying go? The one Eliza said her dad used to use all the time?

If my aunt had balls she'd be my uncle.

You know what I am? I'm just another guy with a guitar trying to make it. Nothing more, nothing less. And the statistics only serve to reinforce my theory. Our first single was promoted meagerly and received less-than-modest air play. No big surprise there. The second single was subsequently released without any promotion at all. Winkle claimed he couldn't justify spending the kind of money it would take on a record that wasn't generating any real heat, meanwhile the industry is such that it's categorically impossible to generate heat without heavy promotion.

It should also be pointed out that Winkle recently signed a nineteen year-old, ample-breasted, singing-and-dancing android from Indiana to a multi-million-dollar, multi-media contract.

There's no way in hell I can compete with that.

Winkle also made the mistake of assuming the Drones tour would do most of the publicity work for him, and sure, we gained a decent number of fans along the way. But the Drones's most recent release has been their least successful to date, and the tour was something of a flop.

There's more. Around the time our record came out, Winkle wasn't generating much heat either. He hadn't knocked out a hit in over a year, and in the record business, Winkles are one flop away from the unemployment line. All the eggs are now in the teen sensation's basket. Bananafish is completely ovum-less. Adding to that pressure, the company's stock is down—maybe people aren't buying mayonnaise and cigarettes like they used to, and how many people still go out and buy new CDs when they can download them for free?

There you have it—the recipe for mincemeat á la Paul Hudson.

To paraphrase: Winkle can no longer afford to take a chance on an artist who could take years to turn a profit when the poor guy needs a sure thing *right now*.

A gold record is five hundred thousand units sold. Platinum is one million.

A year ago this kind of goddamn data was completely unknown to me. Then one day I woke up, knew it all by heart, and wondered where the hell I'd gone wrong.

Probably the biggest kicker of all is that Bananafish's record sales have, at this point, reportedly tapered off at around twenty-nine thousand.

Success is so unbelievably relative. To think that twenty-nine thousand people went out and spent their hard-earned money on a collection of songs that came from my goddamn heart and soul makes me wanna do the Hustle down Broadway.

Winkle considers it a failure.

"Dead," he said for the fourth time in sixty seconds.

"What about the 'career artist' approach? Nurturing the band?" Feldman huffed, his face as pink as a baby's newborn ass.

Winkle had the nerve to say he was doing just that. It was the reason, he said, for sending me back into the studio ASAP.

Studio? I asked Winkle what happened to Europe, and shit, I know I sounded desperate, but I WAS desperate. Getting out of New York was the only thing I had to look forward to. I should probably add that a little over a week ago I gave Jilly Bean the old heave-ho. The more I saw her walking around my apartment in her mishmash of under things, sitting on Eliza's window ledge with a goddamn cigarette hanging from her mouth, the more I wanted to catapult myself off the goddamn roof.

"Europe?" Winkle said the word as if the entire continent had just been nuked and was no longer existent. He yapped for a long time about his reasons for canceling the European tour. Not surprisingly, they all came down to money.

"Do you have any idea how much we'd lose?" he said, looking straight at me and clearly relishing his domination over my life.

Winkle said that between rehearsals, flying us over there, the buses, the gigs, the merchandise, they'd be spending ten times as much as they earned.

"Hell," he said, "even a mid-level band has a hard time breaking even on the road."

Whah, Whah, Whah. He'd started to sound like Charlie Brown's teacher.

I closed my eyes, took a deep breath, and pretended Eliza's hand was on my chest. This soothed me for about half a second, and then made my heart feel like it was being ripped apart by a grizzly bear.

Even now it hurts to think about.

I didn't refocus until Winkle announced he had a big surprise for me, a proposition that was going to make up for all the disappointments.

"The Gap," he said.

I could tell by the look on Feldman's face he already knew about this. He had that "Please, just listen, Paul" expression going on.

Turns out my ex-employer wants to use me and one of my songs in a commercial. It's a "white" campaign: White jeans, white shirts, white denim jackets. Some kind of upcoming winter holiday thing. They think "Avalanche" and I would be perfect.

Winkle said the Gap pays musicians out the ass and clearly thought this was all it would take to convince me. Meanwhile,

HOW TO KILL A ROCK STAR 307

I couldn't figure out how the guy had gotten as far as he had in life, being that he was so goddamn stupid.

I informed Winkle and Feldman that the campaign would have to be white and red if they put me in it, because they'd have to fucking shoot me first.

I think that was the straw that broke Winkle's back. He threatened to shoot me himself. And after realizing that nothing he said was going to change my mind, he shifted back to the new record. He wanted to know how many songs I had in the can.

The whole time he was talking I felt myself retreating from reality. Like in the movies when the camera zooms away from the character on the screen, and the character keeps getting smaller and smaller until he's finally nothing but an undetectable little blip. I was that blip.

Winkle snap-yelled my name and shouted, "Are you listening to me? How many songs have you got?"

I told him I had thirty thousand songs. Then I laughed so hard my eyes watered. It was my only defense. My way of spitting in Winkle's face without having to hock up a lugie.

Winkle asked Feldman what the hell I was on and I told him I was high on life. This is the honest-to-God truth—I'm really trying hard. I haven't smoked pot in three months. And seeing a roadie talk Ian Lessing down from a trip just so he could finish a set was enough to keep me away from the rough stuff forever.

So there I was, sitting at that table. On my left I had Winkle looking like he wanted to kill me. Across from me there's Feldman, probably wondering if John, Paul, George, and Ringo ever gave Brian Epstein this much trouble. My pancreas was burning like a son of a bitch, my career was slipping through my hands, and all I could think about was Eliza.

Pitiful.

I wanted to run out and find her and tell her how much I hated her. And I do. Because I'm sure I could make it through

these cataclysms and survive my undoing with genuine amuse-
ment if only she were down on Ludlow Street waiting for me.

You know what else really kills me? If I didn't know me, and
just sort of happened upon myself, I'd think: Wow, man, that
guy's got it made. He's got a nice fat advance in the bank. He's
traveled the country. Women want to fuck him. He's been on
MTV once or twice, and Doug Blackman knows his name.

Sounds like a pretty fucking great life, doesn't it?

The reality is that I still live in a shithole apartment I'm too
sentimental to move out of, I smoke too much, I don't take care
of myself like I should, I've sold my soul to a devil with cocoon
eyebrows, and I'm probably going to spend the rest of my life
pining for the girl who left me for the son of my hero.

Pitiful.

No joke, the next sentence I threw at Winkle was this:
"Jeeze, Louise, it must be humid outside."

The reason I said that was because Winkle's eyebrows were
fluffier than usual—the cocoon was about to pop and I was
ready to lay ten bucks on the table, with the odds on precipi-
tation by mid-afternoon. Actually, I did lay ten bucks on the
table. I even verbalized the offer. Twice.

"Come on," I said. "Who's with me? Who wants to wager
a bet? Rain or no rain?" I smiled like a harum-scarum career
gambler and nodded for Winkle to ante up. By then he was
making steamy, hissing sounds like an old radiator. I had a
notion he might try to grab me so I stood up just in case.

He called me an asshole and said, "I'll bury you!" like some
comic book villain.

I wanted to fucking scream my head off—I'm not your toy!
Your puppet! Your whore! I'm a human goddamn being and I
expect to be treated as such!

Instead I told him I didn't want to be buried, I want to be
cremated. And I want my ashes stored in a disco ball he can
hang over his desk.

Something possessed me to walk over to the guy, grip his face, and kiss him. It was a good one too, right on the mouth. I even twisted my head left to right like the old-time thespians used to do before they were allowed to suck face for real.

I might have been losing it. I might have been having the time of my life. I'll never know.

I left the room, got in the elevator, and rode it down to the lobby. A husky female security guard with the happiest face I'd ever seen opened the giant glass door for me. She wished me a nice afternoon and I kissed her too.

Now comes the sickest part of the whole day. I left the building and walked north. I live south and east but I walked all the way up Broadway, followed the traffic around Columbus Circle, merged onto Central Park West and didn't turn again until I was on 77th Street.

I'm still here.

That's right. This is WP Hudson coming to you live from 77th and Central Park West.

It's not like I can run into her or anything. I overheard Vera say she and The Thief are in Vermont. Probably on some goddamn love retreat, having sex in the woods, hopefully catching Lyme disease or getting poison ivy on their asses.

I'm just looking at the building. I want to feel close to the woman whose guts I hate. I want to imagine what her life is like in there without me. I want to stumble across something on the sidewalk and pretend she dropped it: a flower petal, a scarf. And then I want to set it on fire.

One thing that did slip my mind—the ex-wife. I parked myself on this goddamn bench with my tape recorder, right in front of the south entrance to the Natural History museum, directly across from Loring's building, and never gave a second thought to Justine Blackman. Ten minutes later, guess who walks out the front door? Justine goddamn Blackman, with a twin on each side. They were all holding hands and I couldn't tell which kid was Sean and which was the other one.

Justine's hair was in a ponytail and when she glanced around for a cab it played peek-a-boo with me from behind her head. I saw her look across the street sort of nonchalantly, then she started to bend down toward one of the boys but she straightened back up, put her hand to her forehead like she was going to salute someone, and peered at me. I probably should've turned away or ducked but I didn't see the goddamn point.

I waved.

Justine waved back, but it was a weak half-wave, like she thought I looked familiar but couldn't place my face. Before she glanced away I saw the recognition hit her. And then the pity. Holy Hell, more pity. Like I don't already have enough self pity— I certainly don't need everyone else's. I folded my arms across my chest, slouched down so that my head could rest against the back of the bench, and waited for her to walk over and offer me an apology, or at least invite me in for coffee. Part of me thinks she should shoulder some of the blame for my maladies. Holy Hell, if she could have learned to appreciate life on tour, if she could have kept her goddamn marriage together, her husband never would've stolen the love of my life, and I wouldn't be sitting in front of her house like the pathetic stalker-freak she probably thinks I am.

For a second it looked like she was going to come over, but the doorman hailed her a cab, she and the kids hopped in, and off they went.

Bye, bye little Blackmans! I waved like crazy. Bye, bye!

That was a couple hours ago. It's completely dark now and I want to get up and go home, but the longer I stay, the less sure I am about where or what home is. I don't even know who I am anymore. Who the fuck is Paul Hudson, anyway? I can't get a grip on how I arrived at this place. This street is alien. These strange uptown Martians offer me nothing but vigilance and hostility as they shuffle their kids to the other side of the sidewalk so they aren't permanently damaged by the weird guy yelling into a tape recorder.

Yeah, I'm talking to you, lady. What, you've never seen a man in ruins before? Open your goddamn eyes. This is New York. They're everywhere.

I must have taken a wrong turn somewhere. That's the only explanation I can figure. I veered left when I should've gone right, but instead of stopping to turn around I just kept going and now I'm so fucking lost I don't think I could get back on track if my life depended on it.

Problem is my life does depend on it.

This is what's going through my head right now: Getting the fuck out. Ending it all. As I sit on this bench trying to figure out which window lets sunlight into Eliza's bedroom, the urge to let go is wiggling itself out from the womb of my psyche, being born into the chaos that is my pitiful goddamn existence.

And you know what? If Eliza was inside that building instead of on a holiday in Vermont, if I could go up to her penthouse and have a five-minute conversation with her, if I could tell her what I'm thinking, even if she doesn't love me anymore, I'm positive she would lower her chin, blink like an angel, and tell me I'm acting like a bastard. Or else she would just kick the notion right out of me. She might even rest her hand on my heart and give me one of her crazy goddamn lectures about being a savior.

As usual, no one's ever around when you need them.

Roger that.

Over.

Doug Blackman turning sixty was big news. Apparently nobody thought he would make it and, accordingly, Loring was putting together a celebration, despite the apathetic cooperation he was getting from the guest of honor.

"Dad, sit down."

Loring was at the kitchen table in the townhouse where he'd lived for the first eighteen years of his life and he didn't recognize any of it. His mother had just redecorated all four floors and it was as if he'd never been there, as if someone had dug up all his roots and planted a shabby chic field where the funky, familiar, mid-century modern furrows had once been.

There was something outrageously disturbing to Loring about no longer recognizing his childhood home.

"Please," Loring begged. "Sit."

Doug had been trying to empty his ashtray into the trash compactor but he couldn't get it open. "Everything's new in here. I don't know how to work a damn thing."

He put the dirty ashtray back on the table, then sat down and let Loring explain the details of the birthday bash—small venue, astronomical ticket prices, the proceeds going to three charities to be determined.

Doug lit another cigarette. His third in half an hour. That's one every ten minutes, Loring calculated. Six an hour. At this rate, his father would go through a pack every three and a half hours. Even if Doug only smoked for six waking hours, which was doubtful, that still equaled close to two packs a day.

Loring watched a trail of smoke billow out of his father's nostrils and then evaporate. He observed his father's hand as it brought cigarette to mouth. He saw thick blue lines running below the knuckles like cold tributaries flowing down into his father's arm. The hands were see-through gray, the same filmy color as the smoke.

Sometime in the last decade, when Loring wasn't paying attention, his father had acquired the hands of an old man. And when one of his father's old-man hands once again lifted that third cigarette to the waiting lips, Loring followed the hand upward and noticed a face that looked as if it had been left out in a cold wind for thirty years.

In a weird way, his father had always seemed immortal. Doug Blackman was more than a patriarch, more than the man who sat at the head of the table, more than the guy who cheered his son at track meets. He was a legend. A storyteller whose imitable songs had changed lives and histories.

He was also a figure that represented something Loring had been born too inside of to fully understand, and felt too overshadowed by to truly appreciate.

For the first time in his life, it occurred to Loring that someday, probably sooner than later, his father was going to die. He couldn't imagine what a world without Doug Blackman was going to feel like, and he resented the fact that all of America would claim the loss as their own and thus, for Loring, losing his father would be completely incidental to the country losing an icon.

"Tell me how this whole thing is going to work," Doug said. "What the hell am I going to have to do?"

"For the tenth time, nothing."

"I'm not performing. I'm retired, remember?"

Doug had promised Lily that the world tour he'd wrapped up in 2000 had been his last, and he hadn't performed live since. But Loring knew there was no way his father would leave the theater that night without singing at least one song. At any rate, he kept this prediction to himself to insure its occurrence.

"All you have to do is get up and thank everybody at the end. Meanwhile, a dozen of your peers will sing your songs, and maybe some of their own as well."

"No singing Happy Birthday."

"I can't promise that. Do you have the list?" Weeks ago, Loring had asked Doug for a list of the artists he wanted to invite.

With the cigarette dangling from the corner of his mouth, Doug reached into his shirt pocket, pulled out a handful of papers, and weeded through them, ripping to pieces everything that wasn't what he was looking for. A credit card receipt, a gum wrapper, an empty matchbook all got torn to shreds. The only thing he didn't tear up was a business card. He handed that to Loring. It was from an investment banker at Prudential.

"Other side," Doug said.

Loring flipped the card. There, his father had penned a roster of names that, because of the small surface area, all ran together like some crazy foreign alphabet.

The list was a who's who of rock 'n' roll: old guys, young guys, the famous, and the infamous. But it was the second-to-last name that made Loring stop and catch his breath.

"Dad, you can't be serious."

Doug stubbed out his cigarette and glanced at the names. "Jesus Christ, Loring, don't get all unglued about that. He's a good kid. He deserves it."

Loring picked up his dad's ashtray and emptied it into the trash compactor, which he managed to open without complication via the foot lever Doug had obviously not seen. He set the ashtray in the sink and turned on the water. "No. I don't want him there."

Doug laughed. "It's not your party. Besides, it's the least you could do after the hell you and your girlfriend put him through."

Loring tried to keep his cool. Evidently his father believed the myth that Loring had stolen Eliza from Paul. He only wished it could have been that simple.

"It's not just me," Loring said. "Eliza's not going to want him there either."

"I already asked Eliza. She didn't seem to have a problem with it."

Loring watched a pigeon flutter and shake on the window sill. The bird looked like it was trying to shrug something off of its back and lost a feather during the convulsion.

Doug fiddled with his lighter, and after what felt like a calculated silence, he said, "Do you remember that night in Cleveland? The night I met Eliza?"

Through the reflection in the window, Loring watched his father reach for another cigarette and light it. He wanted to grab his father's hand and tell him he'd smoked enough, but he knew Doug would have just waved him off and grumbled about being too old to change.

"I left you a message. Do you remember?"

Loring nodded at his own reflection. Behind him, his father's eyes were glued to the tiny red-orange glow of the cigarette's tip.

"At first I thought she was a crackpot, but the more we got to talking, the more I thought, this girl really gets it."

"*Dad—*"

"No, listen. I talked to her for an extra hour because I was waiting for you to show up, but you never did."

Loring felt his toes twisting, his fists tightening, his

insides coiling. It was as though his body was trying to curl itself into a ball.

The ashtray looked clean enough after a little rinsing, but for lack of anything better to do, Loring went over it with a soapy sponge. He wasn't clear on the point his father was trying to make, but guessed it was some kind of comment on fate, and on the obvious fact that Loring had failed to get to Eliza before Paul had.

"What did she say?" Loring asked quietly, still facing the window.

"Huh?"

"Eliza. When you asked her about Paul, the birthday. What exactly did she say?"

"Same thing I just did. It's my party and I can invite whoever I want."

Feigning indifference was one of the easiest skills I ever acquired. There was the cheek-biting, which kept my lips from moving up or down, thus enabling me to maintain a neutral expression. The eyes were a bit trickier, but I found that if I looked directly at a person, they tended to believe what I was saying, even if it was a lie.

These were the techniques I had to employ when Loring broached the subject of Paul's forthcoming attendance at Doug's birthday bash.

"I couldn't care less if he's there or not," I said, folding underwear on the bed, tasting blood in my mouth, yet keeping all traces of emotion from my face.

I tried to assure Loring that Paul wasn't taking part out of spite, or because of some master plan to get me back. "He hates me, remember?"

"Right." Loring sounded like a man who'd just received a draft notice. "Then why did he agree to do it?"

The answer to that question was obvious. "Paul would never turn down the chance to pay tribute to his hero, even if it means he has to be in our company."

Loring was sitting on the chair in the corner of the room. I watched him bend down to tie his shoe. He grappled with the laces, attacked them. "Eliza, I feel like things are good between us right now. I just don't want Paul to swoop down and mess them up again."

I was still biting my cheeks.

"Let's go back to Vermont," he said.

The time we'd spent in Vermont had been something of a Shangri-La: a long weekend of swimming, playing chess, cooking. Loring had even taught me how to ride a horse without using a saddle. But the liberty I'd pretended to feel simply because Paul and I were in a different area code was short-lived, not all that emotionally satisfying, and was followed by a painful recrudescence upon returning to New York. The minute the car crossed the state line, it all came back to me. Paul was in the air. He *was* the air. He hovered above the city breathing on me, stifling me, and providing life at the same time. I was sure Loring felt it, too. That's why, as we were crossing the GW Bridge, he put up the windows for the first time in hours. He was trying to keep Paul out.

Loring got off the chair, positioned himself behind me, and set his arms directly on top of mine, making it impossible for me to keep folding. "Vermont next weekend?"

"Your dad's birthday is next weekend."

"I mean after the show. We'll go the next morning."

"I can't." Michael and Vera were going to Cleveland to visit Vera's parents. I had agreed to stay at their house and dog sit. "Fender, remember? I promised."

The cheek biting was the key, but it only worked under normal conditions. Spur of the moment ambushes made nonchalance more difficult, which was the case two days before Doug's big bash, when Lucy Enfield interrupted a staff meeting to tell me that some guy who looked like a mobster was in the hall waiting for me.

I almost ripped a hole through the side of my face when I saw Feldman pacing near the drinking fountain, his pudgy hands clasped together, resting above his belt as if propped up on a pillow.

He held my hand flat like lunchmeat between two pieces of bread. "Eliza," he said. "Can we go somewhere and talk?"

Something was off the mark if he was calling me by my real name. Leading Feldman downstairs, I walked him outside and we stood in front of a newsstand.

"It's good to see you," Feldman said.

His voice was polite, humble, and frighteningly out of character.

"What's wrong?" I said, suddenly panicked. "Did something happen to Michael? Or—"

I caught myself before I said the name.

"He's fine. They're all fine," Feldman said. "For the moment."

I picked up a newspaper so that Feldman would think I was uninterested in what he had to say, and a byline caught my eye. It was a story about a guy who'd recently survived a plane crash in Peru. The guy's name was Phillip Oxford, and he'd been flying on a small South American carrier. I couldn't fathom why anyone in their right mind would fly on an obscure Peruvian airline.

Feldman said, "Let me start by saying I owe you an apology."

"For what?"

"For not appreciating you as an ally when I had you on my side."

Phillip Oxford was from St. Cloud, Minnesota. To get to Peru, he'd had to book himself on five different flights. This was his first mistake. Since most mechanical mishaps occur during takeoff or landing, and he was racking up five takeoffs and five landings in a twenty-four-hour period, the odds were against him from the start.

Feldman used his hand to push all the hair off his face. One chunk of bang rebelled, clinging to his forehead like a rat's tail on a glue trap. "Have you talked to your brother today?"

"No." Michael had left me a message earlier but I'd been in meetings all morning and hadn't had a chance to call him back. "Why?"

"Paul's quitting."

I stared at Phillip Oxford and tried to act blasé. Hearing Feldman say Paul's name, even under these circumstances, felt like a gift. I hardly ever heard his name out loud, unless it was coming from Loring's mouth, and Loring said it with too much indignation to make it worth anything. "He's quitting the band?"

Feldman was shaking his head. "The band's already kaput. I mean the whole shebang."

"What are you talking about?"

"He's done," Feldman said. "Claims he got more respect as a shirt folder. He wants out."

"What about the new record?" I was trying to keep the shock out of my voice but it wasn't working. "Michael said they spent all last month in the studio."

"They did. Winkle doesn't like any of it." Feldman was still fighting with his hair. "And we're talking powerful fucking songs. Mind-blowing stuff. Not number-one singles, obviously. But bone-crushing shit that would break your heart. Think *Sgt. Pepper's*, the *White Album*. I know you don't believe the music means anything to me, but I've known Paul longer than you have. This is the best work he's done and I don't want to see it sit on a shelf."

In my head I translated Feldman's statement into: "If this record gets shelved, I can kiss my Epstein future goodbye."

"So, get him out of his contract," I said. "Shop him to another label. You shouldn't need me to tell you this."

The weather had been storming outside of Lima when Phillip Oxford's plane went down. I deemed Phillip Oxford an idiot for not getting a weather report prior to departure.

"Winkle has no intention of letting Paul out of his contract. Not without a fight, anyway. And he advanced Paul money for the new record—a third of which has already been spent on pre-production, band, and studio costs. If Paul tried to bail out now he'd get stuck having to reimburse that. And sure, he could sue, but a legal battle would go on for years, it would cost him hundreds of thousands of dollars, and essentially put a stop to his recording career until the case was settled. On top of all that, if Paul signs with another label, Winkle gets a fucking override on the sales of the next album. Assuming Paul could even get another contract. After this, he'll be considered a pain in the ass. Who's going to want him?"

"Jack Stone."

Feldman pointed his little sausage finger at me. "Don't think that doesn't play into Winkle's decision to keep Paul under his thumb."

Finally a smart move on Phillip Oxford's part—he'd booked a seat in the exit row. Only it turned out Phillip Oxford was six foot three. Not so smart after all, just lucky he'd been blessed with long legs.

"I don't get it," I said. "If the label doesn't like the record, and they have no plans to release it, why not just let him go? What's in it for Winkle?"

"Nothing. But he's not losing anything either. He just hit the jackpot with that jailbait hooker from Indiana, so he's in a position to do whatever he wants. And look at it from his point of view—the guy *knows* Paul's a genius. Imagine if he did let Paul go, then Paul hooks up with Jack Stone and his next record sells five million copies. You think Winkle's going to chance that?"

"All right, so where does this leave Paul?"

"In limbo." Feldman seemed on the verge of blowing a gasket. "It's a power trip. Winkle's fucking with Paul's head, and unless Paul compromises, he's screwed."

I almost made a joke about how much Paul liked getting screwed, but thinking about that felt like suffocation. I took a deep breath and focused on Phillip Oxford.

This has nothing to do with me, I told myself.

"Eliza, I don't know how much Michael has told you about what's been going on with Paul these past few months, but—"

"Michael never tells me anything about what's going on with Paul. Michael won't mention Paul's name in my presence."

"Well, to put it mildly, Paul really got on Winkle's bad side, and now it seems the guy's mission in life is to make Paul miserable."

"You mean to tell me Winkle's going to sit on Bananafish just because Paul got pissy with him? Eventually he'll get tired of the game-playing."

"About two weeks ago, I called Winkle and basically said the same thing. Ten minutes later the asshole sent me a fax—the page of Paul's contract that says the deal is void in one instance only—in the event of the death or disability of the artist. Basically it was Winkle's way of saying that unless Paul goes in and makes the record Winkle wants him to make, and says and does the things Winkle tells him to do and say, Winkle owns Paul's ass until the day Paul dies."

Phillip Oxford claimed that before the plane went down there was so much smoke in the cabin he couldn't see the emergency floor lighting. When the plane hit the ground he said it bounced. But Phil was ready. Phil had the exit open before the plane came to a stop. He was the first one out.

"Help me, Eliza. I'm running out of time."

"There's nothing I can do."

"You're the only one Paul ever listened to. At least try and talk some sense into him."

I bit my cheek and stared at the photo of Phillip Oxford.

He had a goofy, unburdened smile, and didn't look like he could maneuver his way out of a sleeping bag, let alone a burning plane. "Believe me, I'm the last person Paul wants to talk to."

I put the newspaper back. I was looking for someplace to store all the things I was feeling—the friction, the contradictions, the unmerciful truth—but my heart, my soul, my eyes and ears and even my toes were locking their doors. They wouldn't let me in. For safety reasons. I had no choice but to throw the feelings away.

Feldman held onto my sleeve and I glared at his hand until he let go.

"I can't see many ways out of this," he said. "Either someone talks Paul into making a few concessions, or something *very bad* is going to happen. I don't want it to come to that, and trust me, neither do you."

There was something sordid in Feldman's eyes—a silent warning I couldn't decode. "What do you mean *very bad*?"

"Paul's not thinking straight. I'm afraid of what he might do. I don't want it to get ugly and I don't want anyone to get hurt."

The cheek biting counterbalanced all the emotions. It was another innovation, using physical pain to redirect the train of memory.

"I wish I could help," I said, my voice firm. "But like I already told you, I'm the last person Paul wants to talk to."

There's nothing worse than falling in love with a person over and over every time you lay eyes on them, especially when you hate their goddamn guts.

It happened yesterday at rehearsal. We'd all been given designated slots for practice. Mine had been set for noon and Loring's wasn't until later so it never occurred to me that I might run into either of them.

Actually, that's a lie. It did occur to me, which is why I'd gone to considerable lengths to avoid an encounter. I looked before I turned every corner, stayed in the hospitality room until the producer told me they were ready for me, kept my eyes to the ground anytime I had to venture down the hall, and all was well until a certain uppity British musician took longer than his allotted time, throwing the whole schedule off.

It's bad enough when people I know fuck with my life, but when pretentious bass players interfere with my destiny, then I really get pissed.

What I'm trying to say is if I'd left the theater when I was supposed to, I never would've seen her. But there I was, loitering around the catering with a bag of salt and vinegar potato chips in my hand, waiting for my turn, and here comes Eliza waltzing into the room with Loring hanging all over her. They didn't see me at first, they were too busy talking, and they looked so goddamn intimate I almost coughed a mouthful of food at their feet.

Doug was behind them, along with some other guy who had a camera in his hands. Doug waved. He was trying to distract me, I'm sure of it, but I couldn't take my eyes off of Eliza. She had this black knitted shawl around her shoulders, and with her chin down and her eyes blinking toward the sky, she looked like a falcon about to spread its wings.

It was all I could do not to fall on my knees and weep like the bastard she always said I was, and I was a breath away from begging her to run away with me. I can't believe I'm admitting this on tape—I was standing at that table, she hit me with that look of hers, and I swear to God all I wanted to do was grab her hand, press it into my heart and say, "Let's get the hell out of here." I was even willing to ride the 6 all the way to Houston Street. No kidding, I was going to take the subway to prove my love. And if she said no, I was going to kidnap her until she agreed to stay.

But then Loring slipped his arm around her waist, she took his hand, and I came to my senses.

Note to self: The past is gone. Let it go.

So there I was in the hospitality room, eating my potato chips, my heart breaking all over again, then Doug goes and throws his arm across my shoulder and for a fleeting second I made believe he was my dad. This felt good until I realized it would've made Loring my goddamn brother and Eliza practically my sister-in-law, which put a tragic, Shakespearean spin on the whole fantasy and I dropped it.

Doug told me I looked well and I announced, more for Eliza's ears than Doug's, that I'd quit smoking. Three weeks without a cigarette. I told them how I've also been running. I could tell Eliza didn't believe a word I was saying.

Doug wanted to know what song I was going to do. He was still trying to distract me. I answered his question as loud as I could, and the guy holding the camera, a photographer whose name I didn't catch, told me "The Day I Became a Ghost" was one of his all-time favorites.

"What a coincidence," I said. "Loring's girlfriend likes that song, too. Don't you, you lying bitch?"

After that little outburst, Loring left the room, but not before he gave me a look of reigning superiority. Believe me, it was no skin off my back to see the guy go, but the way he was able to hold his head up and play Mr. Innocent really burned me up.

Loring looked back at Eliza like he expected her to follow him, but she and I were too busy playing a game of war with our eyes.

Doug cleared his throat and said, "Bonnie Raitt once told me coincidence is God's way of staying anonymous."

At that, Eliza let out a pshaw and told Doug she'd see him later. She scurried away. And I don't know what I was thinking but I actually cut my conversation with Doug short so I could follow her.

Unfortunately, my journey ended in front of a door with Loring's name on it. I stood there for a long time, wanting to knock, but eventually I just walked away. It's too late. My plans have all been made and the last thing I need is Eliza and her dreamy falcon eyes fucking everything up again.

Part of me feels like I owe it to her to say goodbye, but I also know I'm not strong enough to do it in person.

Today, when I got back to the theater, I came straight to my designated area. Of course they gave Loring a legitimate dressing room. This hole they've got me in is smaller than my bathroom and looks like a closet where props are stored. There are all these Western costumes hanging on a rack behind me, along with ten-gallon hats, chaps, and holsters with cap guns.

I put one of the holsters on and tried to see how fast I could draw. Put it this way: I would've made a shitty cowboy.

I still had the holster on when a stagehand named Rick came in and set me up with a fold-out chair, a bucket of ice, two beers, and a bottle of water.

"Cool belt," Rick said. He was being an asshole so I decided to leave it on.

Did you hear that click? I just locked the door. And I'm not unlocking it until it's my turn to go on because Eliza's somewhere out there and I can't risk running into her again.

In less than ten minutes, Rick is going to come back to get me, and once I get on stage I think I'll be okay, but right now I'm shaking so hard I can barely stand.

It's weird—I'm about to perform in front of an audience for what will probably be the last time in my life and I have to say, it seems appropriate, not to mention grimly poetic, that the music that began my career is also the music that's going to end it.

To take that idea a step further, how about the fact that the man who spawned the sounds that saved my life also spawned The Thief who took it away.

Holy Hell, there's my knock.

Over.

The performers had all been billed according to their popularity. The earlier you went on, the less popular you were. Paul was second on the bill. The guy who went on before Paul was an unknown folk singer married to Lily Blackman's niece.

Right before Paul took the stage, a guy with lamb-chop sideburns tested the standing mike and pulled a thick, quilted tarp off of a piano.

I watched Paul as he walked out. He looked absurd, wearing a holster around his waist and a ridiculous orange wool hat, the kind they sell to hunters in the Army-Navy store. The hat was tight-fitting and covered his whole skull, as well as both of his ears. In the front, it was pulled down all the way to his eyebrows. In the back, it reached his neck, and not a speck of his hair was visible. His head looked like the number five billiard ball.

"First things first," Paul said into the microphone. "Happy Birthday to the Man." He bowed to Doug, who was sitting in the front row, off to the right. The audience clapped and Paul waited until they quieted down before he continued.

"It's such an honor to be here tonight. And I need to say thank you to Doug, not only for asking me to be a part of this extraordinary evening, but for giving me so much more than I could ever express with the appropriate level of gratitude." His voice was shaky. "I know I'm not the only one here who feels this way, but there's been so many times in my life when I didn't have anything except one of Doug's songs to help me make it through the night…He's been a friend, a teacher, a shoulder to lean on…"

Paul took a drink of water and I noticed his hand trembling. I had never seen him so nervous on stage.

"Shit. All right. Enough sap." He cleared his throat, rubbed his palms together and said, "God knows where I'd be right now if I'd never discovered this song. Or maybe it discovered me, whichever the case may be."

I was surprised Loring hadn't pouted over Paul's choice of songs. He knew how much "The Day I Became a Ghost" meant to me and could have easily claimed it as his own. As Doug's son, he would have received preferential treatment, but he'd made the mature decision, selecting "Son of Mine" instead—a little ditty Doug had penned as a sixth birthday present to his firstborn.

Paul dove heart-first into the song, and I did everything in my power to stay detached, but my arms were covered in goose bumps before he even started singing.

Ten goddamn seconds.

The difference between the real stuff and the crap.

And the more I heard of the song, the farther back it spanned into my history. The deeper it reached, the more intense the feeling, turning over every experience I'd ever associated with it, swirling the past in with the here and now, moving it toward the future, and yet remaining so timeless that a belief in the infinite nature of things seemed obvious, if only in those brief moments.

By the time Paul got to the end of the second verse, tears were fighting their way down his cheeks and I was sure he was feeling it, too.

I was sitting in the third row, dead center, willing him to look my way. Something told me he knew exactly where I was, but he never glanced in my direction.

Paul finished the song and stood still for an inordinate amount of time. Then he took off his guitar and sat down at the piano.

This was another first. I had never seen Paul play piano on stage.

"I recorded this next one about a month ago," he said. "It was going to be the title track on our new record. It's called 'Save the Savior' and it's a little long so bear with me, or feel free to go to the bathroom, get a drink, whatever blows your hair back."

I was afraid to hear the song, but I couldn't seem to move or run or, at the very least, plug my ears.

The melody was poignant and overly sentimental right from the start, like an ultramodern, atmospheric version of one of the ballads Elton John and Bernie Taupin wrote for the *Captain Fantastic and the Brown Dirt Cowboy* record. But the voice and the conviction was all Paul, and it came out of him like an efflux of flesh and blood and, ultimately, of what I could only describe as surrender.

> *I'll say this much for him*
> *The guy knew when to quit*
> *But Jesus had more guts than me*
> *He carried his cross*
> *And cried to the boss*
> *Who deserted him to set him free*
> *And for what?*
> *The crowds that now gather*
> *Pretend it matters*
> *But the infidels get the last laugh every time*
>
> *So much for deliverance, right, angel?*
> *Save the savior, she cried*
> *But as she bowed her head and stared at the sky*

She left me alone
Left me to die

Judas has nothing on you, babe
But I guess it's not as easy as we thought it would be
A bastard was bound to falter
When even love couldn't erase that scar
On your wrist or in the stars
Or in the sacrifice I'm leaving at the altar

I still think about those nights
Living warm inside of you
Never wanting to say goodbye
Now all I can say is, God have mercy on my soul
The sweetness of the flowers always fades with time

Nobody zoned out. For seven minutes and twenty-two seconds every heart in the theater was ripped wide open, their contents spilling themselves at Paul's feet.

He stood and the audience stood with him, clapping like a rainstorm. Even Doug got up and applauded with his hands above his head.

By then I was racing down the aisle, hoping to catch Paul before he disappeared into one of the dressing rooms. At the backstage entrance I was halted by a security guard and wasted a minute digging through my purse for my pass. When I finally found it, the guy made me peel off the backing and stick it on my shirt before he would let me go in.

I rushed down the corridor in search of the room with Paul's name on it, but stopped when I felt a hand on my elbow.

"We need to talk," Loring said.

"In a minute."

"Now." He steered me into an empty bathroom and

waited until the door closed on its spry hinge. "You didn't even see me, did you?"

I looked back at the door, imagining it had sealed shut. Airtight. To abscond was no longer an option.

"I was standing to the left of the stage during his set, forty feet away from you. At one point, I swore you looked right at me but you didn't even see me."

I was reminded of Phillip Oxford. I thought about how he put his hand on the emergency exit so as to flee the burning plane as soon as it came to a stop. I slid my hand behind my back and tried to reach the door handle. It was too far away.

"I can't do this anymore," Loring said. "I can't pretend that someday you're going to look at me the way you look at him."

I covered my face and shook my head, a dual action born out of self-loathing. Not even when I'd slit my wrist had my self-loathing been so strong. But I hated myself—first, for what I'd done to Paul, second, for what I was doing to Loring, and third, because I had been so unbelievably wrong about everything.

All the decisions I'd ever made were screaming inside my head.

"Eliza, say something."

I knew what he wanted me to say, but I couldn't pretend anymore either. "I told you I couldn't do it. I told you I was incapable of giving you what you wanted."

Loring banged his fist into one of the stall doors and it flapped violently back and forth for a good ten seconds.

I was staring at his shoes, trying to remember which foot his birthmark was on.

"I give up. I'm done," he said.

I took in my surroundings with a heightened sense of awareness: the urine smell of the bathroom, the fluorescent lighting that made even Loring's lustrous skin look sallow, and the leaky sink that sounded like the thrust of a jet engine every time a drop of water hit the porcelain.

This is what it means to be in the middle of love, I thought. Being in the middle of love is like being in the middle of a war zone.

I stood there contemplating how long I had to wait before I could run off, find Paul, and tell him everything.

Twenty more seconds, I decided. I started counting them down in my head. Nineteen Mississippi, eighteen Mississippi, seventeen…

Then the door behind me swung open.

"You've *got* to be kidding me," Loring said.

I wasn't facing the door but I could see Paul in the mirror. He had a backpack thrown over his shoulder and that stupid orange hat still on his head.

"Shit," Paul said, sounding as though he felt foiled by the two people he'd happened upon.

Loring's eyes followed Paul to the sink.

"Hey, don't look at me, Sam. You wanted her, you got her. She's your goddamn headache now. I just need to wash my hands."

Paul silenced the drip by turning on the cold water. Behind his back, Loring snarled, "Fuck you, Paul," and left.

"Damn, he sure is crabby today," Paul said. "What's the matter? You get caught making out with Eddie Vedder or something?"

I tried to meet Paul's eyes but he wasn't playing that game. He seemed to be doing everything in his power to avoid looking at me. I watched him let the water run over his fingers, press the soap dispenser, rub pink goo between his palms, rinse off the soap and then shut the tap so tightly the whole room was as quiet as the inside of a coffin.

He was at the door when I turned and said, "*Wait*."

I could sense his hesitation, but eventually he rotated to

face me.

"I have to go," he said, adjusting his falling backpack.

I took a small step forward and spoke just above a whisper. "Do you think maybe we could find someplace to talk?"

"*Talk*? You wanna *talk*?"

"I'm on my way to Michael's. I'll be there all weekend watching the dog. If you have time, maybe you could stop over."

"I don't have time."

"There are things I need to tell you."

"Tell me right here. Tell me now."

My eyes were on his hand. I saw him tighten his grip on the door. His knuckles were bloodless around the handle. Like Phillip Oxford, he was ready to pull, ready to run.

"I messed up, Paul."

"Holy Hell, you have no right to lay this shit on me now."

"I never meant to break your heart. You have to believe me. All I ever wanted was—"

"*Hold* it!" He let go of the handle and his fist exploded into a shape that reminded me of a spider web. "Break my *heart*? Is that what you just said? I have news for you; you didn't break my *heart*. My heart's *fine*. My heart's in the best shape of its life. You know what you did to me? You took an AK-47 and blew my *soul* open. So fuck you and your fucking *talk* because nothing short of a miracle could take back the last nine months of hell you put me through!"

"I know I can't take it back. I wish I could. What I *can* do is tell you the truth and hope that—"

"Shut your goddamn mouth. You don't know the meaning of the word *truth*." He took another step back. "You know what *I* wish—I wish I'd never *met* you. Better yet, I wish you'd bled to death in your bathroom twelve years ago instead of living long enough to move to New York and assassinate my soul. *That's* what I wish—that you'd never fucking made it here."

I didn't even bother trying not to cry, but to retain some self-respect I pulled my shoulders back and lifted my head high. "No one has ever said anything that awful to me. *Ever.*"

But I was seized by something I saw in Paul's eyes. What lay beneath his gaze didn't match the hate in his voice. There was a trace of regret. A cry for help, maybe. I made one last-ditch effort to hang on whatever it was.

"We *need* to talk. Later tonight, tomorrow, two months from now, whenever you're ready, okay? I'll wait."

He began to quail, like he was being pulled backward against his will, like someone was yanking him by the sleeve.

"Don't hold your breath," he said.

By then he was standing in the hall. He let go of the handle, the door shut in front of him, and he was gone.

A plastic T-bone steak, a yellow ducky, a red fire hydrant, a furry hedgehog. Fender had more toys than a kid, all strewn across the floor like squeaky landmines, and I stepped on every one of them, not because I wanted to play, but because without the noise, the silence was unbearable; without the day to let light in, the house felt like a morgue.

I was alone with nothing to do but obsess over the contradiction of Paul's cruel words against the look on his face. It was *I wish you were dead* versus *Save me*.

I told myself I would feel better when it was no longer dark outside. And Michael and Vera would be back on Monday. The minute they returned I would go straight to Ludlow Street, climb the stairs, use the key that still hung on my chain to unlock the bleeding door, go in, and *make* Paul listen. And afterward, if he still didn't want anything to do with me, fine, I would accept that. But not until he'd been given the facts.

Vera had made up the sofa bed with one of Aunt Karen's afghans. The smell was too much. I stuffed it in the closet and put on one of Michael's sweaters to keep warm.

At some point during the night, Fender began pawing at my arm. The dog's leg looked like a furry chopstick. I figured he had to pee, and I got up to let him out.

It was early October, the weather had been chilly and rainy all week, and through the front window I could see drizzle illuminated by the light of a street lamp.

I opened the door and my eyes were instantly drawn down.

Paul was sitting there, heels on the ground, his toes erratically tapping against each other like two shutters in the wind. His arms encircled his knees, his head was lowered, his back was to the house, and he still had that stupid orange hat on.

I whispered his name and he leaped up and turned around, giving me the impression I'd startled him even more than he'd startled me. He had the dizzied look of an amnesiac, one who didn't know where he was or how he'd arrived there.

Fender scurried out from underneath my legs, jumped on Paul, then darted down the sidewalk and lifted his leg on the neighbor's garbage. Michael had asked me to make sure I wiped Fender's feet before I allowed the dog back inside, but when he came home I let him go right past me.

Paul leaned to the left and peered into the house. "You alone?"

I nodded. "How long have you been out here?"

"A while," he said, monkeying with the zipper on his sweatshirt. "Trying to decide whether or not to knock."

I opened the door a little wider—my way of inviting him in without having to say it—but he stood in place, chafing his palms together as if they were wood and he was trying to start a fire.

"Eliza, about what I said to you at the theater—"

"Forget it." I made a shooing motion with my hand. "I deserve it."

"I just don't want you to be thinking back on *us* someday and believe that's how I really felt. I just had to say that to you, all right?"

I didn't like the way he said *us*, as if *us* was lost forever.

"*All right?*" he said again, desperately.

My mouth was dry from sleep. I let saliva collect around my tongue and then nodded in simultaneity with a deep swallow.

Holding the door open, I walked back into the house and, in a completely calculated move, lowered my chin, widened my eyes, and blinked until Paul's face showed signs of collapse.

"I can't," he said.

"Just for a minute."

He looked over his shoulder, surveyed the sleeping neighborhood, then stepped inside and shut the door behind him, but with a noticeable disinclination to do so.

I reached out to touch his chest, moving slowly to see if he was going to flinch or jerk away. He did neither. He set his palm on top of my hand, lifted it up, and slid it underneath his sweatshirt, placing it directly over his heart. My hand was colder than his skin and he trembled. Then he closed his eyes, and I began edging forward until I was standing so close to him, the back of my hand was pushing into my own chest.

"I shouldn't be here," he said.

Everything happened so fast after that. Within seconds we were kissing and fumbling onto the bed. Then we were undressed; Paul was above me, inside of me, and he was violent, though not in the act itself, but in the intensity with which he performed it.

"Paul…"

"*Shh.*"

I opened my eyes and realized he still had the stupid orange hat on. I tried to take it off but he grabbed my hand.

"What's the matter, you get a bad haircut?"

"Something like that," he said, but his voice contained no trace of good humor.

I wrapped my legs around him and felt him tense up before he came, was able to let go just as he let go.

Moments later I was staring at the shadow of a cross on the bedroom wall, cast by two power lines outside the window. "There's so much I have to tell you."

He dovetailed himself around my body, drew me in, and said, "No talking. Not tonight. Just let me hold you, okay?"

When I woke up I knew, even before I turned over, that Paul was gone, and the first thing I did was call and leave him a message asking him to call me back.

I put the couch back together and then brought the phone into the bathroom in case it rang while I was in the shower. As I was getting dressed, there was a knock on the door, and I rushed to answer it with a towel wrapped turban-style around my head, hoping to see Paul waiting on the porch with coffee and breakfast. I got Loring instead.

Loring stepped inside, looking around. "Michael and Vera aren't back yet?"

It was an odd way to start the conversation considering how our last one had ended. "No. Not until Monday. Why?"

Loring perched himself on the edge of the couch and sighed heavily, his eyes trained on some invisible spot in the carpet. "There's something I have to tell you."

I took the towel off my head and felt droplets of water dampen my shoulders. "There's something I have to tell you, too." I sat down next to him. "It's about Paul."

"*Paul?*" His whole body bent toward me as if pushed by the force of a wave. "You mean, you know?"

"Know what?"

Loring's face went limp. "Eliza, what are you talking about?"

"Paul was here last night," I said, using a penitent tone,

implying there was a lot more to the story.

Loring immediately put his arms around me and cradled me the way he cradled the twins when they cried, rocking me back and forth, kissing the top of my head. And had it not seemed so out-of-place, I might have described his behavior as the utmost in piteous compassion, the likes of which I hadn't seen so intensely since the day I returned to my high school classroom having lost two parents in a plane crash.

Fender started clawing at the door. Seconds later Michael and Vera staggered in looking like two scarecrows weathered by a storm. Michael and Loring exchanged somber glances, and Vera's eyes were red like she'd been crying.

"I just got here," Loring said to Michael, and then he announced that Paul had been a recent visitor.

"*What?*" Michael's head fell back. "He was *here?* Last *night?*"

Michael touched Loring's shoulder as if to say, *Let me*, and the two of them traded places—Michael took the seat next to me while Loring lingered beside Vera. The way everyone was gawking at each other was giving me the creeps. I grabbed my brother by the arm and said, "What's going on?"

"Eliza." Michael's face was pallid. "Something happened this morning."

My body began to shake and my eyes welled up with tears. *An accident*, I thought. *Paul's been in an accident.* I imagined planes colliding in midair, a taxi being crushed by a semi, a mugging gone awry, terrorism.

"Something bad?" I asked, my breath shallow, my heart pounding.

Michael's lips were locked together. He seemed to be trying to keep the words in, as if the ones that wanted out didn't belong in the air.

"Yeah," he said, barely opening his mouth. "Very bad."

part three

Sometimes a
Person Has to Die
in Order to Live
or
(Why are the ones
who need the
most shelter
always the ones
left out
in the rain?)

"Suicide."

Michael said the word, he knew what it meant, and yet all he could feel, at that moment, was anger—anger at Paul for throwing in the towel, and for putting Michael in the position of having to be the one to tell Eliza.

She was shaking her head; tears were streaming down her cheeks.

"No…" she kept saying. "No…"

Michael couldn't look at her. He muttered the word a couple more times, trying to knock it into his head, trying to make himself believe it, too.

Suicide. Suicide.

That's what the cops were calling it. That's what the newspapers would eventually call it. Paul Hudson was no longer a person, he was "a jumper."

Apparently there was nothing too unusual about some crazy asshole vaulting off the Brooklyn Bridge. Even if that crazy asshole was three steps forward and two steps back from being a rock star, the world will still judge him and deem him a fool.

They'll never understand. Not today, not ever.

History can be as cruel as a bully on a playground.

Michael had no clue what else to say, or the right way to say it. And so he just recited what he'd practiced the whole way home from the airport.

Eliza had started crying even before he'd said the word. Eventually she stood up and began moving backward, all the way into the corner of the room, pressing herself so tightly into the ninety-degree angle where the walls met that her body made a triangle.

She grabbed at her shirt—stretching it out, pulling on it, wrestling with it.

"How?" she finally whispered, wide-eyed.

Michael glanced at Vera, who glanced at Loring, who hadn't moved from his station near the door. Loring looked staunch and brave and Michael wished he would step in and take over.

"Feldman called me early this morning," Michael said. "Vera and I went straight to the airport."

As Michael continued to relay the details, he tried to make himself cry, believing it was necessary to join Eliza in a symmetry of pain, but he was too outside of himself to really *feel* anything, too disconnected to appropriately *mourn* his best friend.

"I guess it happened around three o'clock this morning. Paul called Feldman sometime last night, said he was here in Brooklyn and needed a ride home. Feldman came and picked him up."

Eliza's hands were flat against her ears but Michael knew she could hear him.

"Halfway across the bridge, Paul asked Feldman to pull over, said he felt sick."

She was shaking her head again.

"There was an eyewitness. Besides Feldman, I mean. Some guy was driving across the bridge and saw the whole thing."

Eliza reached out to Loring. He went to her and she clung to him. "Tell him he's wrong, Loring. You're smart. *Tell* him."

Loring said he was sorry, he wished he could, and then Eliza buckled to the floor, whimpering.

"Where is he?" she sobbed.

Vera sighed heavily, and Michael regarded his sister with precaution. "They haven't found him yet. And Eliza, there's a good chance they won't."

She cried into her hands and asked if she could be alone. Michael wasn't sure it was a good idea, but Loring nodded and led Vera and Michael into the kitchen.

"I didn't know whether to give her this or not," Loring said, half-closing the door and pulling an envelope from his jacket. "It was in my mail this morning."

Michael caught a glimpse of Eliza's name on the front, and he recognized Paul's handwriting, but his nerves were shot and his head was so messed up he didn't know what to do with it.

"*Damn* him," Michael sighed. "Why couldn't he just let it go?"

The stamp on the letter was a picture of the Statue of Liberty—a gloriously proud nighttime view, illuminated from below with light that bathed Lady Liberty in money-green radiance.

"Give it to me."

Eliza's voice hit Michael like a snowball.

"It's mine," she said from the doorway. "I can see my name."

"Eliza, you don't need to read this right now."

But she walked over and reached for the letter, and against his better judgment, Michael let her lift it from his hand.

There are things we never tell anyone. We want to but we can't. So we write them down. Or we paint them. Or we sing about them. Maybe we carve them into stone. Because that's what art is. It's our only option. To remember. To attempt to discover the truth. Sometimes we do it to stay alive. These things, they live inside of us. They are the secrets we stash in our pockets and the weapons we carry like guns across our backs. And in the end we have to decide for ourselves when these things are worth fighting for, and when it's time to throw in the towel. Sometimes a person has to die in order to live. Deep down, I know you know this. You just can't seem to do anything about it. I guess it's a sad fact of life that some of us move on and some of us inevitably stay behind. Only in this case I'm not sure which one of us is doing which. You were right about one thing though. It's not fate. It's a choice. And who knows, maybe we'll meet again someday, somewhere up above all the noise. Until then, when you think of me, try and remember the good stuff. Try and remember the love.

"Bastard."

I let the letter drop to the counter, then went back to the couch and stretched out as if for sleep.

I could hear Michael and Vera and Loring—their voices were traveling through the open kitchen door. I heard Loring ask Michael why Paul would do such a thing, as if

Michael were the foremost authority on Paul's inexplicable behavior. Michael said he didn't know, but that Paul hadn't been in a positive frame of mind for a long time.

The three of them came back into the room together, with Fender in tow, all of their eyes on me. Even the dog was staring.

"Fuck Paul Hudson," I said.

Back in college, to fulfill my science requirements, I had elected to take a year of psychology. I'd studied the five stages of grief and immediately recognized my current position as somewhere between one and two. Stage one—denial and isolation—was obviously lingering, but stage two was anger and there was no doubt I was feeling overwhelmingly pissed off.

"*Bastard.*"

Loring was now standing above me. "Eliza, you don't mean that."

I wanted to kick Loring. His capacity for mercy was attenuating stage two, but I needed to hang on to stage two for as long as possible. And I was going to skip stage three altogether. Bargaining. An utterly useless stage. Neither God nor the Universe ever bargained with anyone.

The plan was to segue from anger right into depression—a place I knew I could endure for a long time.

Loring lifted my head, squeezed in behind it, and gently set it back down on his lap. He began petting my hair, I closed my eyes, and before I knew it I was watching the shadow of Paul's body hovering over the edge of a bridge. Only it wasn't the Brooklyn Bridge, it was the scene in *Saturday Night Fever* when John Travolta's drunk friend falls off the Verrazano Narrows.

In the dream, Paul was wearing brown sandals. Jesus shoes. His toes beetled over the ledge. His arms were in the air, straight and determined. His fingers were pointing to the sky. He was looking up, not down, and there was no fear on his face.

He hesitated a moment before he jumped, like he'd had a change of heart but was a second too late.

Still, no fear. Just that modicum of reconsideration.

As his feet disengaged from the steel beam and he leaped into the air, I expected him to flap his arms and fly away.

It was a dream. It could have happened.

He dove instead. A dive full of dignity and grace. Olympic. Perfectly straight for the first ninety degrees, with three somersaults and a reverse twist.

This is where I wanted the dream to end. Or else I wanted Paul to break the water in absolute kinetic awareness without so much as a splash, popping back up with a satisfied, gold-medal-winning, cocky-bastard smile on his face.

I saw him hit the water. Then the water returned to stillness and I knew that below the surface of the river, Paul's body lay broken to bits.

That's how it happened, right? Kind of like a plane crash.

It's usually the impact that does you in.

Mid-afternoon, I was still on Loring's lap. Michael, who was crumpled on the floor like a beanbag, looked up at me and said he was sorry, for what I didn't know.

"I'm going to make some coffee," Vera said. Her voice was small and hoarse. She'd been crying again.

I wondered how Paul would have felt about people crying over him. Who was I kidding? He would've pretended to find it irrelevant and embarrassing, but deep down he would have deemed heartache and despair the only appropriate responses to his demise.

"Loring," Vera said, "can I get you some coffee?"

If I would have been able to find the strength to move my tongue, I would have answered for Loring. *No, thank you*, is what I guessed he was going to say. Loring didn't like coffee. He thought it tasted like ashes. What Loring wanted, but was too polite to ask for, was some tea. A nice, sweet, full-bodied cup of Yinhzin Silver Needle, his afternoon favorite, would have made him happy.

"No. Thanks, though."

The doorbell rang while Vera was still in the kitchen, and I felt Loring's body shift to see who was there, but the window that would have allowed Loring a view of the porch was behind him, and to turn all the way around would have meant disturbing my head on his lap.

Vera answered the door, and I sat up when I heard Feldman's voice. He'd just come from the police station, he said. He'd been there since dawn and needed to speak to Michael.

"This is a really hard time for all of us," Feldman said to me. "I know you and Paul were close at one time, and I'm sorry."

I knew *sorry*. I was an expert on *sorry* and I'd never heard a *sorry* more ripe with innuendo. It was a finger pointing in my face. It was *I warned you* and *I told you so* and *Why didn't you help me, you bitch?*

I probably would have gone for Feldman's jugular had he not been right. I had vowed to save Paul. And what had I done instead? I'd metaphorically handed him over to the Romans, stood idly by as the warriors raised their swords, thrown salt on his wounds, and loitered at the foot of the cross while he'd suffocated and died.

"Michael," Feldman said, "is there somewhere we can talk?"

I shook my head. "Whatever you have to say, say it in front of all of us."

Feldman gave me a look and then shifted to address Michael. "Paul's body was recovered about two hours ago."

Much to my surprise, I took the news under the guise of control. Or else I was just too numb to move. Michael lost it.

"No!" He lunged at Feldman. "You cocksucker! You no-good—"

"Michael!" Vera cried. "Stop it!"

Loring grabbed Michael and held him back until he calmed down.

"It's okay," Feldman said. "I understand. He's upset. We all are." Feldman took Michael by the arm. "How about you and I take a walk, huh?"

They were gone maybe five minutes. Upon their return, Michael said he was okay, that he didn't know what had come over him, but I thought he looked worse than when he'd left.

Paul had no family to speak of, and Feldman announced that he and Michael would be handling all the necessary arrangements. The body was being cremated, and a service would be held later the following week, possibly at Rings of Saturn.

"We think it's what Paul would have wanted," Feldman said.

I didn't know whether I agreed or disagreed. Regardless, nobody asked for my opinion, and that hurt. But a crushing voice inside my head said I had no right to an opinion anyway.

Michael walked Feldman to the door and then watched from the porch as he got in his car and drove away.

The second Feldman was out of sight, Michael ran back into the house, grabbed his wallet off the counter, said he needed to get some air, and took off.

He was crying.

"Aside from O.J.," Eliza said, "murderers don't normally attend their victim's memorials."

Loring thought she was making a mistake. If she had any intention of letting Paul go, that is, she needed to say goodbye.

"He blamed me himself. In that song he sang at your dad's birthday. Besides, I'm sure the place is going to be swarming with every girl he had sex with in the tri-state area, and I really don't want to be a link in that chain of fools."

So while everyone else, including Doug and Lily, and even Amanda Strunk, were at Rings of Saturn lauding Paul's short and tragic life, Loring was in Brooklyn, where he had been every day for the last week, sitting on the floor next to Eliza, holding her hand while she watched bad movies and pretended she wasn't crying.

"You look handsome." She said it as if Loring had just walked in even though he'd been there for an hour. He'd worn a suit and tie in case he would have been able to change her mind about going to the service.

For the last fifteen minutes they'd been watching a ridiculous comedy about a UFO landing somewhere in the Midwest. The spaceship had been carrying an alien prince looking for an earthling princess in, of all places, a mall. The alien's body was buff and human, but the creature had the universal extra terrestrial eyes—huge, bulging, almond-shaped, the color of a radioactive swamp; and his face was almost identical to that of a Sleestak from *Land of the Lost*.

Loring watched in frustration as the buff alien browsed the food court. It exasperated him that none of the shoppers seemed to find it strange to see a guy from outer space standing in line at Burger King.

"Lucy called me yesterday," Eliza said, picking a piece of lint from Loring's sleeve. "She wanted to know when I was coming back. And she thought I'd be happy to know there was a surge in Bananafish's record sales this week. God, would that piss Paul off, people buying his record now that he's dead."

Loring put his hands on her shoulders and began kneading the little knots that felt like M&M's under her skin.

"Lucy wants me to write an article on Paul," she said. "He didn't give many interviews. And when he did he used to make stuff up. I once heard him tell a reporter he'd been born on an army base in Germany. Nobody really knew anything about him."

It was a terrible idea, and Loring deemed Lucy a terrible person for suggesting it. "You're not going to do it, are you?"

"Of course I am," she said with no trace of emotion. "And then I'm going to quit."

"Quit?"

"I can't write about Paul and then go back to writing about heathens and pagans." Loring wondered what Eliza would do if she didn't write. He remembered how, in Vermont, she'd gone out beyond the apple trees to gather flowers, which she'd arranged in an old pewter pitcher. She'd said then she thought she might like to work with flowers someday. Loring considered offering to buy her a flower shop.

"Winkle paid for the memorial service," she said during the next commercial. "He sent out invitations and everything, like it was a New Year's Eve bash or one of his obnoxious Labor Day picnics."

Another few minutes went by. Eliza leaned on Loring's chest and said, "You know the worst part? Winkle told Michael he's going to release the album—the very same album that, two months ago, he deemed commercially unsatisfactory. I guess Paul's death was enough to convince Winkle it's a masterpiece. He's probably going to market the shit out of it and send it soaring to the top of the charts."

She disappeared into the kitchen, came back with a glass of water, and set it next to Loring as if he'd asked for it.

"I bet Winkle's glad Paul's dead. I bet he clapped and did a flip when he heard." At this point, Loring wasn't sure she was speaking to him, or just to hear herself talk. The way her shoulders were shaking, he knew she was trying not to cry again, but her voice could have been that of a local newscaster giving a traffic report.

"Loring," she said in the same, unaffected voice. "Why are you here?" On the screen, the female lead was trying to teach the alien how to eat with a knife and fork. "The night of your Dad's birthday you acted like you never wanted to see me again."

"I'm here because I'm your friend, regardless of what happened between us. I don't want you to have to go through this alone."

"Do you feel guilty?"

Until she said it, it had never occurred to Loring that he might have had any bearing on Paul's decision to fling himself off that bridge. "He wasn't pushed. He jumped. You need to remember that."

The alien was shooting something at a cashier. His ray gun made the same sound as one of Sean and Walker's toys: *Pfew, pfew, pfew.*

"I tried to talk to him that night but he wouldn't let me," she murmured. "Then I fell asleep…And I thought I'd have another chance…I really thought…"

Don't we all, Loring wanted to say.

"How come you haven't asked me what happened that night?"

"Asked you what?" Loring said. "If you slept with him? It's not something I want to think about. And anyway, what difference does it make now?"

She put her hand on his cheek but it was too much. He had to take it away.

"Loring, you and I, we can never be. You know that, right?"

Interestingly enough, it was the first thought Loring had after Michael called him the morning Paul killed himself. Notwithstanding the fact that Loring had ended his relationship with Eliza at the theater the night before, he'd done it on an I'm-at-the-end-of-my-rope whim, preserving a small amount of hope that maybe she would wake up the next day, realize how much he cared about her and come back. But as soon as Michael broke the news, Loring knew he'd lost Eliza for good, that Paul's death would only push her farther away.

Loring noticed that the star of the movie, the girl giving the fork-and-knife lessons, was a now-famous actress who had once sent him an email, via his manager, inviting him on a date. *I find you very attractive*, the girl had typed. *Maybe we could meet for a drink sometime.*

He'd never responded, and the girl turned up backstage at his Hollywood Bowl show a few months later. She was flashy and puerile and he'd pawned her off on Tab.

"I have blood on my hands," Eliza said, examining her palms as if they were covered in the stuff. "I can blame Winkle and Feldman, but it's my fault."

Loring lifted her chin. The way her eyes smoldered under her tears made his heart ache. "Listen to me: there had to be forces at work inside of Paul that no amount of love and support would have saved. You've been there. You know this."

"I don't know anything," she said. "Except that desperation and fear make a person do really stupid things."

She loosened Loring's tie and used the thicker end to catch her tears. And as she continued to weep on his chest, Loring knew he was never going to be this close to her again. And he knew she knew it, too. That they were going to say goodbye sometime after the sun went down and he was going to walk out the door and catch a cab to 77th and Central Park West and he wasn't going to come back. Not unless she asked him to come back. And she was never going to ask him to come back.

By the end of the movie, the girl and the alien were madly in love. The last scene was a shot of them flying off in the standard, saucer-shaped UFO.

"Where are we going?" the girl asked her buff, alien Prince Charming.

"Home," he said in a boxy, computerized voice.

"But where's home?"

Then came the most pathetic part of the whole film. The alien showed the girl a pillow he'd swiped from a gift store in the mall. It had a saying crocheted on the top that said: Home Is Where the Heart Is.

Eliza remained riveted, even as the credits rolled.

Finally the music started to fade and the picture cut to black.

For the record, I didn't go to Michael's with the intention of falling into bed with Eliza. I went because one of the most painful needs in life is the need to tell someone how you really feel about them, especially if you're pretty sure you're never going to see them again.

That's the reason I ended up on Michael's doorstep. Because my last words to her had been words I didn't mean, and I couldn't exit her life without telling her the truth.

The truth is I was never, not for one goddamn second, not even when I walked in on her in Loring's arms, sorry that I'd met her.

I'm a better person for knowing her.

I fucking loved her.

No, it's more than that. Not only did I love her, but I'm pretty sure I've never loved anyone *but* her.

Shit. Maybe I didn't exactly *tell* her all this crap. It would have been too risky to say it out loud. But I showed her. Believe me, I rocked her world.

Getting out of that bed that night, getting dressed and walking away, was the hardest thing I ever had to do. But you know what did it for me? I thought about something she said once, it was after a gig at Rings of Saturn. She and I, and Michael and Vera, we'd stopped at Katz's for a late dinner, and someone had left a box of crayons on our table. Eliza picked out a shade called Purple Mountain Majesty and started scribbling on her placemat. All the way across it she wrote the word BELIEVE in big block letters, and she colored them in on the sides the way amateur artists do when they're trying to make letters look 3-D, except the L, the I, and the E were about ten times bigger than the B, E, V, and other E.

beLIEve

She held it up and said, "Get it? Inside every believe, there's a lie."

I think I told her that was the worst thing I'd ever heard her say, but a few months later I found her sucking Loring's face in my apartment and it made a lot of sense.

That's what got me out of bed that night. All I had to do was remind myself that she was a liar, a cheater, and that she'd single-handedly destroyed all my beliefs with lies, and I was gone. Well, after I stood in the doorway staring at the outline of her body under the sheet, that is. Trying to memorize the image for future use in my dreams. And I did it too. I burned her so deep she's as vivid as a painting on the wall in front of me. I don't even have to close my eyes to see her. I can just blink her into focus.

Before I call it a day, I want to document the memorial service.

I know, I know. Showing up at Rings of Saturn was stupid, if not wholly narcissistic. But let's face it, who wouldn't do the same thing if given the opportunity? Besides, I was careful. I slipped in at the end when the crowd's attention was focused on the stage. And it's not like anyone recognized me. Holy Hell, right now I don't even recognize myself when I see my ridiculous goddamn reflection. Mostly, it's the hair. The hair's really throwing me off. You know what, though? I did notice Caelum looking around a lot. He seemed nervous and I wondered if maybe he felt my presence. I doubt it. He's too grounded for that. He was probably still freaking out over the general absurdity of the situation.

I'll tell you who really pissed me off—Angelo. He didn't look sad at all, and he spent the five minutes I was there flirting with some girl near the bar. I was dead and the only thing that ass-hole cared about was getting laid.

Burke made up for Angelo. He bawled like a baby the whole time. Queenie, on the other hand, had a scowl on her face, and she kept rocking back and forth on her heels like she was ready to attack someone. I could tell she wanted to kick my ass, and she was probably thinking up a new ice cream to express her rage: Chocolate Hudson Shit for Brains, Brooklyn Bridge Bullshit, something like that.

One of the coolest surprises had to be Doug. Having my hero show up just about killed me all over again.

I didn't see Eliza anywhere.

But the biggest shock of all was the fans. They made an altar outside the club and sat in a circle with candles and flowers, talking and singing and analyzing my songs. Some kid even made a poster that said I'd changed his life.

What do you know? There are still people out there who believe music is more than just something to dance to. I'm glad I got a chance to see that.

Incidentally, I've been keeping up with the news, surfing the net a lot since my death. It's not like I have much else to do, and I'm stuck here until January.

Besides the handful of aforementioned fans, people are pretty much over me. And rightly so. I didn't expect to make the cover of *Time* or anything. Our goddamn idiot-in-chief is too busy stealing all the thunder anyway, trying to convince the world to let him bomb that evil freak who tried to kill his dad. I'm long gone and long forgotten.

One advantage to cashing in the chips this early: Chances are I'll never be popular enough to be the subject of a *Behind the Music.*

Holy Hell, I still can't believe I actually went through with it.

Like most of my outlandish ideas, the first time this one crossed my mind—it was that day I sat on the bench in front of Loring's building—back then it seemed so ridiculous, so unbelievable, I assumed I'd never have the guts to make it happen. And even if I did have the guts, it was what I call a "futuristic unthinkable." Like when you're ten and someone tells you you're going to be thirty one day. Or you hit puberty and you hear a rumor about this thing called a blow job, but you can't believe any girl is ever going to put your dick in her mouth.

That's the stage I was in on that bench. The "futuristic unthinkable" stage. Nurturing the possibility but still unable to imagine it ever coming to fruition.

Now look at me.

I should go. I'm starting to feel depressed.

Next time, remind me to talk about the body.

There wasn't supposed to be a goddamn body.

Over.

Jesus was waiting with open arms. He was still there, up on the wall, right where I'd left him. But Jesus didn't look so sexy anymore. Jesus looked soggy and worn out. Jesus looked like he'd broken free from his home on the cross, jumped into the East River, swam around in the muck, climbed back up and reinserted the nails, ready to resume hanging in torturous limbo for all of eternity.

I didn't care what Paul said in that song. Jesus was a coward. He'd taken the easy way out. Given up. Surrendered. Wimped out.

Maybe we all had.

I took Jesus down and put him in a box. Then I put Jesus on a shelf in the closet. Jesus and I were over. Finished. Kaput. Ex-lovers to the tenth power.

Across the hall, the door to Paul's room was open. I could see the foot of his bed, where his *Jive Limo* T-shirt lay next to two CDs and a pile of unopened mail.

I walked apprehensively into the room, breaking the vow I'd made to Vera and Michael an hour earlier, when they'd begged me not to move back to the apartment and, losing that battle, made me promise to at least stay out of Paul's room.

"It's too soon," Vera said.

But I knew that "too soon" was a fallacious phrase, implying that I would, in the fullness of time, segue far enough into stage-five acceptance to walk up the four flights of stairs and across the threshold of the bleeding door with the capacity for happiness.

How long does something like that take?

Another month? Another year? Another lifetime?

Desperately wanting to communicate with someone who no longer exists is essentially a lesson in gravity. No matter how hard you try to overcome it, it will always pull you down.

That's the real reason I agreed to write the article. It gave me the opportunity to inundate myself with all things Paul. It was a way to keep him alive for a while longer.

And it didn't take me long to amass an entire folder of information, including but not limited to a copy of the police report that had been filed the morning Paul dove off the bridge, as well as the statement from Will Lucien—the eyewitness who'd been the only other person besides Feldman to see Paul jump. And, as soon as it became available, a copy of Paul's autopsy report, which arrived from the medical examiner's office in a manila envelope, and remained there because I couldn't bear to acknowledge its existence.

Over the course of a week, I interviewed Paul's friends and associates, and even managed to have a civil discussion with Feldman, which wasn't something I'd wanted to do, but since he'd been the one driving the car it was inevitable. He was forthright during the meeting, probably because he knew an article on Paul would sell more records. Unfortunately, he wasn't particularly enlightening, maintaining that Paul was sullen the entire time.

"I could tell something was bothering him," Feldman admitted. "He just stared out the window, tapping his feet on the floor. I asked him if he wanted to talk but he said no. That was the extent of our conversation until he told me to pull over."

I attempted to locate the eyewitness. The police report listed him as hailing from Pennsylvania, but all I had in the way of contact information was the phone number he'd given the police. The area code was northern New Jersey, but no one answered the number when I called.

I didn't figure the eyewitness would have anything new or earth shattering to add to the story, but part of me wanted-ed to talk to him anyway. Part of me was jealous that he'd been present for Paul's last moments and I hadn't.

One of the most unsettling chores of my research had to be seeking out mawkish quotes from various members of the music community willing to laud Paul's overlooked-in-life genius. Lucy had ordered me to make Paul sound impor-tant. This could be achieved, she explained, by getting important people to talk about him.

"A quote from your old buddy Doug would really make Hudson shine."

Doug invited me to his Greenwich Village studio. He was working on a new record and thought I might enjoy hearing some of the songs, but not even the gospel accord-ing to Doug Blackman could elevate me.

During our hour together, I felt obliged to ask how Loring was doing, and Doug managed to sidestep any awk-wardness by saying, "He's been spending a lot of time in Vermont" and left it at that.

Doug spoke eloquently about Paul: "The thing that struck me most about that kid, he had a real pure heart, but his spirit was all moxie. Perfect pitch in a cacophonous world, that's what he was. And you can quote me on that."

Bruce Springsteen, who'd admittedly never heard of Bananafish but had been blown away by Paul's performance at Doug's birthday bash, called Paul "gifted" and "irreplace-able, ya know?"

If my dad had been alive he would've dropped dead when I told him I got to talk to Bruce Springsteen.

Thom Yorke said: "It's always the good ones who get taken away."

Jack Stone contacted me before I had a chance to contact him. He asked me to lunch, eager to discuss his theory on where it had gone wrong for Paul. He saw Paul's death as a cautionary tale of music business ethics and viewed Paul not as a coward, not as a quitter, but as a victim.

"Paul Hudson didn't kill himself, he was murdered," Jack said, impassioned. "Believe me, this is one of the great tragedies of our industry. The artists who need the most shelter always seem to be the ones who get left out in the rain."

Even Ian Lessing, still drunk, had kind words to say about Paul, admitting the world had lost "an unbelievably intense motherfucking performer."

Then there was the hypocrite.

"Paul Hudson was a like a son to me," Winkle said. "I took him under my wing, made him part of my family. We were very close. And he was a *hell* of a talent."

Clearly, Winkle had no recollection of ever meeting me, let alone having been introduced to me as Paul's fiancée. Meanwhile, Feldman and Michael both confirmed on record that they had witnessed blowouts between Paul and Winkle in the months before Paul died. According to Michael, the last confrontation, which began over Paul's refusal to participate in a corporate radio station concert extravaganza, had resulted in Winkle lunging at Paul with a letter opener and swearing that as long as he was breathing, Paul would never work in the music business again.

"You won't be able to get a job tuning a guitar," Winkle reportedly told Paul.

After that mêlée, Bananafish essentially fell to pieces.

"Angelo was first to crack," Michael told me.

Throughout the recording sessions, Angelo had apparently expressed dissatisfaction with the direction of the music. He agreed with Winkle—the new songs were entirely too long and precocious for radio.

"Fuck radio" was Paul's reply.

A day later, Angelo left the band over what he dubbed Paul's "psycho-artist bullshit," and Paul played drums on the remaining tracks. But once Michael and Burke realized the record was probably never going to be released, and the standoff between Paul and Winkle showed no signs of easing up, they had to start making other plans.

Burke got a job working at a holistic pet store on East Ninth Street, and a small gourmet market in the Village was going to start carrying his ice cream.

Michael resumed his post of employment at Balthazar and was contemplating starting a band of his own.

"That was pretty much the end of it," my brother said. "Bananafish snuck in like a thief in the night, made some really great music, then got eradicated. And you know what? Ninety-eight percent of America will never know the difference."

Initially, I thought investigating and writing about Paul's death was going to be cathartic, and maybe bring me closer to stage five. But acceptance requires understanding, and nothing I learned about the last months of Paul's life enabled me to understand, not even in a minuscule way, why he'd done it.

The detail I found most disturbing was that Paul had left a will behind. In it, he'd put Michael in charge of his estate, which contained the money left over from his advances, as well as his personal property, and any future royalties his music might yield.

Until the discovery of the will, I had chosen to believe Paul's suicide had been a decision based on a whim—he hadn't really wanted to die, he'd simply wanted to stop the pain, and then hadn't allowed the moment to pass.

The will made Paul's death look premeditated, as if he'd planned it weeks in advance, as if he'd thought long and hard about his options and still decided there was nothing—and no one—left to live for.

Late November, I ran into Loring across the street from a tea cafe on Rivington, just a couple blocks from my apartment. I was about to exit the Baishakhi Food Corp. with a bag of groceries when I saw him.

It was a windy day. There were fast food wrappers, cups, and newspaper remnants blowing in circles on the sidewalk like little urban dust devils, and I was waiting in the doorway for things to calm down. Outside, people walked, cars moved. I saw TVs on in apartment windows, heard sirens screaming nearby, and wondered how it could be that everything in the city had life, even the garbage. Everything except for Paul.

My gaze landed across the street and on Loring. He was about to walk into the cafe, and he was holding hands with a pretty girl dressed in a bright red, knee-length coat who, from afar, reminded me of Holly Golightly from *Breakfast at Tiffany's*.

I hadn't seen Loring since the day after Paul's memorial, when I'd gone to his apartment to get my things. I'd told him then that I thought it would be a good idea if we didn't talk for a while. He had agreed, and hadn't phoned me since.

I put my eyes to the ground but didn't even make it out the door before Loring called my name. He held up an index finger, asking me to wait, and then said something to the pretty girl, whose compassionate smile told me she knew my whole sorry story.

The girl went into the cafe and sat at a table next to the window; Loring waited for a truck to go by and then crossed the street.

"Small world," he said with a level of comfort I wasn't expecting. "You weren't even going to wave, were you?"

"You looked busy."

He studied me like a scientist would study a specimen. "How is everything?"

"Everything's good," I lied. "How's everything with you?"

"Good."

He sounded like he meant it, and I was unable to hide my smirk. "Wow. So, who is she?"

"A friend," he mumbled, as if he feared saying any more would hurt me.

"It's okay, you can tell me."

He kicked at the ground, but his warm, bashful eyes divulged most of what he wouldn't say.

"Good for you." I laughed and elbowed him playfully. "At least tell me where you met her."

"Believe it or not, I've know her since I was a kid. Her dad's been Doug's lawyer for years. I've had a crush on her since I was twelve."

"Are you sleeping with her?"

He rolled his eyes, and I suddenly remembered how much fun it was to torture Loring with personal questions.

"No kidding," I said, "it would be the best news I've had in months. I'm begging you, tell me you're madly in love and having the best sex of your life, because knowing you're happy would mean one less person I have to feel guilty about hurting."

Loring glanced back at the girl. She looked up almost at the same time, as if she could feel his eyes. She smiled at him in the way you would smile at someone if they'd saved your life.

"Good for you," I said again, although it hurt a little that time.

With his thumb, Loring drew a cross on my forehead like priests do on Ash Wednesday. "Consider yourself absolved," he said.

Through the cafe window, I watched the girl take out a little spiral notebook from her purse. "Uh-oh, don't tell me she's a writer."

Loring laughed. "No. She's an artist, actually. She makes jewelry."

I couldn't have been happier for Loring. Really. But being witness to the beauty of burgeoning love was making me feel hopelessly, impenetrably alone.

"I have to go." I shifted my grocery bag to my opposite hip. "Tell your friend I said she's the luckiest girl in Manhattan, okay?"

He smiled. "Take care of yourself, Eliza."

"Yeah. You, too."

The prospect of spending the rest of the afternoon alone in the apartment was too much to bear, but Vera was busy studying, and I was trying hard to simulate normalcy in front of Michael so I couldn't go to him.

I dropped off my groceries, walked to Houston Street, and reluctantly entered Rings of Saturn for the first time in months.

John the Baptist was busy watching a NASCAR race on the new TV that had been installed above the bar. He didn't notice me right away, but when he finally turned around and spotted me, he smiled the gentlest, saddest smile I'd ever seen.

He shut off the TV and went about fixing me a drink, putting seven olives in my glass. As he slid the goblet across the bar, all he could say was, "Man, oh, man…"

My eyes filled with tears.

"You wanna talk about him or not?" John said. "'Cause I can talk about him all day if you so desire."

I shook my head and John seemed to acquiesce, but seconds later he said, "How about I tell you a story about a friend of mine? Skinny guy with a big nose."

I lowered my chin and peered at him.

"Helluva guy, my friend Saul." John's fake eye was askew. The iris seemed too far to the left. "Saul was here the night before he—well, he had an accident."

"John..."

"Pardon me a sec." He turned his head and adjusted the off-kilter eye. I couldn't figure out how he knew it was crooked, being that he couldn't see out of it. "Last time I saw Saul, he'd just come from a doctor's appointment."

This sparked my curiosity. "Was Saul sick?"

"Nope."

"Why did he go to the doctor?"

"He *thought* he was sick. Claimed he'd been experiencing some chronic pain in the pancreatic region."

I almost laughed. "And to what did the doctor attribute this pain?"

"Anxiety. Stress. Completely psychosomatic. 'Course I could have saved Saul a couple hundred bucks if he would've listened to me—I gave him the same diagnosis a few days before when he came in here with his hand on his hip, moaning like a cow in labor."

That time I did laugh, albeit with difficulty.

"Know what else?" John said. "I saw a lot of Saul before his accident. He spent a lot of time in the seat right next to the one you're sitting on, and let me tell you, there was an uncharacteristic aura of calm about him." John served himself cranberry juice in a glass that matched mine. It looked silly and out-of-place in his hand. "That is, except when he talked about the girl."

I let the tears fall. It was stupid to try and pretend under these circumstances. "What girl?"

"Apparently Saul had developed a bad habit of walking by the building where this one girl lived. Somewhere up in the nosebleed section of town, if you know what I mean. Not a place he felt particularly at home, but he made the sacrifice because he was nuts about her, even though she'd tossed him by the side of the curb like an old piss-stained couch, and was shacking up with some larcenist, as Saul put it."

I sighed. "Please don't bring Loring into this."

"Who the hell is Loring?" John was a good actor. Not a great one, but a good one. "Anyway, Saul contemplated trying to get this girl back."

I felt like I had a ten pound rock in the pit of my stomach. "You're telling me he wanted her back?"

"I just said he was crazy about her."

"Is that so? Then why, right before his *accident*, did he tell her he wished she were dead?"

"Obviously he was hurt. Maybe he wanted to hurt her back, I don't know. Last I'd heard, old Saul had decided the girl was better off with the other guy."

"Jesus, John. Didn't you tell Saul he was wrong?"

"Yes ma'am, I did. But Saul could be pretty stubborn. And a funny thing about Saul, he could talk a cock 'n' bull talk, but he could also walk a scaredy-cat walk."

I took a long, deep breath, and tried to convert my sorrow into something more practical, like anger. It wasn't working. "Did he seem happy to you? The last time you saw him, I mean."

"I'm glad you asked that." John narrowed in on me. "Do you have any idea how many people have sat in the chair you're in right now, wearing the mask of death?"

"The what?"

"I can see it, plain as day. They come in here pondering the end, thinking maybe they're ready for that big old barstool in the sky." John made a fist and pounded the bar three times like a judge demanding order in the court. "*All* of them have come back for another drink. And I like to think I had a hand in that. I like to think my wisdom helped talk them out of it."

My heart hurt. So did my head. "Why didn't you talk Saul out of it?"

"You're not listening. Saul wasn't wearing the mask."

"I don't get it," I said, poking at the olives in my glass.

John dropped the *Saul* jive. He suddenly seemed exasperated. "For Christ's sake, did you know Paul had quit smoking?"

"So he said."

"He'd been running, too. At night. He liked to run right as it was getting dark."

"So?"

"You're not listening, Miss American Pie."

"Please don't call me that."

"Pay attention because I'm only going to say this once." John leaned in so close I could smell a mustiness emanating from his clothes. "I don't know about you, but I'm pretty sure that if I were planning on taking a short walk off a tall bridge, I'd be doing all the things I gave up twenty years ago. I'd be smoking up a storm, eating hot dogs at every meal, tossing back the whiskey, I might even be shooting smack in my arm, and I sure as *hell* wouldn't be watching sunsets at a 10k pace."

I shook my head. "You lost me."

"Good Lord." John made his way to the corner of the bar and began rummaging through the leather jacket that hung beside the cash register.

I was wishing I hadn't come. I wanted to be home, lonely apartment or not. I wasn't in the mood for John's nonsensical barroom Zen. I slid a couple dollars under my glass, hopped off the stool, and tried to slip out.

"Come back here," John said.

I returned to stand beside the seat I'd just vacated. John handed me a small news clipping. "Have you read that?"

It was an obituary that had appeared in one of the local alternative music papers after Paul's death. "Of course," I said. "I saw it weeks ago."

"I didn't ask if you *saw* it, I asked if you *read* it."

"Yes."

"Humor me, Miss American Pie. Read it again."

It took me less than a minute to scan the three-paragraph piece of nothing. Basically, the blurb mentioned Paul's name and occupation, and had a short list of his accomplishments, but it was written in a way that thoroughly diminished their scope. There was a quote from Feldman, the same one from the police report. And a quote from the eyewitness, also lifted from the police report. That was it.

I handed it back to John and resumed my trek to the exit.

"See ya 'round, Miss American Pie."

"Please," I said, halfway out the door. "I asked you not to call me that."

"I know you're in mourning," Lucy said over the phone. "But a deadline is a deadline."

Sonica had thrown in two quick sentences about Paul's death in the previous issue. My more in-depth article on his life was now a week overdue, and despite the tremendous urge I had to slam the receiver down hard enough to cause permanent damage to Lucy's hearing, I assured her that the assignment would be finished by Monday—the last possible day to make publication—and then I politely hung up.

It was Saturday night and I hadn't written a word. I turned on my laptop and spread the contents of the Paul folder across my bedroom floor. With Bananafish's CD as background music, I read the transcripts from my lunch with Jack Stone, the chorus to "Death as a Spectator Sport" a disturbingly appropriate soundtrack. Before the song ended, I jotted down a few points and questions on which to focus:

• Don't paint him as a quitter, a loser, or a rock star.
• Don't glorify his death.
• Has talent become irrelevant?
• Has the industry done to music what McDonald's has done to eating?
• Specifics of the suicide?

That last one was going to require an examination of the autopsy report, which was adjacent to my right foot, just out of reach, and still hadn't been opened, chiefly because the last thing I wanted was a vision of Paul's body as nothing more than a broken vestige of the sublime life it once held.

I stared at the envelope and it stared back like an enemy. Eventually I dragged it in using my heel, removed the eleven-page document, and lifted the cover sheet with a loud exhale as if I were ripping a band-aid from a fresh wound.

The first page contained basic information: the name, address, sex, and age of the decedent. Underneath that was an anatomical diagnosis listing severe trauma to the spine, a crushed skull, and a broken femur as injuries suffered on impact. Below that was a line where the medical examiner had to fill in the cause of death. He'd written: SUICIDE.

My skin felt prickly, my eyes were changing from solids to liquid, and Paul's voice was still bouncing off the walls as I moved on to the next page—a pathological diagnosis that included blood-alcohol and drug test results, both of which were negative. Despite the rumors that circulated around the Lower East Side after Paul's death, one of which had him brandishing a bottle of red wine in his hand and wailing "Bohemian Rhapsody" as he jumped, he had been neither high nor drunk nor singing. I made a note to include this in the piece.

On the following page there were two simple outlines of a male figure, one front-facing, the other back-facing. The examiner had drawn lines to various body parts connecting physical descriptions of markings found on the decedent's body to their specific locations, presumably for identification purposes.

From the figure's left shoulder, a line had been extended out to the middle of the page, next to which the examiner had written: TATTOO ON UPPER ARM. In parenthesis he'd added: SKULL AND CROSSBONES.

I supposed that, prior to his death, Paul had gotten inked again. The choice of a skull and crossbones seemed morbid and cliché, but so did jumping off the bridge, and for this reason I didn't give it a second thought.

Then I resumed scanning the page. Something was wrong. Paul's other tattoos—the man/boy cherub hanging from the butterfly and the Chinese symbol—had gone unnoted by the examiner.

My chest tightened. Small gasping sounds were coming from my throat. And although I could only imagine one fantastic explanation, I was too frightened, too shocked, and too gutless to name it.

I studied the drawings until I could trace every line without looking, but they made no sense beyond the context of the page.

After weighing my options for a long time, I forced myself to call the only person I knew who had gotten a look at the corpse.

"Did you or did you not see Paul's body before it was cremated?"

Feldman paused. "Eliza?" Another pause. "Christ, do I hear Bananafish?"

I turned off the music. "Please, this is important."

"You sound strange," he said.

"Just tell me you're *sure* it was Paul. You *recognized* him."

"We went over all this when you interviewed me."

But we hadn't. I had deliberately refrained from asking Feldman about the body for the same reason I hadn't looked at the autopsy report—I didn't want to know.

"I'm trying to finish this *Sonica* piece. There are a couple things that aren't adding up and I—"

"*Peepers*," Feldman said, "this hardly needs an in-depth investigation. Paul jumped, he croaked, they fished him out of the river. The end."

I wanted to shove a pile of shit down Feldman's throat until *he* croaked. "What about dental records? Don't they use those? Did they ever check to see if—"

"Wasn't necessary," Feldman said quickly. "Paul hadn't

been in the water long enough. I was able to identify his face. And he had a picture ID on him."

"You're telling me you're positive, beyond a shadow of a doubt, that the body you saw was Paul's?"

"One hundred percent." His voice was like a snake slithering down my spine. "Now how about you tell me what's got your panties in such an uproar."

"Forget it," I said, suddenly terrified. "I don't know what I'm talking about."

I hung up wondering why it hadn't dawned on me before. Didn't matter. It was clear to me now.

Feldman was lying.

For the next two days I hardly spoke to anybody, one exception being the call I made to Lucy Enfield, to explain that writing about Paul's death had proven much more emotionally draining than I'd imagined. I told Lucy I wasn't going to be able to do it, and furthermore, I wouldn't be coming back to work.

Lucy sounded satisfied, like she and I had been playing a game all along, one in which she had finally emerged the victor.

Terry called within the hour and tried to get me to reconsider. When I told him I'd made up my mind, he said, "Good luck, Mags. We'll miss you."

Fortunately, Loring had refused to accept rent money from me during the nine months I lived with him, so getting another job wasn't something I had to worry about right away. I could concentrate all my energies on Paul.

The floor was still covered in my notes and I scrutinized every page for hours, but with the exception of the discrepancy in the autopsy report, I couldn't find anything else that struck me as even remotely suspicious.

I needed to talk to someone, but Vera was too sensible,

and I couldn't turn to Michael without more evidence. He was liable to have me committed.

John the Baptist was rinsing out glasses in the sink when I walked in.

"Miss American Pie," he said, a dish towel tucked into his pants, his tone implying he knew I was there for purposes having nothing to do with hydration.

I stood on my toes and leaned over the bar. "What were you trying to tell me the other night?"

He went to the corner, rifled through his coat pocket as he'd done before, pulled out the same news clipping he'd shown me then, and slapped it onto the bar like he was dealing me the ace I needed for blackjack.

I picked it up and glanced over the three paragraphs. Once again, nothing struck me as unusual.

"Jesus, do you have to be half-blind to see it?" John grabbed the clipping, marked a few sentences, and slid it back my way. "One more time," he said. "And when you get to the part I circled, try using a soft, arrogant-yet-bashful sort of voice, why don't you?"

I eyed him curiously.

"Do it," he said.

John had circled the account of Paul's suicide as described by Will Lucien, who was referred to by name in the police report, but in print was known simply as "the eyewitness."

According to the police, there was an eyewitness who had been driving westbound at approximately 3 a.m. the morning of October 12 and saw the events unfold. The eyewitness, who was described by the first officer on the scene as "visibly shaken," corroborated Mr. Feldman's story.

The eyewitness said he noticed Mr. Hudson walking

toward the side of the bridge and slowed down to see if the man needed help. Allegedly the eyewitness called out to Mr. Hudson, who never turned around.

"He stepped over the railing and, without looking back, did a swan dive right off the bridge and into the water," the eyewitness was quoted as saying. "A god-damn swan dive right off the bridge."

I reread the last line three more times and couldn't get a solid breath. Then I met John's eyes, wanting to say what I was thinking, but knowing that to do so could be perilous.

"Please tell me you haven't shown this to anyone else."

"Just you, Miss American Pie," John said. "Just you."

Michael was reaching the end of a long shift. It had been a hectic day, par for the course during the holiday season, but it was the stress, the abstruseness of the last few months that was really wearing him down.

Everything was finally starting to sink in, and Michael was beginning to realize how much he had gained and lost over the course of the year. In effect, he had been handed his life's dream, only to watch it get pulverized. And through no fault of his own. He had been the passenger in a head-on collision. A casualty of someone else's fate. And yes, he was disappointed. But admitting disappointment was asking for trouble. This he'd seen firsthand with Paul. Left unchecked, disappointment had a way of rendering the good things in life meaningless.

Michael had a wife who loved him, they had food on the table, a little money in the bank, and he would never be able to say he hadn't tried.

He made the decision to be oblivious rather than bitter, numb instead of heartbroken. Case in point: just two days earlier, he'd told Vera that his music career was over and he'd already submitted his résumé to a few commercial art and graphic design firms in the city.

It's so much easier to surrender than to fight.

"How's the shepherd's pie?"

The customer's voice seemed to come out of nowhere,

pulling Michael back into the moment. He was about to tell the man that the shepherd's pie was his favorite item on the menu when he felt a tug on his arm and turned to see his sister behind him.

"I need to talk to you," she said breathlessly, as if she'd run all the way there.

He couldn't tell if she was upset or excited. With Eliza it could go either way. He asked her to wait for him at the bar, and after pawning his current table off on a coworker, he went into the kitchen and threw a plate of pasta together.

"In case you're hungry," he said, setting the plate in front of her, taking the seat catty-corner.

She moved the dish out of her way, too busy chewing on a straw to consume food. "Michael, I need you to promise you'll listen to everything I say before you freak out."

"Uh-oh."

"Just promise."

There was passion in her eyes. And she had a glow Michael hadn't seen in a long time. "Eat something," he said, taking the straw from her and asking the bartender for two glasses of water.

She picked up her fork and absent-mindedly twirled a mound of pasta Michael knew was never going to reach her mouth. "Okay, what would you say if I told you there's a chance..." She put down the fork, chuckled once, and then got terribly serious: "Forget it…I'm just going to come right out with this…I think Paul is still alive."

Michael had a mouthful of water. He coughed half of it back into the glass. The bartender gave him a look but said nothing.

"I *know* it sounds crazy," she said, hands flailing like an Italian. "Just hear me out." She pulled a newspaper clipping from her pocket and shoved it at him. "The part that's circled. Try reading it in Paul's voice."

After shooting her a wary look, Michael read the blurb, imparting Paul's prolix verbal style in his head. Two thoughts occurred to him, one right after the other. First, Paul was an idiot. Second, his sister, unfortunately, was not.

"You see it, don't you?"

He set the clipping on the bar and sat on his hands to keep them from shaking. "I don't know what you *think* you see, but let me just say this—Paul couldn't have been the only man in the world who used *goddamn* as an adjective."

"Like I said, I *know* it sounds insane, but—"

"Insane?" Michael shook his head. "How about certifiable? How about *impossible*?"

"Will you at least listen to my theory?"

"I'll give you one minute."

She spoke quickly: "All right, I think Paul *was* the eyewitness that night. I don't think he was in the car with Feldman at all. I think Feldman is lying. I think Feldman is in on it and I think Paul *is* Will Lucien. *That's* what I think."

Michael tried to keep his voice down. "Eliza, Paul was my best friend. I miss him too. But you have to let go. Do you hear me? This isn't healthy."

"You didn't let me finish," she said. "I have evidence."

Michael didn't like that word, evidence. It sounded like something that could occupy space.

"Did you know Hudson wasn't Paul's real name?"

"No," he lied. "What was his real name?"

"I don't know. I asked him a million times and he always said he couldn't tell me until we got married. But guess what? I have a sinking suspicion it's Lucien. Here's something else you might find interesting: his father's name was William, and Paul was known among his BINGO lady friends as Willie." She took a quick sip of water and Michael tried to seize the moment to escape. "Wait. There's more."

"I don't want to hear anymore."

Michael was about to point out that, in case she'd forgotten, Paul's body had been recovered and identified. *There's
some evidence for her.*

She was a step ahead of him. "Tell me something, if Paul
had gotten a new tattoo before he *allegedly* killed himself,
would you have known about it?"

"Probably," Michael answered. "Why?"

"To your knowledge, had he gotten any new ones?"

Michael felt like he had dice tumbling in his chest. He
didn't want to tell her about the tattoo, nor could he imagine how she'd found out about it. But since he had no idea
where she was going with this line of questioning, he had
no choice but to answer her honestly.

"Yes."

At first she looked puzzled, then thoroughly devastated.
"*Yes?*"

"I told him it was ridiculous, believe me. I tried to talk
him out of it for days. And anyway, I thought it ended up
looking more like a train track than a scar."

"*What?*"

Michael took Eliza's wrist and flipped it over. "I don't
know, maybe a little."

Her eyes were expanding, as if someone were pumping
air into her head. "Listen to me Michael, listen *very* carefully…" She drew him in and lowered her voice to a scarcely
audible whisper. "I have a copy of Paul's autopsy report, and
according to the doctor who did the examination, the guy
they pulled out of the East River had a skull and crossbones
on his right shoulder but *did not*—I repeat *did not*—have
'self-portrait hanging from a butterfly' on his forearm *or* a
Chinese *wu* on his shoulder *or* a train-track scar on his wrist.
Do you understand what I'm saying?"

Michael clenched his fists. He understood he had to offer
his sister some kind of logical explanation, he just couldn't

think of one. "I'm sure it was just a mix up."

He also knew he had to do better than that.

"*Mix* up?" she shouted.

The bartender looked again, and Michael shifted Eliza's chair toward the front of the restaurant.

"Yes, Eliza. This is New York. They foul up all the time." Sweat was running down his back. "Don't get mad at me for saying this, but you dumped Paul, remember? You didn't want him when he was alive so why this crazy obsession with him now that he's gone?"

Tears ran down her cheeks and Michael moved over because he figured she was going to try to kick him. "Do you remember the day Paul and I broke up?" she huffed. "When he so conveniently walked in on me and Loring kissing?"

Michael didn't like her intonation. It sounded like another bomb about to drop.

"Do you want to know *why* I was kissing Loring?"

"Not particularly."

"Paul was an hour away from turning down the Drones tour, that's why."

"*What?*"

Now she was nodding. "I wasn't going to let him throw it all away just because I wouldn't get on a plane. Don't look at me like that. I wanted—hell, I don't know what I wanted anymore. But besides that one kiss, I never so much as touched Loring until Paul hooked up with Jilly Bean. Until he'd moved on."

Moved on, Michael thought. *Yeah, that's a good one.*

She waved the news clipping in his face. "Don't you want to at least talk to someone about this? Maybe the police can check and see if—"

"*No.*" His head was pounding and he needed to get Eliza out of the restaurant before he had a meltdown in front of her. "Listen. *Shit.* Can you just let me sleep on this? You really hit me with a ton of bricks here, and what I want you to do, *right now*, is to go home, calm down, don't talk to *any-one*, and let me think this over. *Okay?*"

Michael was barely cognizant of walking Eliza to the door, putting her in a cab, and watching the car drive away.

Back inside the restaurant, he rushed downstairs, directly to the payphone. After making sure both restrooms were empty, he removed a two-by-four-inch piece of paper from his wallet on which he'd written a series of numbers separated by dashes and spaces. He'd been trying to make it look like birth dates, a combination to a lock, a bank account. Anything but a phone number.

They hadn't talked since the afternoon the body had been recovered, when Michael thought there was a possibility it had actually been Paul and called to make sure something hadn't gone terribly wrong.

"*That's* a frightening turn of events," was Paul's response after Michael informed him that his corpse had just been plucked from the East River.

But the only thing Paul had really seemed to care about was how Eliza was taking the news. "Did she cry?" he'd asked over and over, until Michael finally said, "Yes, she cried, okay. And she seems pretty pissed off."

"Pissed off? Holy Hell, that's *so* Eliza. She's a real piece of work, your sister. She's supposed to be crushed, not pissed off."

"Paul, forget Eliza! Someone is dead. We could end up in deep shit if—"

"Stop calling me Paul."

Michael gave Paul a quick play by play of Feldman's visit, starting with the way Feldman dragged him outside, called the body "insurance," and said that his "friends" assured him it belonged to a very bad guy whom no one was going to miss. The last thing Feldman told Michael was that if he knew what was good for the well-being of his family, he wouldn't ask any more questions.

"Holy Hell," Paul had said, his voice shaking. "I don't feel good about this body either. But, realistically, it probably solidifies the story, not jeopardizes it, right?"

Michael and Paul had ended that conversation agreeing that unless an emergency arose, there would be no more communication between them until the week before Paul was scheduled to leave the country.

Michael deemed the current situation a legitimate, five-alarm crisis.

He dialed the number, let it ring twice, hung up, and then dialed once more, per their code.

Paul picked up right away.

"It's me," Michael said. "Are you sitting down?"

How does that goddamn cliché go? If I'd known then what I know now.

Or maybe I should have heeded the opposite warning. Maybe I should have delved a little deeper into *then* back when I was wandering aimlessly around *now*.

The holy truth is that I'm standing in front of a window looking out over Ora—wait, maybe I shouldn't say where I am—Michael told me to stop divulging secrets on tape, which is why my reports have been sporadic. He's right, I know. But I'm stir crazy. I need someone to talk to.

Let's just say I'm in a New-that's-not-York state, I've been holed up in this little apartment for two months, and I just got off the phone with the aforementioned Michael.

First of all, when nobody calls you for like, a zillion days, just hearing the phone ring is a monumental thrill. Michael's voice was a goddamn Verdi opera in my ear. And besides going out for midnight runs, which Michael doesn't know I do, I don't leave this room. Not that I need to. I've got two guitars, a box full of books and music, a computer, enough food to last me through a long war, and about ten gallons of toothpaste and moisturizer. I have no idea why I thought I was going to need so much toothpaste and moisturizer.

Anyway, after my post-death conversation with Michael, we weren't supposed to talk again until after the New Year, when Will Lucien will be kissing America goodbye. Then, about half an hour ago, the phone rings and it's Michael and he's in a panic. He asks me to sit down, I tell him I'm already sitting and here's what he says: "She knows."

I asked him who the hell he was talking about but he didn't answer me and I thought he'd hung up until I heard voices. That's when I realized he was at the restaurant. He was waiting for the people around him to leave.

As soon as it got quiet he cleared his throat and said, "Eliza. She figured it out. You and your goddamn goddamns." Then he commenced a rambling freak-out of questions: What if she goes to the police? What if she blows the whole thing wide open? What if we end up in jail? Is that what I want? To spend the rest of my life in jail? Is it, Paul? Is it? Huh? Huh?

She's a smart cookie, I'll give her that.

Michael said, "Paul, say something."

I said, "Stop calling me Paul."

He told me this whole thing was my gig—that's what he called it, a gig—and that meant I was supposed to be able to figure it out and tell him what to do. But, at the time, a solution seemed like the least important issue. What I was wondering was why Eliza cared enough to figure it out. "What's it to her?" I said.

Michael repeated my question in his dad voice, indicating his annoyance.

"I mean it," I told him. "I want to know. Why the fuck does she care?"

So then he goes, "Jesus, Paul, she's still in love with you, why do you think she cares?"

Talk about a left hook. Talk about a sentence that can really knock a guy on his ass and throw him down a flight of stairs.

And that's not even the half of it. The next question out of my mouth was something along the lines of what about her goddamn boyfriend, and Michael purged a lot more shit, all this stuff about what happened with Loring, how it was all a big sham. Well, at least it started out that way. I guess she eventually gave in and fell for the guy, but not until I commenced spite-fucking Amanda and Jill and, well, never mind the rest.

I have to shut this thing off for a second. I'm getting—what's that Yiddish word for when you're so overwhelmed you can barely speak? Verklempt.

Okay, I'm back. Sorry. Had to compose myself. Where was I?

I think I was about to say that if I ever see Eliza again—and the fact that this is even a remote possibility is—I don't know what it is, a goddamn miracle, maybe? After I kiss her and hold her and let her touch my chest, I'm going to hang her upside down and employ Chinese water torture until she promises never to be so stupid again.

This brings me to the new crux of my life. To echo the words Michael left me with: "You have a really big decision to make."

Michael said he would keep playing dumb with Eliza, stave her off until I make up my mind, but we both know what a pain in the ass she can be. In other words, we don't have much time. Michael suggested I take a few days to let everything sink in before I settle on a course of action. I said I would, and he and I agreed to talk again on Friday.

But come on, who the fuck am I kidding?

I already know exactly what I'm going to do.

Over.

Officer Levenduski offered me a soda. I declined, he opened a can for himself, and then sat down behind the big steel desk.

Based on the family photographs scattered around the tabletop, I guessed the desk didn't actually belong to Levenduski, as the subjects in the pictures were not, nor did they resemble, the man sitting across from me.

When I'd called and requested a meeting, Officer Levenduski had been flippant, claiming he had better things to do than discuss the months-old, open-and-shut case of an obscure rock musician, until I mentioned I was a journalist for a national publication.

"Will I be quoted in the magazine?" Officer Levenduski had asked.

"Of course." I saw no point in telling Officer Levenduski that the article, as well as my job, was null and void.

The police report was sitting on the desk that was not Levenduski's when I sat down. Before opening it, the rusty-haired officer spelled his last name aloud.

"Most people end it with a Y but it's an I," he said.

I knew what kind of man Levenduski was just by looking at him—the kind who relishes his position of authority at work because he has no power elsewhere. I guessed his wife bossed him around, he had kids he couldn't control, a dog that peed on his carpet, but here, behind the big desk, with the big gun at his hip, he was the king.

Levenduski spent sixty seconds browsing the report. "Okay," he said. "Hit me."

To make my visit seem legitimate, I questioned the officer on the details of the night. Then I got to the real reason I'd come. "The eyewitness."

Levenduski looked at his notes. "Lucien." He made the name sound Chinese, pronouncing it "Lucy-In."

"I think that's *Loo-shen*," I corrected. "Tell me what you remember about Mr. Lucien's appearance. Anything at all."

Levenduski had a finger stuck inside his front belt loop. "The guy had a beard. A thick one, like a lumberjack."

I suppressed my overwhelming disappointment upon hearing this. Paul had a better chance of sprouting wings than he had of growing a lumberjack's beard, never mind that I'd seen him hours before and he'd been clean-shaven. But, I assured myself, a beard can be faked. It was a long shot—asinine even—yet completely within the workings of Paul's skewed mind.

"Was he tall or short?" I asked.

"Don't really recall."

"Well, what was his build like?"

"Hard to say. He had a sweater on. But I'd guess he was on the thin side."

"What kind of sweater?"

Levenduski laughed like he thought my questions were the stupidest he'd ever heard. "Something dark."

Paul had been wearing his black hooded sweatshirt when I'd found him on Michael's doorstep.

"Did he have a prominent nose?"

"*Miss*, I had better things to do than take notes on the guy's nose."

"Well, what about his hair? Was it dark and stringy? Sort of in his face?"

Levenduski had the tip of a ballpoint pen in his mouth.

He was biting down on it, stretching his lips so that all his teeth were showing. He looked like a hungry Irish Setter. "No. This I *do* remember." He pointed the pen at me. "The guy was completely bald. Not a speck of hair on his head. Honest to God, I remember thinking, This poor joker's got all that hair on his face but none on his noggin." Levenduski laughed. "Yeah, I remember the guy's head just like I seen him yesterday. Looked like a freakin' cue ball."

My initial reaction was more letdown. Maybe I was wrong. Maybe Will Lucien and Paul Hudson were not one in the same.

My memories of that night were vague. Not moving pictures, more like photographs. I flipped through the snapshots in my mind: Paul on the porch, Paul sliding my hand under his shirt, Paul above me on the bed, Paul grabbing my arm when I tried to take that stupid orange hat off of his head.

"What's the matter, you get a bad haircut?" I'd joked.

"Something like that," he'd said.

I crashed through Michael and Vera's front door ready to report my discovery, certain I was going to convince my brother and astound Vera at the same time.

Michael was sitting on the couch with a TV tray in front of him, Fender resting at his feet. Vera was halfway between the kitchen and the main room carrying a wooden salad bowl.

"Michael, I—" were the only words I got out before my brother stood up and swooped down on me like a vulture.

"Outside," he said, dragging me in the direction of the door.

Vera looked curious, and Michael said, "It's about your Christmas present."

At the end of the block, Michael stopped in front of a vacant basketball court. "Are you out of your *mind?*" he yelled, and then turned his back to me, gripping the chain-link fence and breathing heavily. His head was pressed so hard into the metal I thought he was going to have a fence pattern on his forehead when he turned around.

"I just came from the police station," I said. "You're not going to believe this, but the officer on duty the night Paul—"

"Jesus, Eliza!" Michael spun to face me. There was no pattern on his head, only redness. His whole body seemed shaky. "You didn't tell the police about your little *theory*, did you?"

"I didn't tell them anything, I was asking—"

"Who else *have* you told?"

"No one. Stop yelling at me. Will Lucien was bald."

"*What?*"

"And so was Paul that night. At least I'm pretty sure he was. He wouldn't take off his hat, not even during sex."

Michael rolled his eyes and started frantically pacing the fence line.

"I found this site on the Internet," I said, "it's for lawyers and companies that have to check up on people, I guess. Anyway, for $39.99 you can find out almost anything about a person if you have their name and date of birth."

Michael ceased moving. "*And?*"

"It takes twenty-four hours. I'll have Will Lucien's vital stats by noon tomorrow. And if it just so happens Will Lucien was born in Pittsburgh in 1972, is there a chance you might start to believe me?"

I watched Michael's face.

That's when I saw it. And my mouth fell open.

"What?" Michael said nervously.

The whole time I'd been waiting for a reaction—a flinch, a nod, one of his Abe Lincoln scowls—anything that suggested my brother was starting to take me seriously. Now I saw something else.

His was not the face of a man trying to figure out the

truth. His was the face of a man who knew the truth, but was torn by whether or not to expose it.

"*Damn you…*" I didn't know whether to laugh, cry, or kick his kneecaps in, but I settled on a mixture of the first two options. "You've known all along, haven't you?"

He leaned his body backward, resting all his weight against the fence so that it curved and flexed behind him.

"Michael, this is my *life*! You have to *tell* me!"

"Jesus Christ, it's *my* life too, Eliza!" He rubbed his face and tried to catch his breath. "Please, just sit tight for another day or two. And stop asking questions. *Can you do that please?*"

I didn't want to agitate Michael any more than I already had, but I also thought the world might end if I didn't make one more appeal.

"I swear over my life I won't ask to see him or talk to him, if that's what he wants. I won't ask where or how or why, and I won't tell a soul. I just need to know. I need to hear you say it. Is he alive?"

Michael glanced around, then picked up a rock and skipped it violently down the sidewalk.

"No more police," he said.

I made an x over my heart, and then the tears fell harder, because I knew what Michael was going to say.

"Yes," Michael sighed. "He's alive."

The street lamps in Tompkins Square Park were like electric candles. They gave off heat, Michael was sure they did, because it was twenty-seven degrees outside, but as long as he and Vera remained within the light's radius they could unbutton their coats and still be comfortable.

Michael and Paul had talked that morning. At lunchtime, Michael had called Eliza and told her to meet him at the fountain at eight.

"Eight?" she'd whined. "That's hours away. Can't we meet now?"

"I have some things I need to take care of first."

At 7:49, with Vera at his side, Michael spotted Eliza walking down Ninth Street at a swift, urban pace emblematic of Manhattanites.

Eliza looked stunned by Vera's presence. Her eyes went to Michael, then to her sister-in-law. "*You know too?*"

"Not until today, I didn't."

"Sit," Michael told Eliza, nodding at a bench. He could tell she was nervous, she was biting her cheeks. "First of all, I want you to know I had no hand in the decision-making that led to the deal I'm about to offer you."

"*Deal?*" She eyed Vera, who was fidgeting beside Michael, twisting her hands as if she were wringing out a dishrag. "What does he mean *deal?*"

"Don't look at me," Vera said. "I'm still in shock. It's not everyday someone you know is resurrected."

Michael pulled a standard-sized white envelope out of his breast pocket. Eliza took it and studied her name typed across the front.

The envelope wasn't sealed. She lifted the flap and removed the packet of papers. The next few moments passed in formidable silence, and Michael and Vera watched Eliza's face contort like dough being stretched in all directions as the proviso of the "deal" revealed itself to her.

She was holding a nudge. A dare. Choice in the form of an airline ticket made out in her name for a flight that would be departing JFK right after the New Year.

There was a printed itinerary with the ticket, as well as a voucher for a discount on a car rental the airline must have thrown in.

"Remember, don't shoot the messenger," Michael said.

Eliza remained silent until she unfolded the itinerary. "*Over water?*" she shrieked. "He expects me to fly *over water?*"

Michael flipped the page to where it listed the equipment. "Look, a 767-400. Practically brand new—I checked before I booked it. Oh, and he wanted me to point out you'll be sitting in first class, so you know how much he was willing to spend on you."

"I have an idea…" Her voice was dry and sputtering. "I could take a train to Boston…somewhere on the coast…catch one of those ocean liners and…"

Michael shook his head. "He figured you'd try that. He said, and I quote: 'Tell her no dice unless she gets her ass on the plane.'"

"Those were his exact words? He actually said *ass* and *dice?*"

Vera pointed to the envelope. "I think you missed something."

Eliza looked in and found a small scrap of paper that read: If you want me you're going to have to come and get me.

"Bastard."

coda

Art & Love:
The Only Things
That Can Bring
a Person Back
to Life

I entered JFK's Central Terminal with a scarf tied around my head, covering my eyes, completely obscuring my vision.

Michael carried my bags; Vera held my hand.

I was a soldier being led to the firing squad.

Joan of Arc on her way to the barbeque.

"Eliza," Vera said. "People are staring."

"I don't care. Pretend I'm blind."

"If you were blind, you wouldn't need the scarf."

Vera guided me all the way to the ticket counter, where I listened as Michael gave my name and flight number to the chipper lady behind the desk who sounded so much like Glinda the Good Witch, I imagined the woman wearing a pink dress made of tulle and a big golden crown on her head. It helped.

"May I have a window seat?" I held my passport out until Glinda took it. "I know it's safer to sit in the aisle, but I'm going to need a view of the outside world at all times."

Glinda told me I was in luck. There was one window seat left in first class. And for a brief second I thought I felt brave.

Glinda gave my boarding pass to Michael. "They'll begin boarding in about forty-five minutes," she said. "But before I let her go, I'm going to need to see her face."

"Eliza," Michael said.

I lifted the blindfold a smidgen, allowing Glinda to verify that I was indeed the girl in the passport photo. Glinda was appeased. I, on the other hand, was fearfully taken aback. The appearance didn't match the voice. Glinda was hard-edged, with a crispy mess of hair. Her head looked like it had been deep-fried.

I put the blindfold back on and let my escorts lead me in the direction of the gate. We walked slowly, and then Michael stopped.

"Security checkpoint," he said. "You're going to have to take that thing off."

I untied the scarf, and when I opened my eyes I could have been standing at the entrance to a shopping mall. There were retail stores and fast food counters up ahead, and the only thing that disturbed me was the big machine waiting to make sure I wasn't carrying any weapons.

Michael, Vera, and I took our places at the end of the line. We moved when the people in front of us moved. At the halfway point, Michael put his hand on my back and said, "We should say goodbye here. Only ticketed passengers beyond this point."

I jumped out of line and Michael asked the guy behind me to hold my place. I was panting now. Not only because I was terrified, but because I realized there were questions that needed answers, major issues that, due to the wondrous reality of being reunited with Paul, I had failed to address.

On Michael's advice, I had told Burke and Queenie that I was going to Europe "to find myself," or something asinine like that. But I had never discussed with Michael and Vera how or when I would be able to communicate with them.

"I am going to see you again, right?"

Michael chuckled. "Yeah. I mean, not right away, but yes."

I threw my arms around Vera and the tears came on both sides. Eventually Michael tapped my shoulder and said, "You should get going."

Michael's eyes were watery too, but he pretended they weren't.

"Thank you," I said, squeezing him as tight as I could.

When I let go, he pushed me back in line.

"What if I can't do it? What if I get to the gate and can't go any further?"

"You can do it," he said.

I passed through the metal detector without incident. Then I picked up my carry-on and stopped to take one last look at my family.

"Go," Michael said.

"You first."

Michael and Vera waved without smiling. I waved back. Then Michael put his arm around Vera, and they turned and walked away.

I kept my head down and took small steps, heel to toe, until I arrived at my gate. I chose a seat facing the inside of the airport, to watch the travelers and learn their secrets, and so as not to actually set eyes on the plane this time.

Pilots with starched uniforms and sharp posture passed by. Kids hopped around chairs. An elderly couple waited for their flight. Businessmen paced in corners with phones against their ears. None of them exhibited one iota of concern for their lives.

I tried to tell myself I was no different from any of these people.

Breathe, I whispered.

Every time a plane took to the sky, the walls screamed and the ground vibrated. Nine nauseating takeoffs later, a forty-something airline employee with a high-pitched voice punched in a code on a keypad, unlocked the door to the Jetway, and made a falsetto announcement that anyone with kids, disabilities, and those sitting in the first class cabin were welcome to board the aircraft.

I rose, brushing crumbs from the back of the leather pants I'd purchased for the flight. Then I put on my imaginary blinker, merged into the line of passengers, and before I knew it I'd handed over my boarding pass, shown my passport to the woman at the gate, and was making my way down a telescope-shaped tunnel.

The closer I got to the plane, the colder the air became. There was a loud sucking noise coming from the engines. I was shivering and sweating, something I didn't know a body could do at the same time. And the man behind me was carrying a briefcase that kept banging into the back of my legs.

I stopped and spun around. "Two foot rule," I said, trying not to throw up.

"Sorry?" The man had an accent. Norwegian, or one of those other cold, blond countries.

"You're invading my body bubble, and I really need some space right now. How about taking a few steps back?"

But he couldn't. There were other passengers prodding the man to keep going. He had no choice but to push on, and I let myself get swept up in the horde, knowing that otherwise I'd never make it.

And then, just like that, I was on the plane.

It was big inside. An oversized waiting room.

The air in the cabin was stale and insipid, exactly like it had been on the Lear jet, and I couldn't understand why, after decades of aviation, no one had figured out how to make a plane smell safe or pleasant.

I found my seat, which was considerably larger than the coach seats I could see behind me, and I immediately began the pre-takeoff checklist I'd prepared. First, safety issues: I stowed my carry-on, fastened my belt low and tight around my waist, made sure my seat was in its full, upright position, double-checked that my tray table was secure in its compartment, and memorized the locations of the two nearest exits.

All was good to go. And for what I knew would be a very short period of time, I felt ready. Not calm. Not comfortable. But more ready than I'd expected.

The problem was the passengers. There were dozens of them still boarding, all in a row, like cows on their way to the slaughter. They moved close together with dumb cow looks on their faces, and couldn't seem to find any space for their bags. They spent a lot of time standing around, opening and slamming the overhead bins. I was afraid all the slamming was going to damage the plane. I started sweating again.

A narrow-faced flight attendant humming "Swing Low, Sweet Chariot" brought over a blanket and pillow, a little ramekin of smoked almonds, and offered me a glass of either champagne or orange juice, neither of which I took. The flight attendant's blouse advertised her as Samantha.

I asked Samantha if she was acquainted with the pilot and copilot.

"Yes," Samantha said.

"To the best of your knowledge, are they heavy drinkers?"

I was certain I had just made an enemy of Samantha. "No, Miss—" Samantha perused the papers on her clipboard. "Caelum. I assure you they are not."

To ease my nerves, if that was possible, I reviewed a few of the facts I'd recently learned about the 767-400, mostly from the Boeing website, which meant it was probably propaganda, but it was all I had: The plane had never crashed. Its safety record was impeccable. It sat approximately three hundred and seventy passengers, depending on its configuration. And it was the first plane to implement a vacuum waste system in the lavatory. This was a good thing, I guessed, but not really going to come in handy in the event the plane went into a nosedive.

With departure imminent, it was time for a weather check. Channel Seven had promised that the skies in the New York area would remain clear until the following morning but, tragically, two small clouds were forming directly above the airport.

Things only got worse when the captain's voice came blaring out of the ceiling. He introduced himself as James Morgan, and he sounded nice enough at first. But then he had to go and say he was anticipating a smooth ride once we got to our cruising altitude of *thirty-seven thousand feet*, and I could taste the bile.

I darted to the bathroom, pulled my hair off my face, and threw up in the toilet. If nothing else, the experience demonstrated the merits of the vacuum waste system.

Moments later, there was a tap-tap on the door. A flight attendant who was not Samantha, but an older woman named Vicki, peeked in and said, "I'm sorry. I gather you're under the weather, but we're going to need you to sit down very soon."

Vicki handed me a damp cloth, a disposable toothbrush, and a travel-sized bottle of mouthwash. After freshening up, I stepped out of the lavatory, and Vicki asked me if I was feeling better.

"I'm not a very frequent flier."

"I know," Vicki said, smiling brightly. "Your fiancé told me."

Vicki said she thought it was sweet, the way Paul and I fell all over each other, kissing and laughing and crying like we hadn't seen each other in months.

"But you really need to sit down," she told us.

I hadn't recognized Paul right away. He'd been standing in the middle of the aisle when I rounded the corner, but I was looking to my seat and almost walked past him until I heard him say, "*There's* my betrothed."

He had the green suit on, paired with a dress shirt and a hideous yellow tie that was covered in tiny green golf clubs. He was attempting to look unlike a rock star—an attempt that wasn't remotely successful. No matter how hard he tried, Paul would never be kempt enough to pull off the businessman vibe.

His hair was shorn. Or rather, it was in the early stages of growing back, and it was bleached a pale blond that clashed with his dark eyebrows and lashes. He was also wearing tortoise-colored glasses I was sure he didn't actually need, despite his droll claims to the contrary.

"Tell me you're not going to look like this for the rest of our lives," I said after we finally composed ourselves and sat.

"God, no. Do I look like a salesman, though? I told the stewardess I was a salesman from Peoria."

"You look a little like that dead guy from Bananafish. What do you sell?"

He pointed at his tie. "Sporting goods. With an emphasis

on high-end leisure activities."

Paul took a glass of champagne from Samantha and I caught a glimpse of the new tattoo peeking out from under his cuff. I flipped his wrist and examined the art against my old wound.

"Cool, huh?" he said.

I was about to rest my hand on his chest and kiss him again, but the plane's door shut with a bang that sounded violent and terminal and I screamed. "Please, Paul! Please don't make me do this!"

He took my hand, leaned in, and whispered, "It's probably a good idea if you stop calling me Paul."

The plane started moving in reverse and I felt like I was going to faint, which would have been a blessing.

"Inhale, exhale," Paul reminded me. "We're together, everything's fine, and I love you."

I pressed my forehead against the cold plastic window, imagining my mom doing the same thing years earlier.

"I love you too," I told Paul.

"You're breathing all wrong."

He was right. I was taking in air in short, shallow spurts like someone with emphysema.

"I have a confession," he said.

"Right now?" I half-turned to see what he wanted.

"My dick is hard."

I elbowed him and then went back to looking out my portal. At the same time, I extended my arm behind me so that I could hold his hand.

"I think it's those goddamn pants you're wearing."

"Not now, Paul. I mean it."

"Stop calling me Paul."

Then the captain said, "Flight attendants please prepare for takeoff," and I knew there was no turning back. I dug my nails into Paul's palm until he winced. "You hate me, don't you? That's why you're making me do this. Pure hatred."

"I just told you I love you. What do you want, a formal goddamn decree?" He made me turn and look at him. "Hey," he said, his eyes sharp and sincere. "I'm doing this because I love you. I want you to be free."

I was about to lean over and kiss him once more, but the plane turned onto the runway and I had to refocus on my breathing.

Paul grabbed a handful of almonds. "You know what I've been thinking about all day? What color underwear you'd be wearing."

I found his nonchalance staggering. "Don't make me kick you before we die."

"We're not going to die. But look on the bright side—if we do, at least we'll die together." He peeked down the back of my shirt. "Mmm. Pink. Is that pink?"

The plane started thundering down the runway, picking up speed by the second. "This isn't fair," I sobbed. "If we make it out of here alive, you're taking the Chunnel."

"The what?"

"The subway-train thingy that runs under the English Channel. It's called the Chunnel." I was hysterical, my voice getting increasingly louder to compete with the roar of the engines. "If we survive this, you're going underground!"

"Fine, we'll go tomorrow if you want. Can you keep it down, though?"

The nose of the aircraft tilted toward the sky and I immediately assumed the crash position—head between my knees, hands protecting my skull—until Paul pulled me up and said, "Don't be ridiculous."

The wheels lifted off the ground, and I was instantly aware of the sensation of being airborne.

It felt like a dream.

It felt like my stomach was floating above my head.

I was afraid I was going to throw up again.

And then the coolest thing happened.

I heard music.

Calling Eliza a high maintenance flyer might be the understatement of the goddamn decade. During takeoff, I wondered if I'd made a big mistake, if maybe we should have just hopped on the Love Boat, let Isaac serve us some drinks, let Julie McCoy plan us a few shuffleboard games, and saved ourselves a lot of trouble. She was out of control. Like one of those little rubber balls they sell for a quarter in gumball machines—the crazy kind that, once you dropped it—and you didn't even have to drop it with any force—it would bounce left and right and up and down and diagonally, ricocheting for all of eternity unless you scooped it back up and put it in a goddamn drawer or something. That was Eliza for the first hour of the flight. Forget that she was chained to her seat as tight as the belt would go, she was all over the place.

She was also squeezing my fingers like a vice grip, and I had to switch hands every few minutes, otherwise I thought I might never play guitar again.

All the same, I knew it was my responsibility to keep her amused, distracted, and basically try to get her to forget where she was.

My first attempt was singing. I started right as we were taking off. I was going to do "The Day I Became a Ghost" because of its uncanny relevance to the situation, as well as its sentimental value, but that seemed too obvious so I broke into "Shadows of the Night" by Pat Benatar instead. And get this—even though Eliza was having a breakdown, I still saw goose bumps on her arms.

Unfortunately, the song only pacified her until the landing gear was retracted, at which point she had another convulsion. That's when I changed tactics. I informed her I was still hard— I was—and suggested she might want to throw a blanket over my lap and touch it if she didn't believe me.

It was those goddamn pants she was wearing. And don't forget, moisturizer and free Internet porn were all I'd had in the way of companionship for months.

"Paul," she said, "for the love of God."

I begged her for the zillionth time to stop calling me Paul. Then I asked her to kiss me and she did. This turned out to be a very good thing. Kissing is the perfect distraction because there's no limit to how long you can do it. We went at it for a while, and I figured we'd keep at it until she pulled away, or until the captain shut off the fasten-seatbelt sign. The latter came first.

I put my hands on her face because I couldn't believe she was really there. I told her she was brave and she said, "I'm not brave, I'm in love."

Ha. Same goddamn thing.

Then I pointed at the sky and said, "Look. You did it. Cruising at thirty-seven thousand feet, still alive and kicking."

At first this did nothing except incite another riot, but when she calmed down long enough to look out the window, and I mean really look, I'm pretty sure I saw half a smile.

This is not to say the rest of the flight went off without a hitch. Whenever there was the slightest bump she thought we were a second away from tailspinning into the ocean. Something as routine as an altitude change spurred a grab for the ralph bag. And every time she heard a weird noise, she'd jump and say, "What was that?" and then expect me to give her a dissertation on aeronautical engineering. I had to make shit up. "They're just deploying the spoilers," or "Oh, that? That's the vertical stabilizer." Funny thing is she knows a hell of a lot more about aviation than I do, but she never called my bluff.

For a while she wouldn't eat anything either, but finally gave in when Vicki, our friendly neighborhood flight attendant, wheeled out the dessert cart and told us we could design our own sundaes.

First Class—always the way to go when you're dead and have an advance to burn.

Eliza got vanilla ice cream with butterscotch sauce, whipped cream, and a cherry. She asked me to get chocolate ice cream with hot fudge and marshmallows. This way, she explained, we could share without overlapping flavors. Except she was pretty goddamn stingy with hers. She only gave me one bite. Meanwhile I was supposed to let her eat half of mine.

"Will..." She couldn't keep a straight face when she said my name. Still can't. "We have to talk."

I'd been waiting for this. Knew it was a matter of time. But it turned out to be the best diversionary tactic of all. Every second Eliza wasn't freaking out she was talking or asking questions about our lost months, like she thought we had to cram every day we'd spent apart into the time it took us to fly across the ocean. I tried to tell her we had forever, there was no need to rush, but in case we didn't make it, she said, she wanted me to die knowing the truth the whole truth and nothing but the truth so help her God.

She started off with the day Feldman invited her to the Kiev, then gave me an overview of life in the penthouse, and I have to admit, when she told me what a good friend Loring had been to her, my initial fondness for the guy returned. In my head I wrote him a thank-you note, one that, if not for the circumstances, I honestly would have sent.

"Dear Loring: Please accept my sincere gratitude for taking such good care of Eliza during her period of Paul-less dementia."

But then I made the mistake of asking Eliza if Loring was any good in bed and because all she did was giggle and say "that's completely irrelevant," my sympathies for him vanished.

Jilly Bean was a topic. Amanda was a topic. I even confessed to the two other lapses of judgment I had on tour.

Okay, three.

Okay, four.

These were the times I actually prayed for a little regular turbulence.

We talked for a while about Feldman and why he'd agreed to help me, and for the first time Eliza acquiesced that maybe Feldman had a heart after all. But she felt the need to add that he probably had plans to turn me into the next Nick Drake, too. Twenty years from now my songs will be background music for car commercials, just you wait and see.

Another big topic was where we were going. Nothing was carved in stone. Our immediate destination was only temporary, and we made a plan to travel around until we found a place we want to stay. We both agree that settling in a big city is probably not a good idea, but other than that the world is our goddamn oyster.

How we're going to make a living is still up in the air. Not that it's a real concern at the moment. I've got my goddamn advance to tide us over until we figure things out.

"Why don't you talk about the Chunnel, cocky-bastard?"

That was my betrothed, in case you didn't recognize her voice.

"Go on, I'd really like to hear your version."

Not going there.

"Give me the recorder, I'll tell it."

There's nothing to tell about the goddamn Chunnel. It's a train. Somehow it runs under the water. It goes really fast, it smelled like burning flesh, and it took, like, twenty minutes to get from England to France. Enough said.

"Give it to me."

No. Get your own goddamn—Hey—

"Hi. This is Eliza. I'd just like to say that Will sat on the floor with his head between his knees, moaning and holding his pancreas the whole time."

I did not.

"Did too."

That's because you kept laughing and saying, "How does it feel to be a hundred and fifty goddamn feet under the sea?" All I can say is you better watch out the next time we get on a plane. I'm going to make Ian Lessing look like a saint. Now give me my goddamn tape recorder.

"Here. Take the stupid thing."

Thank you. I apologize for that interruption. Where was I? Plane ride. Eliza freaking out. Talking. Questions. Eliza freaking out. Ice cream. Eliza freaking out. Oh, right. Eliza was calm after the ice cream. Marginally, at least. Enough that I finally felt okay about getting up and going to the bathroom—I'd had to piss for hours. But when I came back she was all melancholy. Not scared so much as just plain sad. I asked her what could have happened in the two minutes I was gone and she confessed that she'd been sitting there wondering if we were cowards, if what we were doing was tantamount to surrender.

My holy goddamn *no* was emphatic. I might be fooling myself, but I truly believe surrender would have meant giving Winkle his hit songs, his Gap ads, his flashy videos, and his power ballads. It would have meant making concessions. It would have meant joining hands with the heathens and pagans in a happy little game of ass-kissing ring around the rosy.

Eliza's afraid that someday I'm going to regret giving it all up. She said she doesn't understand how I could turn my back on what I love more than anything in the world.

I know, kind of sanctimonious coming from her, considering how she fed me to the sharks.

But the way I see it, I haven't given up that much. Am I going to miss the live shows? Hell, yeah. But it's not the end of the world. I'm still going to play my guitar, write my songs, and sing them into my four-track. It's just that, at least until I croak anyway, very few people will get to hear them.

What I love, what it's about for me, and what it's always been about, is the music. Everything else I can use to wipe my ass.

It's pretty simple, really, when you think about it: We all start out as little fishes in our daddy's pants, and we all end up a Thanksgiving feast for the worms, and in the meantime we have to find a couple good reasons to give a fuck.

I've got my girl and my guitar, and for me that's enough.

The rest is yesterday's news.

Eliza was still pondering all this stuff when we started our approach into Heathrow. I could tell by the way her eyes looked. She was also exhausted—neither of us had slept at all. And the first thing she did after we touched down was start bawling. Then she kissed me and thanked me and I thanked her back, and let me tell you it was a pretty amazing moment all around.

As we were taxiing to the gate, she lowered her chin and blinked, and I knew she had at least one more thing to say. I told her to spit it out and she goes: "With a little compromising on your part, you might have been king of the heathens and pagans, you know that, don't you?"

The plane came to a stop, the bell dinged, and I unbuckled my seatbelt. "Wasn't worth it," I said. "Besides, I don't think I ever wanted it badly enough."

She called me an anachronism. She said that if I'd been twenty-nine in 1969, everything would have been different. I might have been a legend.

I stood up and took her hand.

"Yeah, well," I said as we began walking off the plane. "And if my aunt had balls she'd be my uncle."

Over.

The world is filled with people who are no longer needed—and who try to make slaves of all of us—and they have their music and we have ours. Theirs, the wasted songs of a superstitious nightmare—and without their musical and ideological miscarriages to compare our Song of Freedom to, we'd not have any opposite to compare music with—and like the drifting wind, hitting against no obstacle, we'd never knows its speed, its power.

—Woody Guthrie

My thanks go out to all the artists and music industry professionals who spoke so candidly with me about their experiences in the music business.

I also need to wholeheartedly thank my agent, Al Zuckerman, for his undying patience and support. And my editor, Hillel Black, for being such a joy to work with.

Friends, family, and inspirations: If your name is on this list, then you fall into one or more of those categories, and I thank you with all of my being: Mom, Dad, Lisa DeBartolo, Nikki DeBartolo Heldfond; Nashara Alberico, Barry and Jen Ament, Bambi Barnum, Sebastian Beckwith, Jack Bookbinder, Gene Bowen, Seymour Cassel, Teressa Centofante, Corrine Clement, Liad Cohen, Denise Coleman, Jean-Paul Eberle, Jonathan Fierer, Sean Gauvreau, Savita Ginde, Jimmy Gnecco, Elizabeth Graff, Ben Heldfond, Eddy Midyett, Gunita Nagpaul, Peter Prato, Race, Troy Reinhart, Jennifer Roy, Sean San Jose, Scott Schumaker, Kira Siebert, Sasha Taylor, Sep Valizadeh.

To the greatest rock 'n' roll band in the universe, U2, who for over two decades have made it easier for me to believe in love amidst the chaos and contradictions of life. Thank you for never letting me down.

To Asher: may the words of the radio prophets touch your soul.

And last but not least, to JB. Angel and muse extraordinaire.

To contact the author, go to www.tiffaniedebartlo.com

To help music make a difference in the lives of young people, visit www.roadrecovery.com